RICK
MOFINA

THEIR LAST
SECRET

mira

Recycling programs for this product may not exist in your area.

ISBN-13: 978-0-7783-0986-4

Their Last Secret

Copyright © 2020 by Highway Nine, Inc.

This edition published by arrangement with Harlequin Books S.A.

For questions and comments about the quality of this book, please contact us at CustomerService@Harlequin.com.

Mira
22 Adelaide St. West, 40th Floor
Toronto, Ontario M5H 4E3, Canada
www.Harlequin.com

Printed in U.S.A.

*This book is for
Ron Collins,
Helen Dolik
&
Mario Toneguzzi,
my partners in crime.
Those were the days, my friends.*

THEIR LAST
SECRET

"When you murder someone, they never die. You watch their life drain from their eyes, feel the last pulse of their heart, their last desperate gasp. But the dead never stay dead. They live in your nightmares, haunting you for the rest of your life, because of what you did and what you are."

—From the confidential diary of a young killer,
"Girl B"

Eternity: The Story of Homicide in a Small Town by
Benjamin Grant

One

Eternity, Manitoba
2000

Waiting to die. Or dying to get out.

Those seemed like your only choices when fate had dumped you in a small, prairie town where nothing happened and your secret torment burned like a lit fuse.

That's how it was for Janie, Nikki and Marie, best friends born in and, as Nikki said, condemned to, Eternity.

The rest of civilization was at least a two-hour drive east in the metropolis of Winnipeg. Saskatchewan was about an hour west. Nothing to see there but the sky and land so flat you'd think you were driving to the edge of the world.

Drive south for about an hour and you'd see rolling hills, or what some people called mountains, until you came to the North Dakota border. If you really wanted to push things, you could spend a day getting to Minneapolis, Minnesota.

If you were Janie, Nikki and Marie, growing

up in Eternity, there was nowhere to go. You were a prisoner, yearning for something, *anything*, to happen.

They'd all just turned fourteen in the previous months. It was the summer that preceded high school. A fact they were pondering on another scorching day while they considered things to do as they walked through town.

The Windflower Mall was out because last month the clerks at the drug mart had suspected Nikki of shoplifting eyeliner. They couldn't prove it because she'd deftly dropped the evidence in an old lady's bag. Still, security called police. Nikki wasn't charged but they took her fingerprints and her picture, and under some law or rule, banned her from the building for six months. Nikki took it as both a badge of honor and an affront that stoked the rage forever bubbling under her skin. For as long as Janie and Marie had known her, Nikki seemed to be at war with the world, carrying a deep, invisible wound.

"They can ban me for all my life—I don't care," Nikki said. "We see the same people at the food court, nothing to do there but laugh at seniors, Hutterites and cripples."

Besides, Nikki boasted, she'd stolen enough makeup from that place to last years and she piled it on to create the mask she hid behind. With her quickly maturing body, she looked older than Janie and Marie, who believed her claim that she was no longer a virgin.

After Nikki's father died when she was younger,

her mother, who was a cashier at Eternity Market Mart, began drinking and gambling, running up massive debts until she couldn't pay the bills. She met a man named Telforde, a contract painter at the bar, and they moved in with him. That was her family. Nikki smoked, drank her mother's alcohol, read dark books and listened to bands like Exact a Toll and Kill Me Now.

As for Marie, she had beautiful skin and soft brown eyes. She was a smart-dumb girl, a genius at math and science but always missing the obvious in real life. She was self-conscious about being a little heavy. A few years ago, her little brother, Pike, had choked on a piece of apple when the family was having a picnic by the creek. He died right in front of her. Marie felt safest with Janie and Nikki. They allowed her to love NSYNC, the Backstreet Boys and maintain her crush on one of the Hanson brothers. She was always humming "MMMBop," because Pike had loved it.

Janie's battle with zits didn't detract from her almond-shaped eyes and high cheekbones. Of the three girls, Janie's personality was the sweetest. She loved French fries, Coke, ice cream and Elton John. She liked all kinds of music, even—to Nikki's horror—country. But the weird thing was all three of them loved one particular song, an old one, "Ring of Fire." They sang it together, belting out the chorus because for each of them something was burning inside.

The girls had known each other all their lives and while Janie was not sure what she wanted to do with hers, she was resolute in her desire to one day get as far away from Eternity as possible. To move someplace like New York, London or Paris. She was already working on her dream by saving her babysitting money.

Janie and her friends were determined to leave this town for their own painful reasons. But today, they just wanted to escape boredom.

"We haven't been to the cemetery in a while," Nikki suggested, once more forgetting about Marie, not seeing the hurt in her eyes.

Nikki liked counting the graves, guessing how people had died. Once she jumped into a freshly dug grave and lay in it for a while. "It's cold in here." Janie and Marie had to help her climb out.

It was during the last time they'd gone to the cemetery and Nikki was doing her Empress of the Dark thing when Marie couldn't take it anymore.

"I hate it when you do this crap. I don't like coming here like this."

Nikki smirked and shrugged. Fighting tears, Marie ran across the cemetery. Janie and Nikki let her go, then sat under the shade of the tall poplar trees, listening to the birdsong. In the distance they saw Marie kneeling at her brother's grave, which they always avoided when they came here, the breezes carrying her voice as she sang Pike's favorite song.

Some days Marie got so sad about Pike. Other days it was like she was almost glad he was dead. It was a little disturbing.

Now, after digesting Nikki's suggestion, Marie said: "I do not want to go to the cemetery today."

Nikki took stock of Marie's face, reconsidered. "What about the railroad tracks or down to the creek?"

"We've done all those places *to death*," Janie said.

"What about the restaurant at the golf course?" Marie said.

Nikki rolled her eyes and Janie gave Marie a sharp glance, correcting Marie's memory lapse as to why the Eternity Country Club was off-limits.

Janie's mother was a waitress at the club's restaurant, a job she was still clinging to after the incident that happened the first and only time the girls had gone there.

It was in the spring and Nikki had dared them to go. "We're just as good as those rich snobs," Nikki had said. "I bet they've got the best desserts and I've got money from the creep." She waved cash she'd stolen from her mom's boyfriend.

Janie had been uneasy about going to the restaurant because of her mother's caution. "I know you and your friends wander all over town but you are never to go there," her mother had said. "It's not for us. It's not the mall—it's where I work. Do you understand?"

Janie had never set foot in the place.

A few times in the past she, Marie and Nikki had walked up to the gate of the forbidden kingdom, marveling at its vast and perfect green lawns, the trees, the waterfall, people gliding around in the little carts and the clubhouse, a low-standing stone building that beckoned them.

They were curious about what it would be like to go inside.

Maybe it was Nikki's bold defiance of authority that drove her to break rules. The way she saw it, the world owed her a better life than the one she was living, and maybe it was because she seemed older, more experienced, but these forces shaped her persona, never failing to pull Janie and Marie into her orbit.

"Are you little girls afraid to walk in there? Because I'm not." Nikki had challenged them that day.

Marie turned to Janie—it was up to her.

It was a Saturday and Janie's mom was not working at the golf course. When Janie had left that morning, she was still in bed. Janie had figured by the empty bottle on the kitchen table from the night before that she'd be sleeping much of the day. Ever since Janie's dad had walked out on them two years ago, leaving them nothing but bills, her mother had become what Janie had later learned was *a functioning alcoholic*.

"Come on," Nikki said.

"But we're not members," Janie said. "We won't get in."

"We'll get in. I'll do all the talking," Nikki said. "Let's do it. It'll be fun."

Janie saw sparks in Nikki's eyes, felt herself being pulled, felt her resistance crumble. Nikki was their leader and always would be. So they went, setting in motion events that would change Eternity forever.

Two

When the girls got to the host station, Nikki was prepared.

"My dad's finishing his game. He said that me and my friends were supposed to wait for him in the restaurant. His name's William Carruthers."

The host guy gave them a quick, guarded appraisal before he started looking in his book. The air was appetizing, inviting and carried the sound of conversations, cutlery clinking. "I'm afraid he doesn't appear to be listed."

Janie tugged at Nikki's wrist, a signal to abandon the plan. Nikki shrugged it off.

"We're from Winnipeg," Nikki said. "He's discussing business with people here, big business."

"Do you know who he's with, the member's name, perhaps?"

"I don't. But if it's a problem I'll just tell my dad you couldn't let us in."

Weighing her subtle threat and the ramifications, the host smiled. "No. Not a problem. For three?"

"Four. For when my dad comes," Nikki said. "He likes to be by the window."

"Of course. Right this way."

He led them to a corner with floor-to-ceiling windows that looked out to a sea of green. Their table was dark wood with rolled white linen napkins, ornate glass goblets and high-backed white leather chairs. Soft music was playing as their server, a woman Janie did not know, brought them menus. They each ordered sodas and apple pie with ice cream.

"This pie is so good," Marie said. "I feel like royalty."

"Look at them over there showing off their money." Nikki glanced at the other tables, eyeing men as some paid, signing and leaving cash tips. "We're just as good as those rich people, right, Janie?"

Janie had stopped in midchew, emotions swirling as, across the dining room, she saw her mother taking an order. Believing she was home, Janie was shocked. At the same time, witnessing her mother in a servile situation, displaying an artificial smile, one Janie had never seen before, filled her with embarrassment, sadness. And fear.

For upon finishing, her mother turned, recognition flashing like lightning on her face as she moved directly toward their table.

"Oh God," Janie said.

Her friends' attention shifted to Janie's mother.

"What're you doing here, Janie?"

"I thought you were home."

"I took an extra shift. How did you get in?"

No one responded. Her mother's eyes swept over the table.

Nikki grinned and said: "Just relax, Marlene."

Janie's mother's eyebrows arched at Nikki's insolent use of her first name.

Nikki sipped her Coke. "We're not hurting anybody."

"I don't need any lip from you." Janie's mother's face reddened. "Just the pies and drinks?"

Janie nodded.

"Finish and leave. I'll take care of the bill," Janie's mother said.

"I've got money," Nikki said.

Janie assessed Nikki. "I just bet you do." Then, before she left, her gaze drilled into her daughter. "We're not members. None of you are. There are rules. I don't know what you did to get in but don't you ever pull a stunt like this again. Do you understand?"

Janie's mother left and a long moment passed with Janie staring at the eternal green lawn. Nikki and Marie worked on their pie.

"I don't know what she's all lathered up about." Nikki chewed slowly. "We're not hurting anyone." Her focus then went to the vacated tables nearby that still had cash on them.

When they left, Nikki moved toward the tables with unwatched cash.

"Don't," Janie said.

Nikki ignored her, quickly plucking small bills and coins just as someone called out: "Watch it!"

Heads snapped.

Several tables away, Janie's mom, carrying a tray loaded with food, had glanced at the girls, not seeing the man who'd left his table and had stepped into her path. The collision caused a ceramic explosion, launching a starburst of food that splattered on tables, the floor and the man.

"I'm so sorry, sir!" Janie's mother quickly seized a napkin, brushing at the tomato, lettuce, fries and toast that had stuck to his designer golf shirt, unable to remove the mayo splotched on his chest and shoulder. "Sir, I'm so sorry."

"It's okay," the man said. "Just an accident."

Janie's mom got down on her knees, brushing lettuce and chicken from his pants, bacon, tomato and mayo from his shoes. Her hands shook as she gathered the broken plates and food onto her tray while other men applauded and snickered.

"Looks like lunch is on you, Roy," one man said.

The joke brought on roars of laughter.

The incident also brought on the host and a well-dressed unsmiling woman, no doubt a manager. Both of them hovered over Janie's mom, still on her knees cleaning up, as she wiped her face with the back of her hand. She lifted her head, tears in her eyes as they locked onto her daughter and her friends, looking down on her.

* * *

Janie avoided going home until around eleven that night when she was dropped off from baby-sitting at the Landers.

Janie and her mother lived in a rented duplex that was not far from the railyards and the slaughterhouse. On hot days the stench was terrible, like the smell of defeat.

Her mother was waiting in the kitchen, bills fanned over the table next to a glass with ice and a bottle that she was deep into. Her hair was mussed, her face puffy, eyes bloodshot. Janie knew the look and steeled herself.

"Do you know who that man was today?" Her mother poured a drink. "The guy I dumped my tray on?"

Janie shook her head.

"Royston J. Tullock. He owns the Prairie Winds Farm Equipment Center, a big deal in his church, donates barrels of money, one of the richest people around. Oh, and he's on the board of the Eternity Country Club." Janie's mom raised her glass in salute. "Know what happens when your daughter and her friends sneak into the club and you dump food on Royston J. Tullock?"

Janie shook her head.

"You get fired."

Janie's hands flew to her face.

"Here's my day," her mother said. "I overslept and was late for work, then you show up with that slut Nikki and that idiot Marie, then I dump food on Tullock and, ta-da, I'm out of a job."

Janie's voice squeaked as she managed: "I'm sorry."

"It was a good paying job and this year they were going to keep the restaurant open in the winter, but now—" she snatched a fistful of bills "—how am I going to pay these? Credit cards, rent, phone, electricity, groceries? How? With your babysitting money?"

Her mother slammed the table.

"I'm sorry," Janie said again.

"Sorry doesn't put food on the table! I told you never to go there! But you never listen to me. Why?"

Janie was silent.

"You won't listen to me but you listen to that slut Nikki!"

"Don't call her that. You of all people shouldn't call her that."

Her mother's chair scraped and fell as she rose from the table and slapped Janie's face.

"Don't you ever talk like that to me!" Nostrils flaring, eyes brimming, her mother glared at her. "I can't stand looking at you. Get out of my sight!"

Her face stinging, Janie ran to her bedroom, slammed her door, locked it, then climbed out of her window.

Fighting tears, she ran through the night to the apartment building where Nikki lived with her mother and Telforde. It was at times like this that Janie wished she and her friends had cellular phones, but they were so expensive and only a few rich kids at school had them. So she threw pebbles way up at Nikki's bedroom window until she appeared.

In whispered tones Janie related what had happened. Nikki joined her and they walked several blocks to the tumbledown house where Marie lived and did what they always did when one of them was hurting. They summoned Marie to her window and she slipped out the back door with the key to her family's dilapidated RV, resting on cinder blocks at the side of the house.

The girls climbed in, got into sleeping bags and through the night as crickets chirped, they talked about how much they hated Eternity.

"One day we'll show them all," Nikki said from behind the red glow of her cigarette.

"How will we do that?" Marie asked.

"We'll do something big. Something they'll never forget."

On the first Tuesday after she was fired, Janie's mother was circling job ads in the *Eternity Bulletin,* when she was called to the country club.

Thinking it was to collect her termination letter and final pay she was surprised to find Roy Tullock in the office with her former manager, Lila Skripchuck.

At Tullock's request, Marlene recounted what had happened the previous Saturday, carefully withholding any mention of being hungover. "I was not feeling well, I was distracted." Tullock then asked Marlene about her personal situation, and she told him she was raising a teenage daughter alone after her husband had abandoned them. Tullock nodded, possibly reflecting on his own teenage daughter, Torrie, whom, according to local gossip Marlene had heard, was in an institution in Winnipeg.

Marlene finished and Tullock rubbed his chin.

"When I learned of your dismissal and your situation as a single mom, I was concerned," he said. "Having a better understanding of the circumstances, young girls being a handful, we believe we rushed to judgment and that you should be reinstated. Right, Lila?"

"That's right, Mr. Tullock." Lila forced a smile.

"It was an accident. I should've been looking, too," Tullock said. "I believe in forgiveness and second chances."

Marlene's gaze flicked from Lila to Tullock, realization dawning.

"Thank you, thank you both." Marlene shook their hands.

"Yes," Lila said. "Just be more careful. We'll see you at the usual time tomorrow."

"Oh," Tullock said, "Marlene, you'd mentioned that your daughter was fourteen and babysits for Marv Lander, one of my senior managers at the center?"

"Yes, she sits for Mr. Lander."

"Has she taken first aid and CPR courses?"

"She has."

"Good. I ask because it turns out our sitter and her family are moving to Calgary, where her dad's been transferred. Do you think your daughter would be interested in watching our son and daughter?"

"Absolutely."

And that was how Janie came to babysit for the Tullocks in their house at the edge of town, the one with the front lawn almost as big as a football field and the four-car garage. Janie was overwhelmed when she stepped into it with its grand piano, chandeliers, plush carpet and expensive-looking furniture. She got along with Neal, a polite six-year-old, and Linda, who was five and very cute. They had an endless supply of toys but seemed lonely.

Their mother, Connie Tullock, was unlike any woman Janie had met. She spoke in a fake accent, like she was from England, even though everyone said she'd grown up in Moose Jaw. She was involved in a local theater group that put on plays. Janie thought Connie Tullock was weird and also nitpicky.

"You must be extremely careful around the pool," she told Janie that first time they met.

Then she had Janie prove she could swim by having her put on one of her teenage daughter's swimsuits and complete a full length of their inground pool.

Then she gave her a list of what foods Neal and Linda could have, what TV shows they could watch, when to take their vitamins, what time they had to go to bed, a list of emergency numbers, including Connie's and Roy's cellular phones.

Alone with the kids, Janie walked through the Tullock home. She played Chopsticks for them on the piano. Then she studied the framed family pictures. Torrie Tullock was sixteen and pretty. Janie wondered why she was so much older than Neal and Linda, and why she lived in Winnipeg.

"Mom and dad say Torrie's sick," Neal said. "We see her at Christmas."

Neal and Linda liked Janie, so did Mr. Tullock, and she became their regular sitter that spring. Things went pretty much all right except for when it came time to pay Janie. She soon learned that despite their wealth the Tullocks were tightwads. Mr. Tullock never seemed to have enough cash on him, leaving it to his wife to either pay Janie, or top off what he thought he'd already paid her.

It got confusing and soon became common for Janie to be shortchanged. In the early days, whenever she tried to raise the issue, the Tullocks would wave off her concern, saying they'd pay her what they owed next time and include extra. It never happened.

Mr. Tullock always drove Janie home but once when he was busy, Mrs. Tullock drove her home in her silver Mercedes, which smelled new with a hint of her perfume. The road was a little bumpy near the railroad yards when she pulled up to Janie's house. The stench of the slaughterhouse invaded the car as Mrs. Tullock stared at the duplex.

"This is where you live?"

In that moment, with her accent, her tone, her Mercedes, she had reduced Janie to someone to be looked down upon, someone beneath Connie Tullock's station in life.

Someone of less value.

And in that instant, Janie saw her mother in the restaurant on her knees brushing food from Mr. Tullock's shoes and her stomach twisted with an internal scream. She welcomed the horrible stink from the slaughterhouse into the car like an allied force and even though the air-conditioning was on, dropped the window.

Yes, Janie thought, *smell it. Breathe it in. This is where I live.*

"Oh my, that is pungent, isn't it?" Mrs. Tullock said, reaching into her wallet. "Now, Roy's already given you some cash. I believe we owe you another five."

"Another ten for tonight," Janie said.

"No, I believe it's five."

"It's ten."

"Well, look, dear, all I have is this five, twenties and fifties."

"I could take a twenty and get change from my mom or from the store and bring it to you next time."

"Don't be silly. Roy and I will make the adjustment next time, like we always do."

"But you don't—"

"Take this five with our thanks as always." Then subtly placing a finger under her nose, Mrs. Tullock hit the button to raise the window as Janie got out.

That was how it had gone since she began sitting for the Tullocks. Janie tried presenting the problem to them but it was futile—they always dismissed it as honest mistakes. Complicating it all was the fact that sitting for them was tied to her mother's job at the golf course. So Janie never pushed it, but she began keeping a log of how much she was owed. By this point in the summer it had grown to about a hundred dollars, along with her anger as she, Nikki and Marie walked through town that hot summer day aching for someplace to go and something to do.

The cemetery was out. The golf course was definitely out. The Eternity rodeo was long over. They didn't care to watch boys playing street hockey and they'd gone everywhere there was to go a million times.

"All right," Nikki said, "I think it's time."

"Time for what?" Marie asked.

"Time we take serious control of our lives."

"What do you mean?" Janie asked.

"I've been reading stuff, stuff that's a little scary, but we'll do it. Tonight."

"Do what? What're you talking about?" Janie asked.

"I can't explain it." Nikki took a cigarette from her bag and lit it, dragged on it. "But it's really big." She blew a stream of smoke. "We need to get something first. You gotta trust me. Let's go."

Janie and Marie exchanged excited glances, picking up their pace as they followed her, as they always did.

Nikki was the leader.

Three

Eternity, Manitoba
2000

Nikki led them out of town along the path in the fields that bordered the highway. Not far in the distance they saw their destination: The Big Sky Horizon Truck Stop, busy with rows of big rigs with their growling diesels and hissing brakes rolling in and out of the stop, heading across Canada or into the United States. Huge flags flapped from chrome-tipped poles that reached high above the main building where the girls entered. Nikki led them into the big store.

Janie watched Nikki go to the discount jewelry section and study a tray of rings as she and Marie went up and down aisles offering T-shirts, caps, sunglasses, along with country music CDs.

Other sections had stuffed animals and toy trucks; while others had jumper cables, gloves, caps, snow brushes and ice-scrapers, coolers and sunscreen, testament to the fact that the weather in this part of the country was blistering in the summer and bone-cracking cold in the winter.

"The weather here's kind of biblical," Janie had always said.

Nikki found them in the aisle with potato chips and beef jerky.

"Okay, I'm done. Let's go."

"What is it we're doing?" Janie said. "Why're you so mysterious?"

"You'll see. You both need to sneak out tonight and meet me at eleven on the corner near my place. It's important. Be there."

That night at eleven, Janie and Marie found Nikki on the corner smoking. When they arrived she'd reached into her bag, withdrawing a small bottle. Under the streetlamp they saw a vodka label but the drink was orange.

"It's called a screwdriver and I made it extra sweet. You both need to take a gulp," Nikki said.

Janie and Marie each took a drink, shuddering as the sweet fiery liquid warmed their throats.

"Whoa," Marie said.

They walked through the night to the creek and into the woods. Guided only by moonlight, Nikki stopped at a secluded spot. Breezes rustled the leaves; birds and insects cheeped and clicked in the night.

"It's creepy here," Marie said.

"You guys ever kill anything?" Nikki asked. "On purpose?"

"What do you mean?" Janie said.

"I've killed squirrels and birds in here." Nikki

chuckled. "Threw stones to wound them, then I finished them off, stabbing them with a stick."

"That's so gross!" Janie said. "Why'd you do it?"

"To see what it was like," Nikki said.

"Did you feel bad after?" Marie asked.

"Nope. It feels good to have the power to decide who lives and who dies, you know. Drink some more."

The bottle was passed around, followed by swishes and gasps.

"Okay, there are important steps to this and this will only work if we do them all together. First, we have to take off our clothes."

"What? Why?" Marie protested.

"We have to be totally naked."

"But there's bugs and things," Marie said.

"Do it. I'll go first."

In the darkness Nikki stripped down, proving she was serious. Then Janie, feeling the alcohol and a surge of electricity at the illicitness, did the same, and soon they coaxed Marie to join them. Then Nikki reached into her bag for a candle. She lit it and placed it on the ground, collaring it with some stones, the dim light dancing over them.

"Now that we're naked we have nothing to hide. We must each bare our souls to each other. Tell us your deepest, darkest secret and none of us can ever share it. Ever. This will bind us. I'll start."

Nikki watched the candle's flame dance in the eyes of her friends as she revealed how Telforde, her mother's boyfriend, came into her room at night. He would touch her and do things to her, and make her do things to him.

"He said that if I ever told, he would kick me and my mom out of his place because he pays the bills. I so want to kill him."

Tears rolled down Nikki's face glistening in the candlelight. She brushed at them.

"Your turn, Marie."

"Uhm, I don't know if I can."

"Come on, Marie," Nikki said.

"Uhm," she sniffed. "Okay. No one knows this but the day Pike died… I was feeding him the apple. I cut big pieces because he liked them and I kept cutting them bigger telling him he looked funny with all that apple in his mouth." She stopped, her voice quivering when she resumed. "That's when he started choking. I tried to pull the piece out, but it was way down…and then he choked…and it was my fault he died. I never told my parents, anyone, but I think my parents know and they hate me for killing him. They think that I'm just a fat, stupid waste of life, that I killed my little brother and shouldn't even exist for what I did."

Marie wiped her tears.

Nikki and Janie touched her shoulders to console her.

"You know what?" Marie said, her composure instantly regained. Her tears gone. "Maybe I did kill him on purpose. And maybe I don't even care. They always liked Pike more than me so it all evens out." Then she giggled to herself.

Exchanging glances, Nikki and Janie took a moment to absorb Marie's admission, letting a silent moment pass before Nikki turned to Janie, who took a breath.

"One day, I was looking for an old school paper I was going to use for a new assignment." Her eyes locked on to the flame as if she were watching herself. "I was searching through some of my mother's things. I went into her closet and through some boxes and found an old journal my mom had. I began reading it and learned that my dad was not my dad, that he used to beat my mom and she went out and had sex with some jerk she'd met at a bar. She didn't even know his real name. She was going to have an abortion but tried to convince my dad that he was my father." Janie exhaled. "I guess my dad found out that I was not his kid and that's why he left. My mother doesn't know that I know, or maybe she does, I don't know, but it's like this hateful thing between us and I'm not sure I can ever really love her like I should, you know?"

"That's sad. You came so close to not even being born," Nikki said.

An owl hooted in the quiet that followed until Marie said: "I'm getting cold. I want to get dressed."

"Shh. Not yet." Nikki took a half sheet of paper from her bag and set it before the candle. In the light they saw her neat printing but could not read it. "We need to make a circle, hold hands, and you must repeat the words I say exactly as I say them.

This is serious. Do not say anything else. Repeat them together. Ready?"

The girls held hands, nodded, and Nikki began making strange sounds.

"Nema! Live morf su reviled tub... ."

Momentarily taken aback by the gibberish, Janie and Marie repeated the odd sounds in unison with Nikki until she ended with "...ni tra ohw rethaf rou!"

"What did we just say?" Janie asked.

"The Lord's Prayer backward."

"But why?" Marie asked.

"It gives us power from the nether regions."

"The nether regions? Do you mean hell? Are we, like, witches?"

"No, it's in the books I read. We're almost bound. One more thing, give me your pointer finger on your left hand."

Nikki reached into her bag. Something small glinted in the night and without warning, using a sewing needle, she pricked the tips of Marie's and Janie's fingers, then her own, drawing blood.

"That hurts! What're you doing, Nikki?" Marie said.

"Don't be a baby. Touch your bloody tips together with mine over the flame so our blood mingles."

The girls pressed their fingers together. Their blood hissed as it dripped into the melted wax pooled atop the candle.

"All right, now each of us gets a ring. These might be a little big. I got them from the truck stop today. You must always have your ring with you, on your finger or a chain."

They were three different skull rings that bikers and truckers liked. Nikki gave Marie the death's head; gave Janie the sugar skull and kept the skull expressing rage for herself. The girls slid them on their fingers.

"Now it's official," Nikki said. "By this ritual we're secretly known as The Skull Sisters. We're family. We do everything together. Everything we get, we share. We protect each other. We never betray or tell on each other. None of us is better than her other sisters. No matter where we go or what we do in life, nothing will tear us apart, because we've made a blood bond and a pact that are forever."

As the breezes raked through the treetops and the candlelight burned in their eyes, Janie, Marie and Nikki nodded.

Their bond was sealed.

"Now," Nikki said, "the first thing The Skull Sisters are going to do is make sure Janie gets the money the Tullocks owe her."

The next day they met in Prairie Sun Memorial Park. Its main features were the weather-beaten soldier statue and flower gardens honoring local people killed in wars.

In the section of the park with the playground, Janie, Marie and Nikki were on the swings, which creaked with their gentle swaying as Nikki outlined the plan to right the wrong the Tullocks had inflicted upon Janie.

"They treat you like crap and rip you off, right?" Nikki said.

"Yes."

"They look down on you and people like us, right?"

"They do."

"We hate them so much, right?" Nikki said.

"We hate them," Marie said. "They think they're better than everyone."

"They owe Janie over a hundred dollars. All we're going to do is get it."

"How?" Janie asked.

"Simple. You said they're planning to go away soon with their brats."

"To Regina to visit friends."

"So the next time you sit for them and just before they go to Regina, you just make sure a window is unlocked. That's it. And we'll go in and find where they keep the cash. They've got to have plenty in the house, and The Skull Sisters will collect—*not steal*, but collect—what they owe you."

Janie thought about it.

"It's perfect," Nikki said. "If it happens when they're away, it could be anybody—they have no reason to suspect you. And, they're so freaking rich they probably won't even miss it."

"Sounds fair to me," Marie said, admiring her new ring. "It's not stealing if they owe you."

Janie got to thinking how Connie Tullock with her fake accent acted like she was superior to her;

remembered her mother on her knees cleaning Roy Tullock's shoes. Janie thought about the pain she carried about who she was and where she belonged in this world, thought about the Tullocks *keeping her money* and she found herself nodding as anger bubbled in her stomach. "Let's do it."

"Good," Nikki said. "Okay, there's something we need to do."

Emboldened with their bond and their mission, the girls decided to record the milestone. Disregarding Nikki's ban, they went to the mall and directly to the photo booth near the main entrance. Laughing, they all jammed inside, shut the curtain, deposited the money, then did a series of poses. The booth's mechanism hummed and ejected photo strips. They collected one for each of them.

Admiring the photos, Nikki grinned. "This is going to be historic."

Nearly three weeks later, just after midnight, The Skull Sisters met on the corner near Nikki's house where she was smoking. Seeing them, Nikki blew a stream of smoke and held up the vodka bottle with orange juice she'd prepared for the night.

The girls drank as they walked to the edge of town with Janie confirming that the Tullocks had left the previous day for Regina. She said she knew how to work their alarm system and could switch it off when they got there. When she'd sat for them a couple of nights before she'd unlocked a basement window in a storage room that no one seemed to use.

Hearts beating faster with every step they covered the distance across town in no time before they came to the Tullocks' property.

They stood on a small rise overlooking the sprawling yard, the house standing before them, deserted in the darkness, glorious for all it represented. Their rage and private pain burning, they each took last gulps with Nikki finishing the bottle and tossing it.

"Let's go," she said.

They moved toward the house, taking the next steps that would irrevocably change their lives and release them from Eternity.

Four

Orange County, California
Present day

Where's Carson Clark?

Emma Grant checked the time—*ten minutes late*. Students were often late for appointments with the school counselor but as she clicked through his file again, concern seeped into her thoughts.

Carson's grades were slipping, jeopardizing his plan to go into the military as a way to pursue a medical degree. His parents had recently separated; his mother had been in and out of hospital fighting cancer. Fortunately, relatives lived nearby. But Carson had told Emma he was "a bit sad about my folks…sometimes it's like, what's the point?"

She had tried to set him up with a psychologist, just to talk. But Carson smiled that broad smile of his and said: "No thanks, I'm good."

It worried Emma that many of the students who confided in her refused to accept expert help.

Apart from their home lives, they faced so many issues: academic and athletic pressure; stress; online bullying; race, gender and mental health discrimination; along with postsecondary planning. Amid all that, Emma had to navigate around legal, privacy and policy restrictions, to decipher the subtext of what students shared with her to identify those at risk of harming themselves, or being violent against others.

It was never easy but she'd made it her life's mission to help young people. She'd learned long ago from painful, personal experience that one wrong decision could change the course of your life.

Now at thirty-four with a master's degree, and even after taking every new course available to do her absolute best for the kids she counseled, she was lucky if she could get through to even one each day.

But the one she could not seem to reach was the one closest to her: Kayla, her sixteen-year-old stepdaughter. Emma checked her phone. Still no response to the texts she'd sent her.

Emma realized that Kayla would never accept her as her mother, especially after Kayla's dad had married Emma three years after Kayla's mom had died. Kayla's dad had called his daughter's relationship to Emma "a work in progress." But today Kayla had been more distant than usual, picking at the omelet Emma had made for her.

"Kayla, is there anything you'd like to talk about?"

"Not really," Kayla said to her phone. "I gotta go."

She hefted her bag over her shoulder, kissed her dad, then left for school. When the door closed Emma had turned to Ben.

"I'm failing with her," she said.

"No you're not. She's still adjusting."

"We've been married a year. We've been together longer than that, yet she refuses to let me into her life."

"She's still grappling with unresolved grief. She just needs time."

Emma understood but needed to diminish the undercurrent of tension between them. Kayla did not attend Valley Meadow High School where Emma worked, a blessing because it gave them space but it was also a challenge when Emma wanted to talk to her face-to-face. Emma's texts to Kayla suggesting a shopping or lunch date had gone unanswered.

Her thoughts shifted to Carson and the time—*seventeen minutes late*—when her phone chimed with a text. Not Kayla, but one of Carson's friends. Cheyenne, a sensitive student Emma had counseled who planned to become a nurse.

Cheyenne had written:

Thought you should see this message Carson just sent out. We're worried, somebody just saw him cleaning out his locker.

Then a screenshot of a text from Carson came through:

Time for me to check out-don't want to be on this earth any longer. I love you guys.

Emma sat bolt upright, looked up Carson's number and called his phone. As it rang, she put it on speaker, her keyboard clicking as she searched Carson's social media accounts. All had been deleted but one, which had one message: "Bye," next to a sad face with a teardrop.

Carson's phone went unanswered and Emma's focus shot to the protocol for alerting the school to a student at risk of self-harm.

Or harming others.

No, Carson wouldn't do that. Would he?

Then, as if on cue, as if by some fantastic miracle, Emma glanced out her office window and saw him—Carson was outside.

Relief and alarm pulsed through her as she rushed from her desk, ran down the hall, students turning, jaws dropping as Emma burst out the main entrance doors.

Carson was well ahead of her, walking away from the school, moving with big strides along the sidewalk that bordered the busy four-lane boulevard. She saw his bulging backpack, saw him gripping the straps.

"Carson!" Emma called as she ran.

He didn't respond. He was heading in the direction of Meadow Valley Elementary.

What's in his backpack?

"Carson, stop!" Emma called over the traffic, running closer to him.

He turned to her, gripping his straps.

An engine growled as she got closer. Carson raised one hand, flashed his palm; their eyes met as he mouthed the word *Bye*, then stepped from the sidewalk into the path of an oncoming Orange County transit bus as it gained speed.

Blood thumping in her ears, Emma reached out and in a heartbeat clawed at one of Carson's straps, gripping it, saw the bus driver's eyes balloon with horror as he twisted the steering wheel, brakes pealing, wheels locking, thudding, the entire bus dipping, swaying as Emma pulled Carson away and down to the pavement.

The bus just missed him.

The stench of burning rubber and clouds of smoke rolled over them. Horns blared. The bus doors opened, the driver flying out to them. Passengers and students gawked. Someone called 9-1-1.

"What the hell, kid, are you all right?" the driver asked.

Carson was crying, choking, coughing sobs. Emma gently pulled off his backpack and held him for a long moment.

"You're going to be okay. We're going to get help. You will get through this," Emma said to the wail of approaching sirens.

As a precaution, paramedics took Carson to the nearest hospital.

His mother was undergoing chemotherapy miles away at a different hospital in Irvine. The school alerted his aunt and uncle, who rushed to be with him. They'd also reached his father, who scrambled to get on the next flight from Houston.

Emma gave a statement to police, then in accordance with school policy, completed reports and forms. Twice she reached for her phone to call her husband but was at a loss as to what she'd say, deciding to wait until she saw him at home. Afterward Glenda Heywood, the principal, came to her office to speak with her.

"The police told me what the bus driver said. Your quick action saved him, Emma." Heywood touched her shoulder. "How're you holding up? Do you need to talk to anyone?"

Emma shook her head, adrenaline still rippling through her. "We were so lucky. His friends noticed something wrong and alerted me. The signs weren't glaring but they were there."

"He's alive because of you and his friends," Heywood said. "Cancel whatever else you've got today and go home. Want me to call anyone for you?"

"No. I'll be okay. Thanks."

After wrapping up matters and collecting her things, Emma stared at her phone. Again, she thought of calling Ben but dismissed it. Still no response from Kayla.

I'll deal with all of it later, she thought, embracing the warm breeze drifting across the staff parking lot. She got behind the wheel of her SUV and before starting it a chill coiled through her. Glancing at her phone and Carson's farewell text, she knew what it felt like when you *don't want to be on this earth any longer.*

But she was a survivor. It took years but she'd made so many changes so she could crawl out of the dark, fighting to prove that she had value in this world, that she could help people. She was doing that every day, building a life, *a good life with Ben and Kayla.* But beneath the surface she struggled because the scars of her past would never, ever fade.

Emma thrust her face into her hands and cried.

After several minutes she found her composure, searched her bag for a tissue. Using the visor mirror, she tried to regain her composure, then froze at what she saw.

In the distance, far across the street she saw a parked car, a green sedan, with a woman behind the wheel wearing dark glasses and a white ball cap.

Is it my imagination, or is she watching me?

Emma was certain she'd seen her once or twice before…

Anger surging, she opened her door, got out and strode toward her. But before she could cross the street the woman started her engine and drove off, leaving Emma exasperated and perplexed. Cursing under her breath, she returned to her SUV, halting when she noticed something she'd missed before: a small, white envelope tucked under a wiper.

Nothing was written on it.

She tore it open, finding a single sheet of paper with a printed message.

SOON IT WILL BE 20 YEARS. YOUR DAY OF RECKONING IS COMING.

Five

Tires.

The ad for the sale popped up on Ben Grant's computer screen triggering memories of his wife.

The deputies investigating the accident had said that Brooke's tires were worn and the right front had blown when she'd swerved in the rain, likely to miss a raccoon or coyote. She'd lost control; the car had rolled down into a ravine.

Brooke had been on her way to join him and Kayla at their cabin in the San Bernardino Mountains. Two weeks before her crash Brooke thought her tires might need replacing.

"I looked at the wear bars but I'm not sure," she'd told him. "Taking care of our cars is your job, buddy. Will you check my tires?"

"Consider it done."

But in the days that followed he was racing to meet the deadline for his new book and she was overseeing an investigative feature at the *Orange*

County Register, where she was a senior editor. They were putting in long hours and looking forward to getting away to their cabin with Kayla for some family time.

He'd forgotten to check Brooke's tires.

And the next thing he knew two San Bernardino County Sheriff's Deputies were at the cabin door, telling him his wife had been in an accident and that she didn't survive.

The aftermath was a surreal whirlwind, Ben crying out, falling to his knees, his ears ringing with Kayla's shrieks. In the hazy time that followed, it was as if the ground under their feet had given way and they'd plunged into an abyss.

Family and friends supported them. It helped.

Eventually his brain began to function in spurts. He and Kayla became a tight unit of survivors until they got a dog, a golden retriever they named Tug, and slowly they healed together—just the three of them. Then two years after Brooke's death he'd met Emma. She was like grief-soothing balm, helping him move on to the next chapter of his life.

A collar clinked. Tug ambled into his office, set his chin on Ben's lap.

Petting the back of Tug's neck, Ben glanced at the contract next to his keyboard, eyes going to the words Delivery of Manuscript, and the legalese under the heading concerning extensions, failure to deliver and liabilities.

Unease rolled over him.

He had written more than a dozen true-crime books. He wrote his first when he'd covered a sensational murder case while working as a reporter for the *Los Angeles Times*. That's where he'd met Brooke, who was also a reporter.

Ben's debut was a national bestseller. It became a TV series. His subsequent books were also worldwide bestsellers, translated into thirty-two languages. Some became movies. He married Brooke and left reporting to write full-time. Brooke took a buyout from the *Times*, and they moved to Orange County. After she had Kayla, she got back into the business, becoming an editor at the *Register*.

But in the years after her death, Ben had not delivered a new book. He hadn't even started one. In fact, he hadn't even found the right case to write about while his publisher had granted him extension after extension.

"They've been compassionate but I'll give it to you straight, Benjamin," his agent, Roz Rose, had said on the phone from New York. "If we don't give them something soon, they can legally demand you repay them every cent of advance money. Ben, losing Brooke was hard, but you've got Emma and you've moved on, so…"

Tug's collar jingled as Ben stroked his neck.

In the wake of Brooke's death Ben's concern for Kayla never abated. She'd lost her mother at one of the most critical times in a young girl's life, her adolescence. The loss was a cruel and merciless severing from which Ben feared Kayla might not recover.

Look at how she's still struggling to accept Emma.

Ben had met Emma at a book conference in Pasadena. Normally private, he'd become more reclusive after Brooke's death but because he'd known the organizers, he agreed to go. Emma stood in line at his book signing, telling him, "I love your books. You have a deep understanding for everyone touched by the crime—even the killers."

Her observation stuck with him because it was true. Later, he saw her sitting alone and invited her for coffee. He'd learned that she'd studied sociology and psychology before getting a master's degree and becoming a school counselor. She'd grown up far from California—"Oh, I lived here and there." She told him how she had known tragedy in her life and how she had found meaning in his books.

"They're operatic because of their scope, their consequence," she said. "Your writing reaches a part of me."

Ben was intrigued, captivated. With Emma he'd found the light he'd been searching for. It was behind Emma's eyes, mingled with vulnerability. Somehow being with her felt right. It was as if she could show him the way out of his darkness. After talking for nearly an hour, he asked to see her again. They began dating and a year later, they were married.

Kayla did her best to welcome Emma into their lives. Ben knew that for Kayla, Emma's presence had upset the equilibrium of their father-daughter

universe, changed the dynamic of their survivors'
unit. He knew how hard it was. Even now, a year
into their marriage Kayla was still having trouble
making room for Emma in her grieving heart.

Tug's bark pulled him from his thoughts. Someone had come in. He went to the kitchen where he
found Emma.

"You're home early," he said reading concern
in her face. "What is it?"

She stood at the counter, hands shaking, cupping her face. He got her a glass of water and she
recounted her close call with Carson. Listening,
nodding at the seriousness of her ordeal, he took
her into his arms.

"I almost lost him, right in front of me," she said
into Ben's chest. "There I was in my office and
he was a few feet away intent on ending his life."

"But you stopped him, Em. You saved him."

"Yes, but it was just dumb, stupid luck."

Tug barked, Emma lowered herself and hugged
him, letting him lick her face, just as Ben's phone
rang.

"Mr. Grant, this is Shawna Voight at the attendance office of Kayla's school."

"Yes?"

"In keeping with our policy, I'm calling to inform you that Kayla had an unexcused absence
today."

"What?" Ben turned to Emma: "Kayla wasn't
at school today."

"I texted her all morning. She never responded."
Emma got her phone from her purse to check it.

"Are you sure?" Ben said into his phone. "There has to be a mistake."

"She did not attend any classes today," Voight said. "As a result she'll need a handwritten explanatory note when she returns. Because this is her second instance, a third will mean truancy and her case will go to the Attendance Review Board for follow-up action. And, Mr. Grant, looking at her file, a reminder that Kayla's past behavioral incidents, her outbursts at teachers, will be taken into consideration by the Board. Sir, we're aware Kayla lost her mother several years ago and we've been sympathetic but there are policies. Kayla could face suspension."

"I understand. Thank you, Ms. Voight," Ben ended the call.

Momentarily bewildered, he dragged his hand over his face and shook his head, barely noticing that Emma, her back to him at the counter, was staring at a letter before sliding it back into her purse.

"She didn't go to school?" Emma said, turning to him. "Then where is she?"

Six

Tug kept pace with Ben as they moved through Suntrail Sky Park. Ben scoured the grassland hills and tangled brushwood ascending the twisting pathway with a sick feeling squirming in his stomach.

Kayla had to be here somewhere. *Let her be safe.*

In the moments after the school had alerted them to her absence, Ben and Emma launched a flurry of texts and calls. Kayla didn't respond. Ben then tried using an app to locate her phone but it appeared that Kayla had disabled the tracking feature. The last known location of her phone was their house. They'd searched it in vain. Then they contacted the parents of Kayla's friends, along with their neighbors. No one had seen her.

"I'm worried," Emma said. "She seemed so distant, so detached this morning. Where could she be?"

Ben racked his brains for the answer and came to one possibility.

"The park," he said. "You stay here in case she comes home and I'll search with Tug."

Suntrail Sky Park had miles of trails connecting Cielo Valle's neighborhoods, necklacing the surrounding communities of Lake Forest and Mission Viejo on a ridge. It had lush woodland, streams and rock formations along rising slopes that offered unbroken views of the region. Ben and Kayla loved living in Cielo Valle, which translated to Sky Valley. They liked the park for its serenity, a place to think. After Brooke died, Kayla came here to be alone, usually on Brooke's birthday. Or the day she died.

Ben prayed this is where she was.

But today wasn't her birthday or any other important date, he thought, just as they crested a hill. Tug's leash tensed and Ben saw Kayla in the spot where she often came to contemplate the mountains and canyons. Sitting on a flat, sun-warmed rock, she turned at Tug's bark, and Ben let him run to her.

She opened her arms welcoming Tug, then embraced Ben.

"We've been worried. The school called. We tried to reach you."

"I'm sorry, I'm so sorry. It's just that—don't be mad, Dad."

"What is it?"

"It's like…"

Seeing that she had been crying, Ben sat on

the rock and took her hand. "Talk to me. Tell me what's going on."

Kayla brushed at her tears. "It's like you've forgotten Mom."

"What are you talking about?"

"After Mom died it was just you and me, you know? Then when you met Emma, she just… I wanted you to be happy, but it's just that, it's like you let Emma take Mom's place and you've forgotten all about Mom and it made me sad, confused and then angry."

Ben listened as she continued.

"I woke up this morning so angry. Oh God, it was horrible. I needed to be alone." She turned to the view. "So I left school, went to the mall. I walked around to the places I used to go with Mom, then I came here, you know, to be with her, to remember, and I tried to think what our lives would be like if she were still alive, still with us, if you never met Emma."

"Kayla," Ben couldn't find the words as she continued.

"Then," Kayla said, "I thought, what would happen to me if you died?"

That gave Ben pause and he searched the horizon because they knew the cold truth: nothing in this world is guaranteed.

"We have Emma in our lives," he said.

"I know, and I know you love her and everything, and that she's a nice person. I like her, Dad, I do, but she's not my mom."

"I understand. But look, we've talked about

this, Kayla. Emma is not replacing Mom. That can never happen. No one will ever replace her."

"I know but I can't help feeling this way, Dad."

Ben's jawline pulsed with his own frustration. They'd been down this emotional road many times.

"Listen, honey, I understand. You're going through a hard time. Losing Mom was a terrible thing. There's nothing bigger. I know that, and your school counselors know that. And Emma knows that. Want me to call Doctor Hirsch, so she can help you sort some of this stuff out?"

"No, I don't need Doctor Hirsch."

"Honey, I want you to listen because you need to hear this again. I've been married to Emma for more than a year. She's my wife, she's your step-mom and she's part of our family. Your feelings about Mom are important. It's natural to feel what you're feeling after losing her. I don't want you to think of Emma as your mom. But she is my wife, she is in our home, and we need to live as a family."

"I know, Dad."

"Maybe you should try talking to Emma about this. She's a counselor, she knows her stuff and you know she's had a tragic life, too."

"But do we really know her, Dad?"

"What?"

"I just have this weird vibe about her, you know?"

"Stop." Ben let out a long breath and dragged his hands over his face. "Stop this, Kayla. Of course we know her. I know what you're doing—you're putting your difficulty to accept her on her, and that's wrong. Emma is not the problem."

Kayla looked off, her chin quivering.

"Honey, I know you're hurting. I understand and I'm so sorry," Ben said, "but promise me you'll give Emma a chance. It could help."

"It's just hard, Dad."

"I know, I do. I understand, but give it time. And no more acting out or missing class. They're sympathetic but you're on thin ice at school. So the next time you're having trouble, talk to me, or Emma, first. Promise?"

"All right, I promise."

Ben rubbed her shoulders.

"I'm sorry for making you worry, Dad."

"I know. It's all right." He pulled her close. "It's been a tough day. Emma…she saved a boy today at her school."

"Really?"

Ben relayed the incident as they started down the slope.

"See, honey," Ben said when he'd finished. "Your stepmom's really a good person."

Kayla nodded. "Dad, can we maybe go to the cabin some weekend?"

Ben hesitated. Since the accident, they'd only gone a few times, some of them with Emma. He was thinking of selling it in case he had to pay back his advance. But Kayla's request surprised him and he weighed the idea as a positive, given that it was Kayla's.

"We'll see. Maybe later when I get things settled

on the book front. Until that time, why don't we all go to the beach this weekend? How's that sound?"

"I'm in."

"Good, okay. Here." He handed Tug's leash to her as they walked and reached for his phone. "I'll let Emma know we're on our way back."

He texted:

Found her. Safe. On our way home.

Oh, thank God, Emma responded with a heart and happy face.

Seven

On Sunday they drove up the Coast Highway stopping at a beach Ben liked near Laguna. It wasn't crowded. The three of them set up the blanket, umbrella and chairs. Then Kayla and Tug headed for the surf while Ben worked on his tablet.

Emma had a Stephen King hardcover on her lap. She had taken the note left under her wiper at school and had folded it into the pages so she could secretly study it.

SOON IT WILL BE 20 YEARS. YOUR DAY OF RECKONING IS COMING.

Who's doing this? There's got to be a way for me to find out before it's too late.

She strained her mind to think of an answer but hit a wall.

Emma closed her book, keeping the note hidden, when Kayla returned with Tug sometime later, and poured some water for him into an overturned Frisbee. Ben shut off his tablet, got a rubber ball from their bag and stood.

"I'm going to take a walk with Tug. Will you two be okay alone here?" Ben smiled.

"We'll manage." Emma smiled back.

Tug barked his approval and they left.

Watching Ben and Tug walk away, Kayla turned to Emma.

"He's not very subtle, is he?" Kayla said.

"He means well, Kayla," Emma began. "The other day when you needed to be alone, well, I want you to know that I understand, and if you ever want to talk, I'll listen."

"I know."

"About anything, okay?"

"Anything?"

"Yes."

Kayla looked at Emma. "Tell me about your childhood. You grew up in Washington, D.C., right?"

"The greater D.C. area, mostly Maryland."

"And it was pretty rough for you?"

"My dad was never in the picture and after my mom died I got shuffled around in the foster care system until I was old enough to take care of myself, get a job and work my way through college."

"You went to college in Indiana, right?"

"That's right."

"Notre Dame, no wait, Purdue?"

"Gosh, no, I went to a smaller school in Indiana, Darmont Hill College. Then I moved here to California, where I met your dad."

"You were about the same age as me when your mom died, right?"

"That's right."

"And she died in a fire?"

"A gas line ruptured at the restaurant where she worked. There was an explosion and a fire."

"That's horrible. You never told me that part before, only that she died in a fire."

"Yeah, well." Emma shrugged.

"Was your relationship with your mom a good one?"

Emma saw a man some twenty yards away wearing a floral shirt walking along the beach in front of them with binoculars hanging from the strap around his neck. He stopped and raised them to look at the sea. Emma thought he'd been watching her.

"Emma?" Kayla said.

The man continued walking.

"It was complicated. Things between us were unresolved because before she died we had an argument. I was running with the wrong crowd, getting into trouble."

"Oh. I never knew."

"Wild teen stuff." Emma searched the horizon. "You know, if I've learned anything from my job and my own mistakes, it's that you've got to choose your friends wisely. Latching on to bad influences can set your life on the wrong path."

Emma looked at Kayla, who seemed to be coming to a decision to open up a little.

"Dad probably told you that Mom and I argued, too, the last time we talked. I wanted to go to a party at my friend Mallory's house and Mom said no because older kids were going."

"What did you do?"

"I freaked. I said, 'You're ruining my life,' then I screamed at her, 'I hate you! I hate you! I hate you!' Then she left for work and later that day when she was heading to the cabin she…uhm…she…"

Tears rolled down Kayla's face and Emma pulled her close and consoled her.

"But you didn't mean those things, Kayla."

"I was a bratty little bitch and I never got to take back what I said, to tell her I didn't hate her, that I loved her."

"Sweetheart, she knew. Your mom knew you loved her."

"You think so?"

"Yes. You have to work on accepting that you were being a kid. You didn't mean those things. You have to forgive yourself for being human."

Emma looked down the shoreline.

The man in the floral shirt was far-off now, looking through his binoculars. Only now Emma could've sworn they were definitely aimed at her.

Unease shivered through her.

Then she turned in the opposite direction and saw two large kites curling and coiling high in the sky.

What's he looking at?

* * *

After the beach they went to a restaurant. It was dog-friendly and they sat on the patio, where Tug was permitted, "and welcome," their server said, to sit beside them.

Once they'd ordered, Emma got a text from Glenda Heywood, her principal, updating her on Carson, telling her that he would be seeing a psychiatrist and his family was with him.

"Everything okay?" Ben asked Emma as their nachos arrived.

"Yes, my student is getting the help he needs."

"Good," Ben said.

"So Dad," Kayla said. "What do you think? Can we all go to the cabin sometime? We've only been up a couple times with Emma. You'd like to go back, wouldn't you, Emma?"

"It's beautiful there," Emma said, "but it's up to your dad."

Ben thought while chewing on a chip. "I'd like to get my next book settled first. Then we'll see. Okay?"

Ben looked to Emma but her attention had shifted from the table to a white car parked some distance down the street near the end of the block. She was certain the man who'd gotten into it was the floral shirt man from the beach. But he didn't drive off. He just sat behind the wheel.

Is he looking at the restaurant patio?

Is he looking at us?

Ben followed Emma's gaze. Then turned back to her.

"What is it?"

"Sorry. I thought I saw someone from the beach."

"Something wrong?"

"No, it's nothing."

She waved off concerns, reached for a nacho, smiled as she chewed but shot a secret glance back to the man's car.

At home that evening Emma was still bothered by the floral shirt man, fearing he could be connected to the note and the mystery woman watching her at school.

Still, she wasn't certain that the guy near the restaurant was the man she'd seen at the beach.

So what if it was? It would only be a coincidence. Or would it?

Her worry pulled her back to the threatening note.

No one knew about it.

And no one will ever know about it.

Still, it gnawed at her.

I've got to find out who's behind all of it and put a stop to this. I'll protect Ben and Kayla no matter what it takes.

Emma had spent most of her life looking over her shoulder because of who she used to be. She glanced around, taking in the gorgeous home she shared with Ben and Kayla, amazed that she lived like this here in California. When she looked back on her life, where she came from, *what* she came from, she couldn't believe how it all got so messed

66 *Rick Mofina*

up and how she worked so hard to bury that life to find the love and trust she never knew growing up.

Emma knew how fortunate she was that Ben and Kayla had opened their lives to her at a time when they were both—and still were—grieving. She ached to help them, sensing that they needed her as much as she needed them. It had not been easy. But now, if her past were to be exhumed, it would destroy Ben and Kayla, and everything that Emma had worked to build with them. In the end, it would destroy Emma, too. She did believe that Ben, on some level, would understand, if one day she felt she could tell them the truth. But for now she needed to protect them from it.

I've survived this long and, so help me God, I'll get through this.

Tired from their day in the sun, everyone in the house had retreated to their own space. Kayla was in her room. Ben had worked in his office, then went to the living room to watch a game. Emma was alone with her laptop at the kitchen table, the lights dimmed, dealing with her uneasiness.

Double-checking to ensure she was alone, she launched a search. In seconds, something surfaced. Something new.

A headline on the site of a major newspaper in Canada over what looked like an opinion piece.

Anniversary of the Eternity Murders Nears Where Are The Killers Now?

Emma gasped and her heart beat faster. As she read, her mind raced back to the note, the woman and the floral shirt man. Maybe they're reporters?

But the judges and the lawyers guaranteed me that no one outside the system would ever, could ever, know who I used to be. They guaranteed it. Yes, she expected people would write about the case, even after all these years.

But God, somebody knows! "What's that you're reading?"

Emma jumped.

Kayla stood over her shoulder, a fruit cup in her hand.

"You startled me. Goodness…" Emma smiled, casually turning and blocking her laptop. "Oh, nothing, just some history I was looking up for my job, a paper on juvenile justice." She shifted the subject. "I was thinking you and I could go out for dinner and shopping one day after school this week?"

"Sure, that would be fun."

For a moment, Kayla's eyes lingered on Emma's laptop as she closed it. Then they met Emma's.

Eight

Marv Lander and Fran Penner took in the sky as Marv drove toward the edge of town.

A clear morning, the sun was rising.

Glen Campbell's "Wichita Lineman" flowed through the SUV's radio. Marv hummed along, annoying Fran.

They worked for Roy Tullock at the Prairie Winds Farm Equipment Center. Marv, his top manager, had been with the company twelve years. Fran, who'd joined ten years ago, handled the finances. Marv's wife, Gloria, was Fran's sister.

Small town life.

Marv observed Fran clasping and unclasping her hands.

"What is it?"

"I'm nervous about today."

"Right. You don't like flying, do you?"

"No, I don't."

"You can get something at a pharmacy in Winnipeg. You'll be fine."

Marv resumed humming.

Fran rolled her eyes.

Today was a break from their usual routine. Today, they were picking up Roy Tullock at his house, driving to Winnipeg, then flying to Edmonton for a business meeting the next day. A group of investors was impressed with the Farm Equipment Center's model and how it performed. They wanted to discuss a franchising proposal. Roy wanted his best people with him. He'd also arranged for an Edmonton lawyer he knew to join them.

Roy had stressed that he wanted to get to Winnipeg early so he could work in a visit with his daughter, Torrie. Marv and Fran were among the few people who knew that Torrie was being cared for in a private facility. She'd had a history of what Roy had called "disturbing episodes."

Today Marv and Fran would spend time at one of Winnipeg's big malls while Roy visited Torrie. Roy would then take a cab and meet up with them at the airport.

That was the plan.

The Tullock property was west of town on Old Pioneer Road. They drove up the twisting paved driveway, bordered with tall trees. Marv never tired of admiring the grand house with its four-car garage, in-ground pool and the vast, perfect lawn and gardens.

They parked and got out.

Marv rang the doorbell and they waited, listening to the sound of chirping birds.

When they got no response, Marv shrugged. They were about five minutes early. He pressed the button again, hearing the chime echo in the house.

Nothing happened.

"Awfully quiet," Fran said.

Marv knocked hard but still nothing.

"They went to Regina for the weekend, right?" Fran asked.

"Yeah but they were supposed to return yesterday." Marv surveyed the Tullocks' vehicles parked outside: Roy's SUV, his Cadillac, Connie's Mercedes. "All their vehicles are here. They're home."

"Everything seems so…still," Fran said.

Marv took out his cell phone and called the Tullocks' landline.

"Maybe he's in the shower, or they've got the TV going?" He shrugged.

Phone pressed to his ear, his call rang. They could hear it ringing inside the house, ringing until it went to voice mail and Marv hung up.

"This is odd." Marv slid his phone into his pocket. "You wait here. I'll walk around back in case they're at the pool."

"It's so early. You think they'd be there?"

"Who knows? Wait here."

Marv walked around to the back of the house, agreeing it was likely too early for the whole family to be at the pool. *Maybe they're having breakfast there?* That's what he was thinking, *hoping,* as he followed the stone walkway to the backyard fence and opened the high-level latch on the gate.

The beautiful in-ground pool was a picture of tranquility, the calm water reflecting the morning sun, the filter's soft thrum soothing. Marv took quick stock of the lounge chairs, the kids' pool toys.

No one was there.

He turned to the house, stepped closer to the sliding patio doors and called out.

"Roy! Hey, Roy, it's Marv!"

No response.

Again, he reached for his cell phone. This time he called Roy's cell phone. He stood up against the glass of the patio doors, used his free hand to shield his eyes from the sun, looked inside as his call rang.

He didn't see anyone.

Then he paused, lowered his phone, set it on the ground and let it ring and turned his ear to the glass. He stopped breathing and could hear the faint ring of Roy's cell phone coming from somewhere inside.

"What the hell?"

Fran's scream pierced the air.

Marv grabbed his phone and ran to the front. Trotting along the path, this time he'd noticed a seam across the bottom of one of the basement windows, suggesting it was not shut all the way. Before he could take a closer look, Fran screamed again and he moved faster, finding her near the door hugging herself.

"Look!" She pointed a trembling finger to a narrow window at the entrance. "Look inside!"

Shielding his eyes Marv scanned the front interior, spotting a pair of legs on the floor, partially blocked by the staircase.

"Holy sh—"

Marv seized his phone and called for an ambulance as he tried the door. It was locked. The regional emergency dispatcher answered his 9-1-1 call.

"We need paramedics now! We've got a medical emergency in Eternity at the Tullock residence, 1721 Old Pioneer Road."

Marv headed for the garage with Fran behind him.

"We've got to get inside!" he said.

Forcing himself to keep calm, Marv's mind raced. He had watched over the Tullocks' home when they had spent winter vacations in Florida, or took a Caribbean cruise. He lifted the cover on the security keypad for the garage doors, praying that Roy hadn't changed the five-digit code he'd given him.

Hands shaking, Marv opened his wallet to the card where he'd written the code. He punched it in then pressed ENTER.

Nothing happened.

He took a breath, tried again, only slower, with more care, pressing down each digit before pressing the ENTER button.

The signal clicked and the doors rose.

Ducking under the rising door with Fran, he

rushed through the garage, opened the door to the utility room of the house, which led to the kitchen.

"Roy? Connie?" Marv called.

Racing through the kitchen his mind hurled questions. *Did someone fall down the stairs? Did they have some sort of seizure?* Hurrying around a corner toward the stairs at the front of the house Marv's foot caught on something, throwing him to the floor.

Fran screamed.

Marv had tripped over Connie Tullock.

She was lying on her stomach, blood pooled and webbed around her.

A muscle, an electrode, or some neurological switch spasmed in Marv's brain, and his mind went numb, thrusting him into shock, failing to convince him that what he was seeing was real.

Everything moved in dreamlike slow motion.

Fran shouted something about getting a towel for Connie as Marv went to the stairs. Roy was lying on the floor, eyes open wide, fixed on the ceiling. Marv shouted his name, taking stock of his polo shirt encased in blood, shredded, as if repeatedly slashed. His face, arms, hands were laced with blood. The floor was covered with splatters and ribbons of blood.

Marv saw suitcases near the front, opened, clothes and toiletries spilling from them as if someone had rifled through them. Two of the smaller suitcases had colorful cartoon patterns and he suddenly thought of the children.

Neal and Linda.

Marv's focus shifted up the blood-splotched stairs. Fran's whimpers as she got on her knees next to Connie filled the house. Marv followed the blood marks up the stairs. Taking one step after the other he moved into a bedroom that belonged to one of the kids.

He turned to the open doors of the closet and froze.

Six-year-old Neal was facedown on the floor. His face was turned sideways, eyes and mouth open as if he were crying out. Blood haloed around his head and fanned from his body, making Marv think of a snow angel.

Blood angel.

Neal's body lay, almost protectively, at the feet of his little sister.

Linda was sitting on the floor, her back against the closet wall, head bent down, hair covering her face, her T-shirt, soaked in blood, a stuffed toy polar bear on her lap, smudged with blood.

A throaty harsh sob shot from Marv as he fell to his knees and took Linda's small, cold hand in his. His chest heaved, releasing another guttural sob, as he reached out with his trembling hand to stroke Neal's hair and whisper a prayer.

Marv stayed that way, unsure if seconds, or minutes, or all time had passed, his heart hammering as he searched the room, the ceiling, the heavens for an answer to the horror.

Tears rolled down his face. Then his concentration left the closet and the bedroom, going to the hallway, the light hitting the wall displaying three words scrawled there in blood.

KILL THEM ALL

As he tried to process everything, Marv called 9-1-1 again. This time for police, just as Fran's cries reached up from the main floor.

"She's breathing! Marv, I think Connie's alive!"

At that moment they heard the first approaching siren.

Nine

Cielo Valle, Orange County, California
Present day

The pressure on Ben Grant to start a new book was mounting.

The conference call with his agent and editor was not for another half hour. He'd only taken a cursory look at the latest list of crime stories they'd sent him to consider. Nothing really grabbed him.

Searching for a solution he looked to the framed covers on his office wall, to remind himself of what he did for a living.

He chronicled death.

With titles like, *Darkness Waiting*, *The Killer No One Knew*, *A Blood Trail in Australia*, *Devil's Dance in Paris*, *The Lone Star Murders*, and all the others, he had journeyed into society's darkest corners. Visiting realms of horror and anguish had left him with memories of survivors, perpetrators and the dead.

In writing his books Ben had talked with everyone connected to the crimes. Investigators analyzed the facts. The survivors had trusted him with their pain and what they had left to give to honor those they'd lost. The criminals talked out of self-interest because they wanted their story told, or what they presented as their story. No matter what the guilty ones said, or how they framed their role, Ben reiterated the cold, hard truth.

Through it all he believed he had a solemn duty to attempt to make sense of the acts that defied comprehension and illustrate the toll they exacted. He drew upon his university studies of journalism, literature, existentialism, philosophy and a course examining religious responses to death. Not only did they prepare him for reporting on crime, they equipped him for the books he was destined to write.

At times he felt like Virgil, the blind poet who had guided Dante through hell. But Ben had always infused his work with humanity, understanding and compassion. Still, he took into account the old caution about "gazing too long into an abyss," for it had filled him with a secret fear that death would touch him, too.

Tragedy came for him that day four years ago when those two San Bernardino deputies knocked on his cabin door, and he knew, he just knew before the first one even spoke.

Sir, I'm sorry to inform you...

The ground under him heaved, he fell into darkness and in the years that followed he did all he could to protect Kayla. Then Emma came into his life, bringing the light he needed. Her eyes were tinged with sadness, but they also held hope. He loved her for her spirit. They'd bonded on another level for not only had she read each of his books, she'd understood and embraced what he had attempted to achieve. Emma had reached him, brought him back to life.

Ben's love for Emma was deepened by the way she had helped him heal after losing Brooke. In some way he couldn't quite articulate, being with Emma mended him. She possessed a warmth, a goodness that had eased his guilt, just a little, over Brooke's death—made him feel that it wasn't all his fault. Emma had helped him come to terms with the fact he was a good man and needed to move forward and that's why he loved her.

Still, Ben could not ignore Kayla's difficulty accepting Emma. It worried him. Of course he felt Kayla's pain. It broke his heart to see his daughter suffering because he wanted more than anything to help her heal. It tore him up because on one level, he understood Kayla's reasoning for being so resistant to allowing Emma into their lives.

The way he saw it, Kayla's prolonged grieving for her mother had evolved into a subconscious resentment of Emma as an unacceptable replacement for her mother. And Kayla's resentment had manifested itself in many ways, including her troubling behavior and her attempts to cast Emma as a mysterious outsider, a threat to Kayla's bond with him, by saying things like: "Do we really know her, Dad?"

Admittedly, Ben was a little apprehensive when

he first started dating Emma, but that was different. In his work he'd encountered so many disreputable people. As he became well-known he'd met questionable types who'd approached him with questionable intentions, schemers and people with ulterior motives. Emma had never given Ben a reason not to trust her.

Still, he exercised caution.

Early in their relationship, when he started getting serious about her, he had his sources conduct some discreet checking into her background after gleaning a few personal details from her. They looked into her previous jobs, her certification as a school counselor, addresses, her financial situation, if she'd been previously married, widowed, divorced; she hadn't. Ben was satisfied, happy, that everything checked out and looked good.

Now his phone rang.

It was Roz Rose, his agent, and Adam Kane, his editor, calling from New York. He put them on speaker and they passed quickly through a few minutes of small talk before shifting to business.

"What did you think of the list we sent you?" Roz asked.

"It's fine. I know those cases and I didn't see anything there."

His response was met with silence.

"Ben—" Adam's tone had cooled "—you have to know we respect and understand what you've been through, that it's been painfully difficult."

"It's profoundly appreciated, Adam."

"But it's been a few years now. I'm getting pressure from senior people here to get you firmly committed to a new book."

"I get that."

"Ben—" Roz jumped in "—Adam knows this, but your foreign publishers have also been pushing hard for a new book."

Adam continued, "What about these more recent cases in the US? There's the Minneapolis case of the mom who never reported her toddler missing for a month. Then the child's body was found in a suitcase in a forest and the mother was charged. Then there's that case in Boston of the father who came to find his wife and twin sons missing. They have yet to be found but police suspect him. What about those?"

"I know about them from the coverage. I'll consider them."

"Ben, your Swedish publisher suggested one about a husband and wife, both of them doctors, who'd been abducting people and keeping them in a dungeon outside of Stockholm. And we just got this one from your Canadian publisher who suggests you look at an older case of a family murdered in a small town. It's twenty years old but it's got a twist of some sort. Do you know about these Swedish and Canadian cases?"

"No, I don't."

"I'm sorry to be the bad guy here," Adam said, "but we've gone above and beyond the extensions stipulated in the contract. The publisher's message to you today is that if we don't have your commitment and a short outline for your next book in our hands within sixty days, we'll demand return of the advance and end the contract. And Ben, the publisher could also consider legal action to recoup any costs arising from catalog listings and production scheduling."

The seconds passed with Ben saying nothing.

"You understand the seriousness of this, Ben?" Roz said.

"It's crystalline."

"We'll send you summaries of the ones we've just discussed and any others we like," Adam said. He sighed, his voice warming. "I know you can pull this all together."

"Thank you, Adam, and thank you, Roz. I promise to do my best."

The call ended and Tug came into his office and nuzzled his lap just as his computer pinged with the email of the newest story suggestions. They were short and he looked them over. He knew nothing about either of them. The Swedish case involving doctors and a dungeon intrigued him. He saw that the Canadian case from twenty years ago happened in Eternity, Manitoba.

"Eternity," he repeated out loud to Tug. "Now that's an intriguing name."

Ten

The monitor next to Connie Tullock's bed at Alden Memorial Hospital displayed her vital signs in a spectrum of colored waves.

She was unconscious, having undergone emergency surgery for the stab wounds she'd received to her stomach, chest and neck. After operating for nearly four hours, the surgeon put Connie's likelihood of surviving at less than 10 percent.

She was the best lead—maybe the only lead—investigators had to solve the murders of her son, her daughter, her husband—*and probably her own*, thought Sergeant Bill Jurek of the Eternity Police Service.

Since Connie had come out of surgery, Jurek had waited at her bedside with the nurse in case she regained consciousness. He was prepared to obtain a dying declaration, hoping she could identify whoever was behind the killings.

The knot in his gut had tightened because he

knew the Tullock murders were going to hit the community hard. The town had never seen anything like it. Eternity's last homicide was seven years ago when a trucker, Lenny Troy Boghin, smashed Rodney John Street, a biker, in the head with a chair at Harry Hoyt's Bar because he spilled beer on him. Before that, Manford Ellerd Wiebe, a farmer with a gambling problem who'd lost everything at blackjack in Las Vegas, set his home ablaze killing himself, his wife and son in 1972.

To be sure, in 2000, Eternity got its run of crimes, domestic assaults, drug dealing, vandalism and thefts. It also saw its share of traffic and farming deaths, drownings, fire fatalities and occasionally people who froze in the winter. But never anything of this magnitude.

When the call came in, Jurek had been at his desk, earlier than his shift. He'd been awake thinking how his son needed braces, and how even with their dental plans Jurek and his wife, a teacher, faced an out-of-pocket bill of 2500 dollars. It weighed on his mind as he'd arrived at the office, got a coffee and was looking at the overnight log when the radio crackled. Dustin Meyer, a new constable, called in from 1721 Old Pioneer Road, which Jurek knew was the Tullock home.

"We've got three 10-32s, possibly a fourth," Meyer said with urgency.

Eternity's alphanumeric code defined a 10-32 as a sudden death, meaning not by natural causes.

Three 10-32s? That can't be. Jurek got on the radio and called Meyer's unit.

"Say again, 1-8."

Meyer confirmed what he had said, setting everything in motion.

Activating the emergency lights and siren on his marked Dodge Charger, Jurek blasted across town to the address on Old Pioneer Road. Meyer was in front of the house with Marv Lander, who had his arm around Fran Penner, her face contorted in anguish, her knuckles white from squeezing the tissue in her hands.

Being the senior officer, Jurek assumed command, making notes of the time, weather, who was present, and getting debriefed by Meyer. The rookie cop's face was ashen, his voice shaky. Connie Tullock was still alive, Meyer told him. She'd been rushed to the regional trauma center in Alden but the paramedics doubted she would make it.

Jurek then talked separately with Lander and Penner, getting initial statements as Constable Danny Dufrense arrived to help. Jurek assigned him to seal the property and to park his patrol car across the driveway's entrance. Meyer had already cleared the house. "No one in there but the deceased," he said.

Jurek slipped on hooded and booted coveralls, tugged on skintight nitrile gloves, got his digital camera and clipboard, then entered the house, steeling himself for what was inside.

As a boy growing up on his parents' farm in southern Manitoba, Jurek had seen things that stayed with him. Like what coyotes did to chickens, or the time he watched an owl eat a gopher struggling for its life. When he became a soldier, he'd seen what conflicts did during his tours in Bosnia and Africa. As a cop in Eternity, he'd seen the bloated bodies of drowning victims, fire victims burned so badly you couldn't tell if they were male or female. In traffic accidents he'd seen men, women and children, entwined in metal, their blood dripping onto the pavement.

Walking through the crime scene, Jurek now saw a whole new level of horror that would haunt him for the rest of his life, as if evil had rampaged through the Tullock home. He took pictures, made notes and sketches as he studied the main floor before proceeding upstairs and concentrating on the message left on the wall.

KILL THEM ALL.

What was the significance? He took more pictures, then made more notes, stopping to steady himself as the extent of the horror caught up with him.

Then he noticed smears, smudges on the floor, and followed a faint blood trail down into the basement that led to a window that was not fully closed. He examined it thinking it was likely a point of entry and exit.

When he stepped outside, Jurek called Abe Atkin, the chief, and told him what they had. Atkin, who'd attended Roy and Connie's wedding, released a groaned curse before asking: "Was there anything else besides that message?"

"A blood trail, an unlocked window. We need to process the scene."

"All right, I'll be there soon. We'll likely have to turn this over to the Mounties. I'll take care of that. We'll set up a case status, hand-over meeting for first thing tomorrow."

"We can handle this, Abe. We've trained for it. We can lead it. This is our town."

"Bill, they've got the resources. They'll lead and we'll support them. Meanwhile, do only what needs to be done now. Protect the evidence and the scene, seal the place. Call in everyone you need, off-duty, vacation, I don't care. I'll sign off on the overtime. I'll alert the RCMP."

Pushing back on his frustration at having to turn the case over to the Royal Canadian Mounted Police, Jurek called in Eternity's K-9 unit. He needed them now because the suspects were at large and could harm others.

Jurek called in every officer he could reach. He was going to need all the help he could get before things got out of hand because news had spread fast. While making calls, Jurek watched the tangle of nonpolice vehicles, concerned people and gawkers growing on the side of the road. He recognized a reporter from the *Eternity Bulletin* and one from *Sparrow 101 Radio News* in Alden. Danny Dufrense was doing a good job of keeping everyone back and off the property.

So far, Jurek thought, as Meyer got a call advising them that Connie Tullock was still alive and in surgery.

Jurek hurried out of his coveralls, left instructions for Meyer, the K-9 unit and other officers arriving at the scene. Then with sirens and lights going, Jurek made the half hour drive to Alden in half the time, where he sat by Connie's bedside, waiting, hoping, she would awaken.

It was coming up on ninety minutes since the surgery and Jurek was reviewing his notes and checklist. Occasionally, he'd step into the hall and use the phone at the nurses' station to make calls. They needed to get the RCMP's forensic unit in the Tullock house to process everything—the blood trail, the window, the message—to determine where the evidence pointed.

Who could do this? My God, who could commit such an outrage to children?

From time to time he glanced at Connie, bandaged, sedated, tubes and sensors fastened to her body. He only knew the Tullocks socially from attending local fund-raisers. He liked Roy; everyone did. Roy was a decent man. But Connie came off as a pretentious woman and Jurek got the sense that few people liked her. But whatever thoughts he'd had about Connie Tullock dissolved in that hospital room in the wake of what had happened to her son, her daughter, her husband, and to her.

Nobody deserved this. If she lived, a nightmare awaited her.

She still had Torrie, her teenage daughter. Jurek caught his breath.

Connie's fingers trembled, then her hand lifted a fraction from the bed and she released a gurgle.

"Nurse?" Jurek said.

The nurse rose from her chair, tended to Connie while glancing at the monitor, then pressed the button over the bed. Connie stirred. A moment later the doctor arrived and examined her as her eyes blinked open.

"She's regaining consciousness," the doctor said. "Connie, I'm Doctor Patel. You've been hurt—"

Her mouth began moving. Then, rasping, she said: "Water."

The doctor got the water cup and put the straw to her lips.

"Connie," Patel continued, "you're in the hospital and a police officer needs to talk to you. It's very important."

She drank, then closed her eyes.

"Her signs are weak," Patel said to Jurek, indicating that this might be his only chance, nodding for him to approach.

Jurek activated his recorder and got close to her.

"Connie, it's Sergeant Bill Jurek with Eternity Police. Can you tell me who hurt you and your family?"

It was so subtle Jurek almost missed it as she began shaking her head and Jurek drew even closer.

"Connie, who hurt you?"

She emitted a liquidy sob so soft it was barely audible.

"Why?" she managed to ask.

"Connie, we need to know who hurt you and your family."

Suddenly her eyes opened and through her anesthetized fog she stared at nothing, and in a harsh, pained, whisper, said, "Why're you here...in..."

"Connie, we need to know who hurt you."

"What're you doing here?" Her voice trailed off.

She coughed and blood droplets appeared on her lips. Her head lolled to one side. The monitor began beeping, chiming and pinging with alerts as one by one the tracking lines flattened.

Jurek pulled back while Patel led medical staff in a vain attempt to resuscitate her.

It was over so fast.

Still holding his recorder Jurek turned from the bed to the window.

Four deaths now.

Bomber, the canine half of Eternity's K-9 unit, worked with his nose to the ground, leading his partner, Constable Mark Warrin, from the open window at the side of the Tullock house.

Warrin had followed Jurek's instructions to start from the outside at the window and track any leads. Warrin had Bomber on a long line.

The German shepherd's leash jingled and tensed. Warrin knew from Bomber's tail wagging that he'd picked up something as he led him toward the edge of the property. Although Bomber zigzagged, he adhered to a fairly direct path to a small wooded rise.

Bomber threaded around the small stand of trees, stopped and yipped.

"What is it, pal?" Warrin asked. "Whatcha got there?"

Sunlight winked from the ground. Warrin lowered himself to look at a small, empty glass bottle that had held vodka, according to the label. He thought for a moment but didn't touch it. Instead he reached into his vest for a tiny orange evidence flag and planted it near the bottle.

Bomber's line tensed and he barked while staring in the direction of the town and the highway as if signaling that the answers lay in that direction.

Warrin reached for his radio.

Eleven

Orange County, California
Present day

The warning note on her windshield, the mystery woman who appeared to be watching her, continued eating at Emma as she drove to her school.

Who is threatening me?

Theories ran through her mind: Were the note, the mystery woman and the man at the beach all linked? The anniversary was looming and it had to pass like the others, without anyone in Emma's life knowing.

I'll protect Ben and Kayla from my past no matter the cost because the truth would not only destroy me—it would destroy them, too.

Emma had gotten little sleep after searching her mind intensively. She woke with a possible solution.

Pulling into the staff parking lot, she collected her things and headed to the entrance, scanning the spot across the street where she had last seen the woman. Emma didn't notice anything this morning.

Inside the school she didn't go to her office; instead she headed to the end of the admin hallway to the door marked SECURITY.

She entered to see Greg Clifton, the school's security supervisor, standing at the desk of Denise Stadler, the office assistant.

"...those biweeklies will now be monthly," Greg said before stopping. "Oh, hi, Emma."

"Hi, Emma," Denise said.

"Sorry to interrupt."

"Quite all right," Greg said. "How're you doing? That was a great thing you did, saving your student."

"Yes, it was a miracle," Denise said.

"Thanks. Greg, I was hoping you could help me with something. Do you have a minute?"

"Sure," he said, and led her into his office. "What is it, Emma?"

She was counting on the fact that she knew Greg a little. At the last staff retreat they were teamed and came second in the three-legged race. They got along, had fun and had eaten lunch together a few times in the cafeteria.

"It's no big thing, a little embarrassing to be honest," she said. "At some point yesterday I may have bumped someone's car with my own, and left a scratch. I really don't remember doing it, but someone left a note on my car about it. I seem to have lost it, though."

"I see."

"I was wondering if we could review the security cameras and maybe I could recognize the person, or something?"

Greg folded his arms across his chest and thought. "Hmm."

"We could keep this confidential," Emma said.

"Come with me."

He led her across the hall to a room where a woman at a desk was watching several flat screens of activity.

"This is Amber Fry—she's just joined us. Amber, this is Emma, one of our counselors."

They greeted one another before Greg went on.

"Amber, could you excuse us? I need to show Emma something."

"Sure," Amber said, and left.

Greg took her seat and tapped at the keyboards as he explained the system, which had about forty high-definition indoor cameras and twenty outdoor cameras.

"Which staff lot are you in, Emma?"

"B."

"Right." He tapped. "I got you in our system and your space number is fourteen. Here you are live, now." Greg pointed to a monitor showing Emma's SUV. "We'll go back on the footage for your lot."

Footage moved at high speed showing cars parking, people exiting, and then showing Emma. Nothing unusual.

"Doesn't look like anyone hit anyone," Greg said.

Then a blip, a flash of color and Greg tapped more commands.

"Here we go," he said.

A woman with dark glasses approached Emma's car, placed an envelope under the wiper and left the frame.

"I don't recognize her," Greg said. "Let me pull in on her."

"Can you run through it all again, so I can record it?" Emma got her phone.

Greg hesitated. "You won't post it or share it?"

"Just for me."

"All right, just for you."

Emma recorded as Greg ran through the sequence again, slowing it when the woman emerged. Then the camera zoomed closer. The woman was wearing dark glasses, a white ball cap. But Emma could determine her hair was a dark shade of blond. She wore a light blue T-shirt, jeans, pink sneakers and had a good figure. Emma guessed her to be about her age, but didn't recognize her.

"She look familiar?" Greg asked.

"No."

"I don't see her leaving a car," Greg said switching to other cameras, tracking the woman as she left the lot, disappearing from the screens.

"Oh darn," Emma said.

"Wait." Greg entered more commands. "Is it possible you bumped her on the street? We can use our outpost cameras." A few more commands and Greg, with Emma still recording, found the woman walking to the green sedan across the street, the very car Emma had pursued on foot the previous day, and there she was in the frame.

"That looks like you chasing after her," Greg said.

"Yes, but she drove off."

They watched as the woman did just that and Emma stopped recording.

"I guess that's it, Greg. Thanks for trying. I'll get out of your hair."

"Hang on." He tapped a few more commands. "Look, nothing shows you hitting any cars in our camera range. But some of our outdoor cameras can capture license plate information."

"Really?"

"For liability, for security, you name it." He continued tapping and Emma resumed recording. "This woman could be running an insurance scam, you know, give you a note claiming you hit her, but pay her X amount and she'll keep it off the books, that kind of thing."

"I see."

"Looks like she has a Ford Focus, and here's her plate." The camera zoomed in, enlarged the plate. Emma recorded it.

"Let me see," Greg said, carefully tapping the plate number on his keyboard, submitting it to the school's database. "Naw, it doesn't come up as staff, student or parent, or anything flagged on our lists."

"Thanks a million, Greg."

"Now, you could give the plate to your insurance, or I could run it down for you. I know some people. Give me some time, I could get you a name and address, and if she's running a scam on school property, we'll pass it to police."

"No, I want to keep this confidential for now. How about you just get me her information for starters? Maybe it's a misunderstanding. I could just call her, talk to her. If it's something more, I'll get back to you."

Greg considered Emma's request. "All right, if that's the way you want to go."

"And we'll keep this between us. Okay, Greg?"

"We'd better." Greg chuckled and winked.

Twelve

There wasn't much time.

Saturday, Kayla and Emma had been shopping all morning and were having lunch at the new Lemon Palm Grill. After they'd ordered, Emma left their table to go to the bathroom, giving Kayla a chance to continue with a little more detective work.

Curiosity had been fluttering in the back of Kayla's mind for days now, since that evening she'd startled Emma in the kitchen and seen how she had reacted. The way she sat, casually shielding the screen, then closing her laptop. It all looked kind of sketchy. As if she'd been caught at something.

What had Emma been looking at?

Kayla had only glimpsed a couple of words, *anniversary* and *killers now*. So in the short time she had before Emma returned to their table, Kayla picked up her phone and began searching those words online.

Again, all she found was information about anniversary gifts and killer ideas for gifts, leaving her stumped. Emma could've been on a site that was firewalled or accessed by subscription. Kayla didn't even know what she was looking for.

A shadow fell over her.

Emma had returned. She nodded to the bags beside Kayla and said, "Those tops you got today are pretty, and I love those new shoes."

"Me, too."

The server set down their soft drinks.

"This girl time has been fun, hasn't it?" Emma smiled.

"Yes." Kayla looked off, then said: "Can I ask you something?"

"Absolutely."

Kayla took a moment, thought, let out a breath.

"I got to thinking after you said your mom died in the explosion and fire."

"What were you thinking about?"

"Was it like a murder, or arson, like someone did it on purpose?"

Emma's jaw dropped ever so slightly. "Why do you ask that?"

"I mean it just seems so horrible and people do kill people on purpose." Kayla flushed, slightly embarrassed. "I mean, look at what my dad writes for a living. I was just wondering."

Emma shook her head. "No, the gas line broke. It was an accident."

"What was the name of the restaurant?"

"It was called Tony's Diner."

"Where in Maryland was it?"

"You're full of questions today, aren't you?"

Kayla shrugged.

"Tony's was in Beltsville, a small town northeast of D.C." Emma looked off and blinked away tears.

"I'm sorry, Emma. I was just curious."

Emma slid her hands across the table and took Kayla's in hers. "It's okay, sweetheart." Emma hesitated, deciding if this was the right time before continuing. "Honey, I know you're having a hard time accepting me, having lost your mom. You and I are more alike than you realize. I mean, I lost my mom, too, when I was young, you know that."

Kayla remained silent, letting Emma continue.

"My relationship with my mom was so complicated. Most of the time we didn't speak. So many things went unsaid. Kayla, what I'm trying to say is that my heart is filled with understanding and love for you." Emma squeezed Kayla's hands. "I treasure the chance we have here because deep in my heart, I know we can help each other."

Blinking back tears, Kayla nodded. A moment passed, filled with the sound of conversations spilling from other tables and the clink of cutlery. Then Kayla picked up her phone, smiling at messages from her friends, bringing their discussion to an end.

For now.

Their meals came. Lunch was punctuated with small talk about current songs, movies and celeb gossip. As they left the restaurant and walked through the parking lot to Emma's SUV, a woman with a floppy sun hat rushed toward them.

"Emma!" The woman arrived breathless. She was in her late fifties. A man about the same age was catching up but walking. "Go get us a seat, Barry," the woman said to him. "I'll be there after I talk to Emma." Then she turned to Emma. "I'm so glad to catch you. Clara Jean O'Connor from the community association."

"Oh, Clara Jean, yes, of course. How are you?"

"Good." Clara Jean nodded to Kayla. "This will just take a moment. I was going to send you an email, but in person's better."

Emma braced herself.

"You were so kind to volunteer and help us with last year's charity drive, Emma. This year we're uniting with associations across the county for a big three-day sale of donated books with donations going to literacy. It's coming up fast, Jake Gyllenhaal agreed to come to the launch on day one to help draw attention. A friend of his lives around here and set it up."

"That's fantastic."

"Yes, well, turns out Jake had to cancel at the last minute. That leaves us scrambling, so the committee was wondering if you could ask your husband to appear on day one. Just for a couple of hours to sign books, meet people. We'll have a lot of his books there to sell. Benjamin Grant at a book event would draw a lot of TV media attention, which would give us a boost for the next two days."

"Oh gosh, I don't know…"

"I hate asking like this but we're in a bind and it would be a lifesaver, and of course we'd want you there helping in any way. A husband-and-wife team would be good for the cameras."

Concern flitted across Emma's face. "Me on camera? I don't think you need me for that."

"We most certainly do. Oh, Emma, would you ask him, please?" Clara Jean touched Emma's shoulder. "Forgive me. I'm coming on too strong. It's just that we're in a jam."

"No, no. It's all right. I'll ask Ben."

"Oh, thank you!" Clara Jean opened her arms and hugged her. "Come with me to my car—I've got some material."

Before going across the lot with her, Emma first unlocked the SUV for Kayla, who used the time to make another online search.

This time she entered the words *Tony's Diner* and *Beltsville*.

One hit came up for a Tony's in Baltimore. Others came up across the country. But nothing for Beltsville, Maryland. Well, it was a long time ago, and the place burned down.

Kayla bit her bottom lip and looked toward Emma.

I'm not giving up.

Thirteen

Eternity, Manitoba
2000

Marlene was washing the breakfast dishes while Janie returned food to the fridge and cupboards when the phone rang, startling Janie.

"What's up with you?" Janie's mother said. "You're so jumpy. Can you get that? I'm running a bit late and have to put my makeup on."

Janie picked up the cordless handset from the table, listened, then held it out. "It's for you."

"Who is it?"

Janie shrugged. "Some lady."

Marlene looked at the clock on the stove. "Take a message. Tell her I'll call her back."

"Can she call you back?" Janie said into the phone, listened then held it out again. "She says it's important."

Marlene groaned silently, wiped her soapy hands on the towel, then took the phone, saying: "Hello?" A second later, she said: "Oh hi, Lila, I'm on my way in and—"

Janie recognized the name of her mom's manager at the restaurant, and resumed putting away the salt, pepper and butter.

"No!" Marlene shouted into the phone, snapping Janie's attention back. Her mother's eyes widened; one hand gripped the back of a chair. It scraped on the floor as she pulled it out and eased herself into it. Listening, her free hand trembling over her mouth, her face filled with fear and tears came.

"Oh dear God. Oh dear God!" Marlene said, her frightened eyes bulging, staring at Janie. "My daughter was in that house. She babysat for them!"

Janie stared at her mother, shaking inside.

Marlene listened for several moments, before finally saying, "Yes, yes, at the club later, whatever you'd like, Lila, of course."

The call ended and Janie's mother sat frozen in silence staring at nothing, as if the world had ceased to make sense.

"Mom, what's going on?"

A moment passed.

"Mom?"

Her mother's eyes searched for the source of the question, finding Janie, looking at her, then searching for the words.

"That was Lila Skripchuck at the restaurant. She just told me that Mr. Tullock, his wife and—" she choked back a sob "—Linda and Neal were all—" Her hands flew to her face. "They're all dead. They were murdered… Oh God!"

Janie froze as the earth under her feet shifted.

Her mother flew to her, taking her into her arms.

"This isn't real," her mother said. "This can't be!"

Janie's face turned white. She was motionless. Her mother gripped her shoulders and searched her eyes.

"Janie, are you okay?"

Silent and numb, Janie stared at nothing.

As her mother held her, Janie began trembling and shaking with intensity until she was almost convulsing as a guttural sob swirled in the pit of her stomach, clawing upward before escaping.

As if to silence Janie's grief, her mother crushed her to her chest, staring at the ceiling, asking over and over: "Dear God, who did this? Who could do such an evil thing?"

"Marie?"

Standing with her mother in the bakery aisle of Eternity Market Mart, Marie was gripping the shopping cart and staring at nothing.

"We need two loaves of whole wheat. They're on your side there."

Marie's mother—whose face was etched in sorrow since Pike's death, making her look older—pointed but Marie didn't move.

"Hello, Earth to Marie."

Marie didn't respond until her mother nudged her. Then, as if waking, Marie looked around until her mother looked from the list in her hand, repeated her request and pointed.

"Two whole wheat."

Marie placed the bread in the cart and they continued to the next aisle.

"Honey, what's wrong? You asked to come with me."

"Nothing."

"No, you've been kind of out of it recently, like a zombie. Are you feeling okay?"

Marie nodded slowly, thinking how after Pike her mother was often out of it herself.

"Well, what is it? We need mayo, the big jar there."

Marie shook her head and placed the jar into the cart, then turned when her mother's name was called.

"Flo!"

The slender woman wearing oversize black framed glasses approaching them with her cart was Eva Bellday, former librarian, local historian and gossip. She knew everyone in Eternity and their business.

"Oh goodness, Flo, have you heard the terrible news?"

"Hi, Eva. What terrible news?"

Exercising a measure of caution, Eva glanced at Marie, then said: "I suppose with all the violence on TV, the web and those music videos these days, Marie's old enough to hear."

"Hear what, Eva?" Flo asked. "What's happened?"

"It's the Tullock family."

"What about them?"

"Roy, Connie, the kids," Eva reached out and put her hand on Flo's arm. "They were murdered in their home on Old Pioneer! Connie died in the hospital. My niece Rhonda told me. Her friend's cousin was one of the first officers who got there. They don't know who did it."

"Oh no, oh my God!" Flo cupped her face with her hands. "Murdered?"

Eva nodded big nods.

Marie's attention bounced with intensity between her mother and Eva Bellday.

"And the children, too?" Flo asked.

Marie tightened her hold on the shopping cart handle.

"Yes, Neal and Linda," Eva said. "I'm not sure of their ages but they were young."

Marie's mother turned to her. "Your friend Janie would know. She's their babysitter."

Tears were flowing down Marie's face as she nodded.

"I know, honey. It's so sad," her mother said.

Marie lowered her head as she cried. "They were five and six," Marie said.

"Five and six?" Eva repeated. "So young—" Eva caught herself suddenly, realizing that Marie and her mother had been struck by their own tragedy.

"Neal was…he was…" Marie began sobbing harder, her body shaking as she hugged herself and bent her knees, until she was on the floor, rocking on her heels and sobbing uncontrollably. "Neal was the same age as Pike when he died."

Marie's mother knelt down and wrapped her arms around her daughter. Flo's eyes burned with tears as she stared up helplessly at Eva Bellday, whose mouth was agape.

"Dear Lord." Eva put her hands on Flo's shoulders. "Tragedy after tragedy. What's our world coming to?"

"You're flying with the Sparrow on 101 Radio News in Alden..."

Tapping on his calculator, Telforde Rahynes made notes at the kitchen table for his next painting job. His girlfriend, Nancy Gorman, had gotten up early to make his breakfast, along with lunch and a thermos of coffee for his drive to Virden and Brandon to provide estimates. But Nancy liked listening to the radio on the counter as she went about her tasks and it made it hard for Telforde to concentrate.

"You need to have that thing on now? Can't you see I'm working?"

"Just a couple more minutes. After the news, they play the birthday contest. If they draw my month and I call in, I could win two hundred and fifty dollars."

He grumbled something about paying a share of the rent when Nancy's teenage daughter, Nikki, joined them in the kitchen.

Telforde's eyes traveled up and down Nikki's jeans, her tight-fitting T-shirt that accentuated her bust, and her makeup. They stayed on her as she got a can of tomato juice from the fridge.

"You're looking nice this morning, Nik," Telforde said.

Her eyes narrowed and she gave him an icy sidelong glance.

"What're you doing up so early?" Nancy asked.

"Couldn't sleep and I'm thirsty."

As Nikki reached for a glass on a high shelf, her shirt rising, exposing her waist, she felt Telforde's eyes on her.

"I said you look nice, Nik. You're supposed to say thank you when someone gives you a compliment."

"You didn't fix my door," Nikki said to the cupboard.

"I'll get round to it. I got a lot of—"

The radio news began with: *"RCMP are investigating the murders of four members of an Eternity family..."*

"Quiet. Listen." Nancy turned up the radio.

"...after police responded to reports of bodies found in a home on Old Pioneer Road.

"Sources have told 101 News that bodies of three members of the Tullock family were found in the home. A fourth member of the family found in the home died hours later in hospital in Alden.

"Officers from Eternity and RCMP Major Crimes are conducting an ongoing investigation.

"RCMP said no further information is being provided at this time but that a full news release will be issued later..."

"That's Roy Tullock, one of the richest people around," Telforde said.

Tomato juice exploded on the floor as the glass slipped from Nikki's hand.

"Don't move!" her mother said. "You're in bare feet. Let me take care of it."

"Who would kill Tullock and his family?" Telforde asked no one.

Nikki remained rooted to the floor, tomato juice splattered in globs on her feet and the cuffs of her jeans as her mother swept juice-covered shards into a dustpan, then got Nikki's shoes and mopped the mess.

"Goodness, Nikki, what's wrong?" her mother asked. "You're shivering. It was an accident. It's just a glass—wait!" Her mother stared at her. "Doesn't one of your friends watch the Tullock kids?"

Nikki nodded, covering her face with her hands, her eyes brimming. She rushed back to her room, her mother calling after her.

"Leave me alone!" Nikki yelled back.

Closing the door behind her, Nikki cursed because Telforde still hadn't put a lock on it for privacy, like she asked him to do every day. Like he promised every day.

In addition to being a creep, Telforde Rahynes was a liar. Nikki hated him so much.

Her loathing was expressed perfectly in her new ring bearing an enraged skull. Sitting on her bed, Nikki twisted it around her finger.

Then she looked at the tiny pinprick on her hand and thought of the blood bond she'd made with Janie and Marie. She glanced at the photo strip of them together at the mall. She rose from her bed and went to her window. Tapping her ring on the sill, she thought how the three of them were united, as strong as the metal of their rings.

Their pact meant they would protect each other forever.

From her vantage she could almost see Old Pioneer Road.

No one knows anything and no one will ever know anything.

Fourteen

Whoever killed the Tullock family was still out there.

That fact churned in Abe Atkin's gut as he and Bill Jurek watched the officers filing into the grand ballroom of the Eternity Community Lodge.

The same room where people had laughed, danced and celebrated events for years was now the command post for the investigation of the murders of Roy, Connie, Linda and Neal Tullock.

They were Atkin's friends and, God help him, as chief of police he'd vowed to Jurek that they were going to find whoever was responsible, and they would do it letter-perfect, by the book. Under Manitoba's provincial law, every municipality must provide policing by creating its own force, or by contracting policing from the Royal Canadian Mounted Police. Manitoba didn't have a provincial force. And if an incident overwhelmed a local force, then officials could request the RCMP take over the investigation.

And that's what Atkin had done.

He glanced at his watch—nearly 6:30 a.m. Less than twenty-four hours after the discovery on Old Pioneer Road and after Connie had breathed her last words, they were marshalling a massive investigation.

They'd set up at the lodge because it had the largest room available for what was needed. All of the curtains had been drawn, the doors secured, the parking lot closed to the public. Atkin gave it a few more seconds as officers settled in with coffees, juice, fruit and sandwiches at tables that were still arranged for last week's minor hockey awards banquet.

In the room were twelve officers from Eternity's service, another twelve loaned from neighboring towns and more than twenty Mounties, brought in from the Major Crimes unit in Winnipeg and detachments in the area. All chairs were turned to Atkin and the people on the stage sitting at a table.

Everyone looked ready. Atkin went to the podium, running his hand over his white hair and replacing his cap, his stomach straining the buttons of his white shirt. The light glinted off the metal maple leaves, crown and town seal on his shoulder boards.

"Good morning and welcome to those of you joining us today," his deep voice boomed before he was interrupted by the crackle of a police radio. "Whoever that is out there, use your earpiece. Thanks. Now, to say our town is reeling and screaming for justice would be an understatement. We're getting press calls from across the country. You all know what we have to do so let's get to it. Some of us worked through the night handing things over to the RCMP. They are now the lead." Atkin nodded to an officer on the stage, "And RCMP Sergeant Louella Sloan is in charge of the case. She'll lead the primary team of RCMP people that will include several from our service headed by Sergeant Bill Jurek. The rest of you will support them."

The creak of people shifting in their seats and whispered grumbling rippled across the room. Fully aware of old-school attitudes, Atkin sensed resistance to having a woman in command and arched an eyebrow.

"Let me be clear," he said. "Everyone will follow the direction of Sergeant Sloan from D-Division. She has worked in Major Crimes for fifteen years on more homicides than anyone in this room. She also has one of the RCMP's highest clearance rates."

After some coughing and throat clearing among the group, people sat a little straighter. Satisfied his words had sunk in, Atkin continued.

"Sergeant Sloan will give us an update and outline next steps. And I'll state the obvious—to protect the integrity of this investigation, nothing leaves this room. Go ahead, Sergeant."

Sloan nodded to the chief, then took the podium. She was in her early forties. Her hair was tied in a ponytail. She wore a golf shirt, jeans and her old navy patrol jacket. She'd had two hours of sleep since arriving the previous night. She slid on a pair of dark-framed glasses.

"You all got the summary sheets this morning," Sloan said, opening her notebook. "We're building on the solid initial work done by the Eternity Police Service and much of it, such as processing of the scene, is ongoing as we speak. I'll start with a timeline of what we believe transpired based on preliminary interviews with the last people to see the Tullocks here and in Saskatchewan.

"On Friday, the Tullocks had left home for a four-day visit with friends in Regina to return prior to Roy's upcoming business trip in Edmonton. But their son, Neal, was ill and the family returned early after two days. The positioning of the luggage and the bodies indicate that the family's early return had surprised whoever was in the house at the time, resulting in an attack or struggle, with the children fleeing to their rooms. There was no sign of forced entry.

"We believe entry was gained by an open basement window," Sloan said. "A K-9 unit picked up a trail and possible evidence leading from the house in the direction of the town and highway before the trail was lost. Our forensic people have been working at the scene through the night."

Sloan then went through a list of next steps that included a bare-bones news release to be issued to the media later in the morning confirming four homicides were under investigation. They would release a tip line number for the public to call. She said investigators will be interviewing and reinterviewing people familiar with the Tullocks' itinerary and movements in the time leading to the murders. A canvass and recanvass of residents and property in the immediate area would be conducted along with a grid search, including a search of all trash containers. Local motels, restaurants, gas stations and stores would be checked.

"We'll run plates and names wherever possible—someone may have seen something," Sloan said. "Okay, before wrapping up I'll take a few questions."

"Do we have any suspects?" an officer from Alden asked.

"At this point everybody's a suspect."

"Got a murder weapon?" the same officer asked.

"Several items were found at the scene and they're being processed."

"Any indication if this was random, or targeted?" an RCMP Corporal from Brandon asked. "Or the work of cults, something ritualistic, someone with a grudge or vendetta?"

"We can't rule out anything at this time."

"I ask because the word is that a message was found. You made no mention of that."

"I can't discuss that. It's being kept confidential as key fact evidence, something only the person or persons responsible would know."

"We understand," a cop from Virden with a chiseled face said, "that the Tullock's have a teen-aged daughter. Have you accounted for her where-abouts?"

"She currently resides in a facility in Winnipeg, but yes, we have people there following up to confirm her movement."

"Have you ruled out murder-suicide?" a member of the Winkler police asked. "Could Roy or Connie have committed the crimes?"

"We've ruled it out because of the nature of the wounds. The bodies will be removed later today and taken to Winnipeg for autopsies."

"What about Roy's business or the family's social online networks? What if Roy or Connie gambled, had outstanding debts, or may have been blackmailed, anything like that?" an officer from Morden asked.

"We'll look at all of it. We'll be looking at all bank, computer and phone records, and we'll be talking with all friends of the family, including those of the children. We'll look at all employees, all contractors, everyone who worked for the family in any capacity or had contact with them."

"Sergeant Sloan, aren't you overlooking something?" an officer from Winkler asked. "Isn't it basic procedure to get aerial photography of the scene?"

Sloan hesitated, tilted her head. As if on cue the distant thump of a helicopter could be heard.

"That's our chopper and that's your answer," she said.

At that moment the rear door opened. A young Mountie entered. Keys chimed on his utility belt and his radio chattered as he walked with a sense of urgency toward the front, up the stairs onto the stage to Sergeant Sloan. He whispered in her ear and passed her a folded piece of paper. She read it without expression, tucked it into her jacket pocket, nodded her thanks, then resumed.

"Okay, that's it. Get your assignments from the people at the table at the back. The next case-status meeting will be here at fifteen hundred hours. The last thing I'm going to say is that this case is solvable and we will solve it."

Fifteen

A clear blue sky above a farm located amid rolling green hills outside of Stockholm, Sweden.

Pastoral. But looks can be deceiving.

Ben Grant studied the picture on his monitor, then clicked to a video of the scene taken by Swedish police.

The remote farm was located near an ancient burial mound. Beneath the barn was the underground dungeon. Intense light from the camera illuminated the sweating stone walls and the glint of metal clasps and the chains fastened to them. Rats scurried across the earthen floor, disturbing human rib cages and skulls.

In this new Swedish case that had emerged a few months ago, a husband and wife, both surgeons, had befriended drifters, offering them a home at the farm, convincing them that they were being rescued. Instead, the doctors eventually imprisoned them and performed medical experiments on them before killing them. One of their earliest victims was Michael C. Dillman, a tourist from Iowa. So the story also had a US connection.

The information was in the latest stories Ben's publisher had sent him to consider for a book. Ben's reputation among law enforcement had helped the publisher secure the confidential video. The Swedish case had potential but it was gruesome, much like the recent case in Germany about a cannibalistic serial killer who had operated a butcher shop.

Also on the list of considerations: an older case from Canada, and two more recent US cases. They were all strong, Ben thought, when his phone vibrated with a text from Kayla.

Want to get pizza for dinner?

She often texted him when he was in his office working.

Sure, he responded. Is Emma good with it?

She is. I'll order the usual.

Less than an hour later, Ben was enticed to the kitchen by the mingled aroma of baked pepperoni, mushrooms, onions and cheese.

"How did your day of girl bonding go?" Ben put two slices on his plate.

"Good." Emma passed around drinks and napkins.

"We had fun," Kayla said. "I got some clothes."

"Great."

"We met a lady who wants you to do a charity book thing, Dad."

"Yes." Emma nodded, putting a slice on her plate. "Clara Jean O'Connor from the community association. They want you to be their featured guest at their literacy fund-raiser, to help get media attention. But you don't have to do it."

"Do it, Dad. Get this—you'd be filling in for Jake Gyllenhaal!"

"Impressive." Ben chewed, thinking and smiling as he said, "If anyone should be on TV, it's you."

"Me?" Emma said. "Why me?"

"You're a hero. You saved that boy. How's he doing, by the way?"

"He's been released from the hospital. He's home with his family, who have invited me to visit him." She took a small bite of pizza. "But I don't want to be on TV."

"It would be fun."

"No, that's not for me. You're the celeb in this house."

"Tell you what. Tell Clara Jean O'Connor that I'll do it but it's a family deal. We'll all be there to volunteer. It's a good cause."

"Yes!" Kayla said. Tug barked and she slipped him a bit of pepperoni as Ben looked at his wife.

"You're okay with that, Em?"

"Absolutely." She smiled, shifting the subject. "So how's work going?"

"My publisher and agent are pushing hard for me to land on a story for the next book."

"That's right. You had your call with them. How'd it go?"

"Today they turned up the heat, giving me sixty days to get them an outline. I get it and I don't blame them for being anxious."

"So have you got something in mind?"

"I'm looking at a new list of potential cases they sent me. There're a couple of interesting ones in Europe—one in Sweden involving two doctors that's pretty gripping, and a gruesome one in Germany. There are a couple in the US and one in Canada."

"Canada?" Emma said. "What's the case in Canada?"

"Something about an old murder. I haven't dug too deeply into it yet. Why do you ask?"

"No reason. I guess I don't think of Canada as having the type of crimes you'd write about."

"Tragedies happen anywhere," Ben said.

"Yes, they do," she said.

Ben and Kayla glanced at Emma, who smiled at them.

As Ben did most evenings after dinner, he took Tug for a walk.

He went alone, enjoying the fresh air while reflecting on his recent list of cases and Emma's comment about crime stories in Canada, finding it naive. Given his work, and hers, she would know that acts of evil are not exclusive to any country.

An odd thing to say, he thought, feeling Tug's leash tighten at the sight of a squirrel.

"You live a simple life, pal." Ben laughed to himself as his phone vibrated with a response to his earlier call to his daughter's therapist.

Hi Ben: Let's set up a call for you to update me on Kayla and we'll decide where to go from there. Send me times that are good for you. Best, Rachel Hirsch.

Made sense, Ben thought, responding with his thanks.

Forty-five minutes later he was in his office reviewing the cases once again.

He was drawn to the Swedish case of the doctors and the unspeakable things they did. Then he turned to the old Canadian case.

This could be one to consider.

Sixteen

Eternity, Manitoba
2000

"Why?"

Connie Tullock's weak, watery voice had been amplified. The sound filled the small boardroom at Eternity Police headquarters, where the primary team had gathered around the table. The faces of the RCMP and Eternity officers were taut with concentration as Jurek replayed her dying words.

"Why're you here...?"

"Connie, we need to know who hurt you."

"What're you doing here?"

Connie coughed, then mechanical beeping and pinging of monitors overtook the recording before it was switched off.

"Let's hear it again, Bill," Louella Sloan said, making more notes.

Jurek had not yet determined whether he liked Sloan, who'd insisted at the meeting's outset that she be called Lou and she'd call him Bill. "It'll make it easier for us to work together," she'd said.

Jurek had learned from the scar on the back of Sloan's hand that she'd been shot by a killer she'd arrested, and also learned that she was divorced and that her daughter was studying science at the University of Toronto. But while Sloan checked her phone's messages occasionally, she was all business when she stared at him over her glasses waiting for him to replay the brief recording for what must've been the twentieth time.

Again, after it ended, officers drew the same conclusions.

"I don't make anything of it," one said.

"She's too sedated," another said.

Sloan threw a glance to Jurek to see if his response had changed but he shook his head.

"She was really foggy, Lou, barely knew why I was there," he said.

"I don't believe Connie Tullock was talking to you, Bill," Sloan said.

"What?"

All of the investigators looked at Sloan.

"Sometimes," Sloan said, "when regaining consciousness after a traumatic event, victims are thrust back to the moments prior to the event and replay them." She glanced to her notes. "Connie Tullock was talking to whoever was in her house when she and her family arrived home early."

Jurek and some of the others nodded at Sloan's observation.

"Then that means she knew them, that this was not random," he said.

"Exactly," Sloan said. "The crime scene supports this. There are few signs of a struggle."

"The autopsy will tell us more," Jurek said.

"It should. Now, while we can't put blinders on and must remain open to all theories, at this stage we should follow the line that the victims knew the killer or killers," Sloan said.

"Have your people found anything in their emails, phone, credit or bank cards that points anywhere?" Jurek asked.

"Nothing has jumped out yet," Sloan said. "We'll continue to focus on those in the Tullocks' circles who were aware they'd be away, as well as those who might have harbored any ill will against them and where the evidence takes us. As for evidence, that note I received at the case meeting was from our forensic people who'd worked through the night. They've collected clear latents and impressions inside and around the property. Once they're processed they'll be run through the databanks," Sloan said. "Until then, let's interview people who were aware of the family's movements and those with any grudges. We'll go to your team on that, Bill."

Jurek paged through his notes.

"We've got Ritchie Hicks, an ex-employee. Roy fired him three months ago for stealing equipment from the Prairie Winds Farm Equipment Center and selling it in Winnipeg and Saskatoon. After Hicks was fired, he was overheard at a bar saying one day he'd come back and get even with Roy Tullock."

"And where is Hicks? Have you interviewed him?"

"Not yet. Last word put him in British Columbia or Alberta."

"We need to find Hicks and confirm his movements." Sloan went to her file folder. "We're using gas and restaurant receipts to confirm the Tullocks' route, times and dates to and from Saskatchewan along the Trans-Canada Highway. We're also working on collecting all possible security camera recordings at all locations visited by the Tullocks."

"Are you suggesting they were stalked?" Jurek asked.

"Anything's possible. We'll put out an alert on CPIC flagging Ritchie Hicks as a person of interest," Sloan said. "Now, the Tullocks have a daughter, Victoria." Sloan turned to one of the Mounties on her team. "What do you have, Frank?"

RCMP Corporal Frank Cullen flipped through his notebook.

"They call her Torrie. She's sixteen. After she experienced several breakdowns, her parents arranged for her to become a resident at the New Dawn Sunrise Wellness Retreat in Winnipeg. She's been there for five months. Winnipeg police report that Torrie's under supervision by retreat staff. She can leave the facility but only when escorted. So for the last five months she's never left Winnipeg."

"All right. We need you to go there today and interview her for any insights. Go with Lorna," Sloan said. "Let's get back to the family's immediate circle in town and who knew about their plans. Bill?"

Jurek consulted the statements and reports in his files. "We've done preliminary interviews with employees at the center and Tullock's ag operations," he said. "We've reinterviewed Marv Lander and Fran Penner, the senior employees who found the bodies, and we're checking with deliveries, contract people, those who service the Tullocks' grounds and pool. And there's the babysitter."

"The babysitter?"

"Janie Klassyn. She's been sitting for the Tullocks watching Neal and Linda for several months."

"Really?" Sloan removed her glasses, thinking. "Janie would know a little something about the inner workings of the Tullock household."

"That figures," Jurek said.

"Okay, when we finish here, you and I will interview Janie."

Seventeen

Santa Ana, Orange County, California
Present day

Marisa Joyce Narmore.

She was thirty-two years old and lived in a town house in Santa Ana on Williams Street, not far from the 55 freeway, a cream-colored unit with an attached two-car garage in the back.

Emma studied the building, thankful that Greg Clifton had come through, phoning her with the contact information for the mystery woman.

"Thanks, Greg," Emma told him. "I'll call her and clear things up."

"And we'll keep this all confidential, right?" Greg said.

"Totally confidential."

Only thing was, Emma had no intention of calling Marisa Joyce Narmore.

No, she wanted a face-to-face session to get answers.

It had taken a couple of days to plan, but Emma had adjusted much of her schedule and obtained approval to leave for appointments outside of school for the better part of today. Then she made the drive to Santa Ana, zeroing in on Marisa Joyce Narmore's address.

She parked two blocks away. She walked by the town house complex and around the back, seeing no sign of a green Ford Focus. Searching the area a few more times, getting a read on Narmore's unit, Emma reflected on how she had to fight every step of the way to get the life she now had. And now, she had to fight again to protect it; protect Ben and Kayla from whoever wanted to destroy it.

She took the note from her pocket and looked at it:

SOON IT WILL BE 20 YEARS. YOUR DAY OF RECKONING IS COMING.

Her jaw muscles bunched.

Who was Marisa Joyce Narmore and what did she want?

Emma had her suspicions but the fact was she didn't know. Whoever Marisa was, Emma was not going to let her ruin everything she had worked so hard to build. In the darkest years of her life she had learned a thing or two about surviving. Experience had taught her that when someone is trying to take you down, you get in their face fast, hard and smart.

It was now or never.

Emma went to the address, walked up the few steps to the solid door and rang the bell.

Immediately, a dog's barking sounded from inside.

A few seconds later a man's voice ordered the dog to be quiet as Emma heard movement toward the door, then locks clicking and a bolt sliding before the door opened about six inches.

Through the opening Emma saw a man in his thirties, messed hair, unshaven. He was shirtless, his chest and arms tattooed. One hand gripped the door, the other was down behind his back, where she glimpsed the dog, growling and barking. The man's eyes took a slow walk over her.

"I'm not buying anything and I'm not looking for Jesus."

While offering a small smile, Emma caught a hint of alcohol. "I'm looking for Marisa. Is she home?"

The dog barked again, and the man turned his head back. "Shut up!" Then to Emma he said: "Who are you?"

"I'm an old friend of hers."

"What's your name?"

"Is Marisa home? Can I speak to her?"

As the man stared at Emma, she noticed his eyes were bloodshot. He removed his hand from the door to scratch his chin, still keeping one hand behind his back, where the dog was barking again.

"Well, Marisa's friend with no name, all I can tell you is she's out."

"Do you know where she is? Where I can find her? When she'll be back?"

"Whoa." The man half smiled. "You're kind of a pushy thing, aren't ya?"

The dog barked. Emma couldn't see it.

"Leave me your name and number," he said. "I'll tell Marisa to call you. Or maybe I'll call you?" He winked.

Emma bit her bottom lip, thinking, when she heard the dog's paws scratching the floor as it barked louder. Keeping the door only slightly open, the man twisted, pushing the dog back with his foot, Emma glimpsing the hand behind his back.

He was holding a gun in it.

"No, that's fine," she said. "Thanks for your help."

"I'd invite you for a drink but I got some other business," he said.

"That's fine. Thank you."

Emma left and walked to her car.

All right, I know what I'm dealing with. I've got to rethink how I'm going to confront Marisa.

For now, she had another address to visit.

Eighteen

The two-story house was on a quiet cul-de-sac in a small hillside section of the neighborhood.

Emma found the grassy yard with its flower gardens and palm trees welcoming, while she ruminated on her first attempt to confront Marisa Joyce Narmore less than an hour earlier.

Emma had contemplated it during the drive, determining she would keep the prop gun she'd sneaked out from the drama department while reconsidering how to deal with Marisa and her threatening note later. Right now, she had other important matters to take care of.

She rang the bell.

A man in his forties, wearing Dockers and a polo shirt, gray hair feathering his temples, answered.

"Hi, I'm Emma Grant, Carson's school counselor."

After a moment, awareness dawned on him.

"Emma. Oh yes, we're expecting you. Austin Clark, Carson's father." He shook her hand. "Please come in. I just made some coffee—would you like some? Or juice, a soft drink?"

"Coffee's fine, thanks."

He led her to the kitchen, which opened to the dining room and glass doors leading to the backyard, the patio and the pool. Austin indicated the stools at the breakfast bar and Emma took one, glancing around.

"Where's Carson?"

"Upstairs with his mom. They'll be down."

"How is he doing?"

"Good. Cream? Sugar?"

"Just a little cream, please."

"He's seeing a psychiatrist," Austin said. "She's got him on a mild medication and—" The ceramic mug shook a little as he set Emma's coffee before her. "I don't know how to thank you for what you did."

Emma smiled and nodded, turning to the hall, where a woman was watching them. She was in her forties, dressed in a peach sweater and white slacks. A floral-patterned scarf covered her head. Emma noticed that she'd lost her eyebrows and eyelashes from her treatment.

"I'm Sonia, Carson's mom. You must be Emma."

"Yes." Emma stood to shake her hand.

Sonia ignored it, embracing her in a powerful hug.

"Thank you," Sonia said. "For saving our son."

Emma nodded, brushing tears from her eyes.

"Hi, Ms. Grant."

They all turned to Carson. Hair mussed, he was wearing shorts and a hoodie with the hood pulled up. He sipped from a bottle of apple juice in his hand, then stood there, looking at everyone before speaking.

"We know you want to talk to Emma, so Dad and I can leave you guys alone," Sonia said.

"No, we'll go outside."

Carson opened the patio doors for Emma and the two of them went out. They leaned on the counter of the poolside bar, staring at the water.

"I'm sorry," Carson said. "What I did was so stupid and so embarrassing."

"No, no." Emma touched his shoulder. "No need to apologize."

"I felt, well, actually, I felt nothing. Just lost, empty, overwhelmed by everything, you know?"

"Yes. I do. Just about everyone has felt that way. But you wanted to kill the moment, not yourself."

A smile began to emerge on his face.

"What is it?" she asked.

"That's sorta what my shrink said, and I guess there's some truth to it. I've got a lot of things to work on."

"Give it time," she said. "I'm so happy you're still here with us."

Carson smiled that broad smile. "Thank you for saving my life, Ms. Grant."

"It wasn't me. Your friends sounded the alarm. You've got a lot of people in your corner, a lot of people who love you and will fight for you. You're going to come out of this stronger, Carson."

They hugged, then went back inside.

When the visit ended at the door and Carson's parents said goodbye, Sonia hugged her again.

"Words cannot convey what you've given us, Emma. Thank you."

Gripping the wheel, Emma's knuckles whitened as she drove away, battling emotions roiling inside her. She recognized a sense of accomplishment at playing a role in helping Carson.

I want to help people. I want to be a good person—I am a good person. But the note, the looming anniversary, even Kayla with her questions, forcing me to lie...it's closing in.

Emma bit back on her tears, refusing to cry.

I will survive this.

At a red light, she checked the fuel gauge. It showed that she had less than a quarter of a tank. Two blocks later she pulled into a Mobil station and filled up, then went into the station to pay.

Inside, a man wearing torn, stained pants with a bulging knapsack slung over his shoulder was being told to leave by the attendant. While departing, the man asked people in line for money. Dirt encrusted the creases of his palm, his full wild beard was dotted with crumbs and he reeked of alcohol, a scent that triggered the shame, pain and desperate hopelessness Emma had known growing up. When his bleary eyes met hers, she reached into her bag and gave him a twenty. Still waiting to pay, she swiped through her phone for messages when it pinged with a news notice.

Talk about timing.

It was another opinion piece from one of the Canadian newspapers she'd subscribed to. The headline read: Eternity Anniversary Will Open Old Wounds.

Emma began reading it, words flying at her— "How can people ever forget the unimaginable crimes…and how those responsible have gone on to live their lives…" when someone tapped her shoulder. A woman behind her indicated it was Emma's turn at the counter. Emma apologized, slid her credit card from her wallet, paid and returned to her SUV, her stomach in knots.

Behind the wheel she resumed reading the news item when a horn honked. The pickup behind her wanted her to move out of the way so he could gas up. She set her phone down, fastened her seat belt and pulled away, working to clear her mind as she headed home.

Preoccupied with her thoughts, she didn't notice a car that had been parked near the busy Mobil station and was now behind her.

It was not Marisa Narmore's car.

This car was the same car driven by the floral shirt man she had seen near the restaurant when she, Ben, Kayla and Tug had gone to the beach.

It remained half a block behind Emma's SUV, allowing several cars to stay between them as it followed her.

Nineteen

Kayla arrived home hungry and went straight to the fridge for yogurt.

"I'm home!"

No one responded.

She replaced her key on the wooden rack on the wall. Kayla had made the rack for her parents a summer long ago, painting little hearts on it. Her mom loved it. The last peg held the keys to their cabin. Above it was a small photo of the place. Kayla touched it tenderly.

Sliding off her backpack, she saw a note posted on the fridge door: *Gone to the dentist for a checkup,* it said in her father's handwriting.

Oh my God, he's so old. You could've just texted, Dad. You know how to do it.

Kayla rolled her eyes and began eating banana yogurt when Tug shuffled into the kitchen, ball in his mouth, looking for a playmate.

"No, not right now," she said.

Tug then went to his electronic dog door in the kitchen door that opened to the backyard and pool. It was activated by the chip in Tug's collar, unlocking only when he was near. No other animals could pass through it. Tug exited and returned, signaling that he wanted to go for a walk.

"Sorry, buddy." Kayla scratched his head, then filled his water bowl. She resumed eating yogurt at the counter while reflecting on the episode of *Dateline* she'd watched on YouTube last night. It was about people keeping secrets and was so interesting with its great detective work. Thinking of it fueled her deepening curiosity about Emma, which had arisen from their recent conversations about Emma's life.

Do we really know her? Dad's blinded by his love and busy with his work. It's up to me to check things out.

Kayla got her laptop from her backpack and again searched for anything about people dying in an explosion and fire at Tony's Diner in Beltsville, Maryland. Again, nothing came up.

Okay, not everything's online. And it was, like, twenty years ago. But it's kinda strange I found nothing.

Kayla finished her yogurt, thinking.

Dad says I have Mom's journalistic genes. And, like him, Mom was a good investigative reporter.

Putting her empty cup in the recycle bin Kayla considered her situation.

Dad was out. Emma was out. She had the place to herself. She looked at Tug. He barked.

"What's that, Scooby-Doo? You want to do some detective work?"

Tug barked again.

"Let's see, where do we start?"

She considered the small office alcove in the kitchen, where Emma sometimes worked. Emma's laptop was there. Kayla's pulse kicked up as she went to it and considered trying to log in and search Emma's files and emails. No, that wouldn't work. She didn't know Emma's password and if she attempted to hack in she'd risk leaving a sign that she had tried.

Kayla looked in the drawer. Maybe Emma kept something in there.

Sifting through take-out menus, expired coupons, brochures, pens and other odds and ends, she found nothing.

I'm not sure what I'm looking for but I'll know it when I find it.

She continued glancing around, thinking about the places and spaces that Emma used.

In the living room, there were drawers in the end tables that she and her dad never kept anything important in. Kayla checked there and found coasters and a few magazines. There was the credenza in the dining room. Kayla went through the drawers finding candles, candlestick holders, most of which her mom had bought. She checked cupboards, drawers and storage closets on the main floor—nothing unusual, nothing hidden away.

Upstairs, then.

With Tug panting happily behind her because

she had his ball, Kayla checked the guest room, searching the dresser drawers, flipping through the extra sheets and pillow cases. She checked the closet. Not much but blankets and extra pillows.

She found nothing in the upstairs storage closets but bathroom and cleaning supplies.

She entered the bathroom her dad and Emma shared, fragrant with soaps and her dad's cologne, going through the medicine cabinets, the cupboards, seeing nothing that came close to what she was seeking.

In the master bedroom she went through Emma's dresser drawers, sifting through her underwear, socks and things. She poked through Emma's jewelry boxes and accessory organizers.

Nothing there.

Kayla went to the big walk-in closet her dad and Emma shared, confident that if Emma was concealing something, this would be the place.

The air was pleasant with a hint of lavender, reminding Kayla of her mom. She blinked as she stared at Emma's shirts, pants and dresses hanging where her mom's clothes used to be.

Mom used to hide our Christmas presents in here.

The shelf above Emma's clothes held stacks of boxes and books. Kayla took them down and looked through them one by one. Nothing but old bills, and records relating to Emma's school counseling job in California. Replacing the boxes, she pulled down the books. All of them were textbooks about psychology, education, sociology and counseling. Kayla fanned through them.

Nothing.

The lower storage area contained shoes, boots and slippers. To one side was a set of luggage. Next to it was Emma's large storage trunk with its metal clamps and latches, sitting on the hardwood floor atop an area rug. The rug was one Kayla's mom got when they visited Arizona.

Kayla knelt before the trunk. It smelled nice, like wood. She ran her fingers along the metal latches. Was it locked? She pushed her thumbs against the latches. They snapped open.

Tug barked.

Someone was home.

Kayla's heart beat faster. She closed the latches, then hurried downstairs.

Twenty

The New Dawn Sunrise Wellness Retreat, a complex of half a dozen low-rise buildings, sat on twenty tranquil, wooded acres at the city's edge.

"Looks like a campus," RCMP Corporal Frank Cullen said to his partner, Corporal Lorna Bryce, as they'd parked after the two-hour drive from Eternity.

Inside, they waited at the reception desk before they were met by Sharon Narski, a senior manager, who signed them in.

"What happened in Eternity is so horrible," Narski said, escorting them to the administration offices,

Narski was a soft-spoken, petite woman. As they walked with her, Bryce threw a glance to Cullen, who followed her focus to Narski's hand. The manager was fidgeting with her pen, a sign of nervous tension. They came to an empty reception area and a closed office door bearing the plate: Zelda Dupree, Executive Director.

Narski knocked gently.

"Come in," said a woman's voice.

They entered the spacious office with Narski introducing Cullen and Bryce. Dupree stood from behind her desk and came around to greet them. She was tall and poised with silver hair styled in a bouffant. She removed her glasses, letting them fall to a golden neck chain, shook hands with the Mounties and indicated the two chairs before her desk. Narski sat alone on a sofa against the wall.

"Such a tragedy for the Tullock family," Dupree said. "Do you know who committed this unspeakable act?"

"We can't discuss that aspect of the case, ma'am," Cullen said. "We're here to interview Victoria Tullock."

"Of course."

"But first." Bryce opened her clipboard. "When you spoke with my colleague earlier on the phone, you'd indicated that Victoria has not left the facility here since she's been a resident?"

"That's not entirely correct."

"What do you mean?"

"This is not a prison." Dupree smiled. "The last time she was off-site was two weeks ago to shop at the mall nearby."

"She walked out of here two weeks ago?"

"I wouldn't put it that way. She can leave, but only with an escort. She has gone to local malls, movie theaters, but always under supervision.

That's our strict policy for residents in her situation."

The gentle clicking of Narski's pen behind them accelerated.

"And what exactly is her situation?" Cullen asked.

"Privacy laws forbid me from discussing Victoria's case," Dupree said. "What I can tell you is that we provide a range of residential treatment programs, involving therapy, education and myriad other services from our psychiatrists, social workers, counsellors and therapists."

"Treatment for what, exactly?" Cullen asked.

"Addictions, alcohol and drug abuse, post-traumatic stress and mood and anxiety disorders."

Bryce, who'd been taking notes, closed her clipboard. "Thank you. We'd like to talk to Victoria now."

"Sharon will escort you to her room," Dupree said. "However, I have a request from her family. Her aunt and uncle wish to talk with you first."

"They're here?" Cullen asked.

"Yes. Mr. Tullock's brother and his wife. They flew in from Vancouver to be with Victoria as soon as they were notified. Sharon will take you to them."

Paul and Lynn Tullock sat at a table in an empty lounge with floor-to-ceiling windows that looked out onto a forest and stream. The couple appeared to be in their fifties. Paul sipped from a ceramic mug; Lynn tended to a Diet Coke. Their faces were etched with anguish and exhaustion when they looked up as Narski introduced them to Bryce and Cullen.

The investigators joined them at the table. Narski went to the far side of the lounge to the coffee station, out of earshot, giving them privacy.

"Did you find the person who killed my brother and his family?" Paul asked.

"I'm sorry, no arrests have been made yet," Bryce said as she opened her clipboard to take notes.

"It's early in the investigation," Cullen added. "Can you think of anyone who would want to hurt your brother's family?"

Lynn shook her head.

"Sergeant Sloan asked us that when we gave our statements to her over the phone," Paul said.

"We just cannot comprehend what's happened." Lynn's face crumpled. "Torrie's the only survivor, that poor child."

"Has she been told?" Bryce asked.

"Yes," Paul said. "We'll be going to Eternity soon to help plan the funerals."

"It's just not right," Lynn said. "Torrie's been ill and now this."

"What do you mean by ill?" Bryce asked. "Why is she here?"

Lynn looked at Paul, then touched her eyes with a tissue, took a breath, then let it out. "When Torrie was younger, Connie thought she was different. She seemed bored, moody, easily angered, but also took up an interest in math, science and literature at an early age."

"Wasn't she nine when she was reading Shakespeare?" Paul said.

"Yes," Lynn continued. "It all worried Connie, so she took her to psychologists, who assessed and tested her. Turned out Torrie's IQ level was near genius. Then Torrie fell down the stairs and hurt her head. Ever since then Torrie's had problems coping with life. She's had breakdowns."

"Breakdowns?" Bryce asked.

Paul added: "She would sometimes descend into what the people here call a dissociated state. Roy told me that Torrie thought she could walk through walls. At times she'd fly into wild, vengeful rages."

"Vengeful?"

He nodded. "Roy and Connie didn't understand what was happening. They were afraid Torrie would hurt someone, or herself. That's why they brought her here for treatment, to help her so they could eventually bring her home."

Bryce continued making notes. "Did Torrie ever harm anyone, or herself?" she asked.

Paul glanced at Bryce's note-taking and shook his head. "No, nothing, thank God."

"In fact," Lynn said, "her treatment here was working. Torrie was getting well. So well that they were going to send her home in a few weeks and then—" She gasped for breath. "Oh Lord, that poor child."

Paul put his arm around his wife and comforted her before the investigators thanked them and left with Narski.

* * *

As they followed Narski down the corridor of the section where Torrie resided, Bryce and Cullen were reminded of university dorms.

Only here all the doors were closed. No music or pot smell leaked into the hall. Instead, the air was soothing, quiet and calm.

They stopped at number 164, where Narski knocked softly. "Torrie, we have two visitors who need to talk to you."

Seconds passed without a response.

Narski opened the door enough to stick her head in.

"Torrie, I'm going to let two new visitors in to see you."

Narski retreated from the door, then nodded to the Mounties. "There's a keypad intercom next to the light switch. Enter one six four when you're done and I'll escort you out."

"Thanks," Cullen said.

Narski opened the door wide, then left down the hall.

The investigators entered and closed the door behind them.

Torrie was seated at her desk, her back to them. They couldn't see her face; her head was bent over her work and her long hair covered her face.

Bryce noticed the security camera above the door as she set a digital recorder on a bookshelf near Torrie and opened her notebook.

"Victoria, I'm Lorna Bryce and my partner is Frank Cullen. We're so sorry for what's happened."

"Call me Torrie."

"Torrie, we're with the RCMP and we'd like to ask you some questions that may help us find the person, or persons, who hurt your family. Is that okay—do you want to help us?"

Torrie said nothing.

Cullen leaned his head to see that Torrie appeared to have a pencil in her hand and seemed consumed with writing or drawing.

"Torrie, it would really help if you talked to us," Bryce said.

Torrie continued working without speaking.

"We need to know if you can think of anyone who would want to hurt your family."

Torrie didn't answer.

"Did your mom or dad ever mention to you anything about someone who'd want to hurt them?" Bryce asked.

No response.

For several long moments Bryce tried in vain to get Torrie to engage with them but it was futile. Bryce glanced at Cullen, indicating he should try.

"Don't you want to help us?" Cullen asked.

"They're all gone," Torrie said.

Bryce shot a hopeful look to Cullen.

"I'm all alone now," Torrie said as she continued working.

"You have your aunt and uncle, who love you and want to help you," Cullen said.

"I'm not me," Torrie said.

Cullen looked at Bryce with a question on his face.

"What do you mean?"

"I'm not me anymore."

Torrie's right arm shot straight back high into the air, gripping the paper she'd been working on, holding it out for Cullen.

He took the sheet, concern webbing across his face.

The pencil sketch showed the furious expression of a girl, her long black hair shooting out wildly in Medusa strands, her eyes narrowed, her mouth scowling with demonic rage.

Torrie then turned, keeping her head bent down low to her chest, her hair curtained over her face. She lifted her eyes, the whites glaring at the two officers as she spoke through gritted teeth.

"Tell me who you think killed my family!"

Twenty-One

Santa Ana, Orange County, California
Present day

Marisa Joyce Narmore's green Ford Focus was parked in front of her town house and reflected in the driver's side mirror of Emma's SUV.

Emma had been watching it from the end of the block where she was parked in the opposite direction. She'd angled her mirror to capture Marisa's front door, too, thankful to find the Ford there when she'd arrived nearly an hour ago.

She'd been watching and waiting.

It had been a couple of days since her first attempt to confront Marisa but she wouldn't give up.

I'm going to find out who she is and why she's threatening me.

Emma had told Ben and Kayla that she had meetings after school then had a few errands, that she didn't know how late she'd be and for them to go ahead and have supper without her. Before leaving her school for her mission to Santa Ana, Emma visited the drama department to get something she'd need. Given her previous encounter with the gun-holding creep at the door and the dog, she was uncertain what she would face a second time.

She wanted to be ready.

Emma accepted that her plan wasn't the best strategy; that she was taking a risk. Her life with Ben and Kayla was at stake and she could feel time ticking down on her to do something.

A slight movement in the side mirror.

This could be it.

The front door of Marisa's town house had opened and a woman stepped out with something in her hand. When she got to the sidewalk, Emma saw her dog on the leash: a beagle. They started walking.

She's alone—good. Coming this way across the street. I've got to do this now. I might not get a second chance.

Emma slid the strap of her bag over her shoulder, got out, crossed the street and began walking toward the woman, growing more confident with each step. The woman was the same age, had the same build and hair color as the woman in the video. She had the pink sneakers. As Emma drew closer, she was certain it was her.

Do it now, head-on.

"Excuse me, do you have a moment?" Emma said.

The woman stopped; the dog pulled on the leash.

"You're Marisa, right?"

A mix of surprise and confusion blossomed on

her face. In that moment, up close, Emma tried to recognize the woman, who appeared to be the same age as she was. But nothing about her was familiar. The woman was a stranger.

"You're Marisa Joyce Narmore, right?"

"Yes."

"And that's your green Ford Focus parked down the street?" Emma recited the plate number.

"Yes, what's this about? Who are you?"

"This won't take long. I need to show you something." Emma held up her phone.

"I really don't—"

"Please, it won't take long. It's important."

Emma played the school security video on her phone, holding it for Marisa to view.

"See," Emma said when it ended, "that's you placing a note on my SUV where I work, isn't it?"

The color drained from Marisa's face and her dog barked.

"This note." Emma stepped closer, invading Marisa's space, pulling the note from her bag, holding it before her to read. Then Emma thrust the note into her bag, letting Marisa see the gun she had there, as she slid her hand around it, while keeping it in her bag.

"Now, I want you to tell me who the fuck you are and why you're threatening me?"

Marisa swallowed and looked around.

"Tell me what I need to know, Marisa. And don't lie because I'll find out."

"How did you? I can't—I just—I don't know–"

"You're not a cop—cops don't do what you did. Are you a reporter?"

"No. I—please, I can't—just leave me alone, please."

"Do you know the others?"

"The others? Who? What? No, I don't know anything."

The dog barked and was answered by another dog's barking.

"Hi, Marisa, hi, Bailey. Everything all right?"

They both looked to a silver-haired man across the street with a leashed German shepherd.

"Tell him you're okay," Emma whispered.

"Hi, Burt, thanks! It's all good!"

"Mind if Skipper and I join you for a walk?" The man started to cross the street to them.

"This isn't over," Emma said to Marisa before she left.

"Sorry if I interrupted," the man said to Emma as she strode away.

She said nothing, knowing he'd fully intended to intervene.

Emma got into her SUV and drove far down the street, disappearing into a driveway bordered with a hedge that concealed her. She got out and from that distance she saw Marisa walking toward her town house with her dog, talking on her phone while looking up and down the street.

Emma would wait this out.

Some fifteen minutes later, Emma saw Marisa get into her green car and pull away.

She began following her, careful to keep her distance as Marisa drove down Williams Street, then headed east on McFadden Avenue.

She went about three or four blocks to Pasadena Avenue coming to an intersection where the light had gone yellow. Fearing Marisa would speed through it, Emma accelerated only to find that Marisa had stopped and the van she had kept between them changed lanes, leaving Emma's SUV directly behind Marisa.

No.

Waiting for the light to change, or the intersection to clear, Emma saw Marisa look in her rearview mirror, saw Marisa hold her gaze, then turn around in her seat.

It was clear. She knew Emma was following her.

Marisa sped down Pasadena, turned right on Sycamore, racing along the on-ramp merging into the lanes of traffic going north on the 55.

I can't lose her. She could be heading to the answers I need.

Emma got onto the 55, keeping her eyes on the Ford but it pulled farther and farther away.

Traffic was heavy and Marisa kept changing lanes. Emma feared she would lose her at the upcoming exchange—not sure if Marisa would continue on 55 or take the Santa Ana Freeway.

Marisa was really moving and at the last minute had taken the Santa Ana Freeway, constantly changing lanes, cutting people off, accelerating and putting vehicles between her and Emma. For miles Marisa drove as if panicked, weaving dangerously from one lane to another. Horns honked, brake lights came on. But Marisa gained speed and distance, to the point where Emma could barely see her.

Then traffic began to congest as they came upon a construction zone with reduced lanes and options to detour.

Emma slammed her palms on the wheel and cursed. She had lost Marisa completely. Frustrated, she took an exit and headed back to Cielo Valle.

Twenty-Two

Eternity, Manitoba
2000

Lou Sloan's unmarked Silver Nissan Rogue tottered and swayed along the rutted, unpaved section of road near the railway yards where Janie and Marlene Klassyn lived.

Bill Jurek surveyed the street's tired frame houses, punctuated by vacant lots, looking at the low-rise apartments with blistered paint and missing shingles.

"It's a rough side of town," he said.

"I see that." Sloan touched a finger to her nose as the SUV lurched. "I can smell it, too."

"The slaughterhouse is just down there. A major employer," Jurek said.

When they reached the Klassyns' duplex, Sloan's phone rang as she parked out front. She answered. It was Frank Cullen, sounding like he was in a moving car. Sloan put the call on speaker for Jurek's benefit.

"Frank, I'm here on speaker with Bill."

"Yeah, Lou, we spoke with Torrie Tullock and we're on our way back."

"Did she tell you anything?"

"Nothing, but it was weird," Cullen said. "She gave us this sketch, maybe a self-portrait, maybe not. It was strange. The only thing she asked is if we knew who killed her family."

"Did you confirm her whereabouts at the time it happened?" Sloan asked.

"We did. The director said Torrie hasn't left the facility in the last two weeks, and can't leave without an escort. I think we can cross her off."

Sloan turned to Jurek for any other questions and he shook his head.

"Okay, Frank," Sloan said. "Thanks for the update."

Sloan made note of the call and got her bag. Jurek collected his zippered notebook, then they walked past Marlene's parked car and knocked on the Klassyns' front door.

Marlene Klassyn's face was creased with worry. Her hair, tied back into a neat ponytail, exposed the anguish she carried.

"I'm sorry. I'm a wreck. This is so horrible for both of us," she said after letting the investigators in. "I've got coffee, if you'd like some."

"Thank you for agreeing to see us," Sloan said. "Coffee would be fine."

Noticing shoes on a mat by the door, the officers began removing theirs.

"Please don't worry about your shoes," Marlene said.

Sloan glanced at Oxfords and sneakers there, before Marlene led them into the kitchen. Taking seats at the table, they saw Janie in the living room, on the couch, hugging a pillow, her chin buried in it as she consoled herself.

"Do you have any idea who would do this and why?" Marlene asked after setting mugs of coffee on the table then milk, sugar and spoons as if they were customers.

"We're working on it." Jurek fixed his coffee.

"We should get started," Sloan said, opening her notebook.

"I understand." Marlene sat at the table with them.

"How many people reside here?"

"Just me and Janie live here."

"And you're a server at the restaurant in the Eternity Country Club?"

"Assistant manager is my title, yes."

Sloan turned to Janie. "And you babysat for the Tullock family?"

Janie nodded into the pillow.

"Marlene, can you think of anyone who would want to harm any member of the Tullock family?"

"I can't. They were such a nice family." Her voice weakened. "I know some folks resented their wealth, but that's petty, small-town jealously. Roy was such a good man with a good heart. I don't mind telling you that a while back I was let go for spilling a tray on him, but he stepped in and, being a club board member, ensured I kept my job. He's a kind, fair man."

"And how did Janie come to work for him?"

"It was out of that incident. Roy said he and his wife were looking for a new sitter and he asked about her because she sat for one of his managers, Marv Lander."

"Marlene, have you ever heard of Ritchie Hicks?" Sloan asked.

She considered the name before shaking her head.

"Have you ever been inside the Tullock home on Old Pioneer?"

"No, but Janie has, many times."

"You're getting ahead of us." Sloan turned to Janie, then back to her mother. "We're going to need to collect Janie's fingerprints, and yours."

"Why do you need our fingerprints?"

Janie lifted her face from the pillow, worry blossoming on it.

"It's okay." Jurek smiled. "It's routine. We create a set of elimination prints so we have a record of all the prints we'd expect to find in the house and run them against any others we might find there."

Janie's face had turned white, which Sloan noted.

"It really is routine," Sloan said. "We'd like you to volunteer to have this done later today."

Janie was silent.

"Yes, of course," Marlene said. "Anything to help."

"Thank you." Sloan sipped coffee. "Now, I'd

like to talk to Janie alone. We can go in her room and Bill can stay here with you, if that's okay with you both?"

Marlene's back straightened. "Why alone?"

"It's just procedure," Sloan said, "because she was in the house and one of the last to see the family."

Marlene looked at the officers, then at Janie, assessing if her daughter could undergo questioning by Sloan without her present. It took a moment before she decided.

"All right," Marlene said, then to Jurek, "I've got some fresh muffins, if you'd like?"

"Sure," Jurek said.

"Thanks," Sloan said. "Janie, want to take me to your room?"

Still hugging her pillow, she led Sloan into her bedroom, which immediately grew smaller when the investigator entered and shut the door.

Janie sat on her bed holding her pillow. Sloan pulled the desk chair over, taking stock of the room, its peach walls, and posters, her shelves with stuffed animals, pictures and keepsakes.

"You've got a pretty room," Sloan said.

"Thanks."

"I know it must be so hard for you, with all that's happened?"

Nodding, Janie clenched her eyes, squeezing out new tears. Sloan spotted a tissue box and held it for Janie to pull out what she needed.

"I'll try not to take too long. I really need your help. It's important, okay?"

Janie nodded.

"How long have you babysat for the Tullocks?"

"I don't know. I started in the spring."

"So, for four or five months?"

"About that, I guess."

"Did you like sitting for them?"

"Yes. I liked Linda and Neal." Janie sobbed.

"You must've known the family fairly well?"

"I guess." She shrugged.

"As far as you could tell, were there any problems?"

"What do you mean?"

"Did they argue or discuss anything that seemed to be troubling them?"

Janie shrugged again, shook her head. "I know they had their daughter, Torrie, put in some institution in Winnipeg."

"Did they discuss that with you?"

"No. The kids told me, and everyone in town knew."

"Did you ever meet Torrie?"

"No."

"Are you aware of any times she may have visited her family?"

"No, her parents would go to Winnipeg to see her."

Sloan made notes.

"Did you ever hear the Tullocks mention anyone who they disagreed with, or who had an argument with them?"

"No."

"Do you know of Ritchie Hicks?"

"No."

"When you sat, did anyone visit the house, or did you have a strange person come to the door? Or receive any strange calls?"

"No."

"And how did you get along with the family?"

Janie looked at Sloan and her lips trembled. "Fine. I liked Mr. Tullock and the kids."

"What about Mrs. Tullock?"

Fear flitted across Janie's eyes and she took a breath. "I sometimes thought she didn't like me."

"Really? Why?"

Wiping at her tears, Janie thought. "Because we're poor and because of where we live."

Sloan looked at her for a long moment, absorbing her comments, then started a new page in her notebook. "I need you to think hard and help with a time frame, okay? When was the last time you babysat?"

Janie brushed her hair from her face, and her tears. Blinking, she looked at the calendar on her door. "It's marked there with an X."

Sloan looked. "So the Wednesday leading to the weekend when it happened?"

Janie nodded.

"That was the last time you were in the Tullocks' house?"

"Yes."

"And that was the last time you saw them?"

Janie blinked and nodded.

"You were aware they were going away to Regina to visit friends?"

"Yes, they told me."

"Do you know who else was aware?"

"No."

At that moment Sloan's attention turned to the desk and the ring. She leaned closer to study the colorful skull.

"Interesting ring, Janie," she said. "Looks like a sugar skull. I saw them on vacation in Mexico. Where did you get it?"

"At The Big Sky Truck Stop."

Sloan let a few long seconds pass before she nodded and stood. "Cool. Okay, that should do it for now."

As the investigators readied to leave, thanking Marlene and Janie at the door, Jurek reiterated the need for their fingerprints as Sloan's attention went to shoes belonging to Marlene and her daughter. She zeroed in on a pair of white canvas sneakers with pink laces, pink trim, noticing that they had small brownish flecks on them.

"Are those your shoes, Janie?" Sloan pointed. "The ones you wear all the time?"

"Yes."

"All right then, one last thing," Sloan said. "In keeping with the point of fingerprints; we'd like you to volunteer Janie's shoes."

"You want her shoes?" Marlene said.

"Yes, we need to take them and process them as well, the same principle as the prints."

"You want to take her shoes?" Marlene repeated.

"Yes, because Janie's been in the Tullock house. She must have others to wear. Is that a problem?"

Marlene, surprised, looked at Janie, who stared through her tears at her shoes, saying nothing.

"We can get a warrant to obtain them," Sloan said. "But that will take time. If you volunteer, we can process them quickly."

"Yes, I guess that's fine," Marlene said.

"Thank you, I'll get a bag from the car," Sloan said.

In her absence, Jurek smiled at them, thanking them for their cooperation, assuring them that everything was routine for investigations of this nature. Sloan returned wearing blue latex gloves and unfolded a brown paper bag.

Marlene and Janie exchanged glances as Sloan placed the shoes inside the bag.

Twenty-Three

Cielo Valle, Orange County, California
Present day

"It's astounding how you get into the minds of murderers," a woman with oversize glasses told Ben. "It makes your stories incredibly compelling. You have a gift, Mr. Grant."

He smiled, pen poised to sign her copy of *Devil's Dance in Paris.*

"Please make it out to Edna," she said.

"Thank you, Edna," Ben said. "I never forget the toll of the tragedy, never excuse the criminal act. My job is to search for the answers, even in the darkest corners."

After signing, Ben greeted the next person in the long line of patient readers that stretched from his table at the outdoor book sale.

Row after row of folding tables, laden with boxes and crates of used books covered the parking lot of the One Light Redemption Church, thousands of donated books of every sort. Waves of book lovers streamed to the sale. Banners, balloons and flags flapped in the breeze that carried the smells of hot dogs and popcorn.

Ben was happy to be a part of it with his family. But between each signing he searched the crowds, dotted with volunteers in fluorescent green T-shirts, spotting Emma in hers, helping people find books.

For a moment he pondered how Emma was taken aback when he'd mentioned a possible case from Canada for his next book. Odd, but he shrugged it off because he was leaning to the Swedish case.

Watching Emma warmed him. He was amazed at how she had saved one of her students. She was a remarkable woman and he was glad she was his wife.

"Hi, Ben," said a large bearded man with a canvas bag of hardcovers and paperbacks of Ben's books, setting them on the table for him to sign. "I love your books. They're better than any versions of these stories they've put on the screen. Can you sign them to Karl with a *K*?"

"Happy to, Karl."

Before signing, Ben spotted Kayla in her glowing green T-shirt helping a woman lift books. His heart swelled with love and pride in how much she looked and acted like Brooke. She was every bit the reporter.

But he was concerned about how Kayla was struggling with her mother's death and her inability to accept Emma—that she regarded her instead as a mysterious outsider in their lives.

He planned to raise it with Doctor Hirsch when they spoke.

* * *

Kayla grunted, hefting a box crammed with Game of Thrones and Harry Potter books, setting it before a woman who was using a cane. The woman slid on glasses to sort through the titles with delight.

"Bless you, dear," the woman said.

Kayla dragged the back of her hand across her brow. While the woman piled her selections, Kayla looked for Emma, still troubled that she could find no reference to a deadly fire at a Tony's Diner in Beltsville, Maryland.

Was Emma lying?

I've got to keep digging. I need to look inside that trunk in her closet. And there's something else I can try. It's dangerous but it'll prove if she's lying.

"There you are, Kayla!"

She turned to the happy face of Clara Jean O'Connor who took her hand and nodded to cameras milling through the activity.

"The TV people are here! They want to interview your dad, you and Emma. We're going to meet them at your dad's table."

"Do you have westerns?" a man with silver hair, wearing a gingham shirt and a bolo tie, asked Emma. "I'm looking for Zane Grey and Louis L'Amour."

"Westerns are in row twenty." Emma pointed to the sign.

"I thank you kindly, miss."

As the man made his way, Emma's smile faded and she returned to her problems. Angry that Marisa Joyce Narmore had slipped away from her on the freeway before she could get answers about the note. Emma would have to try again with Marisa soon.

Then there was Kayla with her questions about her past. Emma hated lying to her and to Ben. But she had to, to protect them. She hoped one day she could undo her lies and reveal the truth.

But right now her plight was bearing down on her, with fears she was being followed. And, with the anniversary nearing, and every news item in the Canadian media about the case, Emma felt like she was running out of time.

"Emma!" Clara Jean O'Connor approached, waving to her and pointing to TV news cameras. "They want you."

Emma's stomach clenched as she threaded her way through the crowd to join Kayla, Clara Jean and the TV people waiting at Ben's table.

Clara Jean, her face flushed with excitement, indicated the two camera operators and two reporters.

"Wonderful," Clara Jean said, "everyone's here. We're so happy to have two teams from the Santa Ana bureaus of their L.A. stations. This is Maggie and Ron."

"It's Rob, Rob Gallo with KRVZ First News." He offered a dazzling white-toothed smile, shook everyone's hand with one hand while his other gripped a microphone. "Love your books, Ben."

"I'm Maggie Shen, with KTKT." She followed suit. "You've got a lot of people waiting for you, Ben," she said, "so Rob and I decided we could do this together, quickly. Promise to keep it short."

"Sure," Ben said.

"Then when we wrap, we'll talk to you separately, Clara," Maggie said.

"Wonderful," Clara Jean said. "This is our opening day. Please don't forget to tell your viewers we have two more to go."

"Yes." Maggie held up her phone. "It's all here in the news release you sent us." Then to the Grants: "If you guys could get a little closer together."

Ben, Kayla and Emma moved closer.

"Great." Maggie got her microphone ready. "Just look at Rob and me like we're having a regular conversation. Don't worry about the cameras."

The operators hoisted the cameras up on their shoulders.

"Good to go." Maggie smiled. "So Ben, what brings a world-famous author and his family to this event today?"

"The proceeds go to literacy programs across the county. It's an effort me and my family support wholeheartedly." Ben indicated Kayla and Emma, whom he'd noticed had slid on large sunglasses. "We were happy to join the countless volunteers and do our part to launch this three-day event and make it a success."

"Ben, I have to ask," Rob said, "it's been a few

years since your personal tragedy. One could only imagine how you, if you ever do, recover from a blow like that."

Ben nodded, bracing for whatever was coming.

"What I'm getting at is, it's been years since your last book. Can we tell your readers that another book is coming and when?"

"Yes. Well, what I can say is that a new book is being planned."

Emma turned her head to him, listening intently.

"I can't tell you what it will be about, but a new one is being planned."

"Great, will it be a local case or an international one?"

"I can't reveal that yet," Ben said.

"Kayla." Maggie moved her microphone to her. "It's great that you're here helping. Why did you come?"

"Like my dad said, it's a good cause and it's something my mom would've done."

"Have you decided on a career path?" Maggie asked. "Are you going to be a writer, like your dad?"

"I'd like to be a reporter, like my mom and dad were."

"And what about you, Mrs. Grant?" Rob glanced at his notebook. "I'm sorry, Emma. Are you a writer or a journalist? Is that why you're here?"

Emma pushed her glasses closer to her face. "I'm a school counselor. I think Ben and Kayla said it best—this is a terrific cause and—" she cast an arm to the people jam-packed amid the books, as if to divert attention from herself "—you can see, a lot of people support it."

"Indeed," Maggie said. "Okay, I think we're good. Thank you."

The cameras were lowered and Emma disappeared into the crowd, leaving Ben and Kayla to exchange glances and shrug at her donning of sunglasses and hasty departure.

Twenty-Four

Winnipeg, Manitoba
2000

KILL THEM ALL

The enlarged photo showing the blood-scrawled message was affixed to one of the big rolling whiteboards in the RCMP's crime lab.

The facility was housed in a low, wide building with a stylistic cluster of red circular chimneys on Academy Road. This was where a team of experts with Forensic Identification Services had been working around the clock processing the exhibits collected from the Tullock murders, going all out to find who was behind the killings.

Autopsy results provided by the province's Medical Examiner's Office, which was located across the city, had confirmed that all the victims died of stab wounds. Specifically, Roy's left carotid artery was severed from behind, consistent with a cut throat. Linda and Neal died from wounds that had pierced their hearts. Connie died as a result of injuries suffered from multiple stab wounds to her organs. The weapons used were steak knives recovered at the scene from a set belonging to the household.

Given the horrific magnitude of the crimes, given that no suspects had been arrested, the case had been assigned the highest priority and the brass at National Headquarters in Ottawa was monitoring results.

Sergeant Amanda Marsh, the Forensic Identification Specialist who headed the FIS team from the first call to Old Pioneer Road, had been given authority to bring in every specialist and assistant available. Her commanders had arranged for others from Regina and Edmonton to be flown in to help.

Marsh glanced again from her worktable at the chilling message. *Its meaning is for the profilers to decipher.* She then looked at the other forensic experts quietly concentrating on examining and processing material.

Other whiteboards rolled against the wall displayed gruesome crime scene photos, showing positioning of the bodies and the knives. One board held drawings, detailed like blueprints, offering a site plan of the Tullock home, showing the basement, main and second floors, and the yard. The drawings had legends with corresponding color-coded keys, numbers and letters pinpointing "blood drops,"

"blood on grass,"

"blood on windowsill,"

"blood on floor,"

"blood on stairs,"

"blood on wall,"

"blood pooled," and "large pool standing blood."

One of the whiteboards had photos and a map locating the small, empty glass vodka bottle that was discovered by a K-9 unit before it lost the trail leading into town. Another board held charts and checklists.

Much work had been completed, but more needed to be done.

At the scene, they had searched, recorded and preserved latent and visible fingerprints from the knives, the bloodied message, basement windowsill, door handles, doors, walls, kitchen, bathrooms and the vodka bottle. They were submitted electronically to Ottawa for an Automated Fingerprint Identification System (AFIS) search against the national repository of fingerprint and criminal record information. They were also checked against local records and the set of elimination prints volunteered by people who had been in, or had access to, the Tullock house.

Marsh also reviewed the painstaking work on the footwear impressions found in blood at the scene. They'd been photographed and in some cases they'd been lifted using casting silicone. The impressions were then searched digitally against various databases, including those with images from other crime scenes, and those provided by shoe manufacturers.

FIS also worked on the shoes volunteered by people who'd had access to the house, making test impressions and photographing them, studying and recording the outsole size, the pattern and wear, such as cuts, nicks and embedded objects. Further processing involved comparing the impressions with those found in the blood pools and partial tracks throughout the house.

Marsh was confident the team would produce results soon.

At one end of the room she'd posted photos of the Tullock family, aglow in happier times, to remind everyone on the case that they had a profound duty to see that justice was done. For a moment she thought of Torrie Tullock, the lone survivor and what she'd have to live with for the rest of her life. Then Marsh allowed a personal thought of her own family, her son and daughter, her husband, a fighter pilot, and how fragile life was, when her line rang.

"Amanda, it's Teresa. I've got something."

Marsh went down the hall to the workstation of Corporal Teresa Honchar, one of the RCMP's most seasoned fingerprint experts. She'd been at it for twenty-two years. When Marsh entered, she saw two images of fingerprints splitting one of Honchar's two large monitors.

"Okay." Honchar pointed with her capped pen. "Look at the loops, whorls and arches against the sample."

"Consistent."

"Yup, and all minutiae points match. The branching of the ridges match. I got twenty clear points of comparison on this one. It's solid for court as a match. This comes from the knife, the windowsill, the bottle, the message, all over the place."

"And the hit?"

"It's local. The prints come from a shoplifting case." Honchar typed a command. "Here's the record."

Marsh looked at the subject's photos, the ID and the abstract of the incident at a drugstore in Eternity concerning a teenage girl's theft of eyeliner.

"Wow," Marsh said.

"There's more." Honchar entered new commands cuing up new prints on her monitor. "Got a solid match with a second subject whose prints were found in all the same places, in the blood, on the knives, the windowsill."

"And was the hit local or from AFIS?"

"Neither. This came from the set volunteered for elimination."

"From the elimination set?"

"Yup, and here's who they belong to."

Marsh stared at the information.

"Amanda," Honchar continued, "I also have a third set of prints I've been unable to identify, on the knives, in the blood, the windowsill, everywhere."

A short silence followed as they both digested the ramifications of the break in the case.

"This is a heck of a thing we've got here," Honchar said. "I haven't seen anything like this."

Marsh nodded. Before returning to her table, she

was stopped by Corporal Steve Egerton, in charge of processing footwear impressions.

"Was looking for you," Egerton said. "I've got three distinct sets in the blood, tracked in the house and at the windowsill, indicating three individuals involved."

"Three?"

"There's a lot of overlapping so there's a remote, very remote, possibility of four," Egerton said. "But I can confirm three sets and we have a match on one of them. It comes from footwear that was volunteered."

Egerton opened a file folder and handed Marsh the information on the owner of the shoes: one of the two people whose prints Honchar had identified, the ones that had been volunteered.

"Thanks, Steve."

Marsh returned to her desk, taking in the significant developments. Forensic analysis of the evidence showed that at least three individuals were behind the Tullock family murders. They had the identities of two of the suspects. The evidence did not identify who the third person was but when investigators arrested the first two, it would likely point them to a third. Evidence seized from that person may be conclusive.

Marsh was mindful of the fact that the evidence did not show who did what, but it unraveled the mystery on who was behind it.

As Marsh reached for her phone to alert Sergeant Lou Sloan, she stared again at the scrawled message, then the photos of the Tullock family.

This one's beyond comprehension.

Twenty-Five

"I see," Doctor Hirsch said over the line as Ben updated her on Kayla during their scheduled call.

Ben was home alone in his office. He'd shut the door, put Hirsch on speaker and related Kayla's recent history.

"Interesting," Hirsch said as Ben concluded. "It appears Kayla is going through some prolonged grief."

"Prolonged grief?"

"Yes, and entwined in her grief is loyalty to her mother and the subconscious fear that if she should accept and love Emma, her stepmother, it would be a betrayal to her mother."

"Really?"

"That's what appears to be happening. You see, Ben, in these cases the only way for a stepchild and stepmom to have a healthy relationship is for the biological mother to encourage it, in essence to release the child from their singular loyalty."

"Right."

"But in Kayla's case, that permission or encouragement cannot be given for obvious reasons. Kayla reinforces her loyalty to her mom with her rejection of Emma, and it's manifested with her 'suspicions' that she's an imposter, making her an unacceptable replacement. That's Kayla's way of coping and it's also her challenge."

"That seems to fit. It might also explain Kayla's acting out."

"That would also be part of it, certainly. And the more Emma is loving and warm toward Kayla, the more conflicted Kayla becomes because her natural inclination to reciprocate is bound to her loyalty to her mother."

"That makes sense."

"Kayla had done well before our sessions ended a while ago."

"Yes, this new stuff seems to have surfaced after Emma came into our lives."

"All right, then if Kayla's agreeable to come back and see me, we can set up an appointment schedule."

"She may be reluctant. I'll have to talk to Kayla, and Emma, too. Let me first give it some thought."

"Take your time, Ben."

The call ended and Tug came into the office, putting his head on Ben's lap.

"Why don't you go through your door outside to the back?" Ben knew Tug was bothered by the chlorine and wouldn't go in the pool but he liked to trot around it. "Go out and get some exercise."

Ben patted Tug as he tried to process Hirsch's unofficial assessment of Kayla. A moment later his computer pinged.

Need to talk. Stand by. I'll call you soon.

That was all Roz Rose said in her email.

Twenty-Six

Cielo Valle, Orange County, California
Present day

After reading Roz Rose's email, Ben continued studying the confidential files he had acquired on the Swedish case with growing interest.

He'd started work on them prior to his call with Doctor Hirsch.

The story of the married surgeons and the vile acts they'd committed could be analyzed on so many levels. They were devotees of the Marquis de Sade, Nietzsche and Josef Mengele. This was a breakdown of humanity. Two respected, privileged members of society had flourished in secret visiting evil on the vulnerable. After Ben replayed the dungeon video, he'd come to a decision.

This was the one. This story had to be told.

Relieved he'd landed on a case, he began thinking ahead. He'd go to Stockholm, rent a place to stay while he researched the book.

There were many players he'd need to talk to, the investigators, the families—the doctors themselves, if they consented to it. He knew the drill. He also thought about the possibility of Emma and Kayla joining him when he was done—they could take a family vacation across Europe. He'd likely need the break from all the dark elements of the story before he returned to California to write.

Roz and Adam, his editor, would be happy.

This could work out, he thought, feeling a spark of renewed energy.

Ben then typed on his keyboard, went online to the sites of the TV stations, KRVZ and KTKT, and again watched the short reports on the book fund-raiser. It had been a week since they'd been broadcast and posted. They made him smile.

Here we are: a family.

As he watched Kayla, Ben thought about his call with Doctor Hirsch and her observations on why Kayla was rejecting Emma and regarding her as an imposter of sorts.

We're going to have to work on that.

His phone rang. Roz.

"I'm afraid I got some bad news," she said.

"Go ahead."

"The publisher's lawyers had concerns with the stories we'd sent you."

"What do you mean?"

"It started with the Swedish case. Apparently, the defense lawyers for the doctors and the prosecution got wind that you might be considering the case for a book."

"So?"

"It hasn't even gone to trial yet and because

of Swedish laws, and Swedish press practices whereby they tend to protect suspects' identities until convicted—"

"I'm aware of European press ethics. My book wouldn't be released until after the trial, Roz."

"True, but there are concerns that for you to conduct any work on it by talking to key players before it concluded could be potentially damaging to both sides. So Sidney Preston, the publisher's attorney—"

"I know Sidney."

"Yeah, well he suggested that because of the potential legal minefield, Sweden should be put on hold."

Ben shut his eyes and cursed under his breath. "That's the one I wanted to do."

"I'm sorry. We'll just have to push it back."

Shaking his head, he cursed again and steeled himself.

"All right," he said. "I'll look at the others. There's that Boston case."

"That's the other bad news."

"What other bad news?"

"In scrutinizing the list, Sidney and his team noted that all the cases, the banker in Boston, the single mom in Minneapolis, and the butcher in Germany haven't gone to trial yet."

"You know what—" Ben stopped to reconsider his next words. "Okay. I don't get it. I've done research in the US on cases before they'd gone to trial. This is a free country, Roz."

"True, but Sidney cited a ruling, the Kimber case in Idaho or Iowa."

"The Kimber case? What's that? Never heard of it."

"Sidney said it's very recent, hasn't got much attention but it's significant. Anyway, a murder case fell apart because an author writing a book had been privy to information salient to the defense or the prosecution prior to and during the trial."

Ben began searching online for the Kimber case and found a short wire story out of Boise. It didn't have much detail, other than declaration of a mistrial because of information shared with a local writer planning a book.

"So—" Roz exhaled "—given these concerns, Sidney and his team strongly advise you not to touch any cases that have not cleared the trial and conviction stage."

Ben rubbed his chin. This wasn't good.

"I'm sorry, Ben," Roz said. "I wish I had better news. I know time is ticking down on the publisher's ultimatum for a new book but this legal curveball leaves us with nothing for the moment."

Ben slumped back in his chair, disappointment rising, pressure to decide on a story mounting, as he shuffled through his papers for the page with the story list. Finding it, he turned to insert it into his shredder, his eyes glancing over it and the handwritten notes he'd made.

Ben stopped.

"Hang on, Roz. We still have one overlooked case that will work."

"Which one is that?"

"The older one, the Canadian case. The one in Eternity, Manitoba."

Twenty-Seven

Eternity, Manitoba
2000

Something wasn't right.

Unable to sleep, Nancy Gorman woke before dawn, slipped into her robe and went to the kitchen to make coffee. Waiting for the kettle to boil, she looked out the window and in the twilight saw two Eternity police cars creep to a silent stop in the rear service lane.

It's Sunday morning. Something's going on, she thought.

Nancy and her daughter lived with Telforde Rahynes in White Spruce Estates, an apartment complex on the south side of the railway yards. It consisted of three buildings, each housing six units. Most were occupied by low-income, transient tenants. Everyone in town knew the complex as "The Estates."

It was not uncommon to see police here, but for Nancy, this felt different. She moved to the front window of their second-floor unit. There, in the parking lot, she saw four more police cars and a third unmarked car. Uniformed officers had left the vehicles and taken positions surrounding the building.

Suddenly Nancy heard the familiar jingle of the superintendent's keys, the clamor of people rushing up the stairs, then loud knocking shook her door. Leaving the chain secured she opened it a crack to the face of a woman.

"I'm Sergeant Lou Sloan, RCMP, and this is Bill Jurek, Eternity Police," the woman said, holding up a folded collection of pages. "We're here to execute warrants. Please let us in."

"Warrants? What? I don't understand. You've got the wrong—"

"Ma'am, let us in now or we'll force the door open."

Her mind and heart racing, Nancy opened the door. The woman and man entered followed by four officers in plainclothes. One of them closed the door as the superintendent was attempting a better look from the hall and the neighbor across the hall, Mrs. Devries, had stuck out her head.

"Are you Nancy Gorman, the mother of Nicola Gorman?" Sloan asked.

The other officers, wearing latex gloves, began walking through the apartment, Nancy's eyes following them.

"Yes. What's this about? Why do you have warrants? For what?"

"How many people are present in the residence now?"

"Just me, Nikki and Telforde."

Telforde Rahynes, unshaven, hair messed, wearing jeans and a Winnipeg Jets T-shirt, had emerged.

"What the hell's all this?"

"Are you Telforde Rahynes, the primary resident?"

"I pay the damn rent and bills if that's what you're asking."

Sloan handed him some of the pages.

"Mr. Rahynes, we have a warrant to immediately search the premises and require that you and Nancy Gorman seek alternative accommodations for the next forty-eight hours."

"What the hell?" Rahynes looked at the warrant, at Sloan, just as Nikki, wearing sweatpants and a black T-shirt stepped into the living room.

"Are you Nicola Hope Gorman?" Sloan asked her.

"I go by Nikki," she said, her gaze bouncing among the officers.

"Place your hands in front of you." Jurek withdrew metal handcuffs.

Reflexively, Nikki stepped away.

"Don't resist. Hold still," Jurek said, taking Nikki's limp hands, placing the cuffs around her wrists, clicking them to the smaller grip.

Nancy's eyes ballooned with disbelief. "What're you doing to my daughter?"

"What the hell?" Telforde glared at Nikki. "Did you steal from the mall again, you little—is that what this is? Because I don't need this. I sure as hell don't need this!"

Jurek and Sloan exchanged glances, then Sloan nodded.

"Nicola Gorman," Sloan began. "I'm arresting you for the murders of Royston Tullock, Connie Tullock, Linda Tullock and Neal Tullock…"

"What? Oh my God! No! This is a mistake!" Nancy shouted.

Sloan continued. "Nicola, you have the right to retain and instruct counsel…"

Nikki stared at nothing. A blood rush throbbing in her ears drummed out Sloan's words as her world swirled in surreal slow motion. Her mother had dropped to her knees in agony, hands pressed together as if she were pleading and praying.

Telforde's face contorted into shocked anger as he demanded in vain to know: "What did you do? What the hell did you do?"

He's the one who should be in handcuffs, Nikki thought, *for all he's done to me. But he'll beat my mom and put her on the street if I tell. Let them take me. There's nothing they can do.*

Nikki's jaw clenched. She knew how to keep secrets.

With Sloan and Jurek carefully leading her downstairs and outside to one of the cars, Nikki took it all in.

Charged with murder at fourteen.

She knew she should be scared but she wasn't. She'd been arrested before. And with what Telforde

Rahynes had done to her, and her crap life, well, she could take it.

She was calm, looking up at the apartment because she felt protected.

Hcr mother had rushed from the building to the car, hysterical and sobbing.

"It's all a mistake! Nikki didn't do anything!"

Watching from the backseat, Nikki felt tears trickling down her cheeks for her poor, dumb mother.

Nobody knew the truth. Nobody knew what happened in the Tullock place. And nobody would ever know because she was protected by the pact.

Nikki's handcuffs clinked as she twisted her ring, looking down at the enraged skull.

Twenty-Eight

Eternity, Manitoba
2000

Sunday morning, Marlene Klassyn knocked softly on Janie's closed bedroom door.

"What is it?" Janie groaned groggily.

"Can I come in?"

"Yeah."

Marlene surveyed her daughter's room, an adolescent sanctuary with clothes tossed haphazardly on the floor and desk chair. She glanced at the digital clock, the photo strip and that skull ring on her wicker nightstand. The discarded wooden ladder Janie had found had been transformed into a bookshelf, the violet walls were covered with Janie's watercolor art and glow-in-the-dark stars studded the ceiling so she could fall asleep dreaming of better things.

Janie was buried under the sheets.

"Honey, you know I have to go to the restaurant this morning to help with the memorial reception the club's planning, right?"

"Yeah. So?" Janie's voice was muffled.

Marlene sat on the side of the bed, tugged at the sheets to see Janie's face.

"I talked to Lila and she said it would be okay for you to come with me today and help. It would be good for you."

"Good for me?"

"At times like this it's good for people to keep busy." Marlene's voice trembled and she squeezed the tissue in her hand. "When we do something to help comfort people, we sort of comfort ourselves, you know?"

Janie said nothing.

In the silence, Marlene, curious, looked at the photo strip showing Janie and her friends, Nikki and Marie, until a loud sob filled the room.

"I don't know if I can go," Janie cried.

Marlene stroked her hair. "Oh, honey."

"I can't go there. Everybody will be so sad."

"I know it'll be hard. But sometimes we have to do the hard things in life. Please come. Please. Do it for me."

"For you?" Janie sat up, her eyes red. "Why?"

"Because I can't stand the thought of leaving you here alone today feeling the way you do, because—" She paused to think. "Because of what happened. I don't know what I'd do if I ever lost you." Then in a voice softer than a heartbeat, she said, "You're all I have."

Janie stared at her, shaking her head slowly.

"Don't say that. Just don't."

Marlene nodded, a moment passed and their tears subsided.

"You should come." Marlene stroked her hair. "Okay?"

Another long moment passed before Janie nodded.

"Good." Marlene smiled. "Come on, get up, get ready, and I'll make you pancakes."

"I'm not hungry."

"All right. You can always get something there." Marlene patted Janie and let a moment pass. "If there's anything you want to talk about I'm right here to listen."

Janie coughed and sniffed. "I need to take a shower."

Some thirty minutes later they were both ready.

Marlene locked the door to their duplex and they headed to the street. The ever-present smell of the slaughterhouse was light this morning and the air carried the clank and thud of freight cars in the yards.

Their used Corolla—Marlene was its third owner—parked out front was twelve years old, the rear bumper dented, the front fender scratched, rust eating the rocker panels. Winters took a toll but it still ran.

Janie got in. Marlene tossed her bag in the back, got behind the wheel, and in a roaring blur they were overwhelmed. Out of nowhere a siren yelped, a marked police car T-boned in front of them.

"Mom?" The blood drained from Janie's face.

"Get out of the car and put your hands on the hood," an officer said.

Uniformed officers surrounded them as they exited the vehicle. No guns were drawn, but their hands were at the ready, on the grips of their holstered weapons.

Stunned and mystified, Marlene and Janie placed their palms on the Corolla's dirty hood.

"What did we do?" Marlene asked. "Why're you doing this?"

Marlene and Janie then recognized Lou Sloan and Bill Jurek approaching them from another car, badges hanging from neck chains. Sloan carried papers in her hand.

"Why're you doing this?" Marlene pleaded. "We didn't do anything."

Sloan stood before Janie as Jurek moved to handcuff her.

"Jane Elizabeth Klassyn," Sloan began, "I'm arresting you for the murders of Royston Tullock, Connie Tullock, Linda Tullock and Neal Tullock…"

Tears rolled down Janie's face.

Marlene, white with terror and confusion, attempted to rush to Janie but was held in place by two officers.

"Murder? My God, no!" Marlene's voice broke as she struggled in vain. "No, no, no, this is wrong! This is a mistake!"

"Marlene Klassyn." Sloan handed her documents. "We have a warrant to search your property now."

As the handcuffs snapped on Janie's wrists, her eyes met her mother's and in that instant, something between Marlene and Janie strained and broke.

A sudden gust blew, kicking up dirt, carrying the stench of the slaughterhouse and the thunder of the freight cars switching, like the closing of a prison door as Marlene watched her fourteen-year-old daughter being placed into the back of a police car.

Flashing red lights painted Marlene's face as Janie, sitting between the big officers, turned to gaze back at her.

Twenty-Nine

Eternity, Manitoba
2000

Late Sunday afternoon, Ned Mitchell stepped into his driveway, sipped cold beer from a can, then popped the hood of his truck and prepared to change the oil in his Chevy's diesel.

Ned sucked air through his teeth. The beast was showing her age, damn starter had a loose post. He'd order a new one Monday. Had to take care of his Century Wrecker; hc carned his living with it. He glanced at the old RV up on blocks, thinking it was time to sell it.

Starting work, Ned belched and turned on the radio, catching Marty Robbins singing, "El Paso." Then came commercials followed by the news.

"Good afternoon, you're listening to Ten-Forty Primrose Valley and these are the headlines. Arrests have been made in the multiple murder case in Eternity…"

Ned stopped working to concentrate on the report.

"Sources have confirmed to Ten-Forty that two arrests were made this morning in the recent mass murder of a family in Eternity. Two people face charges in the deaths of Roy and Connie Tullock and their two children, Neal and Linda, in a tragedy that has shocked the province. No other information is available. Investigators from Eternity and the RCMP are conducting an ongoing investigation."

How about that?

Ned raised his beer in celebration before taking a swig, glad they got the assholes who killed the Tullocks. He felt a connection to the case because he was called to help move the family's vehicles from the house on Old Pioneer to the Eternity Police impound lot with a Mountie riding with him—something about chain of evidence. The RCMP's forensic people were going to go through them.

Those murders were a hell of a thing, and Ned felt for the Tullocks' relatives because he knew the pain of losing someone and there was no one in this world that he would wish it upon.

Something nudged his ankles and he looked down to see Willow, his wife's cat.

"Git," he said as four police cars, two marked and two unmarked, lights flashing, rolled into his driveway and parked.

"Ned!" Flo, his wife, called from the side door of the house, where she was standing with their daughter and pointing to two more police cars beyond the old RV in the rear alley. Ned looked to the front, to the back, and front again as officers and people in plainclothes approached from both directions. His eyes narrowed on the highest-ranking one he knew, Jurek, an Eternity sergeant.

"Bill, what the hell's this?"

Jurek put up his palms. "Take it easy, Ned. Step back from the truck. Keep your hands where we can see them."

"Why?"

"Police business. Do as I say."

Bewildered but halfheartedly, Ned complied, then eyed the woman with Jurek who was holding papers. She handed some to him.

"Ned Mitchell. I'm Sergeant Lou Sloan, RCMP. This is a warrant to search your residence and property."

"Search warrant—but why? What for?" Ned's eyes swept over legal wording. "Is this because I moved the cars on Old Pioneer?"

But Jurek and Sloan continued on to Flo and Marie. Ned moved to join them but two officers blocked him, one saying: "Stay where you are, Ned. Don't interfere."

"Interfere with what? Someone tell me what the hell's going on!"

In that instant, Ned saw his daughter, her arms fused around her mother as if expecting to plummet from the surface of the earth, her eyes wide with fear as if she had somehow known this was coming. Then Ned, not believing this, heard Sloan say:

"Marie Louise Mitchell, I'm arresting you in

relation to the murders of Royston Tullock, Connie Tullock, Linda Tullock and Neal Tullock…"

"Are you out of your mind?" Flo shouted, moving in front of her daughter protectively, as ready as a mother grizzly to protect her. "She's just a child! This is wrong—"

"Step out of the way," Jurek said.

"Bill!" Ned shouted. "Put a stop to this! Please!"

Jurek and other officers moved in, prying Marie from her mother, fastening her wrists with handcuffs.

"You need not say anything…" Sloan continued "…anything you do or say may be used as evidence. Do you understand?"

"No!" Marie cried out. Her knees crumpled and two male officers half dragged, then all but carried her down the driveway, her toes brushing the asphalt, placing her into the back of one of the cars.

Flo and Ned were blocked by officers from approaching it, leaving them staring at Marie, who'd leaned to the side window.

Her parents' faces were frozen in utter confused agony, piercing her. The only time she'd seen them in such pain was when Pike died.

Neighbors gawked from doors, windows and driveways.

Sloan then began advising Ned and Flo that they would be required to leave their home untouched, aided by police, in preparation for the search—but they weren't listening. They were watching Marie.

As the car rolled away, and as if to underscore the moment, the radio in Ned's truck began playing an Elvis Presley song. "Suspicious Minds."

Thirty

Orange County, California
Present day

Emma guided her SUV through the Valley Meadow High School staff parking lot with a mix of relief and apprehension.

A week had passed since the book sale. The local news had run the story. She'd survived having a TV camera on her, glad it was all behind her. But she had yet to deal with Marisa. In the time after confronting her, Emma had gone by her place twice, even rang the bell, steeling herself, fingers wrapped around a can of pepper spray in her bag, in case the gun-toting boyfriend tried something. No one answered and there was no sign of Marisa's car.

I don't like this, Emma thought, walking across the school lot, glancing at the street, not seeing Marisa's green Ford Focus.

Gripping her phone as she entered the school, Emma submitted "Marisa Joyce Narmore" to an online search. Emma's previous checks of Marisa's name had yielded nothing. What she found this time stopped her cold: the *Orange County Register*'s news feed had a photo of a car wreck, with the story:

Santa Ana Freeway Crash Victim Identified

Marisa Joyce Narmore, 32, of Santa Ana, was the victim in a single-vehicle crash on the I-5 freeway.

Narmore's Ford Focus was speeding northbound, veering wildly in and out of traffic when it entered a construction zone, crashed through barriers, flipped and rolled several times, according to California Highway Patrol and Orange County coroner's officials.

The wreck took place about 10:45 a.m. last Friday.

Narmore, a retail clerk, was also a part-time student at Orange Pacific Community College.

Emma swallowed, her back slammed against the wall as she steadied herself.

Marisa's dead. And it happened while I was following her!

Emma's breathing quickened.

But I stopped following her long before then. I didn't even see her crash. How can I be implicated? I didn't do anything wrong. Police would've talked to me.

Emma's mind raced as she looked down the

admin hall. She went to Greg's office, where the assistant greeted her.

"Hi, Denise. Is Greg around? I need to see him for a second."

"Gosh no, I'm sorry. He's been away for almost a week. His dad passed away and he's in Minneapolis taking care of things."

"Oh no, I'm so sorry to hear that."

"It's so sad. Want to leave him a message?"

"Oh, yes. My condolences. Thanks, Denise."

Emma left, forcing herself to keep calm, to think things through. She gave her head a little shake and started for her office when her phone rang with a blocked number.

"Is this Emma, Emma Grant?" a woman asked when she answered.

"Yes."

"Hi, Maggie Shen from KTKT."

The reporter from the book sale? Why would she be calling?

"Emma, are you there?"

"Yes, hi."

"Thought I lost you." Maggie sounded hurried, calling from a moving vehicle. "We should be there by eleven thirty this morning, okay?"

"Excuse me? I'm sorry, what're you talking about? Be where for what?"

"At your school to interview you for the story."

Emma stopped in her tracks.

"What story—the book sale?"

"No, *your* story. Listen, I gotta wrap something

else up right now. I'm sorry—I assumed your principal told you what's happening."

"No one told me. I'm not in my office yet. What's going on?"

"This just came up. We're doing a story on you."

"On me?" Emma's heart skipped into a gallop. "What? Why?"

"Oh—there—pull over there!" Maggie said to someone else, then to Emma, "Sorry, gotta go. See you soon."

The call ended with Emma fearful for what might be coming.

Emma's mind raced with a million fears when she caught up with Glenda Heywood in the hall.

Demanding to know what the story concerned and why she'd been blindsided, Emma followed Glenda into her office, where the principal deposited a stack of binders on the corner of her desk.

"Shut the door and have a seat," Glenda said, reaching for the tepid mug of coffee on her credenza.

The door almost slammed. "I don't want to sit. I demand to know—is this something personal?"

"Yes. And no."

"What?"

"First—" Glenda sipped her coffee "—I apologize that Maggie Shen got to you before I did. The issue came up late yesterday. I'd planned to alert you, but I got tied up with meetings last night and follow-up calls this morning. Your situation is somewhat complicated."

"It's not. I don't want to be interviewed about anything. It's that simple."

"Emma, please. Sit down."

"Glenda, I have rights. I could take this to the CTA."

"You could. But before you make this a union matter, hear me out. And, understand that what I'm going to tell you is extremely confidential."

Emma took a moment, nodded, but remained standing.

Heywood then confided how a district board member with connections in Sacramento had recently been tipped to potential cuts in education funding in next month's state budget.

"She was privy to some chilling figures, which could mean a serious budget drop for the district, which could mean slashing programs and jobs. School counselors will be on the chopping block. Are you with me so far?"

Emma was listening.

"Factions on the board will align behind issues, classroom size, sports and the arts. It'll get political and nasty," Glenda said. "Board members supportive of protecting school counselors need all the help they can get to make a case for what is looming," Glenda said. "They're well aware of your recent action saving a student. A couple of board members saw you on TV with your family at the book sale and urged us to get media attention ASAP on our school counselors, starting with a story about you. So they tipped Maggie Shen at KTKT."

Emma sat in a visitor's chair, digesting the circumstances. At least it was not about Marisa or her past. Still, she was uneasy. "I don't know about this."

"You have to realize the big picture," Glenda said. "This is more than a fight to save your job and those of other counselors. Think of the students who need you—think of their families. Think if you hadn't been there to save that troubled boy."

Emma weighed it all. What Glenda said was true. Above all, she cared about the students.

"So," Glenda said. "Now that you know what's at stake, will you do it?"

Blinking several times, Emma finally conceded.

"We're good?" Maggie Shen said, nodding to the guy with surfer hair behind the KTKT camera.

They'd crowded into Emma's office and set up there. The camera's light was intense but there was no hiding behind sunglasses this time. This was up close.

"Just like at the book sale, focus on me instead of the camera," Maggie said, her face blossoming with a bright smile. Attempting to return it, Emma nodded, feeling her stomach knot.

"Let's start with you telling us about a typical day in the life of a school counselor," Maggie said.

Emma ran down her daily routine of meetings and reports. Then she gave examples of issues students faced, stressing how counselors strive to make a difference.

"We understand that not too long ago you made

more than a difference with one student," Maggie said. "Our sources helped us get in touch with his parents. We're not using his name but they've agreed to talk to us for this story."

After Maggie asked Emma questions about the incident, they set up a reenactment by having Emma walk the halls when classes changed then go outside and retrace her steps from that day she pulled her student from the path of a bus, waiting until a bus approached the same stop.

After the interview ended, Maggie struggled to make her day a normal one, scrambling to re-schedule appointments and catch up with her work.

For the rest of the afternoon Emma was ill at ease over everything that had transpired.

What about Marisa? How will I find any answers now that she's dead?

Her thoughts then shifted to her TV interview.

How many people will see the story? She wondered as she got into her car, telling herself not to worry. *California is a long way from Manitoba.* But her attempt at consolation was weak because she realized that in this digital world, everything was just a click away.

Emma wheeled out of the staff lot, eager to get home.

Turning onto the busy boulevard and accelerating, Emma didn't notice that half a block behind her, a sedan had pulled out from a parking spot and was following in the same direction.

Thirty-One

Fourteen-year-old Marie Louise Mitchell cut a lonely figure in an orange jumpsuit, sitting by herself, handcuffed at a table in a small white-walled room at Eternity police headquarters.

Tears rolled down her cheeks. Her sniffling echoed in the room and through the microphones in the ceiling. They were connected to the speakers in the adjoining room where, unseen to Marie, Sergeant Lou Sloan, Bill Jurek and other investigators observed her through the one-way mirror.

At Sloan's insistence, they had moved fast on her. The sergeant's hunch of Marie's involvement arose from the photo strips they'd found in both Nikki's and Janie's showing the three girls together. Upon Marie's arrest and execution of the search warrants at the Mitchell home, Marie was fingerprinted, photographed and placed in a holding cell while analysis of her shoes, clothing and other material found in the Mitchell home was accelerated at the lab in Winnipeg.

Within hours, they had verified the physical evidence, confirming that Marie was the third person involved in the Tullock murders.

She was formally charged with all four deaths and advised of her rights again, then left alone in the cell. Sloan wanted Marie isolated so the girl could ingest the gravity of her situation. During that time, Sloan read and reread every piece of information they'd obtained on Marie and her family.

Sloan knew that Canadian high court rulings allowed police to use a range of tactics against a suspect, including misleading, bluffing, even lying, in order to check the suspect's account against the evidence, the facts, and arrive at the truth.

She also knew the accused had the right to silence and a lawyer.

Sloan had to walk a fine line.

As Marie's sniffles flowed through the speakers Sloan observed her, crying with her head lowered, looking every bit the vulnerable adolescent. Then a file folder snapped open and Sloan looked again at the crime scene photos of Roy Tullock, his throat slashed, Neal and Linda, eyes wide, frozen in death. Then she flipped to the photo of the message on the wall: KILL THEM ALL.

She was ready.

Sloan entered the room alone, sitting in the chair opposite Marie.

"Hello again," Sloan said, setting a file folder

and small canvas bag on the table. "Marie, the first thing I want to make sure of is that you see the cameras and the microphones. This is all being recorded."

Keeping her head down, Marie gave a small nod. Her handcuffs clinked as she brushed at hair stuck to her face, her fingertips still ink-stained from being fingerprinted.

"You were arrested and charged because the evidence against you is overwhelming and ironclad," Sloan said. "There are some important things you need to know before this goes any further? Will you agree to that?"

Marie shrugged and mumbled.

"I'm sorry, I didn't hear you," Sloan said.

"Okay," Marie said.

One by one, as if laying down playing cards, Sloan placed photos before Marie.

"We've got your fingerprints on the knife, in the blood all over the house, impressions from your shoes in the blood."

Sloan reached into the bag and withdrew small, clear evidence bags. One held Marie's death's head skull ring, the other, a photo strip of Marie, Nikki and Janie taken in the mall photo booth.

"These pictures were among the items we found in our search of your room at your house. We've arrested Nikki and Janie, too."

Marie didn't move.

"And they're telling us things, Marie."

Marie's breathing quickened.

"What do you suppose they're telling us?"

Marie said nothing.

"Do you know that one of them kept a journal?"

Marie didn't speak.

"That's right. We have it now. We have every-thing and we know everything."

Marie began rocking back and forth in her seat.

"You know what else I know?" Sloan said. "Look at me, Marie."

Marie's eyes shot to Sloan.

"This isn't the first time you've been involved in the death of innocent people, is it?"

Marie shut her eyes as tears flowed.

"There was your little brother, Pike. I looked into his death and you know what I found in the file, tucked deep in a social worker's report on your state of mind and your feelings at the time? That you admitted that you thought your parents loved Pike more than you. That he was their favorite. How did that make you feel?"

Marie's face crumpled and she looked away.

"Angry. Worthless and angry—that's what you told the social worker. That's interesting because when he was choking right in front of you, you never called for help, did you?"

"No, it wasn't like that!" Marie sobbed.

"But you let him die, right in front of you. You killed him. No more family favorite. Problem solved."

Marie began shaking her head, gasping and sobbing.

"It was ruled accidental," Sloan said. "But you knew the truth—just like you know the truth now.

You hated yourself for what happened to Pike and you took your rage out on the Tullocks, didn't you?"

Sloan slapped the crime scene photos on the desk so Roy, Neal and Linda looked back at her in death.

"No! Stop!"

"Did you stop when the Tullocks pleaded for their lives, Marie?"

Sloan let a moment pass as Marie cried.

"You know we can always reopen Pike's case," Sloan said. "Take another look at it and you. Think of your parents, what they're going through right now, and then for us to exhume Pike from his grave…how will they survive all of this?"

Marie's handcuffs began clinking because she was trembling.

Sloan leaned close to her. "Everything is stacked against you. You're going to prison for four counts of second-degree murder. Tell me what happened that night. This is the time to tell the truth. We have the other girls, we have the evidence, and lying will only make things worse for you."

Marie's tears splashed onto her handcuffs.

"Are you ready to tell me the truth?"

Marie cleared her throat. "I want a lawyer. You said that I don't have to say anything to you and that I can have a lawyer. I want a lawyer."

Thirty-Two

Morden, Manitoba
2000

After interviewing Marie, Sloan and Jurek drove east for about an hour through the Pembina Valley to the town of Morden.

Eternity jail facilities were small and investigators didn't want the three suspects held in the same building and possibly talking with each other, so they'd arranged for their custody in separate neighboring jurisdictions.

During the drive, cutting along the valley's rolling hills, Jurek's mind took him back to the scene in the Tullock home. It was beyond comprehension. But as he'd done with the atrocities he'd seen in Sarajevo, he kept his thoughts to himself as he drove, giving Sloan the quiet to work. She studied reports and made notes, finishing when they arrived.

Morden's RCMP detachment was located in a small, tree-shaded building resembling a wood-framed bungalow. It evoked a staid air, standing in contrast to the monstrous events that it was now and forever linked to, for accused murderer Jane Elizabeth Klassyn was its sole prisoner.

She was held in one of the detachment's four cells and was sitting on the narrow bed, looking through the barred window at clouds floating by, when suddenly the locking mechanism of her cell clanked before the steel door opened. A female Mountie, the name Leduc on her name tag, handcuffed her, then transferred her down the hall to a small windowless room with beige cinder block walls. Like Marie, she was wearing an orange jumpsuit that was far too large for her.

She sat in the room alone staring at nothing for nearly twenty minutes. Then Sloan entered.

"Hi again, Janie."

She didn't respond as Sloan placed folders and a canvas bag on the table between them, then proceeded to tell her that the room was making an audio-video recording of everything.

Janie said nothing and Sloan glanced at her notes.

"When we talked in your room, I clearly asked you when was the last time you had been in the Tullocks' home, and you said it was when you sat for them, the Wednesday before the weekend, before they left for Regina. Remember?"

No response.

"You know that's a lie, don't you?"

Still nothing.

"We have your fingerprints on one of the knives, in the blood, everywhere in the house and on the vodka bottle. We have your shoe impressions in the blood. We have this." Sloan reached into the canvas bag and retrieved Janie's personal journal sealed in plastic. Then she opened a folder with photocopied pages in Janie's handwriting and read excerpts.

"'The Tullocks think people like us are dirt, they think they're better than us… Connie's such a lying, cheating bitch who should just die…that bitch owes me money and Nikki and Marie are going to help me get it…'" Sloan looked up from the pages. "That's some powerful anger you got boiling up inside."

A moment passed and Sloan slapped down the photo strips of the girls and the three rings, Janie's sugar skull, Marie's death's head and Nikki's raging ring.

"We've arrested and charged the rest of your girl gang and they've told us everything."

Janie glanced at the photos but said nothing.

"What we need is for you to tell us the truth, admit what you did."

Janie said nothing.

"Maybe you didn't expect the Tullocks to be home that night, maybe you were there to rehearse. But you fully intended to exact revenge and that's what you did."

Janie remained quiet.

"Roy Tullock had control over your mother's job, her life. Connie Tullock owed you money and you hated her. You hated them both so much you wrote *kill them all* on the wall."

Sloan placed the photos of the dead Roy, Linda and Neal on the table.

"Look at them," Sloan said, standing, leaning closer to Janie.

Janie turned briefly to the photos, tears rolling down her face before she looked away.

"There's no way out of this for you, Janie."

Janie's eyes were now focused on something distant, something faraway and so terrifying she began shaking, fearing she was breaking apart. Slowly she shook her head. Her jaw began moving as if struggling to form words.

"I want a lawyer but I have no money to pay for one."

Sloan leaned back in her chair, assessing Janie.

"We can get you a free lawyer. You won't have to pay."

Gasping and sobbing, Janie managed to say: "Thank you."

Thirty-Three

Winkler, Manitoba
2000

Five steps forward.

Turn.

Five steps back.

Turn.

Nikki paced back and forth in her cell like a caged leopard.

The Skull Sisters would survive this.

The police had taken her ring but she wasn't worried.

We're bound forever by our blood pact, protected by the incantation. No matter what they say or do to us we'll never ever give up our secrets.

Or each other.

We're sisters.

Keys jingled.

Nikki stopped.

Someone was coming for her.

* * *

As Nikki paced in her cell, Sloan and Jurek drove the short distance on the four-lane highway connecting Morden with Winkler. The two towns were so close they were known as the province's twin cities.

They headed down Main Street stopping at Winkler Police headquarters, a stone and glass building with blue trim that could pass for a small high school.

"Hey, Bill." Lowell DeWitt, the commander on duty knew Jurek. Then to Sloan: "Welcome to Winkler, Sergeant Sloan." Gold crowns flashed as he greeted them. "This is a god-awful case, all over the national news. Let me know if there's anything else we can do to help. This way."

DeWitt then led them down a hallway, turning to Sloan. "As you requested before you left Morden, we put her in the interview room to let her wait there for you."

The three officers stepped into a darkened room with a one-way mirror. They observed Nikki through it, almost glowing in orange prison scrubs in the brightly lit, stark interview room. A fourteen-year-old multiple murderer, alone, head on the table, buried between her outstretched arms, handcuffed at the wrists.

"Can I get you folks some coffee before I leave you to it?"

Sloan shook her head, focused on Nikki as she organized her files.

"We're good, thanks, Lowell," Jurek said.

* * *

The door opened.

It took a few seconds for Nikki to drag herself up to a sitting position, her head lolling as she eyed Sloan, the cop who'd arrested and charged her.

Her again, what now? Nikki released a bored sigh. *Is she going to give me a futile lecture?* Nikki's focus then went to Sloan's folders and stuff. *It's like she's prepping for a test. This is useless.*

"Hello, Nikki."

Sloan stood at the opposite side of the table holding folders and a canvas bag.

"You've been given your rights and you know this is all being recorded."

"I don't care because I'm not talking to you."

"If that's your wish. But before I leave, you should know what I have here." Sloan opened a folder to let Nikki glimpse a photocopy of hand-written pages. "I can't let you read them," she said, "but let's say we have statements from the other girls."

Nikki knew police could trick you and steeled herself.

I know Janie and Marie would not betray me. I know they're holding to our pact like me and told you nothing.

"I'll just read you a little excerpt," Sloan said. "'The Tullocks think people like us are dirt, they think they're better than us… Connie's such a lying, cheating bitch who should just die…that bitch owes me money and Nikki and Marie are going to help me get it…'"

Nikki's scalp began tingling. Those were Janie's words, hitting her like a gut punch.

If that's Janie's confession, then the cop must have Marie's in her folder, too. I can't believe this! Janie and Marie betrayed me. They broke our pact!

Then, as Sloan had done with Marie and Janie, she set down crime scene photos on the table before Nikki until they formed a horseshoe pattern around her, like the onslaught of unyielding, unstoppable forces coming for her.

Nikki's stomach rose and fell, convulsing with such power she thought it would break through her skin. The room, her world, spinning like the day her father died. All she'd counted on, all she had left in this life had vanished.

We made a pact. We swore we'd never, ever break it. You were my sisters in blood and you betrayed me!

Sloan relayed to Nikki the overwhelming and damning evidence, the fingerprints, the shoe impressions, the message in blood, Nikki's connections with Marie and Janie and the rings, the photo strips. Sloan said that forensic experts analyzed everything.

"Before I leave, you need to understand something," Sloan said. "You are charged with four counts of second-degree murder. The case against you is solid. Open and shut. You'll be going to prison for a long time. And you know what happens in prison to people who have murdered children."

Nikki shot Sloan a look of unease.

"Things might be easier for you if you cooperate with us. The courts could be lenient. Think about it, Nikki. Think of your mother."

Nikki saw her mother in her memory of the arrest, rushing from the building to the police car, hysterical, screaming: "It's all a mistake! Nikki didn't do anything!"

Sloan continued. "Think of the pain she carries and will forever carry for the things you did on Old Pioneer Road."

Her mother screamed like that the day they'd learned her dad had died. Then Nikki thought of that night in the Tullock home.

The night of screams.

"Nikki?" Sloan repeated. "Now is the time to help yourself."

Nikki blinked as if she'd returned from an absence.

"I want a lawyer."

Thirty-Four

Cielo Valle, Orange County, California
Present day

I should've heard something by now.

In line at his local SoCal Seaside Assurance bank to deposit royalty checks from his agents in London and Hamburg, Ben checked his phone, expecting a verdict on the new book. Nothing.

Roz Rose, his primary agent, should've had answers by now.

The line moved. His thoughts shifted to considering setting up direct deposit for Europe, as he'd done with his US and South American agents, when his phone rang.

It was Roz. *At last.*

"Is this a good time?" she asked.

"Hang on."

Ben looked around. Too many people in the bank. The call was important. He gave up his place in line and stepped outside, finding privacy and shade near a palm tree adjacent to the parking lot.

"Go ahead," he said.

A woman transferring her toddler from her van's car seat to a stroller looked at him and he pointed at his phone, then turned away.

"Okay, go ahead, Roz. What did they say?"

"All right. Sidney in legal has zero concerns because it's an old case. It's been prosecuted. There are few legal risks in that regard."

"I figured that."

"And Adam says the publisher likes this one, too, and the fact the case is all but unknown to US and international readers, and your books have a global audience."

"Canadians will know this case, even if it is twenty years old."

"Right, and that's another advantage. Your numbers are strong in Canada and a book by you on the case would be well received."

"So it's all good?"

"Yes. You have a green light. And Adam said they'll restart the clock on the deadline for the outline. It'll be sixty days starting Monday. I'll put it in the updated memo to you."

"I'll have the outline done before sixty days, but thanks for that."

"And your Canadian editor wants you to call her ASAP to discuss it a little further. Everyone's excited about this, Ben."

After the call, Ben got back in line. He was now fifth but it didn't matter because he was relieved.

Finally, he'd landed on a book.

* * *

At home Ben looked through his emails for one from Emily Moore in Toronto, found her signature box with her number and called it.

They'd met a few times at BookExpo in New York and the International Festival of Authors in Toronto. She was among the most talented editors he'd worked with.

"Hi, Ben, this is such good news. Everybody here's so pleased." Emily's voice was warm and positive. "At the same time, it's such a terrible case."

"I know. But everything I write is a terrible case."

"That's true," she said. "Listen, I wanted to have this call to let you know we'll help you in any way we can."

"Thank you. I welcome it. I don't know a lot about Canada. I've been to the big cities for book events—Vancouver, Montreal and, as you know, Toronto—but other than that, Canada's a big, alien land to me."

"You'll do fine. You always do. Look at the other books you did that were set outside of the United States. They've all been critical and commercial successes."

"That's kind of you to say. Thanks."

"It's true. You're one of the best true crime writers in the business." Ben heard the tapping of a keyboard on Emily's end. "There were a couple of books written here in Canada back when the case came out but they've been largely forgotten. I'll

send them to you. Also, I had our staff here pull
up all the recent news items on the anniversary of
the Eternity case that they could find in the databases that we subscribe to," she said. "I'm sending
them to you now."

"That's helpful. I've pulled up a few news stories, myself," he said as his computer chimed. "I
just got yours, thanks. I also have a few Canadian
sources—Mounties, city cops, justice people—
who've helped me when I was writing about fugi-
tives who've fled to Canada, or vice versa."

"Sounds like you're in good shape with this
story. I'll let you get to it."

After the call, Ben made fresh coffee and got
down to work, reading through the stories on the
case. There were a lot and soon he had the basic
facts committed to memory.

In a small windswept prairie town, four people
were killed: Royston Tullock; his wife, Connie;
and two of their three children. The murders were
pure evil, an act of unimaginable dimensions.

As he read, Ben saw the framework emerging,
not only would he provide a story of the Tullock
family, he would profile the community and the
impact the crimes had on it then and the legacy of
the murders now.

The most chilling and difficult aspect of the
Eternity story was that the killers were children.
Younger than Kayla when they committed the
murders.

The Skull Sisters.

As he continued reading, he made notes.

It won't be easy but if I'm going to do this right, I'll need to find them and talk to them.

Thirty-Five

Ian Bristol parked his Harley-Davidson Road King in front of the Eternity police station, relieved no reporters were out front.

He cut the engine, dropped the kickstand, removed his helmet, got his briefcase from the saddlebag and entered the building. He handed his ID to the officer at the counter, who nodded as he checked it.

"Right, we've been expecting you. This way."

The officer took Bristol to a small room with a desk and two empty chairs. Bristol sat in one, opened his briefcase and reviewed the documents in his folders. Within hours of Marie's, Janie's and Nikki's arrests, Legal Aid in Winnipeg had provided each of them with their own lawyer. Bristol's client was Marie Louise Mitchell, aged fourteen, charged with four counts of second-degree murder.

Bristol worked at one of Winnipeg's top firms, had nine years of trial experience and had won 80 percent of his cases. He'd already gone through most of Marie's files before leaving Winnipeg on his Harley. He had reread them when he stopped for coffee at Olek's Diner, where a TV mounted on the wall was tuned to a national news network broadcasting updates over the breaking news graphic: Bloodbath In Eternity, Manitoba: Arrests Made in Mass Murder.

Now, in Morden, Bristol looked up from his work when a police officer opened the door and Marie entered wearing an orange jumpsuit, handcuffs and an expression of fear.

Bristol introduced himself, shook her hand and got on with business.

"I'm going to represent you," he said, nodding to the files. "I've read through everything and for me to help you, I need you to take me through that night, specifically what you did and what the others did. Can you do that?"

Marie nodded and in a trembling voice began recounting everything, describing how they'd made their pact. Stopping occasionally to answer Bristol's questions, Marie continued, tears rolling down her cheeks.

"My heart was pounding so hard. I'd never been so scared in my life. There was blood everywhere."

As Marie spoke, Bristol had her go back over details and asked more questions until she ended by telling Bristol something he'd remember all of his life.

"I'll never forget the smell of the blood. It smelled like the slaughterhouse."

* * *

About an hour east, lawyer Ed Tracy was at the RCMP detachment in Morden sitting across from his client, Jane Elizabeth Klassyn, in a chair that creaked.

Tracy, a white-haired man with bearlike gruffness, had decades of courtroom experience. He exuded gentle confidence and wisdom. He was a partner of a respected firm who, unlike others of his stature, still did pro bono work through Legal Aid. After a brief introductory conversation, he unscrewed his fountain pen then gestured for his client to tell him about that night.

"Go ahead, Janie."

Tracy had a soft but gravel-like voice and blue eyes that could see through her to the truth. After Janie recounted that night, she lowered her head and sobbed.

"There was so much screaming, I thought the whole world could hear it. I couldn't stand it. I had to do something to stop the screaming. Everything became a hazy blur." Janie brushed at her tears.

"So you did have a knife in your hand?"

"Yes. Then we wrote on the wall so they'd think it was a serial killer. After that, we ran to the basement window. We swore to each other we'd keep the pact and never tell. We ran and ran and the whole time the screaming was ringing in my ears, like it was trapped there."

Tracy let a moment pass for Janie to recover before continuing.

"You were involved and were a party to the plan to enter the house and steal money?"

"Yes."

"As part of the plan you left a basement window unlocked?"

"Yes."

"And you participated?"

Janie didn't say anything, but Tracy knew she held an answer because he had all the forensic and police reports.

"Janie?"

"Maybe it was the alcohol, maybe it was fear, or anger, or my life, but I let myself get caught up in the moment because I had to stop the screaming. I had to stop it. Yes, I participated in the murders. I set it all in motion so everything that happened was my fault."

Tracy recapped his fountain pen and slowly screwed it closed while staring at Janie in silence, carefully absorbing, weighing and processing everything he knew so far; everything he'd read and everything his client had just admitted.

It left him ambivalent, contending with opposing feelings about his client and the case ahead.

In Winkler, a short distance down the highway from Morden, Nicola Hope Gorman sat across from her lawyer, Belinda Walker, a former prosecutor who worked for Legal Aid.

Walker was in her forties. Her auburn hair was tied in a ponytail. She had thin, straight eyebrows behind her glasses. Her mouth pressed closed, giving her a poker face, while she listened to Nikki giving her account of that night on Old Pioneer Road.

"It was Janie's idea to sneak into the house and take the money she said the Tullocks owed her."

"Janie's idea? Not yours?"

"Yes." Nikki's cuffs jingled as she corralled the hair from her face. "She left the window open so we could get in but we couldn't find any money, which really pissed her off because she hated the Tullocks, especially Connie."

"Because—" Walker glanced at her notes "—Janie claimed that the Tullocks owed her baby-sitting money?"

"Not only that, Janie said Connie treated her like crap. She loathed that woman."

"You admit that alcohol was involved that night. That you brought the vodka?"

"Yes, because I was scared. We were drinking but we weren't really drunk. We were kind of feeling like we could do anything."

"What happened when you got inside?"

"Like I said, we looked everywhere, couldn't find any money. Then the Tullocks came home. They weren't supposed to get home for days so it just freaked us out. We thought Roy Tullock had guns so we got knives."

"Then what?"

"We had to defend ourselves. When it was finished, we talked about our pact, our blood oath never to tell anyone a word and just went home like nothing happened."

Walker's eyes widened slightly, she pursed her lips, then made notes. Then she took a moment, removed her glasses, pinched the bridge of her nose, replaced them and continued making notes.

But her mind strobed with images police had shared of the murder scene and she saw the blood, heard the screams.

Walker took a breath. Preparing a defense would be challenging.

But the trial and verdict were a long way off.

Before that time, Nikki, Janie and Marie were transferred to larger correctional centers in different cities.

Thirty-Six

"Showtime." Ben pressed the volume on the remote.

A spurt of dramatic theme music burst from the living room TV as KTKT's News at Five began.

Once Emma had told Ben and Kayla about being interviewed for a news profile of school counselors, they insisted on watching it together. As the broadcast got going, Emma assured herself that doing the story was for the greater good, yet she couldn't shed her discomfort at the attention.

Several news items played, while Kayla tapped away on her phone to friends, Tug snuggled at her feet. "When is your story coming up, again?" she asked.

"Maggie Shen said it would be immediately after the second commercial break."

The second block of TV ads played—shampoo, health food, pet care and insurance. The story was up.

Ben, sitting next to Emma on the sofa, patted her hand when she appeared on the screen. It was strange seeing herself again on TV. The item seemed to go on forever but the entire piece was under two minutes. Still, the airing troubled her because it would reach so many people.

Who else would see this—and see her?

It ended with Ben saying, "Well done, Em."

"Yeah." Kayla read her phone. "My friends think it's cool you're a celebrity, too."

Emma's phone vibrated with a text from Glenda Heywood.

Good job, Emma. Checked off every box. Just what we needed.

"Who's that?" Ben asked.

"Glenda, my boss. She liked it."

"Great, then that settles it," Ben said.

"Settles what?"

"You had a successful TV story and I have book news I want to share. We're going out to dinner to celebrate."

They went to a favorite Mexican restaurant of theirs, La Cocina De Mi Prima.

On the way, Emma received more messages on her phone.

Maggie Shen said:

The piece looked good. We're getting a lot of positive feedback online. People think you're a hero. Thanks for your help.

As they were seated, she received a text from Carson Clark's mother, Sonia:

The news report was hard to watch but we feel that if helps one troubled teenager, it was worth it. Your work is so vital, Emma. From the bottom of my heart, thank you. Carson sends his thanks, too.

Emma blushed, sent Sonia a quick message of thanks and encouragement, put her phone away, touched the corners of her eyes as she smiled at Kayla and Ben, then picked up her menu. After taking their orders, their server brought them a bowl of tortilla chips and salsa. They dug in.

"Okay, so what's your news, Dad?" Kayla crunched on a chip.

"We've confirmed a story for the next book."

"The one in Sweden?" Kayla said.

"No, Sweden's been shelved, too many complications right now."

"Wasn't there one in Berlin?" Emma took a chip.

Ben shook his head as he chewed.

"There were a couple here, Minneapolis and Boston?" Emma said.

"No, all of those cases are recent with potential legal issues. It made the publisher's lawyers uncomfortable. So… Canada."

"Canada?" Emma repeated, a shadow falling across her face, drawing looks from Ben and Kayla. She reached for her water glass to mask her dismay, forcing herself to remain cool. Canada was a big country, she told herself, there were a lot of possible crime stories. "Sorry, something went down the wrong way."

Kayla turned to Ben. "What's this one about?"

"It's a terribly tragic case."

"Dad, hello, you were a crime reporter, your books are about murder. They're always terribly tragic cases."

"It happened about twenty years ago. A family was murdered in a small town called Eternity, Manitoba."

Emma felt the earth quake; all the blood had drained from her face.

"Eternity," Kayla said. "Cool name."

"There were three young girls who called themselves The Skull Sisters." Ben said, "Anyway, I was thinking that after I went there and finished researching, you guys could join me. We could take the train that goes across Canada and through the Canadian Rockies and—Emma? Emma, are you okay?" Ben reached for her hand. "What is it? What's wrong?"

Ben and Kayla exchanged glances.

Emma covered her mouth with her cloth napkin and stood. "Sorry, something isn't agreeing with me. Excuse me. I'll be right back."

Forcing herself to keep it together, Emma walked toward the bathroom until she was out of sight, then, with her stomach writhing, she hurried. Rushing into the ladies' room, she startled two women at the sink before disappearing into a stall. She gasped, bile burned up the back of her throat, her stomach heaved and she dropped to her knees and vomited into the toilet.

"Are you all right in there, dear?"

Breathing hard, spitting and wiping at her tears, she managed: "Yes. Thank you. I just need a moment."

My God, my God, my God... Ben's going to Eternity to write about the case! Of all cases—never in a million years did I think he would choose mine. How can this be?

Standing, wiping her mouth with a tissue, drying her eyes with trembling hands, unable to stop the agonizing image of...

...one hand gripping the knife held high in the scream-filled air, its blade dripping blood, another hand fighting frantically against it...

Steadying herself, Emma struggled to gain her composure. She had to do it fast before Ben sent Kayla in after her. Once she heard the two women leave, Emma went to the sink, rinsed her mouth, checked her face and hair.

First the threatening note, then Marisa Joyce Narmore's death, even Kayla asking more questions about her life, and now this—

Stay in control, she told her reflection. *You can survive this if you stay in control!*

Emma composed herself and rejoined Ben and Kayla.

"Look, if you're not feeling well we can go home." Ben touched her shoulder.

"Sure," Kayla said. "We'll get it to go."

Emma waved away their concerns while sipping water.

"I think it was a combination of swallowing the wrong way and nervousness from being on TV."

Ben and Kayla studied Emma for a few seconds—stopping when the food arrived.

"All right, as long as you're okay," Ben said.

"I'm fine and so glad you're going to start a new book," Emma lied.

For the rest of their evening her ears throbbed with a clear, shrill alarm. Her heart thudded against her chest.

I've got to do something. Maybe I can stop him from writing the book, nudge him in a different direction? But even if I can't do that, he still may never learn the truth because my identity was sealed by the court. Let's see how this plays out. I can survive this if I stay in control.

Thirty-Seven

Manitoba
2000

The taxi traveled through the northeast corner of Brandon to its destination: The Brandon Correctional Centre.

Marlene Klassyn paid the fare with a modest tip, reported at the desk, was checked by security, then taken to the visiting room and directed to one of the booths, where she waited on her side of the glass for her daughter.

Minutes later amid electric buzzing and metal clanking, Janie appeared in a prison jumpsuit and took her place. Her hair, longer and stringy, didn't detract from her eyes with those upswept corners, her high cheeks speckled with acne, her beauty. They each reached for the telephone handsets.

"How're you doing?" her mother asked.

"Look where I am. How do you think I'm doing?"

Janie took stock of her mother—her skin and eyes looked yellowish and she'd lost weight.

"You look sick. Are you drinking more? You didn't have to come."

"I wanted to see you."

"Here I am. How did you get here?"

"Bus then a cab. I had to sell the car."

"Why?"

"To pay for the move."

"You moved?"

"Yes, I would've visited you sooner but I had to move. They fired me at the club for obvious reasons."

"Where did you move to?"

Blinking back tears, Marlene said: "I got a room above Harry Hoyt's Bar."

"*That* bar? The bar of the intoxicated conception?"

"Please, Janie." Her mother's face crumpled and she covered it with her free hand. "It was all I could afford. I'm on social assistance now." Her mother fell into a harsh sickly coughing fit lasting for half a minute before she recovered. "I'm doing the best I can to hang on but, Janie, please. I have to know…why? I can't understand. I just can't. Why did you do this horrible, horrible thing? Why?"

"*Why?* I could ask the same thing of you."

"What?"

Janie's eyes widened, her face turned red, tightening as if something inside had erupted, forcing her to stand, adjusting her grip on the phone.

"Why did you sleep with some asshole you hooked up with at Hoyt's Bar? Why? It's why Dad left us. I'm the product of your one-night stand! You don't even know who my father is, do you? Do you know how that makes me feel?"

"I told you it's complicated. It's not the same thing at all."

Janie pointed at her mother, stopping short of stabbing her finger into the glass. "It's the same damned thing! It's all connected. It's why I blame you for all of this!"

"Janie, please!"

Breathing hard, her nostrils flaring, Janie glared at her mother with all the hate she could marshal before slamming down the handset and leaving the booth to wait at the security door to be taken back to her cell.

As the jail door opened and swallowed her daughter, the cold clanking of the steel locks mixed with the gasping sobs of Marlene's demolished heart.

Few words were spoken by Ned and Flo Mitchell during their long drive to Portage la Prairie.

They arrived at the Agassiz Youth Centre, where their daughter, Marie, was being held in a segregated unit. For a moment they sat in the truck staring at the imposing stone building, which resembled a World War One–era high school. Then Ned squeezed Flo's hand and they went in.

Other than one-word responses of "yes," "no" and "thanks" to the officers who checked their IDs, scanned them for weapons and drugs before escorting them to the noncontact visiting area, the

Mitchells were silent. But rules shouted from posters on the wall about contraband and how inappropriate behavior and/or language would terminate a visit.

The room had a large window with a row of stools and telephones. Ned and Flo waited for several minutes before Marie appeared, taking a stool on the opposite side.

Flo pressed her open palm to the glass and kept it there waiting for Marie to press hers there, too.

Marie didn't.

Ned picked up their phone then shouldered together with Flo, holding it between them so they could talk to their daughter.

Marie's voice sounded small and distant when she said "Hello."

Tears filled Flo's eyes—her daughter, the accused multiple murderer.

"I wanted—" Flo's voice trembled. "I made peanut butter cookies for you and wanted to bring them with clothes and books, but they said that I'm not allowed to give you anything. I have to mail them or something."

Marie nodded. "They got a lot of rules."

"They only gave us thirty minutes to visit," Ned said.

"How are you?" Flo said. "I mean here, and with everything?"

"I got a place to myself. I eat in my room. I get a half hour alone in the yard to exercise. It's a little lonely. I wish I had a TV. It's boring."

Ned exchanged a quick glance with his wife, repositioned himself and took a breath.

"Marie, we have to know if it's true," he asked.

She stared at her parents, reading the pain, terror and utter emptiness in their expressions, just as she had at Pike's funeral.

"Is it true? What do you think, Dad?"

"We need to hear it from you."

"My lawyer told me not to talk about it."

"We're your parents," Flo said.

"We got a right to know," Ned said.

Marie looked away, blinking back her tears, sniffling, brushing at her nose. Then she looked back at her parents before telling them in a voice barely audible: "It's true. We did it."

Ned shut his eyes, cursed under his breath and stifled a sob by covering his stubbled face with a shaking, calloused hand.

Stabbed with a sorrow she could not bear, Flo groaned and, straining to breathe, she whispered: "You killed a mother, a father and two little children?"

Marie was silent.

"Why?" Ned's voice creaked with pain.

Marie lowered her head, her hair curtained in front of her face. In a soft voice she said: "It just happened."

"It just happened?" Her father's anguish and anger seethed beneath the surface. He stifled another curse. "I was there to move the cars. I saw cops *bawling* and you tell us, 'it just happened'? God, it's like Pike all over—"

Marie's head snapped up, her eyes locked onto her parents.

Flo seized his tattooed forearm. "Don't, Ned. Don't!"

Ned caught himself, struggled for composure.

"Don't you have any remorse?" Ned asked. "Are you even sorry for what you've done?"

Marie was silent.

"You've ripped the heart out of the entire town," Ned said. "Legal Aid was going to force us to pay for your lawyer. We had to prove we didn't have the money. I would've lost the business, maybe had to sell the house. Do you even grasp the depth of the destruction you and—"

"Stop," Flo said.

Marie's eyes narrowed into slits, intensifying the fire burning in them. Assessing her mother and father, her body shook.

"You won't have to worry about me ever again. I'll be out of your lives just like you always wanted."

"Don't say that," Flo said. "Why're you saying that?"

"Why can't you admit the truth for once? You always loved Pike more than me. You always blamed me for Pike. And it's just like your husband said—this is Pike all over again, only this time with *more* dead people!"

"Please, Marie, don't say that!" her mother pleaded. "Maybe when this is over we can get you the help you need—"

Marie banged the headset against the glass,

dropped it to the counter, flashed both middle fingers at her parents and left.

Nicola Hope Gorman had been transferred to the Manitoba Youth Centre, the largest juvenile correctional facility in the province, a sprawling, low-standing, red brick building in Winnipeg's west side.

Nikki rarely had contact with other female prisoners, who all were under eighteen. She was isolated because of her age and alleged crimes. But secrets seldom survived in prison. The others knew who she was. So when Nikki's caseworker, a broad-shouldered woman named Irene, who'd lost the ability to smile, removed her from her cell and escorted her in handcuffs past other cells toward the visiting area, the other girls mocked her.

"Yo, killer queen!"

"Hey, four-count girl!"

"Super freak!"

Nikki and Irene waited for the unit security door to be buzzed open, then entered the visiting room. Because prisoners held in MYC were longer term, policy did not separate families by glass during visits. But Nikki's case was different. She was taken to an open area and seated at a metal picnic table bolted to the floor. No one else was in the room.

"No contact," Irene said. "I'll be near. This will be supervised."

"Because I'm special."

"Yeah, so special."

Across the room there was a loud electronic buzz, a metallic clank, a door opened and Nancy Gorman entered. Nikki's blank face twisted into a scowl when Telforde Rahynes followed behind. In a reflexive response, Nikki stood to leave but felt a hand on her shoulder and glanced at Irene, who gave a subtle shake of her head. Nikki sat back down.

Nancy moved across the room, her arms rising to embrace her daughter until she saw the flash of Irene's big palm and her icy headshake, underscoring the no-contact policy. Nancy and Telforde sat with their palms flat on the table as instructed earlier.

Nikki's first words to her mother were: "Why did you bring him?"

Nancy was taken aback. "I live with him. He drove."

"This whole thing is your fault," Nikki said.

"What?" Nancy said. "I don't understand."

"Hello, Nikki," Telforde said, his eyes taking a quick walk over her jumpsuit. "They only gave us twenty-five minutes, so show your mother some respect."

Nikki shot Telforde a middle finger. "You're not paying my rent anymore."

Disgusted, Telforde shook his head with a sideways grin.

"Nikki," Nancy said. "Don't do this. Tell me how they're treating you?"

"Like you care."

"Hey!" Telforde said. "Respect your mother."

Nikki's jaw muscles bunched as she stared at them for a long wordless moment.

"You know, being alone in here I get lots of time to think of lots of things, like about how people betray you, hurt you, people you're supposed to love and trust."

She shot Telforde a cutting glance of disdain and he blinked.

"It's time to say it," Nikki decided.

"Say what?" Nancy said.

"You know, Mother, that for the longest time your boyfriend's been fucking me and threatening to kick us to the street if I told anyone."

"Nikki!" Nancy cupped her mouth with her hand and looked to Irene, who seemed indifferent.

"That's a goddamned lie!" Telforde said.

Nikki's handcuffs jingled as she pointed at her mother.

"It's your fault I'm in here because you always knew and you did nothing! *Nothing!*"

"Nikki, stop it!" Nancy shook her head. "Why're you saying these horrible things?"

"Because she's a murdering, thieving, lying slut!" Telforde said. "I never touched you!"

"You're lucky I'm not pregnant. But you can't touch me now. I should report you to my lawyer. Maybe it'll help my case."

"You're a lying piece of—"

"Stop, please stop this!" Nancy said through her hands.

"Maybe when we murdered that family, I was

thinking all along about killing you—*both of you*!" Nikki screamed.

Nancy couldn't hold in her anguish, moaning and rocking. Telforde threw his arm around her.

"All right." Irene stepped forward. "That's enough. The visit's over." Irene nodded to an officer across the room to take care of the visitors.

Nikki stood, looking down on her mother, a broken woman.

As Irene took Nikki's shoulder, Nikki stood her ground long enough to spit in Telforde's face.

After the visit ended, Nancy and Telforde drove for miles without speaking as he guided his Dodge RAM pickup through Winnipeg's western edge.

At first Telforde punctuated their stops at red lights with one-sided conversations.

"I don't know why she's lying, Nancy. I swear I never touched her."

Nancy stared straight ahead, meeting his denials with silence until he turned on the radio, keeping it low. Eventually they got out of the city and onto the highway bracing for the long drive back to Eternity.

They'd gone several miles when Nancy began talking. "I've been lying to myself for a long time," she said.

"Lying about what?"

Tears rolled down her face. "That I needed to live with you because I couldn't pay down my gambling debts and couldn't afford to live on my own with a daughter on what I made at the Market Mart. That was one lie."

"Your debts are huge and I was there to help you, get you into gambler therapy, so what're you driving at?"

"I knew."

"Knew what?"

"Nikki wasn't lying. I knew and I said nothing and did nothing. Oh God."

"Now just hold on, I'm telling you she's a lying little bitch!"

The air cracked because Telforde never saw or expected the stinging whip-snap on his face as Nancy slapped him. He cursed, pulled back. The wheel twisted and the truck swayed.

"What the hell?"

"Nikki's right. It's my fault she turned out the way she did—I can't live with it. I gave my daughter to you, you ruined her, now four people are dead and she's so damaged that—oh God!"

Nancy unleashed a torrent of punches and scratches until Telforde, one hand slipping on the wheel managed to seize her wrist.

"Get hold of yourself, Nancy! I swear I never touched her!"

"I want out now!"

Telforde still gripped her wrist, eyes wide on her, the road, then her. "Calm down!"

"I know what you did!" she screamed, pulling away, closing her right hand into a fist, driving it into Telforde's groin, piston-like, again and again. The pain was blinding, Telforde yowled, his hand tensed on the wheel, jerking it left. Suddenly the pickup was vibrating, the road had disappeared and they crossed the grassy median to the moan of an air horn before they slammed head-on into an oncoming big rig.

It was late the next afternoon before investigators confirmed that Telforde Rahynes and Nancy Gorman were the two fatalities in the accident west of Winnipeg.

The truck driver, who was from Ohio, was not hurt and not at fault.

At the Manitoba Youth Centre, Irene brought Nikki into a room where several grim-faced people sat at a table, including her lawyer, an MYC director, two RCMP officers, two people from Child and Family Services, an MYC psychologist and a chaplain.

The chaplain broke the news to Nikki about her mother's and Telforde's deaths.

Nikki lowered her head.

Any thought to report Telforde Rahynes as a pedophile and rapist had died, too.

Condolences were offered from around the table.

Then the director said arrangements could be made for Nikki to receive a compassionate leave to attend her mother's funeral under police escort, of course.

Nikki's eyes watered but she did not cry. She shook her head.

"I don't want to attend the funeral. She got what she deserved."

Thirty-Eight

This is so risky on so many levels but I've got to do it.

Kayla had cut school midway through the day— "I'm feeling sick," she'd told her teacher—and went home where she would determine if Emma was being truthful about her past.

Emma continued to give her an uneasy feeling with her odd reaction at the restaurant the other night. *Maybe she swallowed wrong, like she said, but it looked to me like she'd gone into shock about what Dad said about his new book, or something.* And Kayla still couldn't find anything on the fatal fire at the so-called "Tony's Diner" in Maryland.

It all seems so suspicious. But I can't tell Dad about it; he'll just try to analyze me and send me to Doctor Hirsch. It's up to me to do this.

Kayla knew Emma would be at her school, knew that her dad was gone for the afternoon to deal with his passport, or something called a NEXUS card. For the moment, she had the house to herself. She'd done a little research and had formulated a plan. Now was the time to execute it.

Tug greeted Kayla at the door, happy to have company, following her upstairs to her room, where she got out her laptop and searched online for Darmont Hill College in Indianapolis, Indiana. She found the school and called the registrar's office, mindful of the time difference. Counting on the office still being open, she exhaled when a live person answered.

"Registrar. Records."

"Can you help me? I'd like verification of the graduation status of a former student?"

"Who's calling and what does this concern?"

"I am an assistant for an author, Benjamin Grant. He's considering hiring a researcher but needs verification of the graduation status of a former student. I'm calling on his behalf."

"This is not military but for civilian employment?"

"Yes, civilian employment."

"Please hold."

Another person came on the line and after Kayla briefly repeated her request the woman said: "Student's full name, please?"

"Emma Anne Chance."

Kayla heard typing on a keyboard.

"Date of birth?"

Kayla had managed to get a look at Emma's driver's license in the kitchen last week. She'd taken a photo of it then and provided her birth date now.

More typing and something happening at the other end.

"Miss, our policy is that Mr. Grant make the request on the business letterhead. Only then will we proceed."

Kayla thought of a way she could do it. "Will you accept it if I scan it and email it to you?"

"Yes, send it to the following email." The woman provided the address and instructions. "Make sure the request includes the student's name, date of birth and the request number I'm going to give to you now. We'll respond to the requesting email but it can take up to two weeks to process."

"Two weeks?"

"Most requests are completed sooner, but we are backlogged."

"And is there a fee?"

"No fee."

"Thank you."

Kayla had a copy of her dad's letterhead in her computer. He and her mom had created it using a free online template he never changed. Kayla duplicated it, then replaced his contact information with her cell number and an email account she'd created on Yahoo: BenjaminGrantBooks. She typed the request on her laptop, printed it from the printer in her dad's office, scanned it and sent it to the address of Darmont Hill College.

Then Kayla let out a long breath.

In about two weeks, I'll know the truth. But I'm not done yet. There's more to do.

Thirty-Nine

Winnipeg, Manitoba
2001

Nicola Hope Gorman.

Marie Louise Mitchell.

Jane Elizabeth Klassyn.

Each of them were fourteen at the time of the murders. But because of their ages, their identities disappeared into the justice system. From the moment they had been charged under the federal Young Offenders Act, it was against the law to use their real names in open court, or for the news media to publish them or their photographs.

Ever.

Their true identities were to be kept secret even after the case concluded, even after all sentences were completed, or they were acquitted.

That was the law.

The court ordered that they be identified as "Girl A," "Girl B" and "Girl C," and nearly a year after the morning of the grisly discovery on Old Pioneer Road, their trial began in a Winnipeg Court of Queen's Bench before Justice John Claiborne.

But reaching that day in court encompassed a pretrial legal odyssey of judicial matters that included intense, closed-door legal disputes among the lawyers about the true culpability of each of their clients, measured against the facts and evidence. Ultimately, each girl had pleaded not guilty to the charge of second-degree murder, then their lawyers' bids to secure pretrial release were denied because of the gravity of the charges. Then the crown prosecutor wanted the girls to be prosecuted as adults because of the severity of the crimes but the court rejected the prosecutor's request because of the girls' ages.

As well, each girl underwent a psychiatric assessment; the reports submitted to the court found they were not suffering from any disorder that would exempt them from criminal responsibility of the charges. The girls' lawyers sought to have the girls tried separately, arguing that there could be a miscarriage of justice if the defendants were tried jointly because "cutthroat" defense tactics could come into play whereby each girl tried to blame the other for the crimes. But the prosecution opposed them, saying that the risk of "cutthroat" defense was limited because the case rested on the same facts for each of the accused. The court agreed. The girls were to be tried jointly.

And now here they were: day one of the trial.

Every seat in the courtroom was taken by relatives, friends and employees of the Tullocks, along with journalists and the public. All attention went to the girls when they entered the prisoner's box. They met the eyes of the jury of seven women and five men. Gone were the prison jumpsuits—the girls were dressed in new tops and slacks. One had a blazer, making them look more like a freshman debating team than accused multiple murderers.

In the trial's first days, the girls' lawyers presented a case of self-defense with the aim of putting doubt in the jurors' minds that the girls had entered the Tullock home intending to kill anyone. But one of the lawyers was secretly anguished, believing that the accounts given to them by the girls were not all true, that one of the girls was not culpable. Yet the lawyer was unable, helpless, under the circumstances, to mount a convincing defense for her. Matters proceeded with all of the lawyers optimistic that their agreed upon self-defense strategy would result in convictions on the lesser charge of manslaughter.

"These young girls never wanted to kill anyone," defense lawyer Belinda Walker told the court. "They were caught in a bungled robbery and scared for their lives."

Lawyer Ed Tracy said that the defense didn't dispute the physical evidence and the fact the girls had gone to the home planning to steal cash that they believed was owed one of them, adding that each of the girls had come from low-income families and had endured troubled childhoods that gave each of them an unreliable moral compass.

Lawyer Ian Bolton said that it was clear the girls had been careful to enter when they believed the home was vacant. They had been drinking, but when it all went wrong they were terrified for their lives, honestly believing Roy Tullock had guns hidden somewhere. Tragically, fueled by alcohol and adrenaline, and circumstances creating a fight-or-flight response, they acted in self-defense.

The defense team did not want the girls to testify—the risk of damaging cross-examination was too great.

"No way were these girls frightened," Erika Stone, the Crown Attorney prosecuting the case, began. "They were angry and pissed off at the Tullocks. The facts and the evidence are unassailable."

Stone, who had a stellar record for winning cases because she was surgically precise, said the girls had formed "The Skull Sisters," in a ritualistic blood pact with the intention of exacting revenge against the Tullocks. To prove it, she quoted aloud from a journal kept by one of the girls: "'The Tullocks think people like us are dirt, they think they're better than us… Connie's such a lying, cheating bitch who should just die…that bitch owes me money and—'" Stone stopped to leave out identifying names, replacing them with "the others" "'—are going to help me get it…'"

A lot of people in town knew Roy Tullock got rid of the guns in his house long ago at his wife's insistence, Stone said, noting "their babysitter would've been aware," suggesting the girls had concocted that fear as a feeble self-defense ploy. Stone acknowledged the girls came from rough childhoods but said that they took out their twisted, exaggerated, misguided feelings of victimhood on an innocent family.

"Their invasion of the Tullocks' house was merely a rehearsal that went live when the Tullocks arrived home early," Stone said, presenting the horrifying crime scene photos to the jurors during closing arguments. "The evidence rests in the Tullocks' blood and it cries out. Their fingerprints are on the knives, their footwear impressions in the blood and their own admissions affirm that they each had a hand in the killings of Neal, Linda, Connie and Roy Tullock."

The case lasted three weeks before it was turned over to the jury.

After several hours of deliberation it returned with its verdict.

Justice Claiborne told the girls to stand.

They were each found guilty of four counts of second-degree murder.

A banshee wail tore through the room causing Justice Claiborne to tap his gavel as the girls turned. One saw her father and mother, consumed with anguish, looking older, weaker and smaller. The second girl met the eyes of a stranger before she realized she was looking at her mother, who was now frail and wasted.

The sobbing and gavel knocking subsided, then Justice Claiborne concluded by saying sentencing would come in several months.

* * *

Four weeks later, in Eternity, accompanied by a caseworker, a child services worker and two RCMP officers, Janie stood in the drumming rain as her mother's casket was lowered into the ground.

Her killer: liver failure.

But Janie knew the truth. She'd had a hand in her mother's death, too.

She was taken back to The Brandon Correctional Centre, realizing that at fourteen she was a hated convicted killer, alone in the world.

Five months later, Justice Claiborne's hands shook a little as he read his written remarks to a packed courtroom as he sentenced the girls.

Blood had dried in a red dot on his chin where he'd nicked himself shaving that morning. The case had taken a toll on him and he'd lost sleep and a little weight.

"The taking of four innocent lives, including those of two small children, was an unconscionable act, suggesting to this court that you had colder blood in your veins icing your souls," he said. "That you were barely out of your own childhoods at the time catapults this tragedy to a realm beyond evil. I therefore am compelled to give each of you the maximum sentence and conditions allowed under the law. Whether you will work your way back to redemption only time will tell."

Under the law the girls were to serve six years and in separate federal institutions, in different undisclosed locations. After their prison time, the sentences called for four years of supervised release into different, undisclosed communities. After that, they would be released on their own but were required to report to the court monthly for two years before being completely free.

"I can only pray that by the end of your sentences something salvageable and meaningful evolves in your troubled young hearts. God help you."

Claiborne tapped the gavel ending the case.

Conversations erupted in the courtroom, with reactions to what most viewed as light sentences. The girls were escorted from the court. Reporters rushed to file stories on the conclusion of the tragedy in Eternity.

Among those in the courtroom was someone very few people knew; an older teen dressed in a dark blazer, her face sober and calm. She sat quietly with her attendant from The New Dawn Sunrise Wellness Retreat.

The teen had watched the proceedings from the first day, eyeing the three people who had annihilated her family, watching, studying and digesting every part wholly and slowly, the way a python devours its prey.

Forty

Ben was planning his first trip to Eternity to examine the case.

This can't be happening, Emma thought.

Why not tell Ben and Kayla everything and put an end to it?

No, no I can't tell them. The truth will crush them. It will destroy all of our lives. No, I have to protect them. I know Ben loves me and I know he will understand, and I can help Kayla understand the truth of what I did, but in time. Right now I have to survive and I'll do whatever it takes.

"Emma?"

Someone said her name. Why was someone saying her name?

"Yes," she said, turning to Val Tyler, a science teacher standing next to her in the staff kitchen.

"Are you done with the milk?"

Emma, standing at the coffee counter, looked at the milk container in her hand.

"Oh yes. Sorry, Val." Emma passed it to her.

"Are you okay? You look troubled."

"Just lost in thought." Emma smiled.

She returned to her office with fifteen minutes until her next appointment. It was enough time. Emma went online researching Marisa's name for anything new.

She found her obituary.

Marisa Joyce Narmore, 32, of Santa Ana, passed away in a vehicle accident in Orange County, California. She will be missed, but never forgotten. She joins her mother Doreen, and father Wilfred, in death. Marisa was born in Long Beach, California and was raised there and later in Santa Ana. She loved music and her dog and was a valued long-time employee at AllanTynes Sporting Goods Outlet. Marisa recently followed her dream of becoming a law enforcement officer and was studying criminology at Orange Pacific Community College. A memorial service for Marisa is scheduled for 2 p.m. Saturday at Vane & Meechum Memorial Chapel in Santa Ana. Click for directions.

Emma read some of the tributes that followed.

This is a heartbreaking loss for our organization, Marisa's family and friends, Ned Lober, owner of AllenTynes, wrote.

I was so proud of her working hard to become a police officer, Avery Dodd wrote.

The obituary was accompanied with a nice photograph.

The memorial service was Saturday in Santa Ana, Emma thought as she read it again.

Forty-One

Eternity, Manitoba
2002

A year after her daughter was sentenced to prison for murdering four people, Flo Mitchell, waiting at the drugstore counter for the pharmacist to refill her prescription, heard women whispering behind her.

"That's the mother of one of them."

"How do you live with something like that?"

In the time since the tragedy, Flo had faced ridicule and ostracism every time she went out shopping. Whether it was the grocery store, the bakery, the drugstore, it didn't matter. The derision from other customers, people who used to be her friends, had grown unbearable.

"What kind of mother are you?"

"Too bad you didn't abort that monster!"

The scorn pretty much stopped her from going out. When she needed to shop, she went to another town. The stress led to her dependence on medication.

Her husband drank heavily, was arrested for drunk driving, lost his license and his towing business. He'd managed to get a job emptying trash and cleaning toilets at the mall. Still, they couldn't make ends meet. They sold their house and moved into an apartment at The Estates.

So that day at the drugstore, Flo did what she always did: pretended not to hear the whispers, collected her medicine and walked home, taking stock of her life in ruin.

No matter how much she begged, her daughter had refused to see her. The last time they looked at each other was in court the day of her sentencing. And the memory of the last time they spoke, ending with her daughter's face contorted with hate, middle fingers jabbed at her, was seared into her soul. It was as if the jagged edges of a rusted tin can were cutting away piece after piece of her heart until there was nothing left.

Late one night, unable to sleep, while Ned was passed out on the sofa, Flo kissed his cheek and left their apartment carrying a small bag.

In the still of the night she walked across the tranquil town to the cemetery. She made her way on the soft, dewy grass to the headstone of her little boy, Pike. She reached into her bag, removed her small bottle of pills and shook every one into her mouth, washing them down with several gulps of whiskey from the bottle she'd brought.

She reached into the bag for one more item, holding it tenderly, staring in the ambient light, smiling as she wept and lay down.

The next day a groundskeeper discovered Flo's lifeless body on top of her son's grave. Her arms were folded on her chest over a framed picture, Flo's favorite of her daughter holding her son on her lap, both of them embodying joy with huge laughing smiles.

Their eyes were shining like dying stars.

Afterward, in a letter sent to his daughter in prison, Ned Mitchell wrote:

I blame you for everything. You are no longer my child.

In her cell, reading it through her tears, she crumpled it and was poised to flush it away. But she hesitated, smoothed it out on her table and tucked it away in a book with her other papers. She began humming the song, "MMMBop," then softly, through tears, she sang all the lyrics, which she knew by heart, liking the line about pain and strife.

In the months and years that passed, word got to her that her father had drifted to Vancouver, Toronto, or to the US, where he had an estranged brother.

They were out of each other's lives forever.

Forty-Two

The parking lot at the Vane & Meechum Memorial Chapel was filling up but Emma found a space. She took a moment to check her face in the mirror.

She wore little makeup; a dark, conservative dress; little jewelry and flat shoes.

Everything looked fine.

She'd told Ben and Kayla that a custodian at her school had passed away and she was going to his memorial service.

Another lie.

Emma slid on large, dark glasses. She was taking a risk, but she didn't have a choice, she thought while walking through the lot. It was busy with people arriving.

I've got to follow this through.

In the chapel she estimated there were more than a hundred mourners. She found a seat in a rear pew and her thoughts churned.

Had Marisa's threat ended with her death? Who

was she? How did she know her and why torment her with her note?

Emma removed her dark glasses, scanned the crowd and wondered.

Is there someone among you who knows the answers? Is there someone among you from Eternity? No, no that's impossible. Yet, Marisa's note...

For nearly an hour Emma listened to eulogies, praise, tributes and songs for Marisa. They were beautiful and heart-wrenching. But nothing in them shed light on Emma's predicament. When it ended, she replaced her glasses and positioned herself outside near the door, studying faces as people exited and gathered into small groups.

Emma floated from group to group, eavesdropping.

"We were neighbors with Doreen and Wilfred, in Long Beach. Marisa was so sweet playing and watching out for our daughter," an older woman told a group of older people.

Emma moved on to another group.

"...this old guy comes to the counter—he'd lost his keys in the store. So Marisa goes around, aisle to aisle, until she finds them by the fishing tackle. And the look on that guy's face, like Marisa was an angel who'd saved his life."

She drifted to a cluster of women, all about Marisa's age.

"What I'd heard was she'd broken up with Preston just before the accident, told him to get out."

"She should've done that long ago. He was a creep."

"Maybe that's why she crashed—she was upset about him."

"It's just so sad because she was doing well at college—on her way to becoming a cop."

"I know, she told me she was working on some extracurricular project she was excited about."

Emma's ears pricked up, and without thinking, she said, "Oh? What kind of project?"

Heads turned to Emma.

"I'm sorry. I interrupted," Emma said.

"No, that's fine," the woman said. "Marisa said she couldn't talk about it. So I really don't know."

"Excuse me, I'm Lee, Marisa's cousin," another woman said to Emma. "I don't believe we met."

"Sorry, I'm Anne. I'm an old friend from Long Beach."

"Oh." Lee eyed Emma, nodding politely.

"It's all so sad. Excuse me," Emma turned to leave but after a few steps felt a hand on her shoulder.

"Are you okay?" It was the woman who'd mentioned Marisa's extracurricular project.

"I'm sorry. It's just so sad," Emma said. "She was working so hard on her dream job, even taking on that project you'd mentioned. What was it exactly?"

"Oh." The woman was startled. "I don't know. She said she couldn't talk about it but she was excited about it. Are you sure you're okay?"

Emma nodded. "Yes, thanks."

Emma accepted the woman's hug and over her shoulder glimpsed Lee staring at her for a moment before Emma left the gathering in front of the chapel.

Was I Marisa's secret project? It could have absolutely nothing to do with me. I have no way of knowing.

Walking through the parking lot, Emma was frustrated at being no closer to the answers she needed. Struggling to think of her next steps, she neared her SUV and saw a flash of white on her door.

Emma froze.

Concentrating, she realized a white envelope was wedged in her driver's side doorframe near the door handle.

She stepped to the door, took up the sealed envelope. Nothing was written on it.

She tore it open to find a single sheet of paper with the printed message.

20 YEARS. YOUR RECKONING IS ALMOST HERE.

Forty-Three

Orange County, California
Present day

Emma's knuckles whitened on the wheel as she drove home while glancing at the note on the passenger's seat.

Who is doing this? What do they want?

A horn blasted. She'd drifted from her lane.

Catching her breath, she concentrated on her driving and her problem.

A second note.

Emma had clung to a faint hope that the threat had ended with Marisa—and that she could unearth more about it. But this new note changed that. It meant there was more than one person behind it.

How do they know about me? How did they find me? My name is sealed yet they've found me. I need to know who they are and I need to know why they're threatening me.

How would she find out?

Unlike at school, she had no chance of gaining

access to security cameras. She didn't know anyone who might help her. What about going to Lee, Marisa's cousin, or her friend? Was Marisa's work on the "secret project" related to this?

How far can I afford to push this?

She didn't dare go to police. She didn't dare go to Ben. She had to protect him and Kayla—she could fix this.

Emma swallowed. *But Ben's going to Eternity.*

The walls of her life were closing in on her; the pressure had her dying for a cigarette even though she'd quit years ago.

Again Emma glanced at the note and wanted to scream.

With the anniversary coming, could it be some kind of tabloid, slimy media types who pay people off for information? But how did they know I would be at the funeral?

Are they following me?

She looked at the traffic in her rearview mirror and vehicles flowing around her.

Are they following me now?

Again she drifted from her lane. Again a horn honked.

Emma corrected her steering, gritting her teeth and making a vow.

I'll survive this. I'll protect my family and I'll survive.

Forty-Four

Cielo Valle, Orange County, California
Present day

I just know something's up with Emma.

The thought nagged at Kayla.

It was Saturday afternoon. Emma had gone to a funeral and Dad was out, meeting with some FBI guy to help with his Canada book. Kayla was not sure when they'd be back.

With her partner, Tug, behind her, Kayla headed upstairs to her dad and Emma's bedroom and the walk-in closet. For a long silent moment she stared at Emma's storage trunk sitting on the hardwood floor atop the area rug Kayla's mom got in Arizona.

Could be something to do with that trunk.

Kayla knelt before it, pushed her thumbs against the latches, opened it, inhaled the cedar air and took stock of the contents, the boots, the hats, blankets and coats. Carefully she removed everything and searched every item. Finding nothing, she ran her fingers along the empty trunk's walls, the bottom, the lid, the lining, feeling for hidden compartments.

Nothing.

She looked at Tug, who sat nearby watching.

She replaced all the trunk's items to their original places.

Kayla closed the lid, then stood. When she took a step to leave, the floor creaked.

She halted.

Then she repeated the step, her eyes going to a seam between the hardwood panels. One of them was loose and lifted a fraction of an inch near the rug's edge. Kayla repeated the action, watching the loose board.

She gripped the rug and slid the trunk aside, then, using her heel, pressed down on one end, forcing it to lift. When she crouched, she was able to get a fingernail, then a fingertip, then her fingers, under its edge. She raised the loose panel, removing it from the floor, revealing a deep gap. Reaching into her pocket, she got her phone, switched on the flashlight, raked the beam over the space, then stopped.

What's this? A book of some kind?

Reaching for it, she saw it was bound with a thick rubber band.

She removed the band, opened the book, fanned its handwritten pages. She went to the first page. It was dated the day after Dad had married Emma. Kayla began reading.

Started a new, wonderful life. Finally and truly, I buried my past. This new journal will be the last of many I've kept in my life. It will stand as testament after I'm gone.

No one knows the truth about me, that I—

Tug sat up and barked.

Kayla stopped breathing. She heard a door. Someone was home.

"Hello!" Emma called from the kitchen where Kayla had left her backpack. "Kayla, are you home?"

Her heart pounding, Kayla closed the book and stretched the rubber band over it. The band snapped, the pieces shooting off. She couldn't find them and had no time to look. She replaced the book then the panel, gripped the rug, dragged the trunk back into place, hurried from the bedroom and trotted down the stairs.

Forty-Five

Winnipeg, Manitoba
2012

She participated in the murders of four people.

Yet the twenty-six-year-old woman in the dark blazer, white top and dark pants, her hair styled in a long bob with side-swept bangs, looked like a young lawyer.

She stood in a Court of Queen's Bench before Madam Justice Sue Crawford in the matter of Girl A, Girl B and Girl C.

"You've come a long way." Justice Crawford looked over her bifocals at the woman.

The judge had read every report and had presided over every review in the case during the last several years, after Justice Claiborne died of heart failure while wintering in Florida. Today's final review was the woman's last court appearance for it marked the completion and final day of her sentence. She was supported by her lawyer, caseworkers and psychologists to attest to her conduct over the years.

Relatives and friends of the Tullocks were in the courtroom to bear witness to the next chapter, along with some of the investigators, members of the public and several journalists, including some who'd reported on the murders in Eternity from day one more than a decade earlier. But few details could be reported today as the case was still covered by laws protecting the identities and privacy of Girl A, Girl B and Girl C. Records concerning the woman standing before Justice Crawford that had been submitted to the court were sealed.

Today's court matter would be replayed two weeks later when a second convicted killer, a woman, aged twenty-six, dressed in a short-sleeved knit blouse and pants, her hair in a side ponytail, appeared before Justice Crawford. Like the previous woman, she'd be accompanied by several people to see her through her last appearance.

Nearly three weeks later, the scenario would be repeated with the third woman convicted in the case. Also now twenty-six, she'd be wearing a white dress shirt and new stylish haircut when she made her final court appearance before Justice Crawford with her support team, while a similar group of people observed from the gallery.

In each instance, the caseworkers and psychologists reported the progress each woman had made on the long, difficult road to rehabilitation.

During their time, each woman, as a condition of their sentences, had been separated from the others, serving six years in federal institutions, including a year credit for time served before sentencing. They then served four years in different halfway houses in separate cities across the county, then they were released on their own but were required to report to police every month for two years—failure to do so meant a return to prison.

Throughout those years, each woman had undergone intensive therapy, which included keeping journals and diaries to demonstrate how they were maturing and making progress by facing the issues leading up to their crimes and the consequences. Each woman completed secondary school and had taken some university and college-level courses which could be applied in pursuit of any degrees or diplomas. Each had found jobs and had matured while coming to terms with the tragedy.

It was noted to the court how, after the crime, each woman, while still young, had suffered the death of a parent.

"While it does not excuse, or diminish their crimes," one of the lawyers told the judge, "it presented additional challenges to be confronted at a young age while incarcerated as a consequence of the offence."

In reports presented to the court, each woman was characterized as being a model inmate while serving their time, with no acts of violence or violations reported against them. Each woman, the court was told, was deemed a minimal risk to reoffend or become a threat to anyone.

At each final review, lawyers read statements from their client to the court.

"'Prison can change you,'" the first woman's statement began. "'My mother died while I was in jail. I had no family. I had nobody, but I learned so much.'"

The lawyer for the second woman, in reading part of the statement, said: "'Some people come out of prison hardened. Some people come out of prison ready to be a better person than they were when they went in. I know what I did. I know the pain I caused. I am now a changed person.'"

The lawyer for the third woman, in reading an excerpt, told the court: "'I was fourteen, I was a stupid kid. I made a stupid mistake and each morning I wake up it's the first thing that hits me—like a hammer.'"

Like Justice Claiborne before her, Justice Crawford had struggled with the horrible dimensions of the case and made similar final statements to each woman, evocative of the poet Omar Khayyám, and the futility of the moving finger of time.

"You will never be able to undo what you've done. No amount of words or tears will change the past. But you've served your sentence, met every requirement, and now this court can only hope that you've truly shed the skin of the vile, vindictive young person you were, to become a stable, functioning adult member of society and make a positive contribution to this world."

In each case, court proceedings did not allow for statements from family, friends or supports of the victims. Their thoughts, if they wanted to voice them, were given outside the court to the news media.

"What they did to my brother and his family," Paul Tullock told the cameras, "what they took from us, was too much. It can never be forgotten and will never be forgiven."

The cameras had moved on but a reporter with an online news site returned to Paul because she'd noticed that with him and his wife was the woman in her late twenties who'd watched all the proceedings. The woman had shunned all attempts by reporters to question her. In fact, thinking she was Paul and Lynn's daughter, few people knew who she actually was. But the national reporter had good sources. She'd learned that she was Victoria, the sole survivor of the Tullock family. The reporter approached Paul and Lynn, going directly to Victoria.

"Excuse me, Torrie. I'm Allison Kessing with the *Canadian National Times*. Can I get your thoughts on today's proceedings?"

Torrie shook her head slowly and her aunt put her arm around her shoulder.

"I understand." Kessing smiled and before leaving said, "It's just that they're all free now and I thought you'd have some feelings about that."

Torrie was well dressed and poised. She'd left the New Dawn Sunrise Wellness Retreat about a year after her family was slain, had gone to college and had been playing a role managing her father's company and living a quiet life since. Reevaluating Kessing's comment, she lifted her head. "Wait."

Kessing returned.

"You know about all their conditions?" Torrie said.

"They're now free to live as any other citizen, do whatever they like."

"They cannot contact or communicate with each other. Ever. If they do so they go back to prison."

"Yes, that was a condition given at sentencing, and I doubt they'll violate it after all this time. It seems clear they're each ready to move on."

"Did you know that each of them have legally changed their names?"

"No. I didn't know that, but it happens in notorious cases."

"And did you know that after their release, if they do not break the law, their records are completely sealed, expunged after five years. So no one can ever know what they did?"

"Yes, I know. So what are your feelings on all of it, Torrie?"

She blinked several times, looked to the sky, then at Kessing.

"They can now disappear into the world as new people, as if the murder of my family never happened. That's not justice—it's a rebirth."

Forty-Six

"Yes, please hold for Chief Jurek. He won't be too long."

Ben switched his phone to speaker and "Let It Be" played while he went through his checklist at his desk.

In the past two days he'd read every news article he could find on the murders in Eternity. With the help of an FBI friend with contacts in Canada, he'd already located some of the people involved in the case, conducted brief, preliminary interviews and secured commitments from them to speak to him face-to-face when he traveled to Manitoba to research the book.

Bill Jurek was a key player, among the first on the scene and was a lead investigator. Ben still had other people to contact, but he needed Jurek and didn't mind holding.

Ben was pleased at how things were unfolding. He'd completed a rough draft of an outline and felt positive about getting back to work, especially after all that had happened in the last few years.

While he was gearing up to throw himself into his book, he was looking forward to taking Kayla and Emma on that family adventure on the train through the Canadian Rockies, once he had things under control.

Tug padded into his office with his ball in his mouth.

"Not now, pal. I'm working. Maybe later." Ben scratched the top of Tug's head just as the Beatles stopped and the line clicked.

"This is Bill Jurek. Sorry for the wait, Mr. Grant."

"Thanks for responding to my emails. I won't take much of your time."

"It's okay. I'm curious—why are you writing a book about this case?"

"To be honest, there were complications with other cases I was considering, and I've had to set those aside. But this case was always a possibility, especially with all the elements it holds, even after all this time."

"And what would those elements be?"

"The terrible magnitude, the enormous toll, the ages of the murderers. I think the tragedy needs to be studied and told. It warrants a record of understanding for history."

After five or six seconds passed with Jurek not responding, Ben continued.

"Will you agree to talk to me on the record for the book?"

Jurek took in a long breath, let it out slowly, then answered. "What happened here wounded everyone in town. What those girls did—" He paused to collect his thoughts.

It was Ben's turn to be silent, sensing that Jurek was still grappling with whatever he carried, that he needed to say whatever it was he needed to say.

"What those girls did cut deep into our community and left a scar. Some of the guys on the investigation, because of the things they saw, had trouble for years with nightmares, PTSD. No different from what I saw when I was a soldier in Africa and Bosnia."

Ben remained silent, letting Jurek go on.

"I've read some of your books, Mr. Grant. I thought they were good. I thought you did a good job."

"Thank you. That means a lot."

"Yes, I'll talk to you and I'll help you as best I can when you come."

"Thank you, Chief Jurek."

"Bill."

"Thank you, Bill, and it's Ben for me. While I have you, can I ask a few more questions?"

"Go ahead."

"How often do you think about the case?"

"Every day. Because for one reason or another I have to drive by the house on Old Pioneer Road."

"And what goes through your mind?"

"I'm pulled right back into it like it was yesterday. The scene, the horror of it. I went to the hospital and was there when Connie Tullock breathed her last words. You never forget something like that. Ever."

Ben let a respectful moment pass.

"Can I ask your help on something?"

"You can ask."

"I'm going to need to speak to the girls. Well, they're women now, but with all the restrictions on their identities at the time, I may have trouble finding them. Would you be able to help me on that?"

Ben heard Jurek make a low whistling sound.

"That could be a challenge. I'm bound by the law. Their records are sealed. Their fingerprints and DNA are in the databases but if they commit no crimes, they've essentially vanished. They really have no conditions. They don't report to anyone, and they've all changed their names and we've got no reason and no authority to track them. They could be living anywhere under new identities without anyone knowing what they did."

"What do you think of that?"

"It's chilling."

Forty-Seven

Torrie Tullock's face glowed in the darkness, lit only by the light of the eighty-inch TV screen before her.

She was alone with her dead family, joining them in the moments of their lives, forever frozen in time.

Here we are in the pool. Me on Dad's shoulders while he holds Linda and Neal in each arm as we yell: "Dad Statue!" before he dunks us in a big splash. Now here's Mom waving at the camera with me, Linda and Neal looking out the gondola window ascending the mountains in Banff.

Torrie smiles at the screen's next images.

All of us wearing mouse ears at Disney World.

Now here's everyone in front of our Christmas tree tearing away wrapping paper. Then candles flickering on a cake, Mom smiling, laughing, Linda and Neal squealing, Dad leading everyone in song, the cake reading "Happy Birthday Torrie."

Suddenly the screen goes white like a nuclear detonation.

They're gone. All of them. Gone, gone, gone. I am alone.

I wish I died that day, too.

I'm not me anymore.

I'm not a daughter. I am not a big sister.

I am no one.

Her thoughts pulled her further into darkness to the last time she was alone, when she was sick and had to go to the Wellness Retreat. She hated being there, hated being away from her family.

The worst of it was when some of the staff, those with some connection to Eternity, gossiped. She'd overheard them saying things like they'd heard that her father had beat her, that's what made her sick and dangerous.

Not true.

Some staff said Roy Tullock was not an upstanding man in Eternity but had had affairs that had produced other children and he'd sent Torrie to the Wellness Retreat because she'd discovered the truth.

Lies.

Why did people say things like that?

Torrie hated the gossipers—she reported them and they were reassigned. But Torrie liked her counselors and therapists. They were nice and had helped her to get better. So much better that they said she was well enough to go home just a few weeks before it happened.

I was going to be with them again. I yearned to go home. I was over the moon.

Then.

Torrie tapped out a few commands on her laptop and the TV screen came to life with old news reports.

"*...we have breaking news of a multiple homicide in Manitoba...*"

Then another news report with aerial footage of her home, over the graphic: *Bloodbath in Eternity, Manitoba: Arrests Made in Mass Murder.*

More commands on her laptop produced more reports.

The day the killers were set free.

Excerpts of their statements were seared in her soul, leaving her seething.

"I made a stupid mistake."

Like spilling milk.

"Some people come out of prison hardened... I am now a changed person."

WTF?

"My mother died while I was in jail. I had no family. I had nobody."

You *had nobody? Are you the victim?*

Pursing her lips and entering more commands, Torrie cued up the news report of what her uncle Paul had said that day and absorbed his words, like a soothing prayer.

"What they took from us was too much. It can never be forgotten and will never be forgiven."

Torrie closed her laptop, switched off the TV and sat in the darkness.

No, it will never be forgotten and it will never be forgiven.

Forty-Eight

New York City, New York
One year ago

Across the country, about the same time Emma had married Ben Grant, Lucy Lavenza stood amid the teetering supply crates and storage shelves in the staff locker room of The Neon Willow Diner.

Fingers working feverishly, she tied her apron, grabbed her order pad, then rushed out toward the dining room.

Diego, one of the owners, stopped her in the hallway.

"What're you doing here, Lucy? We told you on Monday you were done."

"Please, Diego, give me one more chance."

"You've had chances. You missed too many shifts or you came in late and under the influence. You're done."

"Please, Diego, *please*. I'm sick."

Diego looked into her glossy eyes then at the bruises on her jaw and neck, likely the work of her dealer. Her tattoos hid the needle tracks on her arms. Diego had lost a sister to drugs, but for Lucy, he had no sympathy.

"You're an addict. You're fired. Get your final pay from Isabel in the office, get out and get your shit together, Lucy, because if you don't, you're gonna die."

Diego's words held Lucy hostage for a stunned moment. Defeated, she untied her apron and walked past him to the office. The door was open and Isabel let on like she hadn't overheard. She was at her desk talking on the phone. Lucy set her apron and order pad down on the desk. Glancing at Lucy, Isabel, still on the phone, used one hand to yank open a low desk drawer, pluck out an envelope and hand it to her before suddenly turning her back to stand at the file cabinet in the corner, phone to her ear.

"We have the inspector's report, Gavin." Isabel pulled open a top file drawer and searched folders. "I have it. I can get it to you."

Turning to leave, Lucy saw in the still-open desk drawer, the blue canvas money bag holding the week's uncounted cash tips to be distributed. It was unlocked, open and bulging with bills.

As Isabel snapped through the files, she said: "By the way, Gavin, we're looking for a server, so if you know anyone."

Lucy seized as much cash as she could, zipped the bag, closed the drawer and left.

A half hour later, Lucy was on a subway train staring at her reflection in the window as the cars rumbled and swayed uptown from Lower Manhattan.

Fired from yet another job, Diego's words cut through her.

I'm dying.

At her first stop waiting on the platform for her connecting train, she gazed into the stinking, black abyss of the tunnel as if it were her past, her present and her future.

I'm thirty-three and for as long as I can remember I've been spiraling down, down, down and it is all because I was betrayed.

Boarding her connecting train, she found herself again in the window, her car rocking, the shrill metallic scraping of the steel wheels rising like a scream as something cold passed through her.

She yawned. The craving was coming.

Hang on.

She surfaced at her stop in the South Bronx.

In the five-block walk to where she lived, Lucy counted ten rats scuttling in the open, ravaging the trash on the broken sidewalks, darting among discarded appliances in vacant lots. Her apartment was in a decaying low-rent complex.

She walked up the stairs to her seventh-floor unit because the elevator was a death trap. Paint blistered on the graffiti-laced walls, plaster had fallen away in patches and the smell of urine permeated the corners. It was common to see rats and stray cats in the halls. The noise was constant, throbbing music, shouting, the hiss and rush of water through pipes that leaked. Roaches, stains, cracks and mold everywhere.

Lucy's keys jingled as she unlocked the door to her unit, where she lived with her man, Hugo, an unemployed drywall contractor, or mover— she didn't know. She just knew that Hugo got her drugs when she needed them.

Stepping inside, Lucy heard music. Hugo wasn't supposed to be home.

A topless woman was upright on the sofa, bouncing up and down and as Lucy moved around she saw that the woman was straddling Hugo, who was naked and shocked when Lucy cried out.

"What the—" Hugo shifted, tossing the woman to the floor as he tried to reach Lucy.

But she'd fled to the bathroom, locked the door, slammed her back to it and slid to the floor.

She could hear Hugo and the woman yelling, a door thudding, then the music died.

Above Lucy, a toilet flushed and foul water dripped from the ceiling into the tub along a path marked with an aged yellow stain. Then Hugo was at the door.

"Get out here. I want to talk to you."

Lucy could feel her craving growing, her stomach cramping, muscles twitching.

She opened her bag. She had no medicine— that's what she called it. She looked at the money from her final check she'd cashed at the bank before boarding the train. She looked at the tip cash she'd stolen. She hadn't counted it but it was a lot.

Lucy moved fast, opened the vanity door under

the sink grabbed the box of sanitary pads, reached to the bottom, where she hid the cash she'd been saving for months.

Escape money—save-my-life money.

"Don't make me come in there, babe. You know I don't want that."

She carefully stuffed nearly all of the cash she had into the bottom of the box, set the pads on top, closed the box and the vanity.

She stood, took a breath and opened the door to an explosion of stars as Hugo's fist jackhammered her skull, sending her to the floor.

"You told me you were working today!" he said. "You lied. When you lie I have to punish you. Why're you home?"

Her head pulsating, the room spinning, she tasted blood as she moved her jaw to speak.

"I was fired. I got my last paycheck, cashed it. I'm sick, Hugo. I need—"

"Shut up!"

She felt him tugging at her bag, glimpsed him rifling through it, taking her wallet and all the cash she'd left in it, gripping it in his fist, bending down and shoving it at her face.

"This it?"

"That's all they gave me, I swear."

All the air erupted from her stomach when Hugo's foot plowed into it.

He stomped away, rampaged through the house. Closets and dressers slammed; zippers zipped.

Then Hugo was gone.

Out of her life.

Lucy didn't know how long she stayed on the floor before she dragged herself to the mussed bed.

Over the next few days Lucy battled her debilitating craving, writhing, curling into a fetal posture. Gooseflesh pricked her skin and she suffered tremors, nausea, vomiting and diarrhea. Thoughts and images of imminent danger tormented her. She couldn't sleep or eat.

Certain she would die, she begged heaven for mercy.

God help me.

Eventually, as her withdrawal subsided, flashes of lucidity only confirmed that she had descended into hell and would die there if she didn't crawl out.

In the weeks and months that passed, she fought to survive. She sought treatment in a free rehab center and managed to qualify for a room in a shelter.

Lucy knew her life was a cursed one, with a line of abusive men like Hugo. The lies and misfortune that had been forced upon her reached back to her childhood. She haunted New York City despising those she saw entering shops, restaurants, wearing expensive clothes, riding in expensive cars; those living in comfort, living pain-free lives, for they were no better than her.

On the street she survived by stealing wallets from inattentive tourists, using credit cards only once to buy things she could sell fast for cash as she continued building her bankroll.

Then the truth hit her.

It happened on a clear blue Saturday morning. Lucy had come to one of the flea markets in Lower Manhattan on Broadway. She'd been searching for tourists to prey upon when the morning sun found a tray of rings, glinting at the right moment, as if signaling her.

Lucy caught her breath.

Gleaming before her was a huge assortment of inexpensive skull rings. Soon she found a death's head, a sugar skull and one displaying rage. They were so beautiful and Lucy recognized the moment for what it was: a message to act.

She bought three rings.

Later, alone in her room, she admired them for they pulled her back through the years, the agony of flailing in the swirling current that was the river of her life. How she'd changed her name, become a new person. She'd married an older, widowed man from Pittsburgh after meeting him online. She'd moved to Pennsylvania, got documented. The marriage didn't last and Lucy drifted from one large city to the next. And all the while she cleaved to the unshakable belief that she was not to blame for everything that had gone wrong in the past.

None of it was my fault.

My mother failed me.

And when my blood sisters betrayed me, they set me adrift on an ocean of never-ending pain. We swore a blood pact and they betrayed me. The anniversary is coming. Twenty years. For twenty years, I've burned. I don't deserve this life. Enough is enough.

Lucy then looked through her few belongings, digging out her tattered journal from her time in prisons, or what she called institutes of higher criminal development. Remembering all she'd learned, all she'd done, others she'd encountered behind bars in Canada, she recalled one girl especially.

Gina.

Gina was an American who'd been visiting her sister in Calgary when she got involved in a cross-country crime spree with older men that ended in Brandon, Manitoba. Gina had too much attitude. Inside, she'd broken a rule and offended a gang leader. One day two gang members had Gina cornered in the laundry room. Lucy, who by this time was a respected force to be reckoned with, intervened, saving Gina from a severe beating, or worse.

Gina never forgot.

For Lucy, this was money in the bank because Gina was from New Jersey and was connected to people who knew people. Gina had promised Lucy her eternal gratitude and help whenever needed.

Gina showed Lucy ways to reach her once they were back in the real world, but because Gina had enemies she needed to be careful about revealing where she was. Gina wrote instructions in code—like the lines of a poem.

Now, after deciphering it, Lucy went to the shelter's free computers and searched online.

It didn't take long before Lucy made a few calls to Newark, then Brooklyn and Queens, saying exactly what Gina had told her to say if she was ever looking for her.

Within a few hours, one of Lucy's disposable burner cell phones rang with the call she'd been waiting for.

"It's been a long time, Gina."

"A long time. So you're calling yourself Lucy now?"

"Yeah. So Gina, I need that favor now."

"What can I do for you, Lucy?"

"I need your help finding people who don't want to be found. Can you help me with that?"

"No, I can't."

A few tense seconds passed between them.

"But I know people who can."

Forty-Nine

French cabaret music blended with children's laughter from the rotating carousel in Bryant Park, where Lucy Lavenza waited to meet the man who would help her change her life.

It had been a few days since she'd called in her favor from Gina, providing her with the little information she had. In that time Gina called her with updates, telling her: "Be patient, I'm working on it."

Then yesterday, Gina instructed her to go to Bryant Park in Midtown Manhattan, at 2:00 p.m., sit alone directly across the lawn from the carousel with today's *New York Times* laid out on the table.

"A friend, his name is Devin, will meet you. He'll have what you need."

It was now 2:21.

Competing breezes carried the floral scent of flowers, food carts and tour buses.

A baby's giggle drew her attention to the couple settling in several tables away. Laughing and squirming in its stroller, the baby couldn't be more than a year old. The mother looked to be about Lucy's age, a fresh-scrubbed beauty with a glow. The husband had a tanned chiseled jawline, deep-set eyes and a good body. The family exuded a blessed life and made her question if she would ever have a life remotely close to theirs.

"Hey, Lucy?"

A lanky man in his twenties stood at her table. His stubble creased into dark lines when he gave her a little smile. He wore sunglasses, a New York Jets T-shirt, ripped, faded jeans and was sockless in his sneakers. He looked like a bike messenger.

"And you are?"

"I'm Devin. Gina's friends asked me to help you and, well…" He lifted his arms a little, as if to say *here I am*. She noticed the strap of a worn soft leather bag across his chest. "May I sit?"

"Sit."

Devin lifted the strap over his head, set his bag atop the paper. He sat, rested his arms on the leather bag and leaned forward. No one was near enough to overhear; and there was the park and street noise; still, he kept his voice low.

"What you've requested is illegal," he said.

"So? Gina owes me."

"And I owe her. Well, I owe friends of hers. Everybody owes somebody, the circle of life."

"Did you do it?"

"Yes, but not me alone. To do this, she called

on relatives, cops, lawyers, security people, you know how it works."

"Are you a cop?"

He laughed. "No. I'm—let's say I'm a reformed computer expert who got caught in nefarious activities. I paid the bill on that. Now I work in IT security—circle of life again."

"Did you find what I needed?"

"Yes. Once I was given the basic information. You're probably aware that traditionally in most states and Canadian provinces legal name changes are, by law, accessible, but you've got to know how to look."

"You said, 'traditionally.'"

"Yes, getting access to some name changes is not easy. Some cases are flagged, like when courts order protection, making it almost impossible to see the names. To access court-sealed data you need the help of someone with clearance to restricted databases to risk breaking the law. Or you need someone who can gain entry through a back door. It's extremely difficult and risky but once you're in you can collect a world of information."

"Did you find the people I'm looking for?"

"I did. Like I said, Gina leaned on a lot of people, called in favors." Devin undid the straps of his leather bag and withdrew a brown envelope closed with metal clasps and handed it to Lucy.

"All here, all up to date—addresses, property records, status, everything."

Without opening it, Lucy slid the envelope into

her bag, withdrew a smaller one and offered it to him.

Devin waved it off. "I don't want anything from you."

"I may need more help at some point."

"I don't know what you're planning to do with the information I gave you but I'm sure it won't be good."

"Suit yourself." She returned her envelope to her bag and stood to leave. "But will you help me if I call Gina to reach out to you again?"

"No, I won't. We're done."

She leaned forward, pulled off his glasses and looked into his face. "You will, Devin." Lucy lifted the newspaper from the table. Under it was her cell phone, which had recorded their conversation. She seized it, took his picture before anger crept across his face. He grabbed her wrist.

"Don't try anything, Devin, or I'll scream for those two cops behind you. You'll be sleeping in custody tonight."

Devin turned. Sure enough, two NYPD officers were strolling across the lawn.

Devin released his grip and Lucy left the park, her heart hammering.

Fifty

> *No one knows the truth about me, that*
> *I—*

Alone in her room doing math homework, Kayla's concentration slipped again to Emma's hidden journal, or diary, or whatever that book was.

> *No one knows the truth about me, that*
> *I—*

That phrase, written by Emma right after she'd married Dad, was locked into Kayla's memory. And Kayla knew that the handwriting was absolutely not her mother's, or her dad's. She recognized it as Emma's from notes she'd left her on the fridge.

What's the truth? What secrets did she write in that book and why was she hiding them until her death?

Kayla wished she could have read more, that she had taken photos of as many pages as possible but there hadn't been any time. It had been another close call. *So how can I find out what all this means?*

If Kayla came forward and said something, she'd be guilty of invading Emma's privacy. If she told her father, he might not see things in the same light as her and it could all go horribly wrong.

He'd likely send me back to Doctor Hirsch.

Kayla needed more answers, needed to know what Emma had written. And the only way to do that was to read what was in that book.

The next chance I get I'll retrieve that book and read every word on every page.

Fifty-One

Cielo Valle, Orange County, California
Present day

Emma was no closer to solving the mystery behind the threatening notes. Now Ben was preparing to go to Canada and Kayla wouldn't stop with her questions about her past.

"Is something wrong, Emma?"

She turned to Ben, who was waiting for her answer, Tug's leash jingling as they walked along one of the paths twisting through the forests of Suntrail Sky Park, a few blocks behind their corner of Cielo Valle.

He'd invited her to go for an after-dinner walk. It seemed like in the last few days he'd been giving her a hard read and brought her here for an underlying reason.

"What do you mean?" she asked.

"Lately you seem disconnected. Like something's eating at you, and maybe I've been contributing to that."

Emma didn't respond.

"It's no secret that I've been consumed with my book, and I apologize for that," Ben said.

"It's all right."

"Here's the thing. Kayla's still struggling to accept you."

"I know."

"I've talked to Doctor Hirsch about it."

"The therapist who helped Kayla when Brooke died?"

"Yes, and she believes that Kayla feels that accepting you would be a betrayal of her loyalty to her mother and it is likely why she may subconsciously, or even consciously, treat you like an outsider, or an unacceptable replacement."

"I understand that."

"She suggested that Kayla needs to work at finding a way to accept you without feeling like she's being disloyal to her mother. Now, Kayla's resisting, but I think we need her to go back to Hirsch so she can help her."

"Sounds reasonable."

"I'm thinking that in a few weeks I'll have my research under control and we can take that vacation together. That's when we can talk to Kayla without distraction and convince her to get on the right track with Rachel Hirsch. What do you think?"

"It's a good idea."

Ben looked at her and seemed unsatisfied. "Something's still troubling you. I'm leaving for Canada soon and I need to be sure you're okay."

She said nothing and he took her hand. "Emma. I'm your husband."

"Why…" Emma began, stopped and resumed. "Why not do a book based in Sweden or Germany, or even here in the US.?"

"Like I said, there were legal issues with those cases that my publisher wanted to avoid." He was puzzled. "Why're you anxious about the Canadian case?"

"It just seems—I don't know—it's disturbing."

"It's no more disturbing than the Swedish abductions or the cannibalistic butcher in Germany."

"I guess that with the young girls, girls not much younger than Kayla, than the kids I counsel, it's just so distressing, you know? Ben, I'd be happier, relieved even, if you found another case to write about."

Ben thought for a moment. "Emma, I can't do that."

"Why not? There are so many other cases."

"You've read my books. All of them have disturbing elements. I want you to read my outline, then you'll have a better understanding of this case."

A long moment passed before Emma nodded, and for the rest of their walk she grappled with apprehension and dread.

Ben's going to Eternity. I can't stop him. He's going to find out about me. But if I tell him it could ruin him, Kayla, everything we have. She battled the overwhelming urge to trust in love and confess her past, to tell Ben everything, now.

No, my identity is sealed. He'll never find out. He'll never know.

Emma searched the forests, unable to push away her trepidation.

But someone has already found out. And I can't be sure Ben won't find out because he's good at what he does.

With waves of desperation rolling over her, they came to the trail's end at the parking lot. Tug barked and Emma was stopped in her tracks by what she saw in the distance.

A man in a red shirt and khaki shorts had exited the trail they had been on, taking a shortcut through the trees directly to the cars. It looked like he'd been following them and was trying to get ahead of them to leave, unseen.

He looked like the man Emma had seen a while ago at the beach.

She told herself she was being silly, then saw that Ben's eyes had narrowed as he zeroed in on the man.

"I don't know what's up with that guy," Ben said. "But I'm going to find out."

The man could be a reporter who'd somehow found her; her fears flared and swirled.

What if he tells Ben everything here and now?

Emma grabbed Ben's arm.

"Ben, no. Let's just wait till he leaves, then go home."

The leash tightened. Tug threw a bark in the man's direction as Ben started toward him.

"I'm just going to talk to him, Emma."

"I'm coming with you."

The man was at his sedan. He'd opened the driver's door when they approached him.

"Excuse me," Ben said.

The man turned to Ben and Emma. He was wearing dark glasses, looked to be in his early fifties with a trim, medium build.

"Forgive me, but were you following us?"

The stranger looked at Ben, then glanced at Emma.

"No, gosh, no. Uhm, but you're Benjamin Grant, the author?"

"Yes."

"Del Brockway." The man released a little laugh. "This is embarrassing, but I'm a huge fan and I missed you at the charity book sale. I'd read somewhere that you lived around here—that's how I found you—and I wanted you to sign a couple of your books for me."

"So you tracked me down and followed me here?"

"Weird dumb luck, I know, it's embarrassing, and I'm sorry. I'm a collector and, well, I got thinking I should've just emailed you or got books signed in a store, rather than follow you to the park like this."

"So you did follow us?" Ben said.

"I'm truly sorry. I got carried away, Mr. Grant. That's why I changed my mind and was leaving, hoping you wouldn't see me."

Ben looked into the car, noticed four of his hardcovers on the front seat.

"Those the books?"

"They are."

"How about I sign them for you, Del, and we'll call it a day."

"Oh, would you? That would be great. I'm so sorry."

"Signed to Del, *D-E-L*?"

"Yes, that would be fantastic," the man said, reaching into his car for the books and a ballpoint pen for Ben, who handed Tug's leash to Emma.

Ben took the books and started signing them on the trunk of the car. At one point Ben dropped the pen and when he bent down to retrieve it the man turned to Emma.

"I'm so sorry," he said. "Being married to him, you must see all kinds of people?"

Emma saw herself reflected in his dark glasses when she smiled and nodded.

"That's a nice dog you've got. What's his name?"

"Tug."

Tug barked.

"Good name," the man said. "I'm really sorry to intrude like this."

"All done, Del," Ben said.

"I can't thank you enough, Mr. Grant."

Brockway shook Ben's hand, then collected the books, got into his car and drove away, leaving Ben, Emma and Tug in the lot.

"That was strange," Emma said.

"It was. I meet all kinds. I don't always like it but it comes with the turf."

Ben secretly glanced at his left palm, where he'd

written down the man's plate number. Then he took Tug's leash from Emma.

"Let's go."

But Emma didn't move.

Ben stared at her.

All the color was gone from her face.

Fifty-Two

Lucy Lavenza looked out at the cities and towns floating by her window of the Greyhound bus.

Since boarding at New York's bus terminal, she'd been riding with ghosts. She'd also been riding with students, weirdos, drifters and assorted misfits, whom life had discarded. Traveling more than a day now, she'd lost count of the states she'd crossed—New Jersey, Maryland, Delaware, Virginia, North Carolina and South Carolina.

Were they in Georgia, coming up on Atlanta?

At times Lucy's journey felt like Dante's descent into the eternal home of the damned, dragging her back to her life in Eternity, tormenting her with thoughts of her mother. The woman was a failure cursed with problems and sins she'd passed to Lucy. It's the reason Lucy had turned to her friends for sanctuary.

She'd bonded with her sisters.

And they'd sealed their bond forever with their prayer and blood pact.

As the bus wheels hummed on the asphalt, images from that night on Old Pioneer Road burned through her and suddenly...

I'm awash with blood, so much blood, warm blood, hot blood and the screaming...

But no one was supposed to tell.

We were protected by the pact, with undying loyalty.

But I was betrayed.

The truth of what happened that night was rising. Ghosts were coming for her, forcing Lucy to clench her eyes.

The time has come for me to set things right.

Between sleeping and the rest stops, she devoured the material Devin had obtained for her, enough for what she'd needed. She'd read through it so many times, she'd almost committed it to memory. And what she read deepened her anger. The information fed her plan, and her plan had options, depending on how reality unfolded when she confronted it.

Lucy was ready, ready to end the pain that was her life and collect what she was rightfully owed.

With each mile her rage grew.

Again and again, Lucy changed buses—in Atlanta, New Orleans and finally in Shreveport.

Her westbound bus left Louisiana to cut through the swamps, creek beds and deep pine-woods of East Texas before she got off in Lufkin.

She went to The Splendid Rest Motor Inn, which charged thirty-five dollars a night.

"We also offer hourly rates, if you like." The clerk winked. "The pool's just been repaired. We got a Long John Silver's, Popeyes and McDonald's down the street."

Lucy hefted her canvas bag over her shoulder, stepped from the office, passed the ice and vending machines, made her way to room 12. It smelled of disinfectant, had a fridge, TV, microwave and a crack in one wall from the floor to the ceiling. She dropped her bag on the bed, pulled out a few items, walked to McDonald's, ate a Big Mac, then called for a cab.

The cab took her to the edge of town. Lucy paid the driver. He grunted at the meager tip.

She turned to the sign that greeted her, its letters weakened by weather, time and neglect.

Welcome
The Irma Mae Anson Mobile Home Community

Walking along the potholed dirt road she surveyed the trailers, run-down with peeling paint and loose siding that flapped in the breeze. Some had older cars, or eviscerated pickup trucks resting on cinder blocks out front.

She turned her head at the yip of dogs, three of them battling over trash strewn across the roadway, gnawing on bones. One of them stopped to assess Lucy, stiffening, preparing for battle if she was deemed a threat. She found a broken broom handle with a spear-like tip, ready to draw blood if she had to, until she passed unchallenged.

Moving deeper into the park, noticing the occasional satellite dish, she checked numbers affixed to the trailers until she found #36.

No vehicle was visible. It looked old, was a dirty shade of white with steel vertical siding and a metal roof. The front offered a small patch of grass, where flies circled fresh coils of excrement at the dirt edge.

Coming around to the side, Lucy heard a ceramic clink, then noticed the woman tending the flower box on the rickety wooden porch landing.

The woman looked from her work to Lucy.

She was the same age, heavyset, cigarette stuck in the corner of her mouth, lines carved into her face.

She stared at Lucy, her eyes narrowed, her memory traveling through time, passing disbelief, before arriving at an agonizing truth, then alarm.

The cigarette fell from her mouth.

Lucy said, "Hello, Skull Sister."

Fifty-Three

Cielo Valle, Orange County, California
Present day

Kayla was in the kitchen texting her friend Haley when her dad and Emma left to walk Tug in Sky Park.

Got the house to myself. It's now or never.

After the door closed, she said goodbye to Haley and hurried upstairs to their bedroom. She checked her phone. It was fully charged. Good.

I'll go through Emma's journal, photograph every page. I'll read through them all, then decide what to do.

Kayla reached the top of the stairs, that one phrase of Emma's journal echoing in her head.

"No one knows the truth about me, that I—"

Kayla strode into the walk-in closet, went to Emma's trunk, reached down, grasped the area rug and slid the whole deal aside. She pressed her heel down on the loose board, crouched and maneuvered her fingers along and then under its edge and then she removed the panel.

She switched on the flashlight of her phone.

Sweeping the dark, deep gap, Kayla gasped.

There was nothing there.

She got down on her stomach so she could lower the phone deeper into the gap, combed the darkness again and again—and found nothing.

Her breathing stirred the dust, it whirled in the light.

Oh my God, Emma must know. When the rubber band broke, she must've suspected something and moved it.

Beads of sweat pooled on Kayla's forehead.

Stay calm. Be cool. Think.

Fifty-Four

Lufkin, Texas
One week ago

Slowly crushing out her cigarette under her sneaker, the woman in the trailer park continued staring at Lucy.

"How did you find me?"

"Not important, Rita. That's your name now, right? Rita Ruth Purvis?"

The woman's expression told Lucy she was correct.

Rita Purvis looked at her for a long time, then said: "Turn around and go back to where you came from."

"We need to talk."

Rita walked down from the porch and stood within inches of Lucy. Her voice barely above a whisper, she said: "You're breaking the law coming here like this. I don't want to go back to prison."

Lucy released a little laugh. "Look around. Who's going to know?"

Staring into Lucy's eyes sent Rita back through

time, over an ocean of sorrow before returning her to the here and now. "Why did you come? What do you want?"

Lucy raised her hand and opened her palm to reveal a skull ring. "Take it."

Rita leaned back and shook her head.

"Come on, it's for you. Take it and we'll talk."

The sudden savage yapping of dogs carried across the park raising a prickling at the back of Rita's neck.

"Take it, Rita, and I promise, together we'll make everything right."

The trailer was a twenty-five-year-old single-wide that smelled of cigarettes, beer and gloom.

It was clean. Barren and tidy with linoleum flooring and outdated paneled walls. They went to the living room with its coffee table and two small faux leather sofas. Rita set the ring on the table next to an ashtray, then sat on one sofa while Lucy sat on the other. A couple of canvas land-scapes of the twenty-buck variety from Walmart were on the walls. No photos of people anywhere.

The place exuded an aching emptiness.

As the air conditioner rattled in one of the side windows, the two murderers took inventory of each other and what time had done.

"I'm sure you changed your name, too," Rita said.

"That's what people in our situation do."

"What is it?"

"Lucy."

"Lucy." Rita reached over the sofa to the end table for a pack of Marlboros, took one out, lit it and turned the pack to Lucy, who accepted one and the book of matches. Fanning out the match and tossing it in the ashtray, Lucy's gaze went to the pale scars on Rita's inner wrists and lower forearms.

"Has life been kind to you, Rita?"

Rita blew out a stream of smoke. "What do you think?"

"How many times did you try?" Lucy nodded at the scars.

Tears stinging, Rita shook her head and searched the ceiling.

"Once after I got out. Then I was a flag woman working with a highway crew near Kicking Horse in British Columbia. Went out to a bar with the guys, and two of them raped me in the alley. Quit that job, lived on the street, got into drugs and tried once again in a shelter."

She flicked ash in the tray.

"Then I drifted, crap job to crap job, met a trucker from Tulsa. Percy. He was nice. At first. Married him and moved to Oklahoma, even got citizenship. Then one night Percy beat me more than usual. I was in the process of leaving him when he was killed."

She dragged and winced in a smoke cloud.

"Car hit him when he was checking his tires near Memphis. That was bittersweet. Percy left me with debts. They took what he had, the truck, the house and whatever savings, left me with this place. Never knew he had it. Used to be his mom's before she died. I live here on food stamps and part-time work cleaning motel rooms."

"And you live without hope."

Rita's eyes narrowed. "Screw you. Who the hell're you to judge me?"

"I'm your sister, Rita. Remember? No kids?"

Rita dragged hard on her smoke. "Daughter. Tara."

"A daughter?" Lucy looked around as if Tara would appear.

Rita shook her head. "She drowned in the tub when she was ten months old. Percy was watching her and was drinking, got careless. I was at bingo. He said it was my fault and beat me." Rita stubbed out her cigarette, then looked at Lucy. "What about you? I'm thinking you ain't won no lotteries."

For the next ten minutes Lucy recounted her pain-filled life since completing her sentence for the murders.

"So it's been no bed of roses for you, either." Rita shook her head. "And how're you going to 'make things right'?"

"I found our other sister."

"You found her?"

"Just like I found you. But I've come to you first."

Lucy reached into her bag for one of her burner phones, the good one, and began showing Rita a sampling of photos.

"Do you know who she's married to?" Lucy swiped to a photo. "Him."

"Who is he?" Rita said.

"Some famous author."

"Really? But how did she—" Rita stared at Lucy, a new question dawning, then answered. "He doesn't know about her."

"Probably not."

"Well, well, well. That's just—wow, I don't know what that is."

Lucy put her phone away.

"I'll tell you what it is, Rita. It's wrong. She betrayed me. Now, you didn't betray me, did you?"

Rita didn't answer, finding something icy, something decided, something dead, behind Lucy's eyes. Rita swallowed.

"No, I didn't."

"But our sister in California betrayed us. And for twenty years, while we've been burning in hell, look how she's been living. She never gave a damn about us, never tried to find us, to help us, living like she's better than us. It makes her just like the Tullocks in Eternity."

"The Tullocks," Rita repeated before looking away. "All these years, I think if only Connie Tullock hadn't said what she said to us that night, then maybe it wouldn't have happened. But she just had to prove how goddamned superior she was and then it was like a bomb going off for us." Covering her mouth with her hand, she blinked several times. "I see them all the time you know."

"Who?" Lucy asked.

"The Tullocks. Mostly at night before I fall asleep, they come to me. Pleading. The boy and the girl are the worst, screaming and screaming. Anything like that happen to you?"

Lucy's face hardened, and she said, "Shut up with that. You gotta let it go."

"Let it go? Look at how we've lived, how much we've paid."

"We were kids."

"That's right. We all come from the same place. We all hurt the same. And we all know what really happened. Our pact was broken."

Rita stared hard at Lucy, then said: "It was a long time ago."

"And how long do we have to keep paying? We can't go on living like this, waiting to die. It's been twenty years—the anniversary is coming. We've suffered long enough. I've got a plan for all of us to set things right."

Lucy took up the ring and thrust it toward Rita's face.

"We're sisters," Lucy said. "We're bonded by blood. We made a pact!"

Rita stared at her, thinking. "How're you going to make things right?"

"We'll start by confronting her."

"Why?"

"There needs to be a reckoning with the truth."

"We all know the truth, *Lucy.* I'm not going with you."

"You'd prefer to die here on food stamps while cleaning toilets?"

Lucy reached into her bag and set down a slender brick of cash, held together with rubber bands.

Rita's eyes widened a little, then Lucy put it back in her bag.

"You'll get it and more when we see her. I've got a plan and I need you to make it work, to do what we need to do."

"And what's that?"

"You'll find out when we get there."

Rita's mind churned for several long, life-defining seconds.

She looked at Lucy, then took up the ring, slid it on her finger. She stared at it—at all it signified—then looked at Lucy. "All right, sister."

Fifty-Five

Cielo Valle, Orange County, California
Present day

It was all coming together.

The keyboard clicked softly as Ben finished the outline for his new book. Running about ten pages, it flowed nicely.

He was ready for Emma to read it.

As a fan, she had read all of his books. She knew his work, understood what he was trying to do. She was smart, sensitive, and he trusted her judgment. But lately, she seemed preoccupied. There was that incident the other day with that guy in the park, which reminded Ben. Before he'd washed Del Brockway's plate number from his palm, he'd written it down.

The guy was odd. I still need to check him out at some point.

He looked at the time.

Tug padded in and Ben rubbed his head.

Deciding he would give his outline to Emma after dinner, Ben went over his research. The list of people who'd agreed to talk to him face-to-face when he arrived in Canada was growing but he still had more work to do.

He wanted to reach Torrie Tullock, the sole survivor of the family, and needed to follow up on calls he'd made to her aunt and uncle.

Most important, he still needed to locate and talk to the Skull Sisters.

After dinner, when the dishes were done, Emma withdrew alone to their bedroom with Ben's outline and shut the door. Her heart was throbbing.

This is really happening. He's going to write about Eternity.

She'd agreed to read Ben's outline to help him, but more so to see what he'd learned and to find a way to ward off what was looming. Mystery still enveloped the threatening notes. Emma was no closer to finding out who was behind them. And then there was the encounter in the park with that character, Del Brockway.

Was he connected to any of this?

Before Emma started the outline, she glanced anxiously at the closet door, unable to suppress her suspicion that Kayla had been snooping there, had discovered her journal. The rubber band was missing. It could've snapped, or been chewed by a mouse or something.

Still, to be safe, Emma had moved it.

I should destroy it, but I plan to leave it with a lawyer so it stands as a testament after my death. But now, with everything happening so fast, maybe after the anniversary has passed, I could reveal the truth to Ben, so we can rise above it all. I know he loves me. I want to protect him and Kayla from the lies and let them know the absolute truth about what happened. But I need to do it on my terms.

I'm not sure how long I can hold myself together.

Hands trembling, she began reading.

Eternity: The Story of Homicide in a Small Town
(Outline)
By
Benjamin Grant

Emma raced through his strong, clear writing, which so easily encapsulated the facts and major points. Reading it pierced her with anguish, jerking her back to that horrible night, forcing her to stop several times.

As she forced herself to continue, panic began setting in.

How could this be happening? When I fell in love with Ben, for his compassion, for his understanding, I never believed there was a risk he would write about Eternity. Not for a moment. It was separated by so many years, and so many miles. And there were so many other cases in the world for him to consider. So many. And I believed with all my heart from reading his books that even if he somehow learned the truth about me, he'd be the most likely person in the world to understand.

Emma pushed through the outline. Hope rose

when she came to his mention of how a couple of earlier domestic books on the case failed to include input from the killers.

Laws protect their identities. They can never be disclosed...

Emma found refuge in the fact that Ben would never know the entire truth, but as she read on, her heart sank.

...however, a check with justice officials confirms that nothing prevents a biographer from including the voices of The Skull Sisters, now grown women, as long as they agree to be interviewed and their identities remain concealed. The challenge will be locating them.

Gooseflesh rose on Emma's arms.

Even if she proved untraceable... What if he talked to the others?

"Hello."

The voice of the man who'd answered the phone sounded older.

"Hello," Ben said, "Paul Tullock?"

"Yes, I'm Paul Tullock. Who's calling?"

Buoyed at success in reaching Roy Tullock's brother in Vancouver after many attempts, Ben sat up at his desk in his office where he was working while Emma read the outline.

"Mr. Tullock, my name's Ben Grant, I'm calling from California..." Over the next few minutes, he explained his intentions, allowing Tullock a moment to digest everything.

"It's all still as fresh to us as it was on the day

we were told," Tullock said. "You just never get over a thing like that."

Ben respectfully conveyed his sympathies and made his request.

"Yes, we'll talk to you for your book," Paul said. "It just so happens, Lynn and I were planning to go to Eternity to tend to some things. We could arrange to meet and talk to you there."

"I appreciate that," Ben said. "I'm also trying to reach your niece, Victoria. I'd like to talk to her. Could you help me with that? Or offer any direction?"

There was a long pause before Paul Tullock let out a breath. "Torrie? She doesn't talk to anyone, much less about the murders. She's something of an introvert, I guess."

"Do you have a number, email or address for her you could share?"

"Not really, we protect her privacy. She travels, keeps to herself. You see, she inherited the bulk of my brother's estate. His farm equipment operation was franchised and is doing well across the country. She's a board member of the corporation. I was too, until I retired." Tullock exhaled. "That said, I'll see what I can do."

"Thank you."

Ben ended the call and a knock sounded at his office door.

Emma entered holding the outline and sat in the chair in front of his desk.

Putting his elbows on his desk, Ben steepled his hands. "So?"

"It's very good, Ben. A few typos I circled." She handed it to him.

"Thank you for doing this." He took the outline. "I'll give it another look, clean it up. I've got folks in New York and Toronto waiting for it. Was that it, just the typos?"

Emma blinked several times.

"Go ahead, tell me."

"One thing. It's about the identities of the girls."

"What about it?"

"They're confidential and it's against the law if you identify them."

"Right."

"Wouldn't your publisher's lawyers have a concern?"

"No. I've talked with them and with justice people involved in the case. You're correct, the law protects them from being identified but if they agree to talk and their identities are kept confidential, in keeping with the law, then they're free to speak to me, to have input in the book."

"How will you find them?"

"I'm a bit rusty, but there are ways. With some help it can be done."

"What if they won't talk to you? I would think that this is something they would not want to talk about. It might be too difficult for them. What if you can't find them, or they're dead? Wouldn't that weaken the book, send you back to square one, leave you with a lot of wasted time and energy?"

"Boy, you really don't want me to do this book, do you?" Ben smiled.

"I have a bad feeling about it, Ben. It's just so—so—disturbing."

"Listen, honey. First off, I'm contractually bound. Second, you raise very valid points. Yes, anything's possible. But I'm confident I'll find these killers and present them with a chance to open up about that night and how three young multiple murderers have been living all these years as free adult women."

Emma was silent as Ben looked at papers scattered on his desk.

"I just need to book my flight, hotel, car rental." Then his eyes found hers. "Is there something you want to tell me, Emma?"

Another moment passed.

Emma smiled, then shook her head.

Fifty-Six

The flat monotony of the Chihuahuan Desert sweeping by the bus window contrasted with the images Lucy showed Rita on her laptop.

An array of Google photos, Street View and satellite frames of a home in Orange County, California. It was a cream-colored, Spanish-style two-level house with a triple garage. Shaded by palms, it had lush gardens and stone block fencing. Aerial pictures showed the in-ground pool, patio and vibrant flower beds.

"*That's* her house?" Rita asked.

"Yes, and look." Lucy clicked on other photos of a beautiful cabin surrounded by trees. "They got this little getaway in the San Bernardino Mountains, too. There's more."

She clicked to a video of a short TV report from KRVZ about a charity book sale.

"This is a terrific cause and you can see, a lot of people support it…"

"That's her behind the sunglasses. She's Emma Grant now," Lucy said, pointing to the woman being interviewed. "The next one's longer."

Lucy then played the KTKT TV news feature with the reenactment of Emma Grant, a school counselor who'd saved a troubled student's life.

"I try to make a difference every day," Emma said in the piece, while the student's mother, her identity concealed, said: *"What our son's counselor did was nothing short of a miracle."*

After the clip ended, Rita shook her head slowly.

"It's like she's a hero or saint," Rita said.

"And nobody knows the truth about her." Lucy closed her laptop.

Both women pondered their old friend's life, measuring it against theirs.

Somewhere between Pecos and Van Horn, Rita fell asleep again, craving a cigarette. As she dozed and the miles passed, Lucy worked, revisiting and refining her plan.

For twenty years she had crawled and struggled, like something discarded to the dung heap while her blood sister thrived at living a lie.

This had to end. A debt was owed.

Lucy was going to collect.

As they neared El Paso, Lucy saw the distant mountain peaks to the north and south of the city, reflecting for a moment about the city's mass shooting tragedy.

The bus made its way downtown to the station, where they got off to board a new bus for Phoenix.

Rita was relieved to smoke and Lucy joined her. While waiting, Lucy glimpsed the unique sneakers of one of the fellow passengers who'd stepped from their bus.

It struck Lucy that those were the exact shoes of a woman she'd seen on the bus from New York to Atlanta. Exact.

Studying the woman, Lucy noted that her hair was different but above her right ankle was the same butterfly tattoo.

What were the odds that the same woman would also be on this bus?

"What're you looking at?" The woman interrupted Lucy's staring.

"Didn't I see you on my bus a few days ago from New York to Atlanta?"

"You're mistaken. I got on at Abilene. You got a problem?"

"No." Lucy crushed her cigarette under her foot. "No problem at all."

Half an hour later Lucy and Rita, along with some new passengers, boarded the new bus to Phoenix.

Not long after they'd left the western fringes of El Paso, a powerful stench invaded the bus before Las Cruces. The stretch along the I-10 was known as Dairy Row. Manure management was in full swing and it took Lucy back to the slaughterhouse of Eternity.

The memories the smell evoked lingered, stirring Lucy to work on her laptop and her plan.

She paused to look at Rita, asleep next to her.

She hasn't changed. I knew she'd come. I need her to make this work and one way or another, it's going to work. When this is over, I promise you, sister, things will be better. I won't need you anymore. I'll be so done with you. You won't have to clean another toilet for as long as you live. You'll get what you got coming to you.

Fifty-Seven

Kayla was grabbing some green seedless grapes from the bowl in the fridge when her father appeared before her.

"Geez, Dad."

"Come with me for a little ride."

"Why? Where?" She closed the fridge door.

"To the plaza to get my mail from my PO box. I want to talk."

Ben snatched his keys from the peg and headed out with Kayla, who popped a grape into her mouth.

What's this about? Did Emma tell him I was looking in her closet?

Ben was a smooth driver. Guiding the SUV through the streets of their neighborhood, he glanced at her.

"Put your phone away. I want to talk."

Like most teens practiced in the handling of parents, Kayla knew her father's many tones. This was not his stern voice. No, it was softer, more like his there's-something-I-want-to-know voice. And that made her wary.

Sighing, she lowered her phone.

"Thank you," he said. "Look, it's just that I'm leaving in a few days and I wanted to be sure you and Emma will be okay."

Is he fishing? What if she told him she thinks I'm snooping and he's giving me the chance to fess up?

"It'll be the first time you two will be alone together. It could be a chance for you to get closer to each other, you know?"

Kayla said nothing and Ben turned, blinking as he looked out the driver's window. Kayla couldn't read his expression. Was he sad or disappointed that she didn't own up to violating Emma's privacy?

I haven't heard back from Emma's college. I don't have all the information yet. Still, should I just come out with it and tell him what I know?

"What is it, Kayla?" Ben asked.

"Dad, don't you think Emma's been acting a little weird lately? Like how she was the other night at dinner about your book. It's like she knows something and she's not telling us, you know?"

Ben took in a deep breath and let it out slowly. "Kayla, how would you feel about talking to Doctor Hirsch?"

"What?"

"I called her, updated her on your situation with Emma, and at school…"

"What? You talked to her about me, my personal stuff?"

"Doctor Hirsch said it's possible your struggle to accept Emma is because you feel that by doing so you would be disloyal to Mom. So you portray her as an unacceptable replacement, an imposter. But it's a normal response. And I understand that—it's okay to have those feelings."

Kayla was shaking her head. "Dad, listen to me. Emma told me her mother died when she was working at a restaurant called Tony's Diner in Beltsville, Maryland—"

"Kayla—"

"Do you know this? She said it caught fire, that it happened about twenty years ago, but I checked, Dad, and there is nothing—"

"Stop, Kayla, please. I know this is difficult. I know you ache for Mom. God, there are days when I miss her so much. But Emma's helped me to heal, not to forget but to heal, sweetheart. There's a difference. She loves you and can help you, if you let her."

"Dad, are you so blinded by your love for her that you aren't hearing me?" Kayla bit her bottom lip. "Dad I think she's got…the other day I found—"

Kayla's seat belt cut into her as Ben slammed the brakes and tires screeched. A little girl, pink helmet aglow, on a wobbling two-wheeler had sailed from a driveway directly into their path. Ben had stopped the SUV in time as she made it safely across the street, dismounted, sat down and sobbed.

A frantic woman holding a palm to Ben blurred by them to comfort the girl. Amid the wisps of smoke and acrid burning rubber, Ben got out, checked on and consoled the woman and the girl, with Kayla standing over them, shaken and hugging herself.

Tragedy averted.

"Thank heaven, thank heaven!" The mother said over and over as she and her daughter, eyes filled with tears, returned to their home.

The incident had pierced them with gut-churning memories of their own tragedy years ago.

Some minutes later Ben and Kayla, rattled by the close call, drove home in silence—their differences unresolved.

Fifty-Eight

Cielo Valle, Orange County, California
Present day

Night.

Alone in the dark and they came.

Paralyzed with terror, Emma was helpless to stop the scenes as the horror unfolded and...

...screaming rakes the air. The knife is raised, poised to strike. But a hand grips the wrist, in a wild furious fight to stop the knife. Amid hysterical screaming and cursing, the resisting grip reaches the attacker's fingers, the knife's spine is slipping. The knife is winning, the blade flashing, slashing, plunging, blood spurting, the knife rising and descending, tearing and ripping. The Tullocks. Their eyes are screaming as life spills from them, their blood splattering. Their dead open eyes accusing. New screams rising, her screams rising...stop, OH GOD, PLEASE STOP!

Quaking with fear, Emma thrashed in the night until something seized her; someone called to her as she clawed at the evil. Someone was shouting her name and pulling her from the darkness to consciousness, soft light and calm.

"Emma?"

She woke to Ben's face above hers.

"Emma, you're having a bad dream."

Blinking, gasping, Emma searched Ben and the room, allowing the assurance of sanity to envelop her.

"It's all right, Emma, just a bad dream."

Emma sat up, cupped her hands to her face. Then she reached for the glass of water on the stand beside the bed. Her phone displayed 2:20 a.m. Drinking, she saw Kayla in their doorway. Hair mussed, arms folded, her face flush with alarm.

"I'm sorry," Emma said.

"She just had a bad dream," Ben said. "Let's all get back to sleep."

Kayla stared for a long moment before disappearing down the hall, leaving a wake of suspicion and doubt about her stepmother.

Fifty-Nine

Cielo Valle and Los Angeles, California
Present day

The two days after Emma's nightmare had moved fast.

In that time, the Grant household had functioned with as much normalcy as could be expected, under the circumstances and in anticipation of Ben's departure, now just a few hours away.

Ben's outline had been officially accepted.

"You hit it out of the park," Roz Rose had said in her email. "Everybody in New York and Toronto loves it. Good luck researching in Canada."

Encouraged by the positive reception, Ben finished packing, checking that he had his passport, contact list, files, laptop and chargers. Taking care of other last-minute details, his phone vibrated with a new email. The subject was: "Del Brockway."

It was from Cecil May, a now-retired cop Ben had battled at a homicide scene when he was still a crime reporter with the *Los Angeles Times*. Cecil, an icy, case-hardened prick of a detective, was impressed that Ben had "managed to ask intelligent questions," compared with other reporters. They became and remained friends. Cecil had kept his strong ties to law enforcement and was always ready to help Ben.

Now he'd emailed his response to Ben's request that he look into the plate of the oddball fan Ben and Emma had encountered in the park.

Working on it, his email read.

Thanks. Appreciate it, Ben emailed back.

Ben drove their SUV to the airport. In the backseat, Kayla said little, typing away on her phone with Tug beside her, happily watching cars on the freeway. Tug loved road trips.

Stealing glances at Emma, Ben thought she was subdued. Checking his rearview mirror, he thought Kayla was restrained.

Undercurrents were raging.

"Guys?" Ben said a bit loud to ensure Kayla was listening. "I talked with a travel agency and we're set. When I'm done, you two can join me in Winnipeg. School should be done by that time. Then we'll take the train west through the Rockies to Vancouver. We can fly home from there."

"Sounds nice," Emma said.

"Fabulous, Dad," Kayla said.

"It'll be therapeutic for all of us," Ben said. "Then, when we get back, I'll knuckle down on writing the first draft."

Ben glanced at Emma, then patted her leg. She

smiled at him but he felt her thoughts were else-where.

Airport traffic was controlled confusion as he navigated to the upper departures level to find a spot at the curbside, where he got out and unloaded his bags. Taking stock of his family, Ben said: "The time will fly by."

"Ha-ha, nice pun." Kayla hugged Ben. "I'll miss you, Dad."

Emma was touching the corners of her eyes.

"Everything, okay?" Ben asked.

"Yes. Good luck in Eternity and have a safe flight."

Ben looked at her for a long moment then at Kayla. "You guys are going to be fine. Think of our trip through the Rockies."

Tug barked a goodbye. Ben hugged him and Tug licked his face. "You take care of them, Tug."

"Folks," an airport security guy said, "got to move it along."

After their final kisses, Ben grabbed his bags, entered the terminal, turning for a last anxious look as Emma, Kayla and Tug got into the SUV and pulled away.

Some two hours later, Ben was buckled in his aisle seat.

The jetliner's doors were closed. The doors to the overhead storage bins had been snapped shut. Attendants moved along the plane ensuring all was in order as they prepared to taxi to the runway. Then Ben got a message from Emma.

I want you to know that whatever happens I love you and Kayla with all my heart.

Staring at Emma's words Ben couldn't understand their intensity.

He wrote:

What's up? You sound ominous.

Feeling a little shaky right now. I'll miss you. I love you.

I love you too, hang in there. All will be fine.

Before Ben could resume trying to decipher Emma's cryptic message his phone vibrated with another text—this time from Cecil May.

The owner of that tag is not Del Brockway. It comes back to Leo Wicks.

Who's that? Ben asked.

Want me to dig a little deeper?

Ben felt a hand gently on his shoulder.

"Sir." The attendant smiled down at him. "The captain has asked that all devices be switched off."

Ben nodded. But before shutting down his phone he typed one word to Cecil: Yes.

Sixty

"Tullock AgriCorp has seen another exceptional fiscal year."

Colorful graph lines and pie charts filled Torrie Tullock's laptop as the woman in the video conference continued.

"Fourth quarter consolidated revenue is up 6.5 percent and annual revenue is up 5.9," the woman said to the camera from headquarters in Edmonton. "Consolidated comparable sales are up 1 percent in the fourth quarter, and 2.5 percent the full year."

"The company is in a strong position to continue with plans to open new outlets across the country, and proceed with our global expansion study," said a man in the Calgary office.

The meeting moved on to other items. Before concluding, Torrie made one request.

"Is Kern there?"

"I'm here, Ms. Tullock."

The face of a man in his fifties, with short salt-and-pepper hair appeared. Kern Garland, a retired police commander and former justice department security advisor, headed corporate security, encompassing Tullock AgriCorp's business practices, day-to-day operations, network security, human resources and physical security for the company's seventy outlets.

"Kern, could we talk offline later? Call me at nine thirty, my time?"

"Certainly."

"Thank you, and thanks again everyone."

Torrie sipped tea as night descended.

Toronto's sparkling skyline was mirrored on Lake Ontario's calm.

From her sixtieth floor condo she had a God's eye view of the lights of the skyscrapers, the CN Tower, the domed stadium, planes landing and lifting off from Billy Bishop Airport in the heart of the city.

Setting her cup down, she returned to her study of confidential reports, photos, videos and sensitive information pulled from restricted databases for an unnamed security project that had been in the works for nearly a year now.

All promising, she thought.

Her phone rang. The time was 9:31 p.m.

"Ms. Tullock, this is Kern Garland."

"Thank you for calling. What's the status on the project?"

"I'm sure you can appreciate, this is extremely sensitive work."

"Yes, I'm aware, Kern. Your point?"

"We've had some near compromises, one of them tragic. A subcontractor died in a car accident."

"My condolences. Was it related to the project?"

"We're not certain. It could've stemmed from personal issues."

"I see. Where does that leave things?"

"We're putting more resources on it."

"Good. I don't care about the cost. I don't want the project halted. I want you to continue with the reminders, warnings and torment, as instructed."

"We are."

"Yes, I've seen the pictures. When we finish with the first target, we'll move on to the others, one by one."

"With respect to the others, we are in fact tracking movement that we believe suggests a potential reunion of sorts related to the anniversary."

"How wonderfully opportune. I want to see this through. Whatever the cost. Whatever it takes. Is that understood?"

"It's understood."

"Keep me posted. Thank you, Kern."

Pleased that the time for action was nearing, Torrie sipped tea and returned to a recent anniversary newspaper editorial, one she agreed with. She particularly liked the headline:

The Eternal Question In Eternity: Was Justice Done?

Torrie reread the item, absorbing the words:

Those girls, The Skull Sisters, killed the Tullock family because they felt they could…and for their monstrous and merciless crime of killing four people, two of them children, how did the court respond? With the utmost mercy, for in the scale of the killers' young lives they paid a pittance for taking those of four innocents. And now, far from a cemetery with four headstones, they're living anonymously as free adults.

Yes, Torrie agreed. Justice was not served. Instead they received new lives, far from the graves they left behind in Eternity. Well, twenty years was enough. The bill was past due.

Torrie's laptop pinged with an email from her uncle.

Hi Torrie: Hope all is well. We miss you. We wanted to let you know that an author, Benjamin Grant, is writing a book on the case. We've agreed to participate to ensure the family has a voice. He'd like to talk to you. Of course, the decision is yours. Let me know. Lynn sends her love.

Uncle Paul

Torrie's eyebrows rose a little.

Benjamin Grant, the celebrated true-crime author? My word, how the stars have aligned.

She glanced at the neat stack of printouts from the project as she considered the request and then typed her response.

Thank you, Uncle Paul: I have nothing to say to Mr. Grant at this time.
All my love to you and Aunt Lynn,

Torrie

Sixty-One

Kayla couldn't stand it.

Her unease about Emma was growing, and Dad was too deeply in love with her to get it.

She should've told him that she'd found Emma's journal, but after the close call with the girl on the bike, they got distracted and she lost her nerve.

Now, as night fell, Kayla was on her bed in her room, her door shut, Tug at her feet, laptop on her lap, searching online.

Kayla liked Emma but couldn't shake her growing feeling that her stepmother was hiding something, something *big*. No matter how she tried, Kayla was unable to find anything about a fatal fire at Tony's Diner in Beltsville, Maryland. And she still hadn't heard back from Emma's college in Indiana.

I know if I keep pushing this, I'm going to piss Dad off even more. He already wants to send me

*back to Doctor Hirsch. But maybe if I can get Dad
proof that I'm right, he'll see for himself.*

Kayla's frustration with herself and her suspicions about Emma intensified as she ticked off the list of Emma's strangeness.

How she got all superembarrassed about being on TV. Then there were those words Kayla had memorized from Emma's hidden journal: *"No one knows the truth about me, that I—"*

Then how Emma practically went into shock when Dad said his new book was on a case in Eternity; then her nightmare the other night…

Wait. Back up. That could be it.

Kayla stopped, reached back to remember the time in the kitchen when she came upon Emma looking at a news story on her computer about the anniversary of some murders, and how she reacted like she'd been caught at something.

The only words Kayla saw in the headline were *anniversary* and *killers.*

Hmm. Let's add some new search terms.

Kayla began searching with a few new words. A headline came up and her eyes widened as she began reading.

It was such an awful story. But there was nothing connecting Emma to it. Her name wasn't mentioned. Besides, it happened in Canada, and she was from Maryland. Maybe it was about a relative…

I can't stand this.

* * *

With Tug in tow, Kayla went to the kitchen to get a drink from the fridge.

Emma was at the counter, wearing her glasses, looking at her laptop. Kayla glimpsed something about Manitoba on the screen.

If that isn't a sign, Kayla thought.

"Emma, can we talk?"

Emma sat up, removed her glasses. "Sure."

"You said I could ask you anything, right?"

Emma's face tightened a little as if bracing, as she nodded.

"I was just curious why you got all, I don't know, like shy and embarrassed about being on TV during the book sale, then again with the story about saving your student?"

"Guess I'm just not comfortable with the attention."

"But you knew my dad was a famous guy when you dated and got married, that media stuff sort of comes with the territory."

"That's true. But I married him because I love him. I knew he guarded his privacy. A lot of famous people keep their family lives private."

Kayla pondered the label of the drink she was sipping.

"Do you have any family or friends in Manitoba?"

"What? No. Why in the world would you ask me that?"

Kayla nodded to Emma's screen. Emma followed her focus.

"That? Well, it's because that's where your Dad is. I was looking it up."

"How come you seemed so upset at dinner when Dad first told us he was going to write about a murder in Eternity?"

Emma's face flushed.

"I don't think it was about—" Kayla used air quotes "—'swallowing something the wrong way.' Actually, to me, it seemed like you really didn't want him to do that story."

Emma was silent.

"And—" Kayla sipped her drink "—you seemed surprised when I glimpsed that headline you were looking at a while back right here in the kitchen, before Dad ever even said he was going to write about that case."

Kayla set down the bottle, pulled her phone from her pocket, typed a few commands, then held the screen out to Emma, showing her the headline and op-ed story.

Anniversary Of Murders Nears; Where Are The Killers Now?

"This one, about the murders in Eternity, about those skull girls, wasn't it?"

Emma was silent for a moment, then Kayla started reading the story out loud, at which point Emma waved her hands. "Kayla, stop, please. Sure, that story's about Eternity, but it was not the story I was looking at that time in the kitchen. That was something else, for school."

"Really?"

"Yes."

"It wasn't this story, about the Eternity murders?"

"No, sweetheart, it wasn't. You're confusing things. Yes, the truth is, something about the case in Canada that Ben's working on reminded me of my own life, and other things, and it saddened me."

"Speaking of your past," Kayla said. "I can't find anything anywhere about a fatal fire twenty years ago at Tony's Diner in Beltsville, Maryland, where you said your mom died."

Emma blinked.

"Well, it might've been called Anthony's Diner, or Anthony's Grill. I know it kept changing hands. Mom called it Tony's."

As Kayla assessed Emma's answers, Emma stared into Kayla's eyes, softening her voice. "I know you're struggling to accept me. I know how after your mom died, it was just you and your dad against the world. Then I came along and invaded your life. I know it's hard for you. Listen to me— I'm not replacing your mom. I'm not an imposter and I'm not hiding anything. I love you."

Kayla stared at her, and suddenly Emma's attention flicked to the large glass doors that opened to the patio, the pool and the night. Then she looked at the oak cutlery block holding a set of big stainless steel knives.

Emma took one, held it tight in her hand.

Kayla caught her breath, never taking her eyes from Emma or the knife.

Tug barked, then ran to the patio doors, where he barked louder.

Emma followed, gripping the knife.

"What is it?" Kayla asked.

Something in the back had tripped the security system's motion detector, activating extra lighting. The pool and backyard were lit up as Emma stepped outside with Tug.

Tug trotted to the dense shrubs, growling.

Emma searched the darkness beyond the lights. She could feel eyes on her before returning to the house, where Kayla was on her phone.

"Who're you calling?"

"Our security company," Kayla said. "They're dispatching people."

Ten minutes later, two cars with First Pacific Sentry Security logos arrived, lights flashing. The two officers, both barely older than Kayla, wearing police vests with company insignias, used powerful flashlights to sweep the backyard and the perimeter of the property. Then they checked the house and the home system.

"Could've been a coyote from the park that triggered the sensors," the guard with the tag Hawkley on his vest said. "We've had a few coyote reports last couple days. Trash and loose food draws 'em in. Make sure all your garbage containers are secure. All clear now. Good night, folks."

After thanking them and locking up, then checking the locks again, Emma returned to the kitchen.

"It's been a long day," Emma said. "We'll finish talking another time. I'm going to bed."

"Sure, whatever," Kayla said, without looking from her phone.

Upstairs, in her bed, hours went by with Emma unable to sleep. She was assailed with thoughts of Kayla's questions, her fear that she was getting closer to the truth, and her stomach knotted.

The knife in her hand brought it all back—the screaming, the blood.

Ben was in Eternity and the truth was rising to the surface.

Sixty-Two

Ben stepped into the elevator at 201 Portage, got off on the twenty-second floor, walked into the reception area of Levitt, Rhodes and Bristol Law Firm and asked for Ian Bristol.

"Please have a seat, Mr. Grant. He's on a call. I'll let him know you're here." The receptionist indicated the sofas by the wall lined with law books and a large aquarium.

Glimpsing the colorful tetras, rainbows and killifish floating tranquilly, Ben set his briefcase aside. After landing the previous day, he'd rented a car and checked into a Holiday Inn. Before he made the drive to Eternity, he first wanted to meet the lawyers who'd represented Girl A, Girl B and Girl C, as they were known to the court.

All three attorneys were in Winnipeg. Two were still practicing. All three had agreed, albeit with some reluctance, to meet with Ben individually.

He checked his phone. His service was fine in Canada—he had no pressing messages.

"Mr. Grant. Ian Bristol."

Ben stood and took the extended hand of a man about his height, midfifties, shaved head and a salt-and-pepper Van Dyke. Bristol led him to his plush, dark wood office with the view of the city. They sat on opposite leather chairs.

"Welcome. When did you get in?"

"Yesterday."

"Direct flight?"

"No, L.A. to Calgary, then here."

"All right, let's get to it. You'd like me to reflect on the case for your book?"

"Yes."

"I hesitate to do that for several reasons. First, I'm still bound by lawyer-client privilege."

"I understand, but the case concluded years ago."

"True, but given the age of my client at the time, many aspects of it remain protected, and will remain protected, under our young offender legislation law, now called our *Youth Criminal Justice Act*, to be precise. Moreover, my hands are tied. But believe me, there are a lot of things I'd like to tell you about how that whole thing unfolded."

"Such as?"

Bristol smiled. "I just can't."

Ben nodded. "I understand. Look, I'm trying to locate the girls. I don't even have their names—"

"Because they're still protected," Bristol said.

"Yes, I get that, but could you get word to your

client on my behalf that I'd like to interview her for the book, as a biographer of the case? Her true name would be kept confidential, in keeping with the law."

"I would if I could. But after her sentence was completed, she no longer stayed in contact with me. She had no reason to. I believe she changed her name and left the country."

Ben sighed and nodded.

Reading his disappointment, Bristol said: "Ben, I'm sorry. Look, you just arrived in Manitoba and you're going to be here for a while, right?"

"Yes."

"All right, I have your contact information. If I can think of ways to help you, I'll be in touch. Fair enough?"

"Sounds good."

"I am a fan of your work." Bristol pointed to several of Ben's hardcovers on the bookshelf.

"Thanks."

Shield and Sanctuary Legal Services was located in the Polo Park area of the city.

The nonprofit agency, which provided help for low-income clients, had its office in a redbrick professional building, sandwiched between an insurance broker and a dental clinic. Next to the building was a gas station, a liquor store and pet food store.

"Are you sure I can't get you a coffee, Mr. Grant?"

"No, thank you."

Belinda Walker, one of the girls' lawyers, was friendly. In her sixties, the lines time had etched around her eyes and mouth vanished when she smiled. But her hair, now streaked with gray, tied in a taut ponytail, conveyed her seriousness in response to Ben's request for cooperation. Seated behind her desk with its neat stacks of files, Walker steepled her hands.

"You must appreciate that there is little I can say to help you."

"So I gather."

"It was a complex case, a disturbing case. I have thoughts about it that I would love to share with you but the law prevents me from doing so."

"That being said, couldn't you even help me off-the-record with some insights, some direction?"

Walker touched her fingers to her lips and thought. "Their criminal records and personal information have been sealed. I know their fingerprints and DNA are in databases," she said. "However, you could get the trial transcripts. That's public record. You have to pay the copying fees."

"Yes, thank you. I've made a request for the transcripts."

"Still, that won't tell you the whole story, the real story."

"The real story?"

Walker began shaking her head at the memory of it all. "It's very complicated. Let me think more about it, and I'll get back to you if I can help."

Ben thanked her. Then, before leaving, his request for Walker's help to locate her client was met with the same response he got from Bristol.

"I have no idea where she is now, or who she is. I'd heard rumors that after completing their sentences the girls moved to Australia, or the UK or the US. Who knows? They're free women now, free to live their lives and do as they choose."

Ben's next meeting was in Assiniboine Park.

Ed Tracy, the last of the girls' lawyers, lived in a condo overlooking the park.

"Not much I can tell you but we can meet," Tracy had said in his emailed response, giving Ben a time frame and directions to where he'd be.

Now Ben walked along park paths that meandered amid the roses, irises and other flowers, to the fragrant air of the English Garden. He found Tracy was sitting on a bench by the pond.

Ed Tracy no longer practiced law. Now in his eighties, his long white hair spilled under his panama hat. He looked rumpled in his white pants, white shirt, sleeves rolled up, leaning on a cane.

"Mr. Tracy?" Ben said.

Tracy's sad eyes lifted to Ben and he nodded as he sat beside him. "Ben Grant."

The two men shook hands.

"It's beautiful here," Ben said.

"So you want to know about the case?" Tracy's voice was gritty and low and he coughed.

"Sir, I'd welcome any help I could get."

"That's a challenge for us lawyers."

"Today I've been schooled in the laws that bind you to secrecy and protect names and details."

"You've come far for a primer in Canadian criminal justice, Ben."

Ben smiled. "Well I've got a lot of other work to do but, well, I'm getting the sense that there's more to this story than was ever made public."

Tracy looked out to the lush gardens. Hummingbirds flitted from flower to flower everywhere.

"You have good instincts and you write good books," Tracy said. "I don't think any of us, the lawyers for the girls, were satisfied that we'd taken the most effective defense strategy."

"What do you mean?"

"Those girls entered the house to get the money, that's a fact. But then what happened next, what really transpired—well… I think we failed to present an accurate picture for the jury."

"Why's that?"

Tracy looked up and down his cane. "Ben, the answer is fraught with complications and while I'm still breathing, I'm bound to carry all the answers with me to my maker."

"I understand."

"And that won't be long for me."

"What do you mean?"

"Terminal. Doctor gives me one, two months at the most, so your timing is good." Tracy coughed.

"I'm sorry to hear that."

"Don't be. I've had a good life, a privileged life. I miss my wife. She passed five years ago. I've accepted it all."

"I can't thank you enough for coming out here."

"Happy for the company. I just wish I could help you. I really do because this case has weighed on my conscience from the first day."

"Could you help me reach your client?"

Tracy shook his head. "She's long gone into a new life. She never had reason to stay in touch with me. I'm just a reminder of the whole tragic mess."

"I get that."

"But I'll see what I can do. I've got your numbers. I just wouldn't bank on anything."

Ben nodded and enjoyed the garden with Tracy.

Apropos of nothing, the older man said: "How does that bit of Scripture go, from Ecclesiastes? Forgive me, I'll botch it, but something like, 'Vanity vanities. All is vanity. What does man gain by all his toil under the sun? A generation goes, and a generation comes, but the earth abides forever.'"

Ben nodded, reflecting on the quote, then sat with Tracy for several minutes before thanking him. As he made his way out of the park, his phone vibrated with a message from Cecil May in California.

It stopped him cold.

Your book fan, Del Brockway, works with Leo Wicks. They're private investigators.

Ben phoned Cecil. "You think these guys are investigating me?"

"Sure looks that way."

"Your sources tell you why?"

"I haven't got that far yet."

Ben thought a moment. "Could be something related to one of my books. That's happened a couple times before. People trying to prove I got something wrong, trying to discredit me for legal action. Nothing ever came of it."

"But you haven't put out a book for years. Could be something else."

"Like what?"

"I don't know. I'll work on it."

"Keep me posted."

Sixty-Three

In the morning, a woman with dark circles under her bloodshot eyes stared back at Emma from the mirror.

Her head was splitting. She needed coffee.

Watching the kettle boil in the kitchen, Emma fought to control the maelstrom churning around her.

She hated lying, but Kayla was putting things together.

She couldn't have read my journal, though. If she had, she would've asked different questions. And now, Ben's in Eternity exhuming my past. Sooner or later they're going to know. And that shadow at the window—and that guy in the park stalking Ben—or me. Was he a reporter? Last night I felt that something, or someone, was watching me out there.

Emma looked out the window into the brilliant sun reflecting on the tranquil pool.

Steam clouds rose from the kettle, its whistle sounding like a scream.

She covered her face with her hands to steady herself, then made a cup of coffee. Going to the fridge, she discovered they were out of milk.

They were out of a lot of things.

She decided she'd get groceries, right now. Do something normal to clear her head and think.

Emma set a fresh bowl of water and food out for Tug. Kayla was still asleep. She sent her a message, telling her she was going out, got her list and left.

Emma shopped at her local Trader Joe's.

She liked the prices, the quality and the fun atmosphere. And today, she needed it more than ever. But between selecting items on her list, her fears struck like lightning, tormenting her.

Gripping her cart's handle Emma could feel the knife in her hand, her past pulling her back to the horror. She forced the images out of her mind as she went through the checkout line, then pushed her cart through the parking lot to her SUV.

"Hi, Emma."

She stopped. A woman she didn't know appeared between parked cars, standing next to Emma's SUV.

The woman might've been Emma's age, maybe older. She had sunglasses perched atop her head. Was smoking a cigarette, one arm against her chest supporting the other elbow in a posture suggesting she'd been waiting.

"Hello." Emma smiled and moved toward her car.

"You're married to Benjamin Grant, the author, aren't you? I saw you on TV."

Emma lifted the tailgate of her SUV and began transferring the bags from her cart to her vehicle. "Yes."

The woman dragged on her cigarette, blew a smoke stream skyward.

"We know each other, Emma."

Emma grew uneasy. Was this woman one of Ben's readers, another weirdo like the guy in the park?

Be polite, respectful, she told herself as she finished loading her groceries.

"No, I'm sorry. I don't think I know you." Emma closed the tailgate and smiled. "Now, if you'll excuse me."

"Wait. I can prove we know each other." The woman crushed her cigarette under her foot, then held out the object hanging from her neck chain. "I bet this looks familiar?"

"I don't—" Emma shook her head, glimpsed the object and froze.

A skull ring.

Emma's pulse pounded. She fixed her gaze on the stranger with unblinking incredulity until recognition dawned. The woman's face, her features, the same, but ravaged by decades, took Emma hostage, launching her across the years, to the screams, the blood—to Eternity.

"Ahh," the woman said. "There it is, in your eyes. You know me, don't you, *sister*?" She smiled. "I'm Rita now, Rita Purvis."

Emma swallowed and looked around. "I don't know why you're here. But you should go. Go now." She pressed her remote key, it chirped and she started for the driver's door.

Rita blocked it with her body. "You've got a very expensive ride here, Emma. You've got a big fancy house, a very nice life. You're doing very well, aren't you?"

Emma looked at Rita. "Get out of my way."

"Or what? You'll call a cop?" Rita laughed. "We're handcuffed in that regard, aren't we, sister?"

"What do you want?"

"I'll make it quick and simple. Twenty years ago, you betrayed us."

"What?"

"We had a pact and you broke it. Now it's time you made up for it."

"Get away from me."

"Your two sisters aren't doing so well. The years have been agony for us—you have no idea. We want your help."

"We?" Expecting to see another woman, Emma looked around but saw no one. "I don't see anyone else."

"Be assured, both of your sisters have found you and both of us demand compensation for violating our sacred bond."

"Compensation?"

"Your husband, with his books, his movie deals, is worth millions. All we want is one hundred thousand each. That's it."

"What? You're out of your mind! I can't give you a penny."

"Give us the help we need, or everyone will know the truth and your princess life will be over. We know everything about you. Imagine the shame and disgrace for your husband."

A long, intense moment passed with Emma staring at Rita. "Have you been threatening me and my family?"

"Are you listening? We made a pact. We swore a blood oath to share with each other."

"We were stupid kids!"

"It was real! What we did sure as hell was real, and our pact is real, too. So you either share your fortune, or you'll share our pain."

Emma stepped closer to Rita. "Don't threaten me or my family."

The two women stared at each other.

"We're not going to wait. We know how to reach you. And we *will* reach you," Rita said before walking away.

Emma was rooted to the pavement, her heart hammering against her chest, unaware that in the distance the sun glinted on the lens of a camera that had made a video recording of the entire exchange between the two convicted murderers.

Sixty-Four

Slipping from Emma's shaking fingers, the egg carton fell to the floor and splayed open with casualties. Four, to be exact.

Emma stared. *It had to be four broken eggs.*

She'd been putting the groceries away with such fury while processing the incident in the Trader Joe's parking lot, she'd lost her grip. Seeing that girl—the ring, that woman, a ghost from her past —dragging her, and now her family, into a nightmare.

Did it really happen?

Emma wiped the floor vigorously, as if trying to erase an indelible stain, tossed the waste into the disposal.

All these years. After all these years. Why? Why? Why?

Her heart racing, she finished with the groceries, then went to her laptop on the counter and frantically searched for answers, starting with the name Rita Purvis—even though she was unsure of the correct spelling.

Or if that's really her new name now.

It was hopeless. What's the point? There were countless hits.

Are they behind the notes? Were they working with Marisa? What am I going to do? She's extorting me, made contact with me and threatened me. We could be sent back to prison.

Emma would not survive having her past revealed like this. It would destroy her, destroy Ben and Kayla.

Emma stared at her phone.

She could call the police. But was the no-contact condition even enforceable here in the US? What about the Canadian Consulate in Los Angeles? She looked it up. The Consulate General of Canada was on South Hope Street. She could go there, request a confidential meeting, explain that Rita Purvis contacted her, threatened her. Demand they arrange to have Rita arrested quietly, make it all go away, for her family's sake—for their safety.

But the risk of this leaking out was too great. Police always tip reporters. The connection to Ben would make a sensational story, with overwhelming consequences.

Rita said "we" want a hundred thousand dollars each, but Emma didn't see the other skull sister, whatever she was calling herself now. Where was she?

Her laptop chimed with a notification of a new

email. The subject read Your Answer? She didn't recognize the sender.

Yes or no, sister? was all the email said.

Shaking with rage, Emma typed a response.

I'M NOT PAYING YOU ANYTHING! STAY AWAY FROM ME AND MY FAMILY!

Emma pressed Send then thrust her hands into her hair.

"I won't pay. I can't," she said aloud.

"Can't pay what?"

Kayla was standing in the doorway.

Emma's face turned ashen. She'd forgotten about Kayla.

Kayla surveyed Emma, her computer, then Emma again. "What's going on?"

Emma cupped her face with her hands and took a breath. "There are things I have to take care of."

"What things? Can't pay who? See? This is why I feel like you're hiding something from me and my dad, Emma."

"I'm not hiding anything, sweetheart. It's complicated financial stuff and it's a little upsetting, that's all."

Kayla assessed Emma again.

"Financial stuff, really?" Kayla said. "Okay, Emma, but frankly, you look terrified."

Sixty-Five

Eternity, Manitoba, Canada
Present day

The stench of death hung in the air.

"That's the slaughterhouse, still in full opera-tion." Bill Jurek, Eternity's police chief, pointed a finger from the wheel as his SUV got closer to the railyards. "Not much has changed, still a sad side of town."

Ben, riding in the passenger seat, looked out to the decaying houses and run-down low-rise apart-ments before Jurek stopped in front of a duplex with curled shingles and worn frame panels that cried out for paint.

"One of the girls lived here with her mother. The unit to the right."

Ben got out, taking stock of the mournful-looking half of a house. Standing there, he con-sidered the news stories he'd read on the case. He imagined the life of the young girl growing up here, breathing in the stink of the killing operation nearby, enduring the clunking and clanging of the trains, feeling trapped in a prairie prison, resentful of those more fortunate, all of it boiling under the surface until something exploded.

He took photos and made notes before returning to the SUV, his thoughts flashing to California.

Upon arriving in Eternity from Winnipeg earlier that day, he'd received a message from Kayla saying their home alarm had gone off; that maybe someone was in their backyard; how the security people dismissed it as an animal. Ben had sent a message to Emma, who'd assured him that everything was fine. But he considered Cecil May's revelation about private investigators and was uncertain what to make of it all.

For a moment, he wished he was home. But he set his worry aside when he met with Jurek, who'd agreed to show him important locations in the case. "You bet, I'll give you the twenty-five-cent tour of Eternity," he'd said.

Now, after leaving the duplex where the first killer had lived, they didn't go far before they rolled into a neighborhood of small houses and mature shade trees. The air was better here. Most of the homes had well-tended lawns, pretty flower beds. Then Jurek parked in front of a bungalow that had fallen into disrepair. It looked abandoned. Neglected, uncut grass and weeds grew wild in the front yard. A sun-faded For Rent sign peeked from the corner of a cracked picture window.

"Another one of the girls lived here with her parents," Jurek said.

Ben got out. He stepped through the overgrowth around the property, surveying the house, the yard, gaining a sense of the desperation the young girl who'd lived here must've felt before succumbing to the evil in her troubled heart.

As he took photos and notes, he noticed the curtains move at a neighboring house and sensed he and Jurek were being watched.

Ben planned to come back later, to all the addresses, to talk to neighbors. Given that most people in small towns stayed put, he figured his chances were good that a lot of the same people were living here at the time of the murders.

"On to the next one," Jurek said.

Jurek drove through several more streets, taking them south of the railyards to a group of apartment buildings.

"This is the White Spruce Estates. Used to be three, now there are five buildings, mostly people on assistance. We get a lot of calls to The Estates." Jurek nodded to the second building. "The third girl lived there with her mother and her mother's boyfriend. The second-floor corner. To the left. That's where we arrested her."

Ben looked at the apartment from the car. A handful of little girls were playing jump rope in front. Ben likened the rope slapping the sidewalk to the pressure increasing in the young killer's mind before she lost control. He took a few pictures and notes.

"How about some coffee before we move on?" Jurek said.

* * *

As they drove across town, Ben reflected on his meetings with the lawyers in Winnipeg. How they were reticent while hinting that the full story of the case was unknown.

I've got to dig deeper into that.

"All right, here we go," Jurek said as he parked the SUV.

Mary's Prairie Kitchen, a cozy downtown diner, smelled like cooked bacon, had a checkerboard floor, swivel stools at the counter and high-back vinyl booths. A woman in her fifties brought them coffee.

"Who's your friend, Bill?"

After Jurek introduced Ben and explained why he was in Eternity, she rested one fist on her hip and looked him over.

"Come to think of it, I think I saw you on TV once."

"That may well be." Ben sipped some coffee. "This is good."

"So you're going to do a book on those girls?"

Ben nodded as he lowered his cup.

"Those little monsters got off easy for what they did," she said.

"You think so?"

"Everybody does. Did you know they killed more than four people?"

Ben threw a glance to Jurek.

"I'm talking about their mothers," the woman said. "All three women died not long after. Let's see." The woman counted on her fingers. "Accident, cancer, suicide. But I tell you it was the murders. They were too much for them. And every one of the women buried in the same cemetery as the people their daughters killed. The whole mess left a scar on Eternity. Put that in your book. Now, what can I get you, or is it just the coffee?"

"Well," Ben said, "would you happen to know the names of the girls?"

The woman's face whitened. "I do. But we're not supposed to say. There are laws protecting their identities—isn't that right, Bill?"

"It is."

"Yeah, well it's been twenty years and I say, damn it to hell, I'll give you their first names, Janie, Nikki and Marie." She glanced at Jurek. "Gonna arrest me, Bill?"

"Need a formal complaint." Jurek turned to the window.

"Thank you," Ben said to the woman, noting the names.

"You didn't get that from me." Jurek smiled.

A half hour later, before they left the diner, Jurek checked with his office again, made calls, then turned to Ben.

"Lou Sloan's on her way back from Brandon to Winnipeg and she's got time to swing down here and meet us at the Tullocks' house."

Sixty-Six

Eternity, Manitoba
Present day

Ben was surprised that he was going to see Louella Sloan, the RCMP's lead investigator on the case.

In her last message to him, Lou, now a superintendent, had indicated a meeting was unlikely because she was busy preparing for a six-month assignment with Interpol in Lyon, France.

"I put in a good word for you." Jurek winked. "Lou made some adjustments, the timing worked, so there you go."

The Tullock property on Old Pioneer Road was not that far from town and not far from the streets where the girls lived.

"So they walked to the Tullock place that night," Jurek said, giving Ben a timeline of events. "First, they finished off their vodka by that grove." He stopped, pointed. Ben made notes. Then Jurek resumed heading down the winding tree-lined driveway, just as he had that awful day.

"The Tullock family still owns the house. Don't ask me why. They rent it, usually to executives. It's empty at the moment. They gave me permission to show you around."

It was a beautiful house. The grounds were meticulously maintained. A solitary sedan was parked in front of the four-car garage. Jurek stopped beside it and a woman got out and greeted them.

She was in her late fifties, Ben guessed, with short gray hair, wearing jeans and a polo shirt.

"Lou Sloan," she said as she shook Ben's hand.

"Thank you for making time for me."

"Not a problem. But I want to be clear." Quick, sharp eyes drilled into his from behind her frameless glasses. "Whatever I say is not to be attributed to me. Don't use my name in your book."

"I understand."

"I can point you places but much of this case is still sealed and protected. As for Bill—" she smiled at him "—he can take care of himself."

"I sure can."

Resuming with the timeline, Jurek led them along the side of the house toward the pool in the rear, but stopped at a basement window.

"The girl who babysat and claimed the Tullocks owed her money left this window unlocked prior to that night."

They returned to the front door, Jurek unlocked it and they entered.

The air smelled of cleaner. The house was unfurnished. Light streamed through the windows. *As quiet as a mausoleum*, Ben thought.

"The family arrived home early," Sloan said. "The girls used steak knives from the kitchen to attack the parents downstairs here."

Ben shook his head, then took pictures and made notes.

"Connie died in hospital later," Sloan said.

"In Alden, not far from here," Jurek added.

"Upon witnessing the attacks, the two children, Neal, aged six, and Linda, aged five, fled upstairs," Sloan said.

Jurek led Ben and Sloan up to the next floor following the path of the murderers, leading them to a bedroom closet.

"They chased Neal and Linda, killing them here," Sloan said.

Ben nodded as he took photos and made notes.

"You can get it all in the autopsy reports and court transcripts," Sloan said. "They're not sealed."

Jurek led them to the hall and touched his fingertips to the wall.

"Here they wrote 'Kill Them All' with the blood of the victims," he said.

Ben took a breath and let it out slowly, took another picture.

Jurek led them to the basement, showing Ben how the girls fled, going back to the basement window.

Back to the main floor at the inside entrance, all three looked around the empty house and let several funereal moments pass in silence before Jurek spoke.

"Two of Roy's employees, Marv Lander and

Fran Penner, made the discovery," he said. "Dustin Meyer was the first officer on the scene. He's with Vancouver city police now. I can connect you with everyone."

After another few moments, they stepped outside into the sun.

"People actually rent this place?" Ben said. "Aren't there disclosure laws?"

"Not for murder," Jurek said. "Most people are from out of the province, even the country. They're told there were deaths here but they fall in love with the place. Rumor is that when the last family learned the grisly details, the mom had nightmares and that's why they cleared out."

"I can understand that," Ben said.

"I don't mind telling you," Jurek said, "I will never ever be able to shut out the images of Roy, Connie, Neal and Linda, how we found them."

Ben turned to Sloan: "And how about you?"

Biting her lip, she shook her head and looked at the horizon. "I carry it with me every day."

Then Ben said: "I talked to the lawyers for the girls and get the feeling that the whole story about what happened here has never been told."

Jurek and Sloan shot him icy stares.

"Those lawyers," Sloan started. "They tried all kinds of strategies, concocting the self-defense thing. They tried cutthroat defense, pointing fingers at who was responsible for what, as a way to clear each other. That didn't work. The fact was their fingerprints were on the knives, in the Tullocks' blood, their clothes were stained with the

Tullocks' blood and we had a journal containing threats to kill Connie."

Jurek nodded. "The case against them was solid."

"And they were released in their twenties to start new anonymous lives without anyone knowing about their pasts," Sloan said.

"But they did their time under the law," Ben said.

"They did," Sloan said. "But listen, Ben, I was there for much of the trial, the sentencing and their release. A lot of experts debated the findings of the correctional psychologists and caseworkers."

"What do you mean?"

"Any or all of the girls could've hoodwinked the court into believing they were fully rehabilitated. It could have been just an act, and it's possible that whatever disturbing forces they had that drove them to do what they did will never go away and that they could kill again."

Sixty-Seven

Eternity, Manitoba
Present day

That evening a gum-chewing server at the Tel-Star Café brought Ben his order—a club sandwich, which was good.

After eating alone and watching the sunset, he walked across the street to the Snowberry Motel, where he'd checked in earlier. A Good Night's Sleep at a Great Rate, the motel sign promised. His room was spacious, clean and quiet. As night fell, he worked, studying his research material, re-reading his newest notes and creating new files in draft form while thinking about the case.

The lawyers had indicated that the full story of the murders hadn't been told, while the investigators held that the case was solid, suggesting the girls, now women, were free to possibly kill again.

Where are these women now? What's become of them? I need to find them, talk to them.

To do that, Ben needed their full names, which were sealed. He already had their first names. He'd talk to people, check property records of the addresses, school records, whatever he could. There were ways to get the names and sooner or later, he'd have them. He'd get photographs, too, to see what the faces of the young killers looked like then compared to what they look like now. If he could find them and they agreed to be interviewed.

Ben's neck and shoulder muscles ached. He took a hot shower. After pulling on a T-shirt and sweats, he thought of Kayla and Emma, stirring his worry. He considered calling home but he was exhausted and got into bed.

Lights off, room lit only by the glow of his laptop on his chest, Ben swiped through the photos he'd taken that day: the places where the Skull Sisters lived, the smell of the slaughterhouse; the Tullock property, smelling of cleaner, silent, empty of life, with nothing visible to betray the outrage that had descended on the family.

He'd see that tomorrow.

He was meeting Roy Tullock's brother and his wife at the cemetery.

The next morning, Ben was back at the Tel-Star Café having breakfast and reading notes about how the Skull Sisters had taken on new names.

He went online to read up on the laws and the process used to legally change a person's name in Manitoba when his phone rang.

It was Kayla. Ben checked the time difference. She was up early.

"Hi, honey."

"Dad, when are you coming home?"

"Home? I just got here. What is it? Is everything all right?"

"No." Her voice trembled. "Tug's missing. We can't find him."

Ben took a moment, glanced around. No one was near.

"He probably ran off. You know he does that sometimes."

"We looked everywhere, up and down the street, asked the neighbors."

"I'm sure he'll come home."

Kayla said nothing.

"Is there something else?" Ben asked. "Is this about the alarm going off? You're sure the security people did a good check and found nothing?"

"Yes. We saw them looking everywhere. They said they had other calls about coyotes."

"Tug could've run off to chase a coyote. Look for him in the park."

"It's not just Tug—it's Emma. She's been acting strange. Talking to herself about not being able to pay."

"What?"

"I asked her and she said she had to take care of some complicated financial things that were upsetting."

"That makes no sense."

"Then I told her to her face that I think she's hiding something from us."

"You said that to her?"

"Yes, Dad, I did."

"Why did you do that, Kayla?"

"Dad, please don't be mad at me but the other day I found her reading stories about Eternity and—"

"That's because I am here, Kayla."

"No, Dad, this was before you decided to do a book there. And the other day I was in your bedroom closet and—"

"What the hell, Kayla? Were you going through her things?"

"Don't be mad. I found something that I'm pretty sure proves she's hiding something from us."

Ben took in an exasperated breath and let it out. "My God, Kayla, you shouldn't have been invading her privacy!" Ben stopped, struggled to find the words. "Honey, listen to me. I want you to go back to Doctor Hirsch."

"But I just know something's not right, Dad."

"Listen to me. I can't do anything about this while I'm here. But when I get my book work sorted, we're going to set up an appointment schedule with Doctor Hirsch."

Kayla said nothing.

"So I want you to promise me you'll stop this, that you'll stop accusing Emma and remember that she loves you and I love you. All right?"

Kayla was still quiet.

"All right, Kayla? I love you."

After a moment, Kayla said: "All right, Dad. I love you, too."

After hanging up, Ben dragged both hands over his face.

"You look like you could use more coffee." The server smiled, then topped off Ben's cup.

He thanked her, drank some. He checked the time, steeled himself and then called Emma. She answered before the third ring.

"I'm sorry I didn't call sooner. I just got right into the work."

"It's okay," she said.

"So how're you doing? How're things there?"

"Tug's missing."

"Yes, Kayla called me. Look in the park on the trail, there's a spot—"

"The place where Brooke used to go?"

"That's right."

"That's not all Kayla told you, is it, Ben?" Emma said.

"She said you were acting weird, like you're hiding something that you don't want to tell us about."

Now Emma was silent.

"I think…" He softened his voice. "I think my absence has made it even more difficult for Kayla. Maybe we should cancel the vacation and I'll fly straight home when I'm done here and we'll get her to see Doctor Hirsch. What do you think?"

"That might be for the best."

"Good. I'm glad you agree. I think she needs a little help, and I'm out of my depth. The timing of this whole thing… I feel so guilty."

"You shouldn't. You have no control over it."

"Maybe so," he said. "Another thing—that message you sent me about 'whatever happens'? What did you mean by that?"

Emma let a moment pass. "Just that… I guess we've all been a little stressed lately and I wanted you to know that, whatever happens, I love you."

A few seconds went by with thoughts blazing across Ben's mind: Emma's concerns about him writing about the Skull Sisters, the private investigator in the park, Kayla's refusal to accept Emma, and Hirsch's observations.

Pushing it all aside, Ben said, "I love you, too."

Sixty-Eight

Cielo Valle, Orange County, California
Present day

After her call with Ben, Emma knocked softly on Kayla's door.

"What is it?"

"I'm going to the park to search for Tug."

No response. Nothing for a few seconds, then the door opened.

"No, I'll go," Kayla said. "I know where to look."

"I know too, sweetheart. And I think your dad would prefer if you stayed here in case Tug comes home. I know you just spoke with him."

Staring at Emma, Kayla sorted through several thoughts before brushing past her and going down to the kitchen, noticing a backpack on the counter.

"What's that?"

"Dog treats, bottled water and a small bowl, in case I find him. I expect he'll be thirsty and hungry."

"Okay." Kayla went to the kitchen closet. "Take

this." She held up a can of pepper spray. "If you see a coyote."

"Thanks," Emma said, before offering Kayla a little smile of surrender. "I'm sorry so much is happening."

Kayla looked at her, then said, "Just find Tug. I'll wait here."

Walking the few blocks in their neighborhood to Suntrail Sky Park, Emma's problems consumed her.

There was no way she could give in to Rita Purvis's demand. Still, Emma believed their threat to expose her past was real.

I can't let it happen—the scandal, the headlines, it would disgrace Ben, devastate Kayla, and that would destroy me. *I won't let it happen.*

She entered the park, took the trail along the grassy hills and brushwood, found a branch to use as a walking stick and began calling out, "Tug! Tug!"

Kayla was torn. Her heart told her that she should be looking for Tug in the park, at the spot where they scattered her mom's ashes.

Holding back her tears, Kayla whispered a prayer.

Tug, please be safe and please come home.

Kayla checked her phone. Still no response from the college.

What's taking them so long? They could have

the proof I need for Dad to take off his love-blinders and see Emma's been lying to him.

Right now, Kayla had to seize the opportunity she had, being in the house alone, because she was close, so close, to finding out what Emma was hiding from them.

Dad needs more proof and I'm going to get it.

She went in search of Emma's journal.

"Come on, Tug! Tug, come on!"

Emma climbed the twisting path along the rising slope. Deep in the park now, she was suddenly wary of that strange fan of Ben's—Del Brockway—who'd practically stalked them here.

Could Brockway be tied to Marisa and the notes? Could he be helping Rita in extorting me?

She couldn't let herself get overwhelmed. That's not going to help.

What was that noise?

Emma stopped. Held her breath. It sounded like a bark. Faint. Distant.

"Tug! Tug!"

Rooted in place, Emma listened. Another bark. Closer this time.

She didn't know if it was Tug, but she moved in the sound's direction calling for him, stopping to listen. For a minute, maybe more, she picked up the pace, repeating her call, then stopped and listened again.

She heard metallic tinkling, then panting, then she saw him trotting toward her on the trail.

"Tug!"

Kneeling down, Emma took him into her arms, welcoming his happy licking.

"Where have you been?"

He nuzzled her hand for the cookie. Giving it to him, she slid off her pack, poured water into a bowl for him.

She was thinking of texting Kayla when a tiny glint at Tug's neck drew her attention. Running her fingers along his neck, she found his tab key —and something else.

It was new, round, attached to the dog tag clip of Tug's leather collar.

A skull ring.

Ice coiled up Emma's back.

Emma unclipped the ring to examine it in her palm. It was a death's head, relatively new. No markings or engravings. Turning it over and over, her heart beat faster, her mind raced through a million horrors.

This is Rita Purvis's ring and it's a message.

Tug jerked his head up, turned toward the forest below. His ears went forward, twitched, and he barked. That's when Emma saw a microflash of yellow in the distance amid the trees.

Barking again, Tug moved closer, alert, his tail wagging, his eyes wide. His mouth was closed as he stood tall.

Emma searched the woods sloping below the ridge.

From somewhere in the darkened forest came a rustling sound. Tug, hackles raised, tail tucked, ears back, barked, then charged into the woods.

"Tug! No! Come back!"

Emma thrust her hand into her backpack, pulled out the pepper spray and a serrated knife she'd packed from the kitchen. With the spray in one hand, the knife in the other, she hurried down into the steep sloping forest after Tug.

Following the jingle of his collar and his panting, she navigated through the trees, branches slapping and pulling on her as she continued going about thirty yards down the slope.

Then she screamed.

Sixty-Nine

Eternity, Manitoba
Present day

Am I making a mistake?

Should I drop everything and fly home?

Ben drove across town beset by how Kayla's refusal to accept Emma into their lives fueled her suspicions that Emma was hiding something.

Am I missing something? Am I being a fool?

He glanced at his briefcase and contemplated flying home, while at the same time thinking how he'd just gotten started on his research, how he'd set up so many things, how badly he needed to work on this book, for so many reasons.

No, he couldn't go back to California. Not yet.

Then he thought of Cecil May, looking into the private investigators from the park for him. Ben pulled over, sent Cecil a text.

What's the status on Brockway and Wicks?

When he didn't get a response he continued driving.

Eternity's cemetery was in a windswept part of town. Wheeling through the stone gates of the entrance, Ben looked out to the lush green lawns dotted with tall willows, maples and poplars. He found Section B, spotted a shiny Mercedes-Benz waiting off to the side and parked behind it. A man and woman in their early seventies got out and greeted him.

"Ben Grant," Ben said.

"Paul Tullock." The man took Ben's hand in a firm grip. "My wife, Lynn."

When she took Ben's hand, he said, "Thank you for meeting me."

"We reached Torrie," Paul said. "I'm sorry but she doesn't wish to participate in the book."

"I understand."

"All of this has been especially painful for her," Lynn said.

"I can appreciate that."

"This way," Paul said, and led Ben to a grave site shaded by a tall maple. It was modest, marked with three rose-colored granite headstones. In the center, a companion stone bore the names: Royston Jackson Tullock and Constance "Connie" Tullock. A smaller separate stone was to the immediate right with the name Neal Jackson Tullock and a similar stone to the left with the name Linda Constance Tullock. Each stone had a cross and roses on the front. Each showed the Tullocks' birth dates and each bore the same date of death. Fresh flowers were at the base of each stone.

Ben held up his camera, as a way of asking permission to photograph the site. The Tullocks nodded.

"We wanted to talk here, Ben," Paul said, "so you'd have an understanding of the toll taken on our family."

"I remember the day we buried them like it was yesterday," Lynn said. "Four caskets, two of them small. I never got over the fact that the children had witnessed their parents' murders. In some ways it gave me peace of mind that they didn't have to live with it for the rest of their lives."

"My brother was a good man. Everyone in town loved and respected Roy. He worked hard to build his enterprise and it was taking off." Paul shook his head.

"Torrie had been getting better," Lynn said, "and was looking forward to being with her family again when this happened. It changed everything. They stole everything from her. It changed her into a sad, solitary person."

Taking notes, Ben pushed aside his own emotions. Standing there in a cemetery, he suddenly felt the anguish of the guilt he carried for his wife's death. There are things in this world that are impossible to forgive.

If only I'd taken care of Brooke's tires like she'd asked me to do.

He glanced around at the lake of headstones,

thinking how there was no stone for his wife in California. Brooke never wanted that.

I'll be with you wherever you are.

That's what Brooke had said whenever they had talked about death, never once believing it would happen until they'd each lived to 100. But now, standing here working again, touched by the gentle breeze, Ben felt Brooke's presence, felt her guiding him.

Keep going. Keep working on your book. Finish what you've started.

"The girls who did this," Ben said, "were fourteen at the time. It's been some twenty years. Have you forgiven them?"

Paul pursed his lips, blinking fast and looked away.

"Those girls," Lynn said, "were evil masquerading as human teens. They were released to start over, given new lives." Lynn pointed to the stones. "Our family didn't get a second chance. So our answer is no. We can never forgive them."

Ben took notes. "I understand that the mothers of the girls died and are buried here, as well," he said.

Paul's jaw clenched. "We fought it back then," he said. "Hired lawyers to lobby the town council to prevent burial here or move their graves. Offered to donate land at the edge of town for another cemetery but we lost that fight because some on council said the mothers had no role in the crime and should not be stigmatized for it."

"So they remain here?" Ben cast around.

"Yes."

"I apologize, but I had to ask."

"I'll show you where their graves are but I won't set foot on them," Paul said. "Give me your notepad."

Paul drew a map to the sites, then pointed.

"Thank you. I just need to get pictures and I'll be right back."

The graves weren't far. Ben walked past ponds, flower gardens and benches and found headstones for Nancy Alice Gorman, Florence Dolores Mitchell and Marlene Judith Klassyn.

But he didn't know who their respective daughters were.

After taking pictures and writing the names down, he returned to the Tullocks.

"Did you get them?" Paul said.

"Yes, thank you," Ben said. "Again my apologies for doing this now. But it's part of my work and, well, it would help my research, my effort to be as accurate as possible, if I had the full names of the girls. I know there's a publication ban, there are laws protecting them, but since their mothers' names are in full public view, I was wondering if you knew the girls' names and could share them with me? I won't have to say where I got them. I'm sure everyone in town knows them and I will get them eventually."

Paul and Lynn exchanged looks.

"Those names are burned into our memories," Lynn said. "We'll never be able to erase them. And the way we see it, they don't deserve to be protected. Not anymore. Give me your notes, Ben."

In clear block letters Lynn printed:
NICOLA HOPE GORMAN
MARIE LOUISE MITCHELL
JANE ELIZABETH KLASSYN

Seventy

Cielo Valle, Orange County, California
Present day

Still alone in the house, Kayla searched with renewed intensity because she knew she was close to answers.

She went to the closet in Emma and her dad's bedroom, moved the trunk, lifted the loose panel, turned on her phone's flashlight and raked the hiding spot on the floor. Nothing.

She looked under their bed. Nothing. Under the mattress. Nothing. Emma's nightstand. Nothing. Emma's drawers, sifting through her clothes. Nothing. Back to the closet, checking pockets, clothes, suitcases. Nothing.

In the hallway closet she checked the folds of blankets, towels, washcloths. Nothing. She checked closets with cleaning supplies. Nothing. The laundry room. Nothing.

Emma hadn't returned yet.

Kayla had no idea how much time had passed, or how much longer she could search without risking Emma surprising her again. She continued looking in every room, nook and storage area she could think of. She went to the garage and searched there.

Nothing.

As she stepped back into the house, she heard a noise and stopped dead.

Someone's in the kitchen.

Retreating to the garage, she looked for something, *anything*, to use as a weapon. Spotting a claw hammer on her dad's workbench, she grabbed it, then went back into the house.

Using extreme caution, and with the hammer raised behind her head, she inched her way quietly toward the kitchen. With her free hand, she held her phone, poised to hit 911.

Moving closer to the kitchen, she heard slurping. *Familiar* slurping.

She glimpsed a tail.

Tug lifted his head and barked at her.

"Tug!"

Rushing to him, Kayla dropped to her knees, crushed him in her arms, wrapping him in a happy frenzy of kissing and licking.

"Where'd you go, you stupid dog?" Kayla brushed her tears of joy. "Are you okay?"

Kayla pulled back and in a quick inspection ran her fingers over his head, his coat, checked his pads. All seemed to be in order.

"Are you hungry? Thirsty?"

Tug barked and Kayla went to the counter, put

fresh water in his bowl, then began opening a can of dog food for him.

"Don't ever run away again!"

The back door opened. Emma had returned. Kayla glimpsed her over her shoulder.

"Emma, Tug came home!"

With the open can and wooden spoon in her hand, Kayla turned and stared at Emma, who'd steadied herself against the counter. Blood was trickling from Emma's arm and hand. Scratches bloodied her temple and cheek. Her shirt was torn, streaked with blood and dirt.

"Oh my God! You look like you've been in a fight—what happened? Was it a coyote?"

Kayla put down the can and spoon to pass her a dish towel.

"No. After I found Tug, I tripped and slid down a hill." Emma shifted off the backpack, plopped it on the counter and sat down. Kayla saw the backpack was smeared with dirt, loosened at the opening.

"Are you all right, Emma?"

"Just a few scrapes." She smiled. "I found Tug on the trail near the spot where we expected, but as we got closer to home, he ran ahead of me."

"I saw him alone in the kitchen," Kayla said. "Thought he came home by himself. It's good his collar key still works on his door."

Kayla spooned the food into Tug's bowl, set both down, then took his head in her hands to nuzzle him. "I'm so glad we've got him home."

A long moment passed while Tug ate, and Kayla

turned to Emma and gave her another assessment. "That must've been a nasty fall. I'll get the first aid kit."

"No, no, I'll take care of myself. Just need a bandage or two. I'm fine."

Kayla stared at her for a long time. "You don't look fine, but suit yourself."

"Tug's home safe—that's what matters."

Kayla shook her head slowly, then looked at Tug, nearly done chomping on his meal. Then she looked at Emma.

"All I know is nothing around here is making sense," Kayla said. "Come on, Tug." She led him upstairs to her room.

Alone in the kitchen, Emma reached into her pocket for the ring and pondered it in her shaking hand.

In her room, Kayla got on her phone and wrote her dad a message.

Emma found Tug in the park, like you guessed, but she came home a bloody mess. Says she fell on the trail. She's acting SO STRANGE! WTF Dad?

Kayla knew he didn't like her swearing but if ever there was a time…

Minutes went by without a response from her father. She looked at Tug. Then she threw her arm around him, nuzzled and kissed him. "If only you could talk."

Almost fifteen minutes went by, with Kayla

playing games online and thinking. Deciding her dad must be too busy to respond, she returned with Tug to the kitchen to possibly try to talk to Emma—but Emma wasn't there.

She wasn't in the living room, or Dad's office.

Kayla went to the bottom of the stairs and called up. "Emma?"

No response. The house was so quiet.

Did she go out?

Kayla looked in the garage. Emma's car was there.

Walking through the house, Kayla saw her outside by the pool on a chair and watched her.

Emma appeared to be on her phone texting furiously, then looking toward the hills in the park before covering her face with her hands and sobbing.

Seventy-One

Orange County, California
Present day

Tug was barking the next morning as distant thunder evolved into loud thudding when a helicopter passed over the Grants' house.

Emma and Kayla went out to the back, standing poolside looking to the sky and the lettering on the chopper: Orange County Sheriff.

"Looks like it's headed to the park near the trails," Kayla said after it passed by.

Emma watched it disappear from view.

"What do you think it is?" Kayla said.

"A missing hiker?" Emma said. "I don't know. We should get going."

Taking quick stock of Emma—the bandages on her hands and arms, a small one on her temple, the red scrapes on her cheek and her sober expression—gave rise once again to Kayla's concerns that something was going on with her. Last night she'd texted her dad, updating him on Tug and Emma. But when she had finally heard back from him, it didn't help matters.

Happy Tug came home, he'd replied.

Hope Emma recovers from her fall. Sorry, honey, busy here, got things happening. Love you.

Emma was dropping Kayla off at her school before heading to her own.

They didn't say much to each other on the drive, glancing up as a news helicopter passed overhead toward the park.

Emma had the radio tuned to a soft rock station and was submerged in her thoughts, frequently checking the rearview and side mirrors.

Kayla was on her phone.

They were stopped at a red light when the radio station news began with a breaking story.

"A body has been discovered in Suntrail Sky Park. A spokesperson for the Orange County Sheriff's Office has confirmed that the body was found this morning by a man walking his dog in the park. The park borders the communities of Cielo Valle, Lake Forest and Mission Viejo. No other details have been released."

"Wow," Kayla said. "That's near our place. So that's what all the action is about. Wonder what happened?"

She turned to Emma, who was staring straight ahead when she said, "It's terrible."

After the news, weather and sports, the station played "Spirit in the Sky" by Norman Greenbaum.

By the time the song ended, Emma had stopped in the drop-off area of Kayla's school. Kayla didn't move, her thoughts kept her seated before she turned to Emma and said: "How are you? I mean after that fall... Are you all right?"

"I'll be okay." She gave her a little smile.

"I saw you yesterday by the pool, crying."

"Oh, I had a little pain from the fall."

She took a moment. "No, that's not it. I know you're hiding something and it's starting to freak me out."

Emma looked at her. "Kayla, I'm not hiding anything. We've been over this and I understand why you have trouble accepting me, but we're a family. Okay?"

Kayla pushed back her tears and nodded.

They let a moment pass and ended things with a hug.

"You're going to be late," Emma said. "I'll pick you up later."

"Thanks but I'll get a ride or take the bus."

Checking her mirrors, Emma said: "No, I'll be leaving school early today. I'll pick you up after your last class."

"All right, whatever. Bye."

Kayla got out, took a few steps toward the school doors before she stopped and watched Emma drive away.

She began a text to her dad but abandoned it.

I'm definitely on my own here.

* * *

At Valley Meadow High School, a few people noticed the scrapes on Emma's face as she got on with her morning, meeting with students, taking care of appointments, returning calls, completing reports and evaluations, struggling to focus on her work. At midmorning she went to the teacher's lounge to get an apple from the fridge. The few people there were all watching a breaking TV news story. Orange County Coroner personnel were moving a gurney holding a body shrouded in a sealed bag out of Suntrail Sky Park and loading it into the coroner's van. The camera pulled back to a reporter Emma recognized: Maggie Shen, with KTKT. She was holding a microphone and reporting from the crime scene tape.

"KTKT can confirm the body is that of a woman and sources tell us this is a homicide…" Maggie touched her earpiece connecting her to the news anchor. "No other details are available but we'll continue to follow this story."

Emma slowly lowered herself into a chair. She reached into her pocket to run her fingers over the skull ring.

Seventy-Two

The bell sounded and classes changed.

As Kayla threaded her way through the busy halls from math to history, she checked her phone. A new message had arrived in the Yahoo email account she'd created for BenjaminGrantBooks.

She stopped.

It was from Darmont Hill College in Indianapolis—finally—an attachment of an official letter in response to her request on behalf of her dad. Students bumped into her as she opened and read.

Dear Mr. Benjamin Grant:

I am pleased to provide this document as verification that Emma Anne Chance graduated from Darmont Hill College. She successfully completed all required course-work...

The letter went on detailing Emma's completion date, her being awarded a Master's Degree and her accomplished rank among all students in her graduating class, adding that a transcript would follow in the regular mail. It ended with:

> If you have questions, please feel free to contact me.
> Sincerely
>
> Clinton Parkerfield
> Director of Records

Kayla read the letter a second time, a mixture of confusion and disappointment rippling through her. This was not the result she'd expected.

She covered her mouth with her hand.

This proves that Emma's telling the truth and I was wrong.

But what about the deadly phantom restaurant fire? Maybe it did happen and she'd simply failed to find a record of it. What about Emma's concern about Dad's book and reading stories about an anniversary and killers? And Emma's journal? "No one knows the truth about me"?

Perhaps she had misinterpreted it, and it was nothing more than a personal reflection.

Kayla was jounced by a few more students, then the chaos of the hall subsided, leaving her staring at the message, conflicted.

Maybe Doctor Hirsch is right. It's me. I can't accept Emma because I don't want to be disloyal to Mom.

Seventy-Three

Eternity, Manitoba
Present day

In his motel room on his phone holding for a clerk at Manitoba's Vital Statistics Agency in Winnipeg, Ben was encouraged.

Getting the full names of the Skull Sisters from the Tullocks was a breakthrough.

Having them was critical to determining the killers' new identities and tracking them down.

Wherever the women are living now, I'm going to find them.

Things were coming together fast, Ben thought, as he scrolled through his notes, then clicked on the photos he'd taken. But his concentration shifted to California, Kayla and Emma.

He kneaded the muscles at the back of his neck.

The problems at home weighed on him at the same time things were moving well here with his work. He was making progress. He had to keep going. It was clear from his research so far that the girls had changed their names at some point during their incarceration or after their release.

Ben was familiar with how the process for a legal name change worked, based on the research that went into all of his books. He'd found that the basics were similar in most US states and most countries. A person usually applied to the court in the jurisdiction where they were living, then they provided required documentation and notice of the name change was made public.

But if the names of the killers from Eternity were flagged by the courts, then that would keep their new names secret, he thought.

"Mr. Grant?" The clerk returned to the line.

"Still here."

"Thanks for holding. As for your request, we have no record in the *Manitoba Gazette* for the names you provided."

"Nothing?"

"I'm sorry, nothing, sir. You can search archived editions yourself for free, if you like. They're public. I'm sending you a link now."

"Great, thank you."

Seconds after ending the call, Ben's laptop displayed the page for the *Manitoba Gazette* and the window to search archived government documents and notices.

One at a time, he submitted the names of the girls: Nicola Hope Gorman, Marie Louise Mitchell and Jane Elizabeth Klassyn, going back to the years they would've changed their names. After numerous attempts, he gave up on the database.

Nothing came up. Zip. He'd hit a wall.

They could now be living anywhere. Tapping his forefinger to his lip, Ben realized that he needed help.

He needed Tessa Fox in Washington, D.C.

Ben found her number and called.

He'd hired Tessa to conduct research on a number of his books. Tessa had worked for the FBI, Homeland Security and the NSA. Now retired and living in Georgetown, Tessa was a forensic genealogist. She'd worked on proving identity in cases involving descendants of victims of the *Titanic* and the Holocaust; she'd located fugitive war criminals, assisted investigators finding next of kin in major disasters and cold case crimes. Tessa's expertise and extensive network of colleagues gave her access to an ocean of archives and databases both public and restricted in over fifty countries.

"This one sounds interesting," Tessa said, after he'd explained the case and given her all the details on the girls that he had, including names and approximate year of birth.

"I need to find these women now. You can charge more than your usual rate if you can expedite it."

"That won't be necessary, Ben. We're only talking about a couple of decades. I just finished a contract, so your timing's good. If there are no complications, this shouldn't take me too long. I may have to access a few restricted databases."

"Thank you, Tessa."

"I'll get going on this right away."

* * *

Next, Ben called Manitoba's Justice Department to follow up on his request.

"Yes, Mr. Grant," an official with the department said, "we're arranging to send you court transcripts both printed and in a compressed digital file."

"Thank you, and my other requests?"

"Your request to see evidence in this case, and the journals and other writings of the defendants while they were serving their sentences, is being reviewed. I must again remind you, much of the material remains sealed under court order. However, I've been advised that it's possible that some items may be released. It will require further review."

"Thank you."

Ben ended the call, collected his things and got into his rental car.

Seventy-Four

Eternity, Manitoba
Present day

Ben drove to a neighborhood lined with tall shade trees, stopped at a tidy two-level frame house and knocked on the front door.

Now that he had names, he needed to confirm which girl had lived at which address so that he could learn more about the young killers. Waiting for a response, he looked next door at the run-down bungalow with the unkempt yard and the For Rent sign in the window. He was knocking at the door of the house where he'd seen a curtain move when he was here earlier with Jurek.

Nosy neighbors tended to know things.

Ben was about to knock again when the door was opened by a heavyset woman in her seventies or eighties with white hair piled in a bun. She eyed Ben guardedly.

"I'm not buying anything, mister."

"I'm not selling anything." He smiled. "I'm a writer."

"A writer?"

"Ben Grant." He gave her his business card.

She looked at it. "From California."

"Yes," he said. "Have you lived in this house a long time?"

She raised her chin a little as if to indicate she had an idea why he was here. "Forty years, why?"

"I'm researching a tragic part of Eternity's history."

He let that register, waiting for her reaction.

"You're talking about the Tullock murders."

"I am." He nodded to the bungalow. "I understand that one of the killers lived in that house beside yours. Did you know her family?"

Looking toward the bungalow, cupping her hand to her cheek, she blinked several times as if something long buried had been unearthed. Tears stood in her eyes and she nodded slowly. "Yes, I knew them."

"Would you talk to me for the book I'm writing?"

Turning his card over in her hand, she studied Ben's face for a moment before deciding.

"Show me your driver's license," she said. "So I can see if you are who you say you are."

Ben reached for his wallet and she studied his California license, his photo, reading his address like a traffic cop. "Can't be too sure, you know." She gave it back to him. "Would you like some coffee?"

Her name was Hedda Murdoch. Her house was done up great-grandmother style, doilies under everything, plastic on much of the furniture, the faint smells of soap, cedar and mothballs. Shelves and tabletops were shrines to her family, holding framed photos: a daughter in Chicago, son in Toronto, grandchildren and great-grandchildren. Hedda's husband, Larry, a plumber, had passed away twenty years ago.

"The Mitchells started off as a happy family." Hedda set down two mugs of coffee.

The Mitchells.

Ben made a note that it was Marie Mitchell who'd lived next door and nodded for Hedda to continue.

"Ned operated a tow truck business. Flo was a nice girl, worked part-time here and there but mostly stayed home with the kids. Then their little boy, Pike, died when he was around six."

"How?"

"Choked on an apple. His sister, Marie, was the only one with him when he died. There were rumors."

"What rumors?"

"That Marie killed him because she was jealous."

"What do you think?"

Hedda shook her head. "I don't know. Police called it an accident." She looked off. "Marie was a quiet girl, smart but lonely. Like the other two, Nikki and Janie. The three of them used to be up to no good, shoplifting at the mall or sitting up all night in Ned's RV in the driveway there. One of them babysat for the Tullocks—that's how it started."

Ben nodded as he took notes.

"Most everyone liked Roy Tullock, a rich but kind man. His wife was another story, stuck-up, like she felt she belonged in New York, not Eternity. But I'm not saying they deserved what happened. Lord no."

Hedda shook her head, remembering.

"At first no one believed that those little girls, just fourteen, could do such a thing. Most everybody refused to believe it. I saw them arrest Marie." Hedda stared into her coffee cup. "It just shakes you to your core, you know? Reporters from all over came here when it happened. Then there was the trial, then came the TV crime show people. And always the rumors flew."

"The rumors?"

"That the girls made some sort of Satanic pact. Then there was the rumor that the Tullocks' teenage daughter, Torrie, slipped away from the institute in Winnipeg and came home and killed her family. But the other Tullocks used their money and influence to protect her and avoid the shame it would bring on the family name because it had happened when Roy was making some big business deal."

"Really?" Ben took notes.

"Who knows the truth?" Hedda said. "This is a small town. I'll tell you something I know for sure is true. The murders wrecked Marie's family, too. Flo committed suicide. Ned lost his business, lost his family, just gave up. Last I heard he was living on the streets somewhere."

"What about Marie?" Ben asked. "It's been years since her release. Would you, your family or neighbors know where she's living right now?"

Hedda shook her head.

"Would you have any pictures of Marie and her family, or Marie with the other girls?"

"I had a few but I got rid of them. Don't want to be reminded."

Ben understood, and after finishing his coffee, he got Hedda's number and mailing address. Closing his notebook, he thanked her and explained that if he used her name in the book he'd send her a release to sign.

Because it was near, Ben drove to Eternity's public library.

The librarian got him copies of the school yearbooks he'd requested. They were for the years around the time of the murders, only he never said why he wanted them. Still, the librarian regarded him with a twinge of apprehension.

Alone at a table, he flipped through the albums, typical school yearbooks, filled with head and shoulder shots of students along with pages of sports teams, school clubs, events and trips. Careful to look alphabetically, Ben froze when he came to the *G*'s. Where he should've seen the photo for Nikki Gorman, he found a perfect postage-stamp-sized square hole. Someone had used a razor-sharp knife to remove it. He found the same thing had happened for Janie Klassyn and Marie Mitchell.

Wow. Whether this is to respect the law, or something else, it's like a metaphor for a wound.

Ben took photos of the pages, then checked to get the name of the company that made the school yearbook. It was in Winnipeg. It should have unaltered copies on file. He'd request to buy one.

Or he could track down former classmates.

He took more photos of pages of students and teachers.

Ben then drove to the far side of the railyards to the White Spruce Estates. Figuring it unlikely someone would be living here for more than twenty years, Ben went to the manager's office in the middle building. Sure enough, the superintendent confirmed the longest any tenant had lived in the complex was nine years.

"We got a high turnover," said the man with the toothpick tucked in the corner of his mouth. "If you want to check the records, you gotta call head office in Brandon."

Ben thanked the man, then drove north of the railyards, picking up the smell of the slaughterhouse as he made his way by the dilapidated houses and shabby apartments, stopping at the ramshackle duplex Jurek had shown him. He got out and knocked on the door of the unit attached to where one of the girls had lived.

No answer.

Enduring the stench, Ben leaned on his rental car trying to guess if Janie or Nikki had lived in this unit. He'd have to find out who the landlord was at the time and check rental records. Or he could go to a municipal office and request a search of property records. Ben took out his notebook when his phone rang.

It was Tessa Fox.

"Is this a good time, Ben?"

"It is."

"Got some results for you."

"Already? You're fast."

"I pushed my best contacts, people with high-level clearance and access to restricted databanks, so you must protect your sources, Ben."

"I always do."

"All right, now some of this information goes back a few years so I can't confirm if it's up-to-date. I'm still working on it. I'll send you all the spellings and details in an email but I wanted to share what I've got so far."

"All right."

"Nicola Hope Gorman became Noreen Nicole Gruning and moved to the US."

"The US?"

"All of them moved here. Hold on. In the US, Noreen Leslie Gruning changed her name to Lucy Isabel Lavenza. That's her current name. Moved around. I'll send you details and spelling. Her last known address: New York City. The Bronx."

"Good."

"Now, Marie Louise Mitchell, was changed to Melinda Spencer-Glantz, then changed again to

Rita Mae Purvis. Lived in Oklahoma but moved to Texas. Last known address, Lufkin, Texas.

"And Jane Elizabeth Klassyn was changed to Sheila Beth Stratton. But that was changed to Vanessa Claire Prather. I have her in Maryland. I'm still following her, she moved around, as well. I'll send you last known contact information that I have for all of them."

"This is fantastic, Tessa."

"I'll get back to you."

Ben stared at the names he'd written down.

He was getting close.

Seventy-Five

Cielo Vallee, Orange County, California
Present day

Emma struggled to focus on her work that morning.

Eating an egg salad sandwich at her desk for lunch, she went online to look for the latest on the homicide in the park. Nothing new on the news sites.

Wait. The *Register* had posted an update ten minutes ago.

Detectives Appeal for Help in Homicide
Orange County homicide detectives are appealing for witnesses and information in the stabbing death of a 34-year-old woman whose body was found this morning in Suntrail Sky Park.

The woman's body has been taken to the Orange County coroner's office to determine official cause of death and identification. However, sources have told the

Register that the victim is Rita Mae Purvis of Lufkin, Texas.

Rita Purvis.
Emma's eyes widened. Her mouth fell open as she read.

A man walking his dog at dawn made the discovery in a wooded section of the trail that winds along the communities of Cielo Valle, Lake Forest and Mission Viejo.

"We'll be canvassing surrounding neighborhoods, talking to residents, checking security cameras," said a source with the Orange County Sheriff's Department.

Anyone with information concerning the case is asked to call the Orange County Sheriff's Department or submit an anonymous tip through the crime line website.

Emma's heart beat faster; dizziness rolled over her in waves.

Balling her shaking hands into fists, putting them to her mouth, thinking. She went numb.

"Emma." Roxanna, the office admin, stood in front of her. "Are you ill? You don't look so good. Want me to call the nurse?"

Emma looked around as if waking. "No, umm." She shut down her computer, closed and gathered files. Got up and put them away. "Thank you, Rox. Please cancel everything I have this afternoon. I'm going home."

"No problem. Are you okay to drive?"

"Of course."

Slipping her bag over her shoulder, Emma walked fast to the parking lot, casting around, looking across the street for anyone watching her. As she drove, Emma checked her mirrors.

Stay calm. At least Rita is out of my life now and forever.

Wheeling through her neighborhood, Emma took extra care not to speed as she scoured the streets for any signs of police going door-to-door.

Nothing.

She could hear a helicopter but couldn't see it.

Police? TV news?

In the house, she was greeted by Tug, and welcomed the fleeting relief of his affection. She got him some treats and fresh water. She paced in the kitchen, taking deep, shaky breaths.

Rita's dead but that doesn't end the threat. When she confronted me in the parking lot, she said 'we.' I have to do something. Come on, think.

Emma halted.

She'd glimpsed the backpack she'd used in her search for Tug sticking out from the closet, and a memory came tumbling back.

No.

Emma seized the backpack, finding the treats, bowl and empty water bottle—*but no knife.*

The knife I took with me. Where is it?

I must've lost it on the trail—and Rita's ring... I still have it. It's evidence.

Rubbing her forehead, she paced again when

her phone vibrated and chimed with a new email. Emma didn't recognize the address.

The subject said: LIFE & DEATH

She read the first part of the message:

Look at this and where it's going. Soon the whole world will know the truth about what YOU AND RITA did and what you are! LYING BETRAYERS!

A video was embedded.

Emma's shaking fingers hovered over her keyboard as she considered whether it was safe to play it, ultimately deciding she couldn't afford not to.

It showed Rita Purvis and Emma in the Trader Joe's parking lot. It pulled tight on Rita's upset face, then tight on Emma's face. The clip of their exchange had no sound. It lasted twenty seconds.

The rest of the email continued beneath the video.

Rita Mae Purvis was last seen arguing with Emma Grant in the parking lot of a Trader Joe's in Cielo Valle, Orange County.

Under it was a tower of email addresses for the Orange County Sheriff, and several news outlets.

The email signed off with: Your lying life is over!

Seventy-Six

"The number you have reached has been changed, is disconnected, or is not in service. If you feel you have reached this recording in error—"

That was as far as Ben got with Lucy Lavenza in New York.

It had been the same for Rita Mae Purvis in Texas and Vanessa Prather in Maryland.

He tapped his phone to his chin.

One step forward and two steps back.

But he'd made progress with the names today.

And all in good time, thanks to Tessa.

Leaning against his rental car and staring at the duplex where one of the Skull Sisters had lived, Ben thought the smell of the slaughterhouse was not so bad now.

Unless I'm getting used to it.

Taking it all in while listening to the clunking of the railyards, there was no question this was a rough part of Eternity to grow up in.

Four doors down, Ben saw two people working in the flower beds in front of their small house.

He headed toward them.

The woman was in a sundress, wearing a floppy straw hat. The man wore a Panama hat. Both were on their knees, weeding.

"Excuse me," Ben said.

They turned to Ben. He figured them to be in their late fifties, maybe early sixties.

"Sorry to trouble you, but I'm researching local history for a book. Have you lived in this neighborhood for very long?"

The couple exchanged glances, then the man nodded.

"Did you know the people who lived in that duplex?" Ben pointed to the place. "The one four doors down?"

The man nodded but the woman shook her head, admonishing him.

"We don't want to talk about anything that has anything to do with those people." The woman stood. "It was a long time ago. No need to stir things up."

She disappeared into the house, leaving the man alone. He got to his feet slowly.

"My apologies for upsetting her," Ben said.

"She doesn't rile easily but anything to do with the Klassyn girl just sets her off."

"Janie Klassyn lived there. I wasn't sure."

"Yes, with her mom and all their problems," the man said. "The thing of it is, our daughter played with Janie a little bit and we thank the Lord every day that she never got caught up with that crowd."

"Would you tell me about it?" Ben began taking notes.

The man held up his palms. "We're not talking to you. I hope you'll respect that, sir."

Ben stopped. Saw the resolution in the man's gray eyes, then put his notebook away and nodded. "I do. Again, my apologies. Thank you."

Returning to his car, Ben considered the silver lining.

He now knew that Janie Klassyn lived in the duplex, which put Nikki Gorman in The Estates. Another step forward.

At that moment his phone pinged with an email from Darmont Hill College. Emma's college in Indianapolis. The subject said: Important Please Call Me ASAP. It was from Clinton Parkerfield, Director of Records.

This is strange. Why would Emma's college need me to call?

Ben dialed Parkerfield's number.

"Thanks for calling, Mr. Grant," Parkerfield said. "I'm following up on our emailed response to your recent verification request on the graduation status of a former student, Emma Anne Chance."

Ben was puzzled. He remembered when he'd first met Emma, how he quietly looked into her background. He'd checked her California driver's license, her addresses in California, marital history and professional certification. He scoured his memory.

I never checked her college because I saw her diploma in her apartment when we dated and by this time everything else had checked out.

"I'm afraid you're mistaken, Mr. Parkerfield. I never made such a request."

"We have it here in writing. Your researcher made it on your official letterhead but I can't seem to contact her."

"What?"

"So I decided to try to reach you directly. I used your website contact."

"I'm not following—you said my researcher?"

For a moment, Ben wondered if it had something to do with the work Tessa Fox was doing for him when Parkerfield continued.

"Yes, a Ms. Susanne St. John. I had trouble trying to reach her."

Then it dawned on Ben. Susanne was Kayla's middle name. St. John was Brooke's maiden name. Kayla had done this. His stomach twisted, he clenched the phone. Biting back on his anger, Ben swallowed.

"Yes, go ahead."

"This won't take long and it's kind of embarrassing. You see, my wife's a huge fan of your work. Well, I am, too. It's kind of why I'm calling you personally. Anyway, I'd mentioned your query and we thought that if it had something to do with a book you're working on then there's something you should know."

"And what's that?"

Ben's annoyance with Kayla for crossing a line competed with his attention.

"Well, it's none of my business of course," Parkerfield said. "And, I am going outside school rules. Can we keep this call confidential, Mr. Grant?"

What's with this guy? "Yes, but I'm pressed for time."

"It has to do with Darmont Hill College's Student Names Policy."

"The Names Policy?"

"Most schools have such policies. Former students can request a name change to their records and diplomas. It's mostly common when they get married, or change their name for other reasons, as long as they supply the proper documents."

"I see."

"Mr. Grant..." Parkerfield lowered his voice. "The woman you enquired about, Emma Anne Chance? She didn't attend and graduate from Dalton under that name."

"What?"

Now Parkerfield had Ben's full attention.

"No, not long after she graduated she requested and received a name change. All of her records were changed to be under the name Emma Anne Chance and we issued a new diploma with the changed name."

Ben swallowed hard. "Do you know what Emma's name—I mean Emma Chance's name was prior to her changing it?"

"Yes, it was Vanessa Prather."

Ben shook his head. He was shocked into a moment of silence, but then realized it must be a co-incidence, and forced himself to recover. "Is that her full name?"

"Full name is Vanessa Claire Prather."

His heart pounded. "You're certain?"

"Yes. She's originally from Maryland."

"Spell out her full name."

Parkerfield spelled it out. It matched the name Tessa had found.

Ben's stomach heaved, his knees buckled and he staggered, slamming his back against the car door, his shirt bunching up his back as he slid to the sidewalk, staring at the Klassyn duplex as Clinton Parkerfield's tiny voice called to him from a million miles away.

Seventy-Seven

Orange County, California
Present day

Striding back and forth in her living room, hugging herself, Emma battled to calm the tingling in her chest.

Her throat had gone dry, constricted as if a noose were tightening around it.

Through the front window, she glimpsed an Orange County Sheriff's car rushing down her street.

Time was ticking down on her.

Her first thought was to get her passport, and Kayla's, and fly to Canada to join Ben.

I could figure things out there. But could I survive going back to Eternity?

She rushed upstairs, grabbed suitcases. As she packed, she abandoned the idea of going as far as leaving the country now. Still, she got the passports just in case.

After packing, she placed her phone and laptop on the kitchen table. Then she made a few quick calls from their landline.

Glad she'd parked in the garage, Emma went through the kitchen, loaded the suitcases and Tug into her SUV, then she silenced her phone and laptop, then completely shut them down before intentionally leaving them behind.

She drove through the neighborhood, counting three marked police units; saw deputies going door-to-door with tablets and clipboards. Guessing the investigation was not at the stage of roadblocks, she was relieved no one had stopped her.

Several minutes later, Emma wheeled into the lot of the SoCal Seaside Assurance bank, parking in a palm-shaded spot.

After tying Tug's leash to the wheel, she lowered all the windows almost halfway and locked the doors.

"You stay here. Be good. I'll be right back."

Tug barked and Emma went inside, her mind racing while in line, remembering that there were federal laws concerning large cash withdrawals over ten thousand dollars. A large amount would draw suspicion.

"I'd like to withdraw five thousand in cash," Emma told the teller when it was her turn.

"Five thousand?"

"Yes, we're getting work done on the house with contractors."

The teller held Emma with a cool gaze for a second, nodded, got the cash and counted it out.

In the lot, Emma found a man wearing dark glasses and a ballcap beside her SUV. He had bent down to tie his shoe and when he stood he was staring at Tug.

"You know, lady, you shouldn't leave your dog unattended in the vehicle like that."

"Yes, I know."

"It's not good for them. There are laws, you know."

"I know, thank you," she said before buckling up and pulling out of the lot.

Driving off, she checked her mirrors for anyone who might be following her but saw nothing.

Ten minutes later, Emma, stopped at a cream-colored strip mall bordered with a trimmed hedge. She parked in front of Irina's Home Away From Home. She took Tug's leash and they entered. Irina's smelled of dog and shampoo. They went to the counter where a teenage girl smiled at Tug.

"Hi. I called about boarding my friend Tug here."

"Oh yes. We remember Tug." She looked in her computer. "For thirty days?"

"Yes, to be safe. We should be back by then. Emergency family trip."

"I see we have all Tug's information from last time. Any medications?"

"No."

"Any special instructions, considerations?"

Emma reached into her bag for Tug's blue rubber ball, handing it to the girl.

"He likes to play catch with his ball."

"Ahh." The girl took it and smiled at Tug.

"He's an easygoing guy," Emma said. "I'll pay in advance. How much is it?"

"Six hundred."

Emma paid in cash, then lowered herself and gave Tug a crushing hug.

"I love you so much, buddy!"

Tug licked her face before she handed his leash to the girl.

Driving away, Emma brushed tears from her eyes.

She then went to Walmart, where she bought a few groceries and several disposable burner phones.

Checking her SUV's digital dash clock, she saw she had just enough time to pick up Kayla at school.

Seventy-Eight

Eternity, Manitoba
Present day

Sitting on the sidewalk, his back against his car, Ben stared at his phone in stunned disbelief.

His stomach hardened and twisted as he raised his focus to Janie Klassyn's duplex.

Emma...one of The Skull Sisters?
My wife...a convicted murderer?

Shaking his head, he refused to accept what Clinton Parkerfield had just revealed to him.

It's a mistake. A computer glitch, a typo, an error, duplicate names. It's not true. It can't be true.

Standing, staring at his phone, Ben called Tessa Fox to double-check without telling her the reason.

"Hang on, Ben."

He could hear Tessa's keyboard clicking through the line.

"Yes, the name is correct: Jane Elizabeth Klassyn became Vanessa Claire Prather." Tessa spelled out the full name and it matched what Parkerfield had given him. Then she added: "Just before you called I tracked her from Maryland to Indiana where she enrolled in Darmont Hill College. This girl seems to have changed her name more times than the others you gave me. Not sure why. I haven't confirmed any further name changes yet but I'm working on it. Did something come up? Why did you need me to check again?"

A moment passed.

"Ben? Is something wrong?"

Ben lifted his head to the sky and gulped air before managing: "Thank you, Tessa. Keep me posted."

Ben lowered his phone, looking at the duplex, pierced by the revelation.

It's true. Emma changed her name so many times, re-creating herself, shedding her past each time, to hide a monstrous lie.

Who is the woman I married?

A cloud of flies hummed on a breeze, bringing with it the foul smell of the slaughterhouse, sending his thoughts swirling, dropping them on one fact: *I've got to get back to California.*

Scrolling through his contacts, Ben made a flurry of calls to airlines and travel agents, desperate to get to Los Angeles as soon as possible. It was late in the day. After checking with multiple airlines, he discovered there were no remaining flights departing for Los Angeles today, none that still had seats. He was looking at longer flights to Minneapolis, Denver and Calgary with connections to L.A.

"One moment, sir. We may have found something," one agent told him. "West Sky Canadian, the new airline, had a cancellation. A seat is available. It leaves later today, departing Winnipeg in five hours arriving about midnight Los Angeles time. It's direct but the ticket is quite expensive, sir."

"I don't care. Book it now. Thanks."

Ben wasted no time getting back to his motel, checking out, then beginning the long drive to Winnipeg.

His world had been knocked off its axis.

I'm an idiot. I'm a fool.

Taking a deep breath as he drove, he clenched the wheel and his mind went into overload.

Kayla was right all along. I was so blind. How could I have been so stupid? I missed every sign.

The relentless prairie rolled by, empty, eternal and without answers.

He had to craft a strategy. Think. Stay calm. Be rational.

The Emma he knew, the Emma he loved, was a good person. She had a good heart. She was kind to his daughter, loving and devoted to him. She saved a boy's life.

But why did she hide her past from us?

Ben dragged a hand over his face.

It's obvious. If she'd told me about her past, would I have married her?

Ben rubbed his face hard—she participated in killing four people, two of them children.

She did her time. She paid for her crime. She left her past behind. But do people really change?

Ben screamed a curse.

Right now he just had to get Kayla away from Emma so he could figure out how to deal with this.

He tried calling Kayla's phone. No answer.

He dictated and sent a text:

Are you there, honey?

Miles, make that kilometers, went by, with no response. Ben tried again, dictating another text. Nothing. He tried an email. Nothing. Then he tried calling his home phone, the landline. It rang through to voice mail. He didn't leave a message.

He thought for a moment, then tried calling Emma's phone. It rang and rang with no answer.

He dictated a text to Emma:

Are you free to talk?

Nothing.

What was going on?

Thinking about Emma, he saw his phone display her older text, sent to him when he was leaving Los Angeles.

I want you to know that whatever happens I love you and Kayla with all my heart.

Ben went numb.

Her message was clear to him now. *She knew I was going to find the truth.*

* * *

Ben arrived at the airport without having received a single response.

He dropped off the car, checked in and passed through security. In preboarding he continued charging his phone and resumed trying to reach Kayla and Emma without success. His heart hammering, he looked at the other passengers biding their time and envied their boredom. When the gate agents began with boarding calls for his flight, he thought of another possibility.

Calculating the time difference in California, he estimated that Kayla and Emma should've finished at school.

As he lined up to board, he scrolled through contacts for Kayla's friends. He had their numbers as part of the deal when Kayla had gone to parties or concerts.

He found the number for Cheyenne Brady. Hi Cheyenne, it's Kayla's dad. Is she with you? Trying to reach her. Can you tell her to call me? Not serious, just need to talk to her. Thanks.

He sent a similar message to Regan Peters.

Staring at his phone as he inched closer to the gate, Ben was getting his passport and boarding pass ready when his phone vibrated.

Hi Mr. Grant. I saw K getting a ride home after school with her stepmom.

Cheyenne ended the text with a smile emoji.
Ben texted his thanks.

His phone vibrated again with another message, this one from Regan:

She got a ride after school with Mrs. G. Trying to reach Kayla too—maybe her phone's off, or died.

"Boarding pass and ID, sir?"

Ben looked up at the agent, then gave him his passport and pass.

Seventy-Nine

Manitoba and California
Present day

On the plane, Ben connected his phone and charger cable to the outlet at his seat.

Once the jet leveled off, a flight attendant confirmed that access to Wi-Fi was available for purchase on the flight. Ben couldn't make or receive phone calls but he could send and receive texts and emails. During the flight Ben resumed trying to reach Kayla and Emma.

No responses.

What's going on with them?

Wishing the jet would go faster, he turned to his window, gazing through the clouds at the patchwork of fields below as the sun neared the horizon. The flight's duration was over five hours. The woman beside him in the aisle seat with white hair, in her late seventies, was sound asleep.

Ben lowered his tray, opened his laptop and angled it so she couldn't see. Contending with the knot in his stomach, he began reading his research notes and reviewing all the photos he'd taken in Eternity.

The Tullock home, the cemetery. The unspeakable horror of it all. The homes of The Skull Sisters.

Where my wife was raised.

Everything took on new meaning now. His pulse racing, he reached for his phone. Still nothing.

How could I have been so stupid? So blind. Kayla had locked onto all the signals: Emma's reluctance to discuss her past. But everything in Emma's history that I looked at checked out. I didn't dig deeper because I had no reason to suspect her. But Kayla picked up on something. There was Emma's aversion to being on TV, her reaction when she learned I was doing a book on the Eternity murders.

On her case.

Kayla said she'd discovered something private that Emma had written about her life. What was it?

Emma has been lying to me all along. I've been such a fool.

Ben's anger rose in his chest. He wanted to punch something. He took a shaky breath and scrolled through his phone.

Again he read Emma's last message to him:

Whatever happens I love you and Kayla with all my heart.

He went to Kayla's last series of texts to him when Tug was missing.

Emma found Tug in mom's spot, like you guessed, but she came home a bloody mess. Says she fell on the trail. She's acting SO STRANGE! WTF Dad?

Setting his phone down, Ben cursed under his breath, swallowed and dragged both hands over his face.

Ben looked to the clouds, remembering when he first met Emma in Pasadena, signing books at a conference. How she'd told him she loved his work.

"You have a deep understanding for everyone touched by the crime—even the killers."

Even the killers...even the killers.

He couldn't believe what was happening. This was a nightmare.

The sun had set and the plane traveled in the twilight.

Examining his situation, Ben was looking at his phone when it vibrated with a message from Cecil May.

Hi Ben. Got an update. Can you talk?

I'm on a flight and can only text. Go ahead.

Del Brockway, your 'fan,' has been removed and it appears other investigators are working on the case.

Is it related to one of my books? Am I the target?

No & no. From what I've learned, it's your wife, Emma.

Ben went completely still, before resuming.

Do you know why?

Not yet. Working on it. You have any ideas?

Ben's mind raced with questions and fears.

Could the PIs be working for a news agency? Could they possibly know what I know about her? Given the anniversary of the murders, maybe someone's trying to track her down—like what I was doing for my book. That would also explain Emma's behavior.

But Ben kept his thoughts to himself. He replied:

No, no idea. Maybe her rescuing her student is tied to a lawsuit or insurance claim?

Could be, I'll keep checking.

Ben had another concern and a thought, but he didn't want to involve police—not yet anyway.

Cecil. This is making me a little uneasy. Can I impose upon you further?

Impose away.

I'm out of town, having trouble reaching my wife and daughter. I'll be home late. Could you go to my house to check on them and get back to me?

Say I asked you because I'm a big worrier. Could you do that?

Sorry, buddy. Out of town myself. I'm in Sacramento for a meeting.

Ben bit his bottom lip then texted: OK no problem.

Why don't you call Orange County for a welfare check?

No it's OK. It's probably a phone glitch. I'll be home in a few hours. Thanks Cecil. Keep me posted.

Will do, partner.

Setting his phone down, Ben let his head fall back on his headrest and gazed outside into the night.

Who hired private investigators to surveil Emma?

Ben struggled to think, looking head-on to the fact he should stop being an idiot and contact police.

And tell them what? My wife is a convicted murderer from Canada and I can't locate her or my daughter. The crime was twenty years ago—she's served her time, done nothing wrong, is a model citizen now, but…but what?

She hid her past from me.

Ben shut his eyes and took a slow deep breath.

Then he took up his phone and stared at a recent picture of Emma, smiling. Happy. Beautiful.

Exhausted, Ben put his phone down and shook his head, gazing outside to lights below.

I'm losing it. No, no police. Emma would never hurt Kayla. I just know it. I need to talk to Emma.

The pilot made an announcement about starting their descent into Los Angeles.

Attendants distributed customs cards to be completed before entering the US.

It was a smooth landing. Ben made good time clearing customs and called an Uber to take him home.

As the car sailed along the freeways of greater Los Angeles and into Orange County, he continued trying to reach Kayla and Emma without success.

Eighty

The exterior lights of Ben's house were on when he arrived home about 1:30 a.m.

They were preset with a timer switch.

All was quiet when he got inside. He walked through the house to the interior garage door and opened it. His car was there. Emma's car was gone.

He went upstairs. Their bedroom was empty. Kayla's bedroom was empty. He checked every room upstairs.

No sign of anyone.

He went downstairs to the living room and kitchen, switching on all the lights. No sign of Tug. No notes on the fridge. He checked the landline. No messages. The only calls showing were the ones he'd made.

Looking around, he saw Emma's phone and laptop on the kitchen table.

What the—

He thought about logging on to Emma's devices but didn't know the passwords.

Ben went back upstairs and searched for Kayla's phone in vain.

He had an idea. Hurrying downstairs, Ben unzipped his bag, pulled out his laptop. He knew it was possible to track Kayla's phone and her location. He went to the accounts for the family phones, zeroing in on Kayla's. He went to the instructions on how to track a missing or stolen phone, reading as fast as he could.

He cursed.

With the type of phones and package they had, Ben couldn't track Kayla's phone if the battery was dead or it was off.

However, he could get its last known location.

I'll take it.

Ben clicked on the locater mode and a map blossomed on the page with a red circle pointing to a location. Ben clicked on the icon and it gave him more details.

It was a gas station, a ViroClean Pacifica outlet yesterday afternoon, located on a boulevard near Kayla's school. It was open twenty-four hours. Ben knew where it was and headed for the garage.

At this hour, few cars were on the street in this part of Cielo Valle.

Unsure of what he expected to find, Ben had no other choice but to check out the gas station where Kayla's phone was last located.

He parked at the pump and gassed up, using the

time to think. No other cars or customers were around. Crickets were chirping when he went inside to pay. The clerk at the counter had a wispy beard, looked to be in his early twenties. He was wearing a navy ViroClean Pacifica golf shirt with a name tag that read Noah.

After paying, Ben said, "Hey, Noah, could you help me?"

"I dunno, can I? My powers are limited."

"I think my daughter may have lost her cell phone here. Did someone find one?"

As Noah leaned back and looked under the counter, Ben saw the small bank of security monitors. Noah put a cardboard box on the counter with keys, paperbacks, vapes and a bracelet.

"Sorry. No phones."

"What about those cameras? She was here yesterday afternoon between noon and six. Could you review them and let me see? Maybe she lost it near the pumps?"

Noah shook his head. "Sorry, sir. You gotta call corporate. I'll give you a card."

"Would you let me have a quick look for two hundred bucks?"

Noah smiled. "Show me the green."

Ben paid him and Noah went to a keyboard. "You said yesterday afternoon?"

"Yes." Ben craned his neck, eyeing the monitors from the counter as Noah cued up the time period. They watched vehicles come and go at the pumps in high speed before Ben recognized Emma's SUV.

"Hold it—that's my wife's car."

Ben got his phone out to record the footage as Noah rewound and replayed it in real time. Ben's heart lifted. There was Kayla leaving to go to the bathroom, while Emma gassed up, then cleaned out the car. It looked like she was tossing magazines and newspapers into the trash before Kayla returned and they drove off.

"Keep it going," Ben said, wanting another few minutes to record other vehicles.

Okay, they're together and safe.

"Thank you, Noah."

Walking back to his car, Ben stopped at the pumps and picked up the trash can Emma had used. He emptied the contents onto the pavement, felt a clunking just as the intercom clicked with Noah's tin-voiced protest.

"Hey, dude, what the fuck?"

Ignoring him, Ben sifted through the cans, bottles, wrappers, diapers, take-out wrappers and bags, magazines and newspapers, finding a laptop and phone.

Kayla's laptop and phone.

Ben stared at them as questions swirled.

He cleaned up his mess, washed his hands in the bathroom, collected Kayla's devices, then left.

His heart was thumping as he drove home along the empty streets, searching the night for answers.

Seeing Kayla and Emma together on the camera footage gave him a measure of relief but it was eclipsed by worry as he glanced at Kayla's laptop and phone, fetched from the trash.

At home he scoured the internet for tips on how

to gain access to Kayla's laptop and phone, hoping to get an idea where they had gone and why. He read everything he could find, studied videos. Hours went by. It was futile.

He called the twenty-four-hour tech support line of their provider. There was little that could be done because of privacy policies and security safeguards. The tech guy cautioned Ben that repeated attempts to guess a password would lock him out, which he already knew.

Ben then scrutinized his phone and the gas station footage he'd recorded of the cars and people, hoping for a clue as to whether Emma was being followed.

He couldn't find anything.

Nothing was working and the sun had risen. Ben hadn't slept. He felt the full weight of the day crashing down on him, his shock, his worry, his jet lag.

He took a cold shower. As water rushed over him, he thrashed in a storm of self-recrimination. The karmic wheel had turned on him. Devoting his life to recording tragedies, he was haunted by Nietzsche's warning about pursuing monsters and gazing long into an abyss, because "the abyss also looks into you."

What have I done?

Once he was dressed, Ben made strong coffee. Then his landline phone rang.

Eighty-One

California
Present day

Morning light pierced the seam of the drawn motel room curtains.

The strange firmness of the motel's bed, the laundered smell of the sheets, told Kayla that it really happened.

This is no dream.

She replayed yesterday's events when Emma had picked her up at school.

After saying goodbye to Cheyenne and Regan, Kayla had opened the door to Emma's SUV, and seen luggage and groceries in the back.

"What's with all that?"

"Get in, sweetheart. Something's come up," Emma had said. "We need to go somewhere."

"Where? What's going on?"

Kayla got in, reached for the car's charger cable, connecting it to her phone. Her battery was low. Then she buckled up. Emma checked her mirrors and drove off without answering. They didn't go far before they pulled into a gas station.

"We need gas. If you have to use the bathroom now's a good time," Emma said.

"Where're we going, Emma?"

"You'll find out on the way. Do you have to go?"

"Yes." Annoyed, Kayla shot her a look when she left the car. But when Kayla returned she couldn't find her phone and began searching the SUV. "Do you have my phone?"

"We have to go."

"Don't go anywhere, Emma! I think someone stole my phone!"

Emma looked at her and started the car.

"Shut it off!" Kayla looked at vehicles at the pumps, then the store. "Someone stole my freakin' phone!"

Emma moved the gearshift into Drive.

"Stop!"

She sped off, merging into traffic.

"Dammit, stop!" Kayla pounded the dash. "I have to find my phone!"

"I had to get rid of your phone, your laptop. I left mine at home."

"Why? My life, my homework, everything's in there!"

"It's extreme, I know. I'm not an expert. I did think of removing the SIM card, but I had to take quick steps. So we can't be tracked."

"Can't be tracked? What the hell're you talking about?"

"I'm protecting you."

"From what? Have you lost your mind? Go back!"

"We can't go back. Kayla, I'm so sorry. Soon you'll understand. Right now I need you to listen to me. Someone may want to hurt us. So we're leaving home for a while. Remember our security alarm going off? Well, before that, there was a strange guy your dad and I encountered in the park. It's all connected to your dad's books."

Emma checked her mirrors.

"We're not going very far for now. We just need to leave the house. I'll explain more when we stop."

They accelerated onto an eastbound freeway only going a few miles before they exited and pulled into this sketchy motel. Kayla didn't know exactly where they were, just that they'd only traveled a few miles from home. After that, Emma spent much of the evening attempting to explain why she was doing what she was doing.

"Do you know what extortion is?" Emma had asked her.

"Yes, blackmail."

"It appears that someone is trying to extort your dad—something to do with one of his books. They're claiming he knowingly published lies about someone."

"Oh my God! Does Dad know? Shouldn't we call the police?"

"Ben knows. And he thinks he knows who's doing it. More important, that they're completely wrong and just want money from him. He told me he can handle this without police, but that to be safe, you and I should leave town for a while. He'll come home as soon as possible."

Kayla took a few moments to process everything before accepting Emma's explanation. And Kayla took solace in the fact she had backed up much of her phone and laptop on the cloud.

"I guess this makes sense now."

"We think it happened after someone saw us on TV at the book sale."

"I know Dad has some scary fans."

"I just want to protect you, sweetheart. Get some sleep."

Now, with morning here, Kayla shifted in her bed to see Emma dressed, sitting at the foot of her own bed watching the TV with the sound off and a phone in her bandaged hand.

"Is that my phone, Emma?"

"No, it's a disposable one, a burner phone." Emma nodded to the desk. "There are muffins, a bagel and yogurt if you're hungry."

Kayla got a bagel and took a bite. "Where's Tug?"

"Boarding at Irina's. After you eat, take a shower if you like, but we have to go."

Chewing on her bagel and feeling strange without her phone, Kayla noticed that Emma was watching a TV news report on the discovery of a woman's body in the woods. Reading the graphic, the locater map and crawler at the bottom of the screen, she saw that it was a homicide in Suntrail Sky Park.

"That's near our house where we saw the helicopters," Kayla said.

Emma said nothing as Kayla watched, reading the graphic naming the victim: Rita Purvis from Lufkin, Texas. Kayla had no idea who the woman was but she was curious: "Hey, when you came back from there looking for Tug you were all bloody."

Emma turned to her. "I know. Right near our home where I fell. The whole thing's so sad, isn't it?" She shook her head. "Come on, get in the shower. Let's get going."

Kayla stared at her, unsure what to think. Her mind was reeling from recent events, including the letter from the college confirming Emma's attendance, leaving her conflicted concerning her doubts about her stepmother, with a feeling of unease niggling at her.

Emma patted Kayla's lap. "We're going someplace safe to wait for your dad so we can figure things out."

Kayla's eyes went to Emma's burner phone.

"Can we at least let Dad know we're okay in case he's trying to reach us?"

"He's still in Canada." Emma stared at the phone in her hand, smiled and nodded. "But it's a good idea to let him know we had to get a new temporary number so that he doesn't worry."

They took a selfie together, then Kayla tapped out a message.

Hi Dad. It's us. We had phone trouble and got a temp phone and a new number. We're fine. Talk soon. Love you. K and E.

While Kayla showered, Emma packed up.

Then she went to the window. Keeping the curtains drawn, she surveyed the motel lot.

A few guests were departing.

Emma saw nothing unusual.

Twenty minutes later they were in her SUV, heading for an eastbound expressway, unaware that a car from the motel across the street was following them.

Eighty-Two

Cielo Valle, Orange County, California
Present day

Ben's phone rang. He snapped it up hoping it was Kayla or Emma.

"Have I reached Benjamin Grant?" asked a man whose voice he didn't recognize.

The number was blocked.

"Yes, who's this?"

"Chuck Doan, ABC News, Los Angeles. Mr. Grant, is your wife, Emma Grant, the school counselor?"

Oh God, were they in an accident? Wouldn't I hear from police first?

As a former reporter, Ben knew police were not always the first to call. He squeezed his phone. "Yes. What's this about?"

"I'm calling for your response to the case involving your wife?"

Was ABC onto the Eternity case so fast? They couldn't be…

"What case?"

"Police want to question her in relation to the recent homicide."

Recent homicide?

"I don't know what you're talking about."

"Rita Purvis. Her body was found in Suntrail Sky Park not far from your home. Would you comment for our cameras? We have a crew..."

Rita Purvis...

Suddenly, the floor felt like it was shifting, Ben forced himself into a chair.

"No." He swallowed hard. "I've no comment at this time."

Ending the call, Ben cupped his hand to his face, blinking at the fear enveloping him.

My God, what's happening? Emma wanted for questioning? Rita Purvis. Nothing makes sense.

Ben looked around the kitchen, seeing nothing except—*my laptop.* He went online to news sites and within minutes he'd devoured the reports of the investigation into the homicide of Rita Purvis, of Lufkin, Texas.

One of the Skull Sisters.

Her body was found in Suntrail Sky Park. Indications were that she'd been stabbed to death. There was a breaking development on all sites: recently obtained video taken a short time before Rita Purvis's body was found. The video had no sound but showed Purvis in an exchange with a woman in a parking lot.

Emma.

Confusion flooded Ben's brain when his phone

rang again. Praying Emma was calling, he answered.

"Hi, this is Juliet Williamson with the Associated Press. I'm calling for Benjamin Grant—"

Without speaking, he ended the call and thrust his hands into his hair when the doorbell chimed. He went to the front of the house and looked through the window. Several vehicles were parked on the street including news vans for KTLA, KRVZ and KTKT.

On his doorstep, he saw a man and woman. They made eye contact with him. Ben gave his head big negative shakes to convey *no interviews* when the man held up a badge and pointed at the door.

Detectives.

Ben's gut twisted and he opened the door. Standing behind them he recognized Maggie Shen, who shouted over their shoulders.

"Ben, Maggie Shen! Could we just have a minute, please?"

"I'm sorry, I've got nothing to say."

According to their IDs and business cards, the detectives were from Orange County. Oscar Garcia, a large man with sharp eyes, and Lilly Webb, red hair tied in a tight ponytail, sober expression.

"Just need a moment," Garcia said.

Ben led them into the kitchen.

"Is your wife home?" Webb asked. "We'd like to speak with Mrs. Grant."

"No, she isn't. I don't know where she is."

"Why's that?" Garcia said.

"I've been out of town. I just got home."

"Can you call her for us?" Garcia asked.

"I don't think she has her phone with her."

Garcia nodded to the two laptops and cell phones on the table. "Does anything there belong to your wife?"

"Yes, those belong to my wife and daughter."

"Really?"

"Where's your daughter, now?"

"She's not home, either."

"And do they usually leave home without their phones? Do they have others?"

Ben dragged his hands over his unshaven face.

"You look worried, Mr. Grant," Webb said. "Is there something on your mind?"

"Look, I just got back from a business trip late last night and I have no idea where my wife and daughter are, and I can't reach them. They could've been in an accident or had car trouble somewhere."

Webb and Garcia traded glances.

"Would you allow us to look around?" Webb asked.

Things were moving too fast and Ben was walking a tightrope. He was at a disadvantage. His stomach was churning with worry, Emma was a convicted murderer, Rita Purvis was murdered near their home, Emma and Kayla were missing, and now detectives were sitting in his kitchen.

I need to investigate this myself. I need to find them.

Ben didn't know what Garcia and Webb knew but he was aware of his rights.

"No. And look, with all due respect, I know I don't have to talk to you."

"Sure, if that's how you want to play it," Garcia said.

"It's not like that. I'm not being uncooperative, it's just that, here…" Ben reached for his bag and gave Garcia his boarding pass. "I was out of town and got in late last night, early this morning actually. I really don't know anything. But when I see Emma—"

"Winnipeg?" Garcia said. "What were you doing in Canada?"

"Research for a book."

"Really?" Garcia said. "What's the case?"

Ben said nothing.

Garcia pressed him: "How long were you out of the country?"

"Look, I'm sorry. I really have nothing more to say."

"Do you want to report your wife and daughter as missing persons, Mr. Grant?" Webb asked.

"No, because I'm sure there's probably an explanation."

"How'd you get home from LAX?" Garcia asked.

"Uber."

"You say you got home early this morning," Garcia said. "Were your wife and daughter home then?"

"No."

"Ben, do you know Rita Purvis of Lufkin, Texas?" Webb asked, cuing up her phone to show him a screen grab from the parking lot video. Then she played the video.

Staring at it, Ben battled not to let his face betray anything, his heart pounding, a drop of sweat trickling down his back. He shook his head. "No, I don't know Rita Purvis. I've never met her."

"How does your wife know her?" Garcia asked.

Ben shook his head. "I'm sorry. I just don't feel comfortable with this because I don't know anything. Maybe I should be getting a lawyer."

"Why?" Garcia asked. "You know how that looks?"

"I don't care. I know how things can be distorted, misinterpreted."

"Where are you headed with this?" Garcia asked.

"Nowhere. I just got home. And I know my rights."

Garcia leaned forward, closer to Ben, his face lifting into a small smile, warming a bit. "Look, no one's under arrest, or under any suspicion," he said. "Fact is we just received that video around the same time as the press. It was sent anonymously. We verified the time and location with security video from Trader Joe's. I'm telling you this because that much is public. We have no control on how your colleagues in the media will 'interpret' things. You know that better than most people. We're giving you the opportunity to help us."

"Mr. Grant, all we want is to talk to Emma about it," Webb said. "The video shows she was one of the last people to see Rita Purvis. We need to know the relationship between them, if there is one. Why they met there, what they talked about. We need her to help us with a timeline, movements, state of mind. Of all people, you know how this works."

"I do, and I am cooperating as much as I can."

"Will you let us look around? Volunteer your family's electronic devices?" Webb asked.

Ben knew "look around" meant bringing in an evidence team to process the house, everything in it, and he wasn't ready for that.

"No."

"If need be, we'll get warrants," Garcia said.

"I expect you will. But I'm hopeful we can clear this up before that becomes necessary."

The detectives looked at Ben for several moments. Then they nodded their thanks, shook his hand and left.

Alone in the house, Ben slammed his back against the wall to keep the room from spinning.

Garcia and Webb couldn't know who Rita Purvis is. They couldn't know about Emma's past. Could they? Their records don't exist. They were sealed by the court in Canada years ago. They can't know. At least not yet. But what was Rita doing here in California? How did she find Emma? Or did Emma find her? Where are Emma and Kayla? Are they safe?

Ben's cell phone vibrated and chimed, indicating a text. He picked up his phone from the kitchen table. Thinking the message was from the press, he swiped to delete it when he glimpsed the first words.

Hi Dad.

Catching his breath, he read.

Hi Dad. It's us. We had phone trouble and got a temp phone and a new number. We're fine. Talk soon. Love you. K and E.

He opened the photo, his heart lifting, smiling when he saw Kayla and Emma. He sent a response.

Where are you? Something came up. I flew back home and can't find you. I want to talk. Please call me now on my cell.

One minute passed. Then another. He called the number without a response.

Where are they? Is Kayla really safe?

While waiting, he took stock of the kitchen, his eyes stopping at the key rack on the wall. Something was different.

The hook for the keys to the cabin was empty.

He never touched them. The cabin keys never moved from their hook unless they were going to the cabin.

Ben seized upon a hope: Emma and Kayla had gone to the cabin.

Was Emma hiding to be safe? Or running from something she'd done?

Nearly twenty minutes had now passed without a response. He could no longer bear the agony. Time was ticking down. He had to do something.

The cabin was his best shot—his only shot.

He grabbed his phone, hurried to his garage and pressed the button for the garage door.

With an electronic hum, the big door lifted, like the rising curtain to a latter-day tragedy. Stopping at his SUV door, he looked to the end of his driveway.

A cluster of reporters and cameras awaited the next chapter in his unfolding story. The realization washed over him like a powerful wave, for he knew how his life—his family's life—was being interpreted, and probably was live right now with the banner *Best-selling True Crime Author's Wife Sought In Murder.*

So be it.

Ben took a breath, got in his car, slowly driving off, not caring if they followed or not.

One way or another he would find his family.

Eighty-Three

San Bernardino County, California
Present day

After their SUV left the freeway and began ascending the highway that twisted into the San Bernardino Mountains, Kayla knew their destination.

"We're going to our cabin, aren't we?"

Emma nodded, her face brightening but still tense because she knew she was digging a deep hole for herself by telling Kayla lie after lie. She hated doing it but she had to, because Kayla would freak out if she revealed the truth to her right now. Later, when Emma could get a handle on everything, and talk to Ben, she could repair the damage. But right now, Emma had to do all she could to buy time.

"Yes, we're going to the cabin."

Kayla loved it up here in the mountains, drinking in the spectacular views, the trees, the streams and waterfalls as they rolled by little diners, campgrounds and villages. The region was so vast, you could still find remote spots.

Traffic was sparse along the winding two-lane road. They couldn't go too fast, which gave Kayla time to think. Driving to the cabin was bittersweet for her, especially as they got closer to their destination. Kayla eyed the roadside carefully when they came to a particular sharp curve.

"Slow down." Kayla leaned forward, searching, spotting it under a tree on the right. "There! There it is! Pull over."

Emma checked her mirrors and pulled over. A few cars passed. They got out and stood before a wooden white roadside cross just under three feet tall, rising straight from the ground in the shade of a pine tree. The cross was weatherworn.

"Dad and I made it."

"Yes, I know."

Emma read the small, engraved plate in the center. Brooke—Forever In Our Hearts.

Kayla caressed the plate.

"Maybe we can come back later and put fresh flowers on it?" Emma said.

Smiling, Kayla nodded.

They drove for another four miles before they came to a bend in the highway marked by a car-sized granite outcrop, shaped like a bear's head.

Emma slowed and signaled for a right turn near the rock formation, at the mouth of a narrow dirt road.

The cabin sat on the site of a long-abandoned prospector's trail. Shaded and bordered by dense pine forests, the earthen road snaked for some sixty yards to their cabin.

Kayla's parents had bought it after Ben's first movie deal. It was a low-standing ranch-style cabin that had belonged to a film actor, who had it custom-built in the 1950s. The front wall was nearly all glass with floor-to-ceiling windows. It was spacious, beautiful and Kayla loved it.

"You stay here." Emma got out, her keys jingling. "Let me go in and check it out."

"Why?" Kayla looked around. "We're totally alone here."

"Humor me. Then we'll get our stuff inside."

Kayla let it go with a long, tired sigh.

Unlocking the door, Emma went in. The air was stale. Dust danced in the columns of light flooding the inside. The front opened to a large living room–dining room area with a cathedral-style ceiling and a stone fireplace on the far wall. The area was bordered by an island that flowed into the kitchen. It led to the hall, the utility room and two bedrooms separated by a full bathroom. Next was the large master with an en suite bathroom and beyond that, a den, where Ben wrote. Every room had enlarged windows with a mountain view.

One by one Emma inspected the rooms. She was satisfied each one was empty until she reached to the last door—the den.

Emma hesitated.

A rustling noise sounded from the inside.

Emma held her breath, listening.

More rustling.

She clasped the door handle, turned it, thrust the door open.

The rustling became loud flapping as a crow flew off from its perch on the exterior windowsill.

Sighing with relief, Emma was now certain the cabin was secure and returned to the front.

"Let's get those groceries in first and see if anything spoiled overnight," she called to Kayla in the car. "There's stuff we need to get into the fridge. Can you bring the bags to the kitchen and I'll put things away?"

"All right."

Kayla opened the tailgate, hauled the first two bags to the kitchen counter.

"Once we take care of everything, we'll try to call your dad, if you like, okay?"

"Okay. I know service is spotty here. They were supposed to install more cell towers."

Kayla returned to the SUV and was reaching into the back when she heard an engine and turned.

A car pulled up next to the SUV.

Kayla blinked. A woman was alone at the wheel. She didn't recognize her.

"I'm sorry," the woman said, holding up a folded map, "but I'm lost and my phone's dead. Can you help me?"

The woman seemed friendly, but for her eyes. Kayla thought they looked a bit off. Her pupils were like big black holes. Maybe she had a condition, or was on medication, and that's why she was lost.

The woman got out, looked around. "You have a lovely place here."

"Thanks…"

The woman placed her map on the hood of her car so they could lean over it.

"My first time here," the woman said. "It's gorgeous."

"Yes." Kayla leaned over the map with the woman next to her. "What're you looking for?"

"The truth."

"What?"

The woman slid her arm around Kayla's neck, locking her in a grip, crushing her windpipe, raising a knife to her face.

Eighty-Four

San Bernardino County, California
Present day

At that moment, Torrie Tullock, the lone survivor of her family's murder, was four miles from the Grants' cabin.

Driving alone in her rented Ford sedan, glancing at the car's erratic navigation system, and her handwritten notes on the console, she realized she'd overshot her destination.

The property she was looking for had a "bear-shaped" rock formation near its entrance along the highway.

Torrie stopped, made a three-point turn and resumed driving in the opposite direction, watching the shoulder for the landmark. Her calm demeanor did not betray what was boiling inside.

For much of her life, her anger over her family's murder had grown, building with volcanic force until it became a part of her identity. The people who killed her mother, her father, her sister and her brother had not paid enough for what they did. No, instead, they were given a gift, the gift of new lives.

Minute by minute, hour by hour, day by day Torrie's rage gnawed at her, ripping away pieces of her, transforming her into what she now was, the embodiment of vengeance.

She had used her wealth, her resources, to find the so-called Skull Sisters.

Kern Garland, her well-connected security chief, had contracted and subcontracted, and subcontracted again, the best investigative agencies. She'd instructed Garland to use every means possible to hunt the women down, put them under surveillance and secretly, psychologically, torment them about their crimes whenever possible. All the while Garland updated her on every change, every movement and every breath they took.

Torrie was regularly provided their current names, addresses and photos.

I know them well. They are my prey.

When Torrie learned that all three were in Southern California, everything had aligned. She might never get another opportunity like this so she flew to Los Angeles.

And now one of them is already dead. Reap what you sow.

In California the investigative work intensified, Torrie's people on the ground had alerted her to the possibility that the remaining two would be together—they'd covertly installed tracking devices on their vehicles.

Of course the monsters couldn't stay away from

each other. Of course they'd break the law to get away to the mountains—to plot something evil.

Now was the time to act.

Too many agonizing anniversaries of what they did to my family have come and gone. These inhuman beings have lived long enough.

Torrie adjusted her grip on the wheel.

Her team had taken care of her requirements for what she needed to do—some of them not so legal.

I don't care what happens to me. I've lived in a prison most of my life. One way or another, I'll avenge my family and I'll be free.

Torrie glanced to the floor on the passenger side, at the Glock 17 with two magazines each holding 17 rounds.

It won't be long now.

Eighty-Five

Driving as fast as he could, Ben had made good time and was now some four miles from the cabin, guilt and remorse clawing at his heart as he neared the location.

He'd pulled over to visit the roadside cross at the spot where Brooke died and had lowered himself to touch the engraved plate. Up here, inhaling the sweet pine-scented air, it felt as if Brooke was part of the mountains and her spirit was near.

I have no right to ask, but help me find them. Please.

Pressing his fingers to his lips, he touched them to the plate.

He returned to his car, resumed driving. He hadn't gone far when his cell phone rang loud and clear.

Eighty-Six

Inside the cabin Emma checked her phone, thinking she'd have to request time off from school, when she found Ben's response to the picture they'd sent him.

She caught her breath.

Why's he back so soon? What did he discover? Things are moving so fast—I've got to tell him the truth.

Emma texted Ben telling him they were at the cabin and to meet them there.

I want to talk, too. There are so many things I need to tell you.

After sending the message, Emma's tension melted ever so slightly as she put the groceries away.

The cabin could stand a good cleaning, she thought, finding a measure of comfort in the mundane notion because it indicated that with chaos whipping around her, she felt safe here.

Even though Rita Purvis's murder loomed large and Emma's world was spinning out of control, she believed with all her heart that after she confessed her life to Ben and Kayla, there'd be hope.

After twenty years, I knew this time would come. I could feel it haunting me. Only now I'll put it all to rest. I'll show my journal to Ben and Kayla. I'll tell them everything. I know he loves me for who I am not what I was. I did everything I could to protect them. I'll survive this. I'll rise from the ashes like I did before.

She would trust in love.

Emma took a deep breath, letting it out slowly, puzzling at why Kayla had not come in with more groceries.

Going to the window and looking out, Emma's jaw dropped at what she saw.

For a millisecond she thought the woman hugging Kayla was a fan of Ben's from the town or a resort. Determined fans of famous people always find their private property. It had happened to movie and rock stars, and a lot of writers, like J. D. Salinger and Stephen King.

But in the next half second, Emma's heart stopped.

Kayla was struggling against the woman's stranglehold—like the kind Emma had seen in prison.

A knife at Kayla's face glinted in the sun.

Emma flew out the door. "Let her go!"

"Stop!" the woman said. "Or I'll cut her."

Processing the scene, the familiar voice, registering a face from Eternity she could never forget.

Nikki.

Glaring at Emma, Nikki said, "Hello, sister."

In a heartbeat Emma rocketed back to that night in the house on Old Pioneer Road to the horror of what really happened all those years ago, all of it replaying in half a second…

They were there for money, looked everywhere and couldn't find any. This was a mistake… Janie saying, 'We need to leave now!' Nikki refusing, continuing to look. They didn't hear the car, the door. Suddenly the Tullocks were home. No time to leave… Nikki saying, 'Roy's got guns!' Nikki and Marie got knives… Connie saw them, said: 'Why're you here? What're you doing?' Then Connie, that stuck-up pretentious bitch let them know how much she loathed people like them and shouted: 'Why are you here? What are you pieces of filthy trash doing in my house?' And it was like she'd detonated a bomb, an explosion of white-hot fury illuminated everything the Tullocks had and everything they were against every anguish, abuse and heartbreak the girls had suffered in their young lives. A wild, growling animal jumped Roy from behind. It was Nikki, her knife flashing, cutting his throat, blood spraying… Connie screaming, Janie screaming, trying to stop her, too late… Marie and Nikki attacking Connie, Janie trying to save her, gripping wrists in a wild, furious fight to stop the knife, but the knife winning…blade flashing, slashing, plunging, blood spurting…the knives rising and descending, tearing and ripping. Stop! Stop! Connie screaming, her children screaming... Nikki and Marie chasing Neal and Linda up the stairs and Janie sobbing, 'Stop! Stop!' Running after them into the bedroom, Neal and Linda hiding in the closet, holding each other, screaming, crying... Janie trying to stop Marie and Nikki stabbing and stabbing...the children's eyes...blood everywhere... Nikki writing in blood on the walls like a serial killer...the pact...sisters...we did this together...no one tells... EVER!

And in a heartbeat the face from that night had returned and was now going to kill her stepdaughter.

Eighty-Seven

As he drove, Ben glanced at his ringing phone secure in its holder in the console. The number was a 204 area code. Manitoba? Using his app for his voice-activated hands-free option, he answered.

"Ben, this is Ed Tracy in Winnipeg." The lawyer for one of the girls. "Have you got a minute?"

"Actually it's not a good time, Ed. Can I call you back?"

"We should do this now... Doctor says my time's coming. Pretty soon lawyer-client privilege won't matter, so you can use this in your book after I'm gone."

Ben considered pulling over but kept driving. He activated the record function on his phone. "Ed, I'm sorry to hear that. Please, go ahead."

"One of the girls didn't kill anybody."

"Say that again."

"One of the girls is innocent of killing anyone."

"Innocent? But—"

"She tried to stop the other two that night, fought with all she had. That's how she got her prints on the knives, got all bloodied. She went along with the plan to steal money because she felt she was owed, and was mixed up with the other girls in that blood bond."

"I don't understand."

"It's complicated. In the early stages of the case, she broke down and confided to me in a private moment that she never killed anyone."

"So what did you do?"

"She would not allow me to defend her on that basis. Didn't want people to think she was trying to lie her way out because she was consumed with guilt. No one knew that she was not a killer. My strategy was to get her second-degree murder charge reduced to aiding and abetting. That way I could've argued that she didn't know of any intent to kill, had in fact taken steps to prevent or stop it under the abandonment principle."

"Why didn't you do that, or appeal or something?"

"Again, she absolutely refused to let me."

"She *wanted* to be found guilty of murder?"

"During the entire case, she went along with being lumped in with the two killers, accepted being guilty because she felt guilty, and in her mind, she *was* guilty, for initiating the circumstances. Janie had a tough life before that night. She blamed herself for the entire tragedy."

"Wait." Ben caught his breath. "You said Janie?" That was Emma's previous name…

"Jane Elizabeth Klassyn. She was no saint, but my God, she was no more a killer than you or me, Ben, and that's the truth that I wanted you to know."

Ben felt his heart filling with warm relief.

She didn't kill anyone.

After thanking Tracy and signing off, Ben accelerated.

Guilt. It's what Emma's been carrying all these years and has been afraid to tell us. I understand guilt—believe me, I get it.

He dragged the back of his hand across his mouth.

But who killed Rita Purvis? Where's the other Skull Sister, Lucy Isabel Lavenza?

Ben's phone pinged with Emma's text.

Emma and Kayla were at the cabin.

Ben increased his speed, praying that they were safe.

Eighty-Eight

San Bernardino County, California
Present day

Kayla was battling Nikki's lock on her neck, gasping for breath.

"Let her go, Nikki!" Emma said. "She's got nothing to do with us!"

Appearing to be in a drug-altered state, Nikki bared her teeth; her eyes flashed fire.

"All these years, finally we find you and what do you do? You deny us. Your sisters! You broke our bond and now Marie's dead because of you!"

"We were children, misguided, stupid children! Our old lives are gone—"

"And you've been living a lie ever since!"

Kayla let out a weak cry as Nikki's crushing grip tightened.

"Each of us paid a price," Emma said. "Let my daughter go. Let her go!"

"We're the Skull Sisters—forever! We were supposed to protect each other! Never betray each other! None of us is better than the other sisters.

Remember? But you turned on us! You go off and live like the Tullocks! The people who *loathed* us! The people we despised! But I never got a chance at a life like you. It's not right. If I can't have a good life, then you can't have one either!"

Struggling with Kayla, Nikki sobbed, her grip momentarily loosening. Kayla twisted free, punching her in the stomach.

"Run, Kayla!" Emma screamed, tackling Nikki.

Kayla fled down the road, into the woods, watching as Emma and Nikki battled for the knife. Emma gripped Nikki's wrists in a frenzied struggle, the blade flashing in the air. But Nikki, surprisingly agile and strong, slashed Emma's forearm with the knife before Emma climbed on top of her, clasped her hair, smashed her head into the ground, then fled after Kayla to protect her.

"Run, Kayla!"

Nikki scrambled to her feet and pursued them, knife in her bloodied hand.

Kayla ran through the trees, branches slapping and pricking at her clothes and face. Her throat aching, her lungs sore with panicked breathing she made it to the highway, unsure of which direction to go, praying for a car to wave down.

Branches crackled, telegraphing that Emma and their attacker were close behind.

Kayla ran for her life down the middle of the road toward an oncoming car.

There it is.

Following the detailed directions her team had

given her, Torrie Tullock rounded a curve in the highway, spotting a bear-shaped rock formation.

She eased off the accelerator. Not far down the highway a girl—*a terrified girl*—was running toward her, waving her hands. Two other women were running behind her—*no, chasing the girl.*

Both women were bloodied.

Slowing her car, Torrie concentrated on the women with full focus, recognition dawning—they matched the faces in the most recent photos her investigators had taken.

It's them. The women who killed my family!

Immediately Torrie pushed down on the gas pedal, accelerating, aiming her car at the women, keeping one hand on the wheel while reaching to the floor for her gun and thinking of what they wrote in her family's blood.

KILL THEM ALL

At that moment, driving faster than the limit, Ben suddenly came up behind three people running on the highway in front of him with a car bearing down on them from the opposite direction.

What the f—

It happened instantly, so fast, too fast for Ben's circuits to react—before his brain issued the order to lift his foot from the gas to stomp the brake, before his jaw opened…

Before his hand spasmed on the wheel, before he formed the cognitive command to swerve, the opposing car was plowing into the women with heart-sickening thuds, bodies flying into the air, shooting to the side in blurring screaming horror as the car blasted with metal-crunching force into his…turning everything…

Blank.

The air was hissing, smelling of burning rubber and plastic; something dripped like raindrops. Ben's ears were ringing, his head dizzy, his chest aching and his pained breathing shallow. He was compacted by the seat against the deflated air bag and dashboard, coming in and out of consciousness with voices around him.

"Hang in there, buddy. Help's on the way!"

"Dad!"

Kayla?

"Can you hear me, Dad?"

Someone's shaking hand had taken his.

"Dad," Kayla sobbed. "Stay with me, please, Dad!"

In and out, everything went dark then bright to the sound of sirens.

"We got to cut him out!"

The clank of equipment bags, hoses dousing hot metal, rubber boots, gloves pulling debris away, firefighters, the deafening high-powered grind and sparks, rescuers cutting into metal.

"We'll have you out real soon, sir."

Ben passed in and out with a blurry glimpse of a TV camera, a news photographer, more faces. A voice shouted, "Get those press people back!"

A gurney rattled, expert hands extracted him, fashioning some sort of harness and brace, placed him on a board then a gurney. Ben glimpsed ambulance doors while floating on the gurney toward them, Kayla's face above him surrounded by sky. She was holding his hand and crying.

The cross for her mother was four miles away.

"Dad…"

Ben tried to smile through his pain, ask her, "You okay?"

She nodded, tears flowing. "I'm okay, Dad."

"Em—" Ben winced.

As Ben was hoisted into the ambulance, he heard Kayla. "But I want to go with him."

"I'm sorry. You've got to go with the deputies, sweetie."

The doors closed. Ben passed in and out.

In the ambulance a paramedic tended to him, quickly fixing him with tubes, an IV, a blood pressure cuff, an oxygen mask. Then she moved forward to read monitors and talk to the hospital on a cell phone.

Ben turned his head to see another patient on a gurney across from him.

Emma?

No, it was a strange woman, bloodied, dirty, grass and twigs in her hair, oxygen mask accentuating the dark eyes staring at him.

"Ben," she moaned, "Ben Grant."

He nodded, not knowing who she was.

Weakly she lifted her arm to take his hand, trying to squeeze it.

"Ben, listen to me." Her voice was hoarse. "Your wife killed Rita Purvis."

Ben was jolted. *I must be delirious, not hearing correctly.*

"My real name is Nikki Gorman…" She gurgled and coughed. "Your wife's name is Janie… get away from her…she's a murderer."

Ben's eyes widened with disbelief.

"Your wife was going to hurt you and your daughter. I came to save you…"

The woman lost consciousness, her monitor began beeping, her hand fell.

Ben saw a ring on her finger.

A skull ring.

The siren wailed.

Eighty-Nine

California
Present day

The next morning Ben stared from his bed at the clock on the wall.

He was in the hospital at Big Bear Lake. He'd been in a car wreck. He'd suffered fractured ribs and his daughter had minor injuries, the doctor and nurses had told him the previous night.

But my wife?

The doctors and nurses made no mention of Emma as Ben was being sedated. He recalled moments from the crash but his memory was a puzzle with missing pieces emerging slowly, not giving him the full picture.

Not yet.

A new nurse was tending to him this morning.

"What about my wife, Emma?" he asked her. "And the other people? There were other people."

The nurse's eyes were shining, heavy with sorrow. "Try to relax, Mr. Grant."

Then the door opened and two San Bernardino deputies and a doctor came into the room.

They were accompanying Kayla, her face bearing cuts, scrapes, bandages on her chin and neck. She kissed him and took his hand.

The doctor looked to one of the deputies, then cleared his throat. "We're very sorry Mr. Grant, but your wife did not survive her injuries. She passed away."

The earth stood still.

Ben could not believe the doctor's words because he had shut down.

All he could manage was: "What?"

Kayla caressed the top of his head, then leaned her face to him, gently touched her head to his.

"Emma's gone, Dad." She sobbed. "She's dead."

It's not true.

Ben couldn't believe it, beseeching God to intervene, to let it not be true. Breathing hard, lightning flashed in his mind, pulling him back to when he had first met Emma, her first words to him.

"You have a deep understanding for everyone touched by the crime—even the killers. Your writing reaches a part of me."

Ben opened his mouth to speak but ceased his effort.

He was deaf to what the deputies and doctor were now saying, a new icy thought piercing him: Kayla. This was the second mother she'd lost. The second wife he'd lost—only miles apart.

The karmic wheel had turned on him.

Again.

After everyone but Kayla left, Ben hugged her while wrestling with his grief. And confusion.

"Dad," Kayla said, tears rolling down and over her bandages, "I'd be dead too, if Emma hadn't pushed me out of the way. She saved my life and sacrificed hers."

Three women, including Emma, were killed, and two people, Ben and Kayla, were injured in a two-car collision involving pedestrians. That was the first confirmed report released out of San Bernardino's Big Bear Sheriff's Station.

Ben declined all media calls that came to the hospital.

Anguished in his recovery, Ben hadn't yet revealed to anyone what the woman dying next to him in the ambulance had claimed: that Emma, his wife, was a cold, calculating, remorseless killer.

How could this be?

Ed Tracy had told him Emma hadn't killed anyone.

What should I believe?

Saying he wanted to thank first responders, Ben managed to speak privately with the paramedic, Lauren Fenton, who had been in the ambulance when he was transported after the crash. Ben asked her what the other patient had said.

"I was on the phone at the time," Fenton told him. "I never picked up on what she said."

"Nothing?"

"Not a word. If it helps," Fenton said, "people say all kinds of things when they're in a traumatic situation, and often it doesn't make sense."

Ben then told police all he could recall, including the claim made by the dying woman.

Kayla had also recounted for police the events leading up to her flight with Emma to the cabin, and the actions and ramblings of the disturbed woman who'd attacked her. Kayla's attacker had been tentatively—they stressed *tentatively*—identified as Lucy Isabel Lavenza of New York City.

The deceased driver of the opposing car had also been tentatively identified as Victoria Tullock, a Canadian citizen, from Toronto. San Bernardino County was working with the FBI, and other investigators, to confirm Torrie's identity and determine her actions prior to the fatalities, including her possession of a firearm and links to tracking devices on Emma Grant's car and Lucy Lavenza's rental.

The story drew news headlines around the world, lighting up social media.

Ben declined the mounting interview requests he'd received when he was released and got home with Kayla to Cielo Valle.

Tug was overjoyed to see them but whimpered when he searched the house for Emma.

In the days that followed, they received cards, flowers, calls and messages of condolences from Emma's friends and colleagues, Kayla's friends, Ben's agent, publishers, his readers, along with actors, directors and writers involved in screen adaptations of his books.

Some asked about funeral arrangements. But

Ben delayed holding any kind of service for Emma because he was tormented by uncertainty arising from the incident in the ambulance and awaiting results from investigators.

I refuse to believe that I was married—and in love with—a deranged murderous liar who deceived me. Have I been staring too long into the abyss?

To pursue the truth, Ben continued telling investigators every single thing he knew about Emma, his work on the Skull Sisters case, everything. He continued demanding updates from detectives in San Bernardino, Orange County and the FBI, who were looking into Rita Purvis's homicide, Torrie Tullock and the deaths near the cabin.

Ben tried calling Ed Tracy for more information, but he'd already passed away. He tried the other lawyers in the case but they couldn't offer much more than what he already knew. He called Torrie Tullock's relatives. They were shocked by the tragedy and in mourning yet again, but knew nothing. He tried reaching Lou Sloan and Bill Jurek, but they were working with US investigators, telling him that everything would be passed to them.

In the end, Ben had made little progress and felt as lost as Tug, watching him with his ball looking for Emma, or roaming the house with her sweater in his mouth, until one day his phone rang.

"Ben, it's Oscar Garcia at Orange County. We'd

like to update you. Can we drop by this afternoon with a few other investigators?"

A few hours later, Garcia and his partner Lilly Webb arrived with law enforcement people from San Bernardino, the FBI and a Royal Canadian Mounted Police sergeant, who was a liaison officer from the Canadian Consulate in Los Angeles. They gathered in Ben's living room and relayed what they knew.

Canadian authorities had DNA and fingerprint records of the three women known as The Skull Sisters on record. US and Canadian investigators, working with the coroners in San Bernardino and Orange County, had positively confirmed, and reconfirmed, their identities.

The murder victim in the park, Rita Mae Purvis, was born Marie Louise Mitchell.

The woman who attacked Kayla at the cabin was Lucy Isabel Lavenza, whose birth name was Nicola Hope Gorman, otherwise known as Nikki.

Emma Anne Chance, or Emma Grant, was born Jane Elizabeth Klassyn, known as Janie.

"This confirms your wife, Emma, was Janie," Garcia said.

He went on to relate that a knife belonging to Lavenza was recovered near Ben's cabin and submitted for DNA analysis and was found to be the knife used to kill Rita Purvis. Additionally, footwear impressions where Rita Purvis's body was discovered were made by shoes worn by Lavenza.

Investigators noted that footwear impressions

belonging to Emma, and a knife from the Grant home, were found in the vicinity but not at the murder scene. Investigators believed that Emma was startled and fell when she'd spotted a man in the wooded distance, who, it turned out, was most likely the dog walker who had discovered the corpse of Rita Purvis.

Continuing, investigators said they tracked the car rented by Lavenza to a motel, where they found a laptop, a video camera, notes and other items leading them to conclude that Lavenza was responsible for Rita Purvis's homicide and threats to Ben's family, arising from her perceived betrayal of their pact as teens. It was always Lavenza's intention to kill Rita Purvis, using her as an expendable resource to frame Emma Grant for her murder.

"So Lavenza, or Nikki, set this all up?" Ben asked.

"Yes," Garcia said. "As for her dying claim in the ambulance, it appears Lavenza, or Nikki, was making a final attempt at revenge against your wife. From Lavenza's discovered notes, she wanted to find Emma, extort her, frame her for murder and destroy the life she had."

"But why?"

"We suspect Lavenza could not stand to see her succeed and be happy in life. Perhaps we'll never know. It was as if Lavenza was locked in time, never outgrowing her life as a tormented fourteen-year-old." Garcia looked at his notes. "Lavenza had written: 'I've got nothing to lose and I'll do anything to win in the end.'" He looked at Ben. "It seems clear that she wanted to control the Skull Sisters to her very last breath."

"My God." Ben took a moment to grasp what he'd been told. "And Torrie Tullock?"

"Still under investigation," the FBI agent said. "We're working with the RCMP on her case but it's clear that she had hired a team of investigators, including Del Brockway, Marisa Joyce Narmore and Leo Wicks, to locate and follow those responsible for her family's deaths, intending on committing an act of vengeance on all three women."

Despite holding a memorial service for Emma, it took Ben and Kayla weeks to absorb and process what they'd experienced.

Together they went to a counselor, who had helped them come to terms with it all, coming to the bitter relief of acceptance and healing.

Ben reached deep inside for the strength to resume working.

He hired lawyers who made successful legal applications in Canadian courts for all the court and prison records he could get concerning the Skull Sisters, including all of the journals they'd kept while incarcerated, using the argument that because they were deceased, Girl A, Girl B and Girl C no longer had identities to protect.

The court agreed, and all the requested records were released to him.

Then one day while Kayla was doing laundry, she scooped to the bottom of the large box of powdered detergent and found a clear plastic bag containing the journal Emma had started after she and Ben were married.

Tears came as she read the few words and shared them with her father.

Started a new, wonderful life. Finally and truly, I buried my past. This new journal will be the last of many I've kept in my life. It will stand as testament after I'm gone.

No one knows the truth about me, that I set in motion all the steps that led to unthinkable, horrible events: The murders of four people. I tried to stop it. I tried so hard. I never killed anyone but I will always feel responsible. I buried Janie, the person I was, long ago, to work on being a better human being. But for as long as I live, I will never forgive myself...

Ben stared at his wife's journal for several moments.

"Dad," Kayla said. "She saved two lives. Remember that."

The next day, Ben and Kayla went alone to the spot near the cabin where she died and erected a roadside cross.

"While we will never forget all the terrible crimes that touched us all, we hope she's finally at peace and has found the absolution she sought," Ben said.

* * *

Fueled by heartbreak and passion, Ben held nothing back, ensuring that every aspect of the truth, including his own, went into what would be his most powerful and successful book.

Eternity
The Story of Homicide in a Small Town

* * * * *

Acknowledgments & A Personal Note

In writing *Their Last Secret*, I took creative liberties with police procedure, jurisdiction, the law, technology and geography. For example, the communities of Eternity, Manitoba, and Cielo Valle, California, are fictional.

And while history holds a number of true life cases of unspeakable crimes committed by young people, the stories of Janie, Marie and Nikki, as well as Benjamin Grant's books, including, *Eternity: The Story of Homicide in a Small Town*, are imagined. But in my effort to make *Their Last Secret* ring true, I drew upon my real experiences as a crime reporter in Canada and on assignment in California, and the kind help of the Royal Canadian Mounted Police, D Division. In areas where police procedure seems accurate, thanks goes to the Mounties. In areas where it doesn't, you can blame me.

In bringing this story to you, I also benefitted

from the hard work, generosity and support of a lot of other people.

My thanks to my wife Barbara and to Wendy Dudley for their invaluable help improving the tale.

Very special thanks to Laura and Michael.

My thanks to the super brilliant Amy Moore-Benson and Meridian Artists, the ever-talented Emily Ohanjanians and the incredible, wonderful editorial, marketing, sales and PR teams at Harlequin, MIRA Books and Harper Collins.

This brings me to what I believe is the most critical part of the entire enterprise: you, the reader. This aspect has become something of a credo for me, one that bears repeating with each book.

Thank you for your time, for without you, a book remains an untold tale. Thank you for setting your life on pause and taking the journey. I deeply appreciate my audience around the world and those who've been with me since the beginning who keep in touch. Thank you all for your kind words. I hope you enjoyed the ride and will check out my earlier books while watching for my next one.

Feel free to send me a note. I enjoy hearing from you.

Rick Mofina

www.rickmofina.com
facebook.com/rickmofina
twitter.com/RickMofina